Pra

Unm

"Erotically wicked! Spellbinding! A unique retelling of *The Phantom of the Opera.*" —Bertrice Small

"Colette Gale leads us through a labyrinth of dark, extravagant eroticism, to the romance at the story's heart. Grandly conceived, wildly inventive in its smallest details—I, for one, will never hear harp music in quite the same way again."

—Pam Rosenthal, author of *The Slightest Provocation*

"*Unmasqued* is a very wicked and original look at an age-old story. Readers will be entranced . . . a very dark thriller with a well-written cast of characters. . . . The pageantry and politics of nineteenth-century Paris and its wealthiest citizens are well-described, drawing the reader right into the drama. . . . This reader was well able to envision a time and people of a bygone era. Lush and sensual from beginning to end, erotic and romantic in the extreme, *Unmasqued* is sure to please fans of historical fiction as well as erotica. If you like your historical romance with a 'dark' and erotic bent, you will be well-pleased with the purchase of this one." —Erotic Romance Writers

ALSO BY COLETTE GALE

Unmasqued

Master

An Erotic Novel of the Count of Monte Cristo

COLETTE GALE

A SIGNET ECLIPSE BOOK

SIGNET ECLIPSE
Published by New American Library, a division of
Penguin Group (USA) Inc., 375 Hudson Street,
New York, New York 10014, USA
Penguin Group (Canada), 90 Eglinton Avenue East, Suite 700, Toronto,
Ontario M4P 2Y3, Canada (a division of Pearson Penguin Canada Inc.)
Penguin Books Ltd., 80 Strand, London WC2R 0RL, England
Penguin Ireland, 25 St. Stephen's Green, Dublin 2,
Ireland (a division of Penguin Books Ltd.)
Penguin Group (Australia), 250 Camberwell Road, Camberwell, Victoria 3124,
Australia (a division of Pearson Australia Group Pty. Ltd.)
Penguin Books India Pvt. Ltd., 11 Community Centre, Panchsheel Park,
New Delhi - 110 017, India
Penguin Group (NZ), 67 Apollo Drive, Rosedale, North Shore 0632,
New Zealand (a division of Pearson New Zealand Ltd.)
Penguin Books (South Africa) (Pty.) Ltd., 24 Sturdee Avenue,
Rosebank, Johannesburg 2196, South Africa

Penguin Books Ltd., Registered Offices:
80 Strand, London WC2R 0RL, England

First published by Signet Eclipse, an imprint of New American Library,
a division of Penguin Group (USA) Inc.

First Printing, May 2008
10 9 8 7 6 5 4 3 2 1

LIBRARY OF CONGRESS CATALOGING-IN-PUBLICATION DATA:

Gale, Colette.
Master: an erotic novel of the Count of Monte Cristo / Colette Gale.
p. cm.
ISBN 978-0-451-22412-5
1. Revenge—Fiction. I. Title.

PS3607.A412M37 2008
813'.6—dc22 2007039978

Set in Adobe Garamond
Designed by Spring Hoteling

Printed in the United States of America

To all the women who knew Haydée
was nothing but a midlife crisis.

Biographer's Note

Not long after I finished compiling the documentation that became *Unmasqued*, in which was revealed the true story of *The Phantom of the Opera*, I was fortunate enough to acquire some personal effects that shed new light on another familiar tale: that of *The Count of Monte Cristo*.

Alexandre Dumas' novel of betrayal and revenge tells the story of the horribly wronged Edmond Dantès and his bid for vengeance against the villains—his friends—who sent him to prison for fourteen years. The tale has been adapted for film and television, and it has been translated and republished, abridged and dissected in numerous ways since its initial publication in serial format through the mid-1840s.

However, through my acquisition of the personal diaries and letters of one of the most pivotal players in the narrative,

I've discovered that the story told by Dumas—along with its other adaptations—is incomplete and misleading.

I have had the pleasure of studying and organizing into a fleshed-out, chronological tale the diaries of Mercédès Herrera, the first and true love of Edmond Dantès. To my astonishment, through this study, I have learned that she was as much a victim of the events told by Dumas as Dantès was. Perhaps even more so.

Her diaries, along with her personal letters from Valentine Villefort and a journal that belonged to Monte Cristo's servant, Haydée, bring to light a much different and more accurate chronicle about what occurred in her life during the years of Dantès' imprisonment. The letters and journal in particular also expose certain other events that occurred when he came back to Paris as the wealthy, learned, and powerful Count of Monte Cristo.

Thus, within this volume is my attempt to make public the true story—with all its explicit details taken directly from her personal effects—of Edmond Dantès and Mercédès Herrera, a pair of lovers divided by greed, jealousy, tragedy, and revenge.

It is the story of *The Count of Monte Cristo* as it has never been told before.

—Colette Gale
May 2008

Prologue

Prisoner No. 34

1819
Château d'If
Off the Coast of Marseille, France

He knew every gray stone in his prison cell, every mortar-filled line between each of them, every change in topography of the dirt floor beneath his filthy, cold, bare feet.

He had stopped counting the days of his imprisonment after one thousand of them, for he no longer cared to keep track of what had become this eternity of worm-filled black bread, dank water, and horrible, dark solitude.

He'd spoken to no one for an aeon, since the day he'd gone mad at the jailer, demanding to know how he'd come to be here, incarcerated—what he'd done, what crime he'd committed, who had sent him here, what horrible error had been made. But the only answer he'd received had been being thrown into this cell, even smaller and darker than the one he'd previously occupied.

He had nearly stopped reminding himself of his own name.

Edmond Dantès.

His lips moved silently, for there was no one there to hear.

But the name that did come to his lips, in a quiet, gentle murmur, like a lifeline to a drowning sailor, was the talisman he'd clung to all these days, these *years.*

"Mercédès."

He said it again, no more than a release of breath in his silent world. "Mercédès."

How many times had he spoken her name?

At first, with anguish . . . he'd been taken from her, from the woman he was to marry, without a chance for farewell.

Then, with despair. Would he ever see her again? Touch her?

With pain. Would she wait for him? Had she tried to find him?

For a time, the only noises he made were the syllables of her name, desperately sobbed into the threadbare blanket, woven with dust, his lips dry and cracked and tasting dirt. Would she remember him?

At last . . . reverently. As if her name, her memory, were a light in the blackness of his life. Something to fixate upon, to yearn for, to live for. A talisman. To keep him sane.

"Mercédès."

When his mind verged on madness, when he longed to end his life but had no weapon with which to do it . . . when he gave up all hope, he remembered her lively, dark eyes, filled with intelligence and laughter. The smooth, sweet curve of her golden arms, the oval of her beautiful face, reminding him of the painting of the Blessed Virgin Mary hanging in Église des Accoules, the church in which they'd meant to wed.

Her lips . . . God had made them full and red, surely designed to fit Dantès' own mouth. He saw them wide with happiness on the day he'd come back from the sea and told her he'd been named captain of his own ship . . . then soft and pliant under his own mouth later that afternoon.

How could he have known he'd be taken from her only two days later?

Who had done this to him? Who had betrayed him?

He remembered how his hands, rough from handling the lines at sea, had smoothed up her warm arms, drawing her close to him on the hidden hillside, bringing her so that he could feast on her mouth, draw cries of pleasure from those sensual, promising lips. Gently tease her so that he could see the light of love in her chocolate eyes before the sweep of her thick lashes came modestly down like the shutters on her little weather-beaten house.

Even now, God knew how many years later, Dantès clung to the memory of the slip-slide of their kiss, the rhythm of his tongue mating with hers in that warm, wet cavern that echoed the tight, musky one between her legs.

He was there again, as his hands drew away the simple peasant blouse she wore, the undyed linen creamy against her sun-drenched skin, baring a simple gold cross and two lovely breasts, along with the faint scent of kitchen smoke mingled with lemon. Her breasts . . . the size of oranges, with their own pebbling flesh tightening under his palms, dusky nipples pointing up to the sun as he loved her there in the thick, warm grass and crushed chamomile.

She arched toward him as his hands smoothed down her narrow back, her chin tipping up and the bundle of walnut hair loosening beneath her skull. As he bent to close his lips around an offered nipple, Dantès' own desire surged when he heard her soft cry of pleasure turn to a deeper one of need. Her legs shifted, opened slightly next to him, her bare thigh brushing his salt-crusted seaman's trousers. He hadn't even bothered to change before coming to take her away to their reunion on this secluded hillock.

He sucked and licked, slowly swirling his strong tongue around the point of her nipple, taking all the time he needed and wanted, feeling the comfortable heaviness of his cock as it filled and swelled. One of her hands had loosened the thong that held his dark hair back; now it fell over his face, curtaining it as he bent to her.

Mercédès untied the fastenings of his shirt, her breath quickening when his hand crept to cover her other breast. He spread his fingers over it, then lightly brushed the backs of his nails over her nipple as he gave a long, deep tug on the other one. She moved restlessly, shivered as he toyed with her, the sun hot on the back of his head and his suddenly bare back.

"Edmond," she murmured, pulling him toward her, away from her breasts so that she could look in his eyes. The expression there filled him with such joy, such anticipation and love that he nearly wept as she guided his face back to hers. She rose beneath him, lifting her mouth, her swollen, puckered lips ardent as they fit and slipped and sucked against his, her hand surprising him as it slipped down the front of his trousers.

Time blurred for him then, but it was a vortex of sensation—her fingers brushing his hot cock, their mouths mashing together, her low, deep moans, the silky warmth of her bare skin.

Then, somehow, he lay on his back, the brilliance of the blue sky cut by a hovering olive tree above. Mercédès rose over him, her slender torso and glorious breasts half-covered by the fall of her rich dark hair. Her red lips parting to show white teeth, straight but for a crooked one on top that gave relief to her perfection.

He helped her move, straddling him, felt the tight slickness as she fit over his waiting erection. Watched the way her eyes half-closed and her teasing smile sagged into wonder and pleasure.

Oh, the pleasure.

And he moved beneath her, slowly at first, his hands on her hips, her thighs bent next to his torso. She reached above, her breasts rising, her fingers brushing the low-hanging olive leaves as her face tipped up, her lips parted, her breath came faster. His world centered at the place where they'd joined, slick and hot and rhythmic. He moved, she moved, and the beauty of it all uncoiled slowly, like a line dropping its anchor to sea until suddenly they were both crying out, both trembling, sweaty and warm and collapsing together on the grass.

"Mercédès," he remembered whispering, pushing the hair away from her face, "I love you."

She rose to kiss him again, her breasts full against his chest, her work-worn hand skimming his shoulder. "I'll always love you, Edmond."

How many times he had relived those glorious moments during the dark years in this dungeon. The memories, the images had been all that kept him sane those early days . . . and now . . . now perhaps they tugged him into madness, a deep well that he welcomed, for surely it would be a relief to be insane rather than to imagine he'd never see daylight again.

He prayed for death.

He stopped eating.

On the fourth day of his determination to commit suicide, he stared at the plate of black bread and the cup of brackish water. In his wavering, sick mind, he saw two cups, then three. And multiple hunks of bread taunting him. He swore he saw a light in his cell. He felt Mercédès' touch, saw the face of his beloved *père.*

And then, somewhere, he heard a faint scratching.

And, long hours later, a small section of the stones that made up his cell crumbled away, and an elderly man's head poked in.

"I am Abbé Faria," he said. "And apparently, this is not the way out."

One
A Purse of Red Velvet

Ten years later
Marseille, France

Mercédès Herrera Mondego, Comtesse de Morcerf, turned in to the wide walkway that led to the grand entrance of the House of Morrel, a well-known shipping company.

Perhaps she could do nothing to help the family, but Monsieur Morrel had been so kind to Edmond when he sailed on Morrel ships, and to his father and Mercédès when he had been taken away more than fourteen years ago, that she felt compelled to be there on this tragic day.

The family would need a friend.

On her arm, she had a basket of oranges, purchased fresh from the market, and some ribbons and lace she'd brought from Paris that Julie might like. Simple gifts, but ones the family would appreciate. They were much too proud to take any monetary offerings.

Bad luck and misfortune had struck the business over the last years, and it showed in the empty corridors and silence of the once-busy company. Four of their five ships had been lost at sea, and now the future of the twenty-five-year-old firm was in jeopardy. How poorly the years had treated the Morrels since Edmond had sailed their ships!

How poorly the years had treated Mercédès herself.

No longer the simple young woman who'd waited for her love to return from the sea, Mercédès was thirty years old and now a comtesse. She'd learned to read and draw and to play the piano. She'd hired tutors to help her learn to speak better French, as well as Italian, Greek, and Latin. She'd learned mathematics and geography, and studied literature—rather masculine pursuits, but her education had distracted her from the years of grief and anger and darkness.

After learning of Edmond Dantès' death in prison nearly fourteen years ago, she had agreed to marry her cousin Fernand Mondego, who had climbed his way up the ranks and through the French navy to become the Comte de Morcerf. They lived in Paris, in a beautiful house on rue du Helder, grander than anything she could have aspired to if she and Edmond had married.

She would have preferred *Père* Dantès' little house here in Marseille with one crooked shutter and a tiny yard, or to be sailing the sea on her husband's ship, as she and Edmond had always planned to do. To see the world. Together.

Julie Morrel, the shipmaster's daughter, was peering out a window when Mercédès came up the cobbled walkway. She beckoned frantically to Mercédès to wait, and then she disappeared from the window.

Moments later, she reappeared from the rear of the building, walking quickly down the pathway, bareheaded and gloveless. It was much too warm for a spencer or cloak; Mercédès carried a fringed white parasol to keep the sun away in lieu of a bonnet.

"Mercédès—Lady de Morcerf—what can you be doing here? And without a driver?" Julie asked, slipping her arm around Mercédès' wide puffed sleeve and directing her back down the walk.

Julie was a beautiful young woman with sparkling dark eyes and a gently plump figure; today those eyes were dull and worried.

"I remembered that today was the day your father's debt is to be called," Mercédès replied, walking along with the young woman, their full skirts swishing in tandem. Despite the fact that they were separated in age by a decade, the two women had become friends and confidantes, and it was only because Julia had mentioned her family's dire straits in a recent letter that Mercédès was aware of the looming tragedy.

It had been that letter that brought Mercédès from Paris here to Marseille. "How is Monsieur Morrel?"

"He has locked himself in his office and refuses to see anyone, even Maximilien. The debt is to be paid at noon today, and it's already past eleven o'clock. There is no hope."

"But where are you going?" asked Mercédès, wondering why such a loving daughter would be leaving her father at such a time. "And where is your brother if he is not with monsieur?"

"Maximilien paces outside of Papa's office door, but there

is nothing he can do. But I . . . I have one small bit of hope. Come, we must hurry."

"Where are we going?"

"To the Allées de Meilhan, to a certain house there."

Mercédès looked at the young woman in shock, but kept her pace. "Julie, what are you about?"

"You know that my father's debt is to be called today, but I didn't tell you all of the story. The debt was actually due to be paid three months ago today, but something quite extraordinary happened that day. My father had a visitor—a man who introduced himself as Lord Wilmore—who came to deliver the news that he had purchased Papa's debt. While he was in the office, the news about the *Pharaon* came."

Mercédès felt a wave of sorrow. The *Pharaon* was the last ship Edmond had sailed, and when it had returned to the harbor those fourteen years ago, Morrel had named him its captain. That was the day she and Edmond had made love on the hillside, and it was two days later that her lover had been taken away by the authorities—during their betrothal party.

"What happened to the *Pharaon*?"

"It was lost in a hurricane, and while Lord Wilmore was with my father, the three sailors who had survived the accident came to bring the news." Julie looked up at Mercédès, shielding her brow with a plump hand. "My papa, though it was his last ship, and his only hope for salvaging the company, cared not for the loss of the ship but for the loss of lives that had accompanied its destruction. He paid the wages for his good sailors out of our last bit of money, and made a small stipend to the widows of the ones lost at sea. Then he turned to Lord Wilmore."

"But he did not call the debt, did he? If it is due today, he must have given your father an extension."

Julie nodded, gesturing for Mercédès to turn with her down Via Meilhen. The houses here were crowded plaster ones, with narrow stoops and irregular walkways. The smell of baking bread wafted from one of the nearby windows. "My father did not lower himself to ask for an extension, but Lord Wilmore offered it and Papa accepted gratefully. But there was little he could do. He went to Paris to see Baron Danglars—do you know him?"

Mercédès did indeed know Danglars. He had been a purser on the *Pharaon* with Edmond and now did business with her husband. "Did he not once sail for your father too?"

"Indeed, but now he has become a successful banker, and my father thought that due to their past business relationships he would grant him a loan. But Danglars turned him away. And there is no one else."

Mercédès' lips tightened as she hurried along. It surprised her not in the least that the sly man with pinched eyes and groping fingers would refuse to help someone in need—especially someone he'd once worked for. He'd been visibly envious when Edmond was given the captaincy of the *Pharaon*, instead of himself. "So the three-month extension is for naught?"

"Perhaps. But there is more to the story," Julie said. "And, voilà, we are here." Mercédès followed her young friend up the short walkway and was surprised when Julie opened the front door and walked in.

Mercédès followed more cautiously, but when she heard a soft cry from Julie, who'd walked into the next room, she ran after her, her soft little shoes slipping on the polished wood floor. In the next room, she saw Julie standing in front of a fireplace mantel, holding a red silk purse.

She was sobbing.

Mercédès put an arm around her friend and brought out a fine lace-edged handkerchief to wipe away the tears. Certainly, there would be more to come.

But when Julie raised her face to look at her, Mercédès saw that rather than sorrow, her tears were ones of joy. She was smiling rapturously. "We are saved!"

"I don't understand."

Julie thrust the purse at her, and Mercédès took it. "I've seen this purse before! This is one your father gave to *Père* Dantès, filled with money, when Edmond was taken away. How did it come to be here?"

"Sinbad the Sailor," Julie said cryptically, smiling through her sobs. "He sent me a note only one hour ago! Come, we must get back before noon. I must show my father before—before he does something tragic."

Mercédès opened the purse and inside were two pieces of paper . . . and a diamond! The size of a walnut! *"Dios mio!"* she said, lapsing into her native language.

She pulled out the papers. One of them was a bill for two hundred eighty-seven thousand, five hundred francs—and it was marked *paid*. And the other was a handwritten note that said: *For Julie's dowry*.

"Now I shall be able to marry Emmanuel!" Julie said, pulling on Mercédès' arm to drag her out of the house, fairly dancing down the walkway.

Clutching the red velvet purse, Mercédès hurried along with the ecstatic young woman, scarcely able to believe what she held in her hand. How could this be? And who was Sinbad the Sailor?

She peppered her friend with questions as they rushed back to the House of Morrel, skirts flapping. But she received only bits and pieces of the story, tossed over Julie's shoulder while they hurried along.

From what Mercédès could understand, Lord Wilmore had spoken briefly with Julie on the day of his visit and told her that she would hear from a man called Sinbad the Sailor, and that she should do exactly as Sinbad instructed.

"And this Sinbad told you to come to this house in Allées de Meilhan?" Mercédès asked incredulously. "And you would have come here alone?" Would she have ever done something so foolish, so blind, when she was Julie's age?

And then she remembered sneaking out to meet Edmond when he was courting her, avoiding the sharp eyes of her mother, and lying to her cousin Fernand when he would have followed her. For the Spanish-Moorish Catalans kept to themselves, away from the French residents of Marseille, even though they lived on the outskirts of the city. They lived and married among themselves and kept their own traditions and cultures. For her to be trysting with a non-Catalan woud have been cause for reprimand.

Sí, she would have done the same. She'd been young and adventurous then. The whole world and its possibilities had been open to her.

The two women burst into the House of Morrel in a manner that would have caused any spectators about to stop in surprise—especially to see a distinguished comtesse in her fine Parisian clothing haring about on the heels of the younger, less fashionable woman.

"Papa! Papa!" cried Julie, clattering up the steps to the upper offices. "Papa, we are saved!"

"What are you about?" asked Maximilien Morrel, who stood at the top of the landing. He was a youth of seventeen, on the verge of manhood, and Mercédès saw that his handsome face had gone beyond worried to gaunt and was striped with perspiration. "He will not let me in, and it is one minute until noon! I swear I have heard the click of a pistol, for Papa has said he will die and be remembered as an unfortunate, but honorable, man."

"Papa! You must open the door! We are saved!" cried Julie, banging on the heavy wooden door.

"See this," Mercédès said, giving the red velvet purse to Maximilien. "She is right—you are saved."

Monsieur Morrel had cracked open the door. The kindly man, his gray hair brushed neatly and his face shaved smooth as if he were ready to attend church, rather than his own suicide, looked out. "Julie—"

But Maximilien shoved on the door, opening it fully. "Papa, put that weapon down! Julie is right. We are saved. Look at this!"

And no sooner had Monsieur Morrel opened the purse and comprehended its contents, and the family was sharing tears of joy, than Mercédès knew it was time for her to leave. She placed the basket of oranges and the small packet of ribbons on a little table at the foot of the stairs and made her way out onto the sunny street.

What a miracle! What a miraculous thing to have happened to such a good family!

When Edmond had been taken off by the officers of the

court from the midst of his own betrothal party, Monsieur Morrel had immediately gone to the crown prosecutor's office to plead his innocence, to post his bond, and to demand information about the charges and his disappearance.

The crown prosecutor, Monsieur Villefort, had been able—or willing—to give Monsieur Morrel little information about Edmond, despite several visits made by the shipmaster. The only thing he had told Morrel was that Edmond was being held on charges of being a rabid Bonapartist, and that Morrel's incessant attention to the matter shed an unflattering light on himself and his shipping company.

Monsieur Morrel had visited Mercédès and Edmond's father, providing the old man with the very same red velvet purse filled with enough francs to feed him for months. But *Père* Dantès would not eat, and within weeks of hearing that his son had been imprisoned, he died of starvation.

That had been a dark time.

Yet Mercédès' life had become even darker since she had gone to Prosecutor Villefort to ask for information herself.

Shouts drew her attention, and she realized she'd begun to walk the short distance from the House of Morrel to the wharf. Ship masts striped the horizon, thrusting up from the cluster of vessels at the docks, and the familiar tang of sea salt reminded her how much she'd missed the simplicity of this bustling seaside town. Paris was full of pretension and fashion and falseness, to her mind, and she'd never felt completely comfortable since she and Fernand had moved there.

That was part of the reason she'd immersed herself in her education—it was a way to keep distance from a life she hadn't been born to, and didn't fully understand. She would have been perfectly content to remain in her little house in Marseille, growing her own vegetables and herbs . . . or sailing with Edmond.

The shouts had become more excited, and Mercédès tilted her head, straining to understand what the men were calling.

"The *Pharaon*! The *Pharaon* has returned!"

Frowning, she picked up her heavy skirts, crinolines and all, and ran toward the docks. Julie had just told her that the ship had been lost. . . . How could this be?

But when she reached the docks, the familiar sight of Edmond's last ship—looking gleaming, and as if it were brand-new—sat, golden and proud-masted in the harbor. People were running and shouting and staring in disbelief.

"Tell Morrel!" someone shouted. "It is a miracle!"

Another miracle for the Morrels. Surely some angel had smiled down on them at last.

Mercédès felt a surprise tear sting the corner of her eyes. Where was her angel?

She was sincerely glad for the Morrels and their good fortune, but suddenly overcome by her own problems and fears. She missed her son, Albert, who was safely ensconced in their opulent home in Paris while she tried to determine a way to bring him with her. But Fernand would never allow it—he loved his only child too much.

If she could figure out a way to do that, she would never return to Fernand.

Mercédès saw Julie and her family as they rushed onto the scene, Monsieur Morrel stumbling along as though he'd just awakened from a dream. As she pushed through the crowd, which had continued to grow due to the miraculous news, she caught sight of a tall, dark-haired man ahead of her.

She stopped, her heart pausing for a moment, then continuing on in a painful, rapid beat.

Edmond.

From behind, he'd almost looked like Edmond for a moment there.

The man turned, and she couldn't stop watching him as he moved gracefully through the crowd. His eyes were shadowed by the hat he wore low on his forehead, and he sported a dark, well-trimmed beard and mustache. His garb was not that of a common sailor, but the loose-fitting clothes of the Orient: sleeves and trousers of pale blue silk, gathered at the wrists and ankles. Dark hair fell in a braided queue from the back of his neck well past his shoulder blades.

Perhaps he felt the weight of her gaze on him, for he paused, turning to look in her direction. She, in turn, felt his attention settle on her as if to determine why she had been staring at him so boldly. Before their eyes met, Mercédès' manners won out, and she quickly averted her attention to the joyous Morrel family, moving through the throng of well-wishers to get nearer to them.

It was an odd thing for her, a distinguished comtesse: pushing through a crowd of ordinary people, smashing her skirts and crushing the very full sleeves of which the fashion mavens were so proud, scuffing her slippers in the dirt.

Fourteen years ago, Mercédès would have thought nothing of moving about alone, or with a single companion; but along with her wealth and power had come propriety and restriction.

A sense of freedom such that she hadn't had for years settled over her. She was here in Marseille, the city of the happiest—and most sorrowful—times of her life. She was alone, without constraints, without a schedule, without expectations.

Alone.

A short while later, when she looked over again, the man was gone.

And her chest felt tight once more, her grief from the loss of Edmond opened like a new wound to the flesh.

As the merrymaking at the *Pharaon*'s return came to an end—for the sailors and townspeople alike seized upon any cause for celebration on a humid summer evening—Mercédès found herself drifting from the wharves, her feet following a familiar path.

Before she quite realized it, she had walked for some time, and made her way along the narrow, uphill street that led past *Père* Dantès' house. Here, Edmond had courted her, brought her from the close-knit Catalan world into his. She hadn't been along this street for more than twelve years.

Suddenly, she realized the sun had dipped behind the irregular row of houses between this hill and the bay, and a narrow thoroughfare that had only moments ago been bathed in soft golden light was now browning. Shadows fell in thick blocks on the cobbled street, casting doorways and small yards into darkness.

The street was curiously empty and silent, and Mercédès felt the lift of hair on the back of her neck. A quiet scuff behind her had her heart thumping faster, and her parasol at the ready. She turned and saw three figures suddenly a mere two houses away. One man leaned nonchalantly against a low plaster wall covered with ivy. Another stood next to him, his hat brim low over his face.

And the third in the center of the empty street had his hands on his hips.

Even from her distance, Mercédès could tell that they were roughly dressed and had likely either just put in from a voyage, or bore the remnants from an evening of celebration.

But where was everyone else? The street was empty.

Her heart began to beat faster, and she closed her fingers tightly around the parasol. Its pointed tip would make a fair weapon, but it was all she had.

And it was obvious she would need one.

The man in the street began to walk toward her, purpose in his step, and Mercédès picked up her skirts and started to run. But even as she did, another figure moved from the growing shadows and stepped into the street in front of her.

She stumbled to a halt, but began to angle slightly toward the edge of the street.

"What be your hurry?" drawled the man behind her. "Don't you want to keep us a bit of company?"

"A fine ransom the bitch'll fetch us," commented the one in front of her. "From the looks o' her clothes." He swiped toward her, grasping a handful of her generous sleeve.

"Release me," Mercédès said in a voice much calmer than she felt. "You'll receive no ransom but a visit from the authorities if you do not let me on my way. My husband is a very powerful man."

The one who'd come from behind was much closer now. He laughed and gestured for his companions to come closer. "Now, my fair lady, wouldn't ye like to see a bit of the world? From the deck of a ship, perhaps? We've got room on ours, and we be shipping out in the morn."

The others laughed, and suddenly they were pulling at her, flipping something heavy and cloaking over her head, a hand slamming over her face to muffle her screams and smother her very breath. She managed to get one good strike with the parasol before someone jerked it out of her hands and the enveloping cloth wrapped tightly around her arms. Her flailing foot slammed into something soft, but she couldn't revel in that minor success, for she was upended over someone's shoulder and her face was full of prickly wool.

Suddenly, she heard the pounding of a horse's hooves and felt tension in the man who held her. Though she could not see, the sounds told the story: The horseman galloped up, drawing his mount up next to her abductors with an elegant clatter. A sharp click of metal, and then a low, accented voice: "It would be best for you to release the woman, else I shall have to tell Luigi Vampa that you have tread beyond your boundaries."

Then she felt the hold on her change, and the man—her rescuer—grasped her by the waist and lifted her against his hip and thigh. Suddenly, they were cantering off down the street, Mercédès still wrapped in the mean cloth, her parasol left behind.

He seemed to hold her easily against his leg, her hip half-wedged against his, with a single arm. If she expected he would stop and uncover her rather immediately, thus releasing any strain on his arm, she was to be disappointed, for they continued through several twists and turns and must have gone some distance away.

As she hung there, in such an ungainly manner, Mercédès began to wonder if she had been rescued only to be captured again! She was afraid to struggle and be dropped beneath the horse's hooves, or in some other dangerous position.

But at last, when she was just about ready to take the chance, their mount slowed and then stopped. She felt the jolt as he dismounted, and then the swoop as he tossed her over his shoulder like a sack of barley—which surely she looked like, still wrapped in the cloying wool.

At that point, she began to struggle and kick again, and was rewarded by being dumped unceremoniously onto . . . not the floor . . . but something soft. Immediately, she began to fight her way out of the cloth.

"I did not intend to frighten you," he said in that odd accent; it wasn't English or Italian or anything that she recognized. She felt him as he moved toward her, his hands sure and warm as they unraveled her from her covering.

She looked up, pushing strands of hair out of her face, and gasped. Despite the dim light, she recognized the bearded man in Persian clothing from the docks. The one who'd reminded her of Edmond.

He was looking down at her just as boldly as she gawked up at him.

"You," she began. "I saw you . . . at the docks."

"And I saw you." His voice sounded uneven. "You were foolish to walk off alone. Where is your husband?"

Mercédès realized belatedly that she had been tossed onto a bed covered with an array of large cushions and pillows, and she pulled herself into an upright sitting position. "He is not here," she replied firmly.

"Not here? He allows his wife, the Comtesse de Morcerf, to wander about Marseille alone?" His voice was smoother now, and there was a decidedly mocking tone beneath that lilting accent. Yet she sensed a tension underlying his sardonic tone.

"How did you know my name?"

He shrugged, spreading his hands nonchalantly. She noticed that his silken sleeves had been rolled up his forearms, showing thick golden bands at both of his wrists. His hands were wide and tanned, funneled with veins and tendons and rough from work, so different from Fernand's soft lily-white ones. And so much like the sailor's hands of her lost Edmond.

What would it be like to have such rough hands smoothing over her skin again?

"It was not so difficult to learn your name. You are a friend of the Morrels, and I have some acquaintance with them as well." His eyes, dark in color, and lined with a narrow stripe of black around the lash line, were steady on her. The space in the room seemed heavy, as though pressing them together.

"Then perhaps you might provide me with your name," Mercédès replied frostily. Her heart still pounded rapidly, but her fear had begun to abate. Her mouth was dry, and she felt a subtle fluttering in her belly.

"I am called Sinbad. Sinbad the Sailor."

Perhaps she shouldn't have been surprised, but she was; after all, the man looked like the legendary Persian Sinbad. He wore a beard, and his skin looked as though it had been sunburned and then tanned. As she grappled with the web of thoughts spinning through her mind, she stammered the first one she was able to seize. "You . . . how did you come by the red velvet purse? With the money in it, for the Morrels? It belonged to *Père* Dantès."

Sinbad loomed tall over her, and she noticed the lean muscles of his forearms. "It was given to me by an old abbé named Faria. And so, Countess . . . where is your husband?"

"He is . . ." Mercédès paused. If she told him that she'd left

Fernand in Paris, and that he didn't know where she was, what would he do? If he knew that she was alone and unaccounted for, would that put her in other danger? "He will be arriving from Paris tomorrow, with our son."

"Your son? And how old is this future count?"

"Twelve," she replied automatically. "He is twelve."

"And only one child, in how many years of marriage to this count of yours?"

Mercédès thought she detected a hint of malice in his voice; but for what reason, she couldn't fathom. "Nearly thirteen years," she replied. Thirteen years of misery and humiliation and abuse. No, perhaps only twelve years. The worst had not truly begun for some time after their wedding. Yet she'd known pain and misery even before she agreed to marry Fernand.

But that was not something to be revealed to this stranger, who looked at her with such an expression in his eyes . . . an expression that seemed to shift from heated to angry to uncertain, and then masked itself into a mocking one.

"What do you want from me?" she asked suddenly, feeling the tension of the room bearing down on her again.

"Want?" he asked, his voice liquid. His fingers closed; she saw them crumple the light silk of his trousers. "From you? Nothing, my dear countess. I want nothing from you."

But his voice had become steely and the expression in his eyes harsh. Suddenly Mercédès became frightened again, frightened, and yet . . . expectant. Apprehensive and . . . breathless.

Yes, her chest filled and tightened, and she couldn't breathe for a minute. And then she looked away, her heart slamming in her bosom, her fingers shaking behind the folds of her rumpled skirt.

"Then I shall be on my way," she told him, standing and starting boldly toward the doorway of the room they were in.

Sinbad stepped to one side, blocking her path. He was much taller than she. Sturdy, muscular, and he smelled of the sea.

"If you want nothing from me, then let me pass," she said with a calm she did not feel. Her heart was racing, her palms damp, her belly aflutter.

"You do not wish to show any gratitude to your rescuer?"

She swallowed, refusing to look up at him. Instead, she focused her attention on the broad shoulder in front of her, covered by pale blue silk that clung to the muscles of his chest in a way that cotton and linen would not. The collarless shirt was buttoned up to the throat with simple silk knots. "I have a few francs with me, but more at the—"

"My dear countess, I am in no need of your money. That is, in fact, the last thing I want from you."

Mercédès gripped her hands tightly in the sides of her skirt, feeling the pounding of her heart all the way down her arms like the beat of a funereal drum. She'd glanced up at his words, but the mockery in his eyes sent her gaze skittering away and suddenly she found it locked on his mustache and the hint of fine lips beneath it.

He smiled and those lips stretched, quirking at one corner, drawing the dark bristles up and away in a fascinating, sensual movement.

"Perhaps," he continued in a low voice, "I should ask you what it is you want from me."

"Nothing. Nothing but to pass you, to leave."

"Then pass. Do not stand there like a frightened cat. If that is what you truly wish, then walk on by, Countess."

She hesitated only a moment, then stepped toward him. He'd positioned himself directly in front of the door; the only way she could move past would be to brush against him, to touch that silken sleeve, and for her skirt to bell over his slippered foot.

"But I don't believe that is what you truly wish . . . ," he whispered as she came closer.

She was touching him now. Her pink linen sleeve, which puffed out three times wider than her upper arm, was crushed as it slid against the blue silk; her skirt crinkled against his leg.

He put out his arm between her and the door, effectively stopping her. "Is it?" He pivoted toward her, and so they were standing toe-to-toe, chest to bosom, silk brushing linen.

She felt his warmth and smelled the sea tang on his skin and the gentle scent of man mixed with something like nutmeg. Edmond. Just like Edmond.

"Kiss me, Countess," he said softly. His flexed fingers trembled against the wall. "You want to."

She did want to. . . . Lord have mercy, she did.

A woman who had never, despite all he'd done to her, betrayed her husband, wanted to kiss the silken-clad, salty, sweaty sailor who stood in front of her. She wanted to lose herself in the memories, the faint familiarity he brought with him.

"Let me pass," she said again. "Please."

His arm dropped back to his side. He stepped away, leaving the doorway open. "You are a devoted wife, Countess. How fortunate your husband is."

She gathered up her skirts and hurried past him, her heart still slamming in her chest, and found herself in the same room she and Julie had been in earlier that day—where Julie had found on the fireplace mantel a red velvet purse filled with the miracle that had saved her family.

Clearly this man was who he claimed to be—Sinbad.

Mercédès turned back to see that he'd followed her, and stood in the doorway between the two rooms. He leaned against the opening, arms crossed over his middle, his eyes dark and their lids at half-mast. A fire burning in the fireplace gave off unnecessary heat and the only illumination in this room besides a small oil lamp.

Before she realized what she was doing, Mercédès was walking toward him, back toward Sinbad and the temptation he represented: the mysterious pull, the incessant draw, the desire to indulge her sorrow and grief and memories.

He straightened as she came toward him, understanding glinting in his eyes, but he said nothing. Only waited.

His shoulders trembled when she spread her hands on the front of them, her fingers curling just over the top, skidding the fabric a bit against his warm skin. He didn't move except to look down at her, and she couldn't read—didn't even try, truth be told—the expression in his eyes. She just raised her face, closed her own eyes, and brought her mouth to his.

At first, she barely brushed against the soft bristles of his mustache and beard and the smooth line of his lips, just to see what it was like. It amazed her to feel the tremors in his body as she touched him. Then she pushed closer, pressing her mouth against his, angling to the side so that they fit together better, her lips parted just enough that his upper lip slipped between and she could taste him.

Something happened, and a great burst of warmth, a rush of emotion and desire, trammeled through her as though unleashed. The pungent smell of the sea was in his hair, on his salty skin; his lips were moving beneath hers now, no longer tentative but hungry and demanding. She was lost in the kiss, caught in the swirl of sensations: her fingers slipping over silk, making warm friction, feeling the swell and dip of muscles beneath . . . the slick, hot dance of their tongues . . . his fingers clutching her waist, digging into her skin . . . the tightening and heaviness of her breasts beneath layers of corset and chemise and linen.

Mercédès didn't protest when he swung her up in his arms and brought her back into the room they'd just vacated, once again depositing her on the large cushionlike bed. But this time, he came with her, his hands holding her shoulders to the mattress as if to be certain she wouldn't rise up and attempt to leave.

But she had no intention of doing so.

It—he—was so much like Edmond, her lost Edmond. . . . It was his rough fingertips catching on the delicate skin of her neck, and the salt on his clothes, the smell of his hair as she tugged it from its queue, and even that of his skin, moist there at the juncture of neck and shoulder. The way he tipped his head to kiss her . . . when she closed her eyes, and she let herself go, she was back on that hillside with Edmond on that last glorious day . . . .

Her hands reaching up into the olive branches above, looking down at his dark, tanned torso and its little patch of hair down the middle of his chest. The lazy smile he gave her from below, his teeth gleaming and amazingly straight, the feel of him full and hard inside her as she rocked back and forth. His weather-beaten hands on the delicate skin of her breasts, the rasp of cracked and peeling knuckles as they turned to brush along the sides. . . .

Now, though, brought back to the world she lived in today,

Mercédès noticed the fumble as this man, this compelling stranger, worked at the mother-of-pearl buttons at the back of her dress. She felt the tightening and shifting of her bodice as he pulled and twisted to loosen it from behind, his hands smashed between her back and the cushion.

At first, she tensed, turning her head to break the kiss. No, no, she couldn't let him do that. . . . And as if sensing her reluctance, he stopped, moving his hands up to lift her shoulders, pulling her closer toward him. His hips pressed into the tops of her thighs, and she felt his erection straining beneath the silk of thin, loose trousers. A sharp spiral of surprise, and desire, shot down from her belly to her sex, where she automatically shifted to let him rub against her there.

He murmured a soft groan against her mouth, and slid one hand around to cup her breast as he rocked gently against her. Mercédès gasped when she felt the awakening between her legs, the lust swell there, burgeoning and lifting after so many years of nothing.

There were so many layers between his hand and her breast—corset, chemise, bodice—that she could barely sense the thumb that tried to stroke over the top of it, yet she felt the tightening and heaviness grow, the surge of sensation gathering in her nipple. She arched, bowing her back, pressing up into his palm, pushing away everything but the beautiful, living sensations channeling through her, all centering into the moist throb of her sex.

Mercédès pulled at the tiny silk knots that acted as buttons on his shirt, looking up as he raised his face to the ceiling and released a long, shuddering breath as if recognizing her final acquiescence. Beneath the silk she found warm, smooth skin, the muscles there flexing beneath her fingertips as he held himself up on trembling arms.

"Let me," he said, rolling to the side, then off the bed, his shirt flapping with his sudden movements. He shrugged it off, and it fluttered down into the darkness beyond the bed as he came to kneel next to her. She saw his chest, the dark tan marks from rolled-up sleeves and the vee of an unbuttoned shirt, and the pale white of the rest of his skin, fairly glowing in the faint light. He was lean and rangy, with wiry muscles roping along his arms to the gold bands at his wrists, and boxy shoulders, and a flat belly with only the narrowest trail of hair leading down to his trousers.

Pulling her to sit upright, he moved around behind her, and again she felt the tightening and loosening of her bodice . . . but this time she didn't hesitate. Mercédès pulled off her slippers and unrolled her silk stockings as she felt the final give of her bodice. As it opened and fell away from its high neck and the covering of her shoulders and bodice, she was aware that he was already unlacing her corset, tugging and jolting urgently as if unfamiliar with such trappings.

Suddenly, two warm, raspy hands slid around, cupping her breasts from behind. The chill of his golden armbands was a shock to her as they brushed against the sensitive skin beneath her arms, and she gasped . . . but then she forgot everything but what he was doing.

The brush of long whiskers—softer than Fernand's short, bristling mustache—and a warm mouth on the side of her neck, sucking and licking just beneath her ear, just at her most sensitive spot. . . . How could he have known? How could she have forgotten?

He nibbled and sucked and licked, and she gasped and closed her eyes, feeling her pip swell even further, knowing that her legs were getting damp from its moistness. He caught each nipple between a thumb and forefinger, gently tweaking and caressing, teasing them into hard points and making her breathing come faster and harder.

She twisted in his arms, her sagging dress and corset a bundle of confused fabric and lace and boning. Their mouths met again, and she slipped her hands down between them, grasping his heavy cock where it strained through the silk.

Dios mio, she thought. . . . How could a man hide his arousal in trousers such as this? It was almost as if he were naked. She could feel the ridge of his head, slide her fingers along the sweet curve of the erection that jutted freely. The silk made warm friction, and he tensed and stilled as she thumbed over the foreskin of his cock's head, down over the front, where she felt the smallest dampness, and back up and over.

His breathing was heavy and raspy, and hers matched; the room was tight and close again, and suddenly he had her back on the cushions, pulling away from her teasing hands and lifting her skirts. He wasted no time, bringing his hands up her thighs, under the layers of skirt and crinoline and chemise, finding that pulsing wetness of her sex. She let her legs splay open and felt the weight of her dress and its undergarments lifted from her hips and piled on her belly. His hands were gentle but firm on the insides of her thighs, spreading them just at the juncture where her sex was now bare to him, to the open room.

He used his thumb to slide up along the front of her sex, slipping and sliding sensuously, slowly and thoroughly between her labia, into their folds, and around her tight pip, down inside her quim. Mercédès moaned, closed her eyes, and let her hips thrash as much as they could under his relentless thumb. Up and down, around and down and in and out, it moved, slowly, easily . . . and she felt her pleasure gathering there, building and throbbing and pounding.

Sinbad murmured something. She couldn't understand what he said—it almost sounded like her name—and then his hands moved along her thighs back to her knees, as if in a gentle farewell. A low, frustrated wail built in the back of her throat, and her eyes flew open in time to see him whipping open the tie at the waist of his trousers, and in the low light, she saw the silhouette of his ripe cock spring free.

After that, there was no hesitation. A lift of her hips, the grasp of her buttocks, and, kneeling in front of her, he slid inside.

Mercédès cried out, shocked at the intense slam of pleasure . . . and then he pulled back, then filled her, then back, and in and out and in and out until it burst and she shuddered, crying out again, biting her hand to keep from calling the name on her lips.

Edmond.

He arched into her one last time, and with a sharp, pained cry came pouring into her, pulsing inside for a long moment. Sinbad's hands had moved to the sides of her torso, and he bent over her, head sagging, hair hanging in long, messy strands on either side of his face as he breathed in and out as if he'd just run up a hill.

Mercédès lay there, slowly coming back to herself. The rolls of pleasure ebbed away slowly. He pulled himself away and scooted off the bed to stand.

She realized he wasn't looking down at her; instead, he was looking out the window. His profile, shadowed but vaguely visible, reminded her sharply, painfully of Edmond: his nose was long and straight just as Edmond's . . . but his chin jutted with the thick beard, and his hair hung down in stringy waves where Edmond's had always been shorter and brushed back over his ears and forehead. As wiry as he was, this man was still broader and more solid than her love had been.

The reminder of Edmond brought Mercédès back to her reality: not just to the end of the pleasure, but to her life. And what she'd just done. She rolled to the side of the bed, gathering her clothing to her body. There was no way she could dress herself . . . and would this silent, strange man help her?

Would he even let her go?

Yet her quim continued to throb pleasingly between her thighs, and she felt an unfamiliar looseness to her limbs. Her body, at least, was satisfied.

As she stood, he moved behind her, silently, helping her dress slowly and clumsily. But his hands were warm and still raised shivers over the back of her shoulders, and Mercédès wondered again at what she'd done. Yet she did not regret it. Not really. Not the pleasure she'd received, nor the chance to forget today and remember her youth.

There seemed to be no reason for words.

Sinbad finished the last button, and made no protest when Mercédès started toward the door, back out to the room with the mantel, hurrying suddenly to get away, to get back to the small inn where she had let a room. Where she would be safe from Sinbad the Sailor and the memories and emotions and wanton pleasure he evoked in her.

For the second time on that long, eventful day, she walked out the front door of this little house in Allées de Milhein and hurried down its short, uneven walkway.

She didn't look back.

If she had, Mercédès would perhaps have seen the bearded Sinbad following silently behind her, staying to the shadows until she safely opened the front door of a small public inn.

His fingers still trembled, his body still hummed. The corners of his eyes were wet, but his mouth was hard.

"And now . . . farewell, goodness, humanity, gratitude, nostalgia," he murmured, watching her as she disappeared into the inn. "Farewell, those gentle feelings of the heart. Now let the avenging God make way for me to punish those who have wronged me."

Two

The End of an Agreement

Ten years later
Paris

One evening in late November of 1839, a splendid fête was in progress at the grand residence of the Comte and Comtesse de Morcerf. The four-story mansion at number 27 rue du Helder was filled nearly to bursting with the cream of Paris' societal crop.

Lights sparkled from every one of the sixty windows that faced the carriages lined up along the rue, and the shapes of ladies in bright gowns and the gentlemen in long-tailed redingotes mingled behind the uncurtained windows. It was too chilly to have all of them opened, but several had been lifted to allow a cool breeze to filter in, and the noise of the party to filter out. Music from a full orchestra, along with bursts of gaiety and conversation, wafted louder every time the door was opened to admit a new guest.

Mercédès hadn't had a moment to catch her breath since early that morning. Even so, she wouldn't have dreamed of slipping away from her son's bon voyage party if she'd not been cornered by the handsome Comte de Salvieux near one of the doorways to the ballroom.

"Mercédès, *mon amour*, I have been trying to get you alone all evening," Georges murmured, planting his hand firmly at the back of her slender waist. "If I didn't know better, I would believe you were avoiding me." Skillfully, he guided her out of the packed room, and around a small bust of Julius Caesar that stood in the hall. His familiarity with the Morcerf residence aided him in hurrying her into one of the only empty chambers: that of the comte's library.

She freed herself, smoothing the elbow-length glove he'd mussed, and looked at him. She'd hoped to avoid this conversation tonight, for she had so many other things on her mind. But apparently Georges was not to be avoided, though, God help her, she'd done her best.

But before she could speak, he stepped closer to her again, gathering her up against him to press sensual kisses into the curve of her neck and shoulder. "It has been too long, *mon amour*," he murmured against her skin. The soft rasp of his sideburn brushed her cheek, and his tongue flickered out for a quick swipe into the swirl of her ear. When he took her earlobe into his mouth, the chunky emerald there clicked against his teeth.

"Georges," she murmured, successfully keeping the annoyance from her voice, keeping it smooth and low, "I must get back to the guests."

"But I have not seen you for three weeks," he said, looking at her with a masculine pout on his sensual lips. Those very same lips had been the ones to attract her several months ago, but now she could easily dismiss the man's charms. "I have had only that very expensive daguerrotype of you walking along the Rive Gauche to keep me company."

He was young and energetic—a decade younger than her forty years—and most definitely handsome. Georges was also more than capable between the sheets, and in the carriage, and even in the moist grass of the summer gardens at Chevaulx, much to the detriment of her favorite lavender day dress. But Mercédès was no longer interested.

That was, alas, how it always happened for her. She would keep herself aloof and private for months, often years, ignoring the flirtations and courtship offered by men she came in contact with. She'd make her stark loneliness a firm shield to keep the interested men—and her emotions—at bay. But at last, the need for affection and love would overcome her resistance, and she'd succumb to the need to be touched, and loved, and cared for. Thus she would try again to find what she'd had with Edmond and, fleetingly, with the sailor Sinbad . . . that awakening, that brief but emotional connection that had left her trembling for hours afterward and that still laced her dreams ten years later.

"I will not see my son for more than six months," Mercédès told Georges, stepping back, extricating herself from his firm grip. "And so I do not wish to be drawn from his side any more than I must this evening. He leaves tomorrow."

"But, Mercédès, I have missed you so," Georges said, reaching for her hand again.

She neatly avoided him by lifting her hand to pat at the intricate figure eight of hair at the back of her head.

"Georges," she said, looking at him seriously, "I must be truthful and tell you that it is time for our attachment to end." It was, for she hadn't found what she'd craved, and their intimacies had become awkward and meaningless to her. She'd begun the *affaire* hoping . . . but in the end, it was nothing but emptiness and disappointment.

"End? No, you cannot mean that!" This time, she wasn't fast enough, and he was successful in capturing her hand. He pulled her toward him, but she resisted, giving him a clearly annoyed look with raised brows—similar to one she'd give her son just before a reprimand.

Dear Albert! She couldn't believe he would be gone for at least six months, traveling throughout Switzerland and Italy. He was twenty-two years old now, a handsome young man of whom she was inordinately proud. Her only child. How she'd dreaded this day.

How she would miss him.

And what would happen after he was gone?

The old nausea twisted her stomach as she remembered the contemplative way her husband, Fernand, had been looking at her these past few days.

But she would not think about that now.

"Now, Georges, please," she said in the motherly tone she could adapt when it pleased her. There were benefits to being a lady of a certain age, and Mercédès had learned how to use them as needed. She could be gay and flirtatious, appearing as fresh and lovely as a young debutante, or she could cock a maternal eyebrow and adopt a sterner attitude when the situation warranted. As this one did.

"Please don't mean it," Georges said. He looked completely

undone, and Mercédès felt a twinge of guilt. "Please, Mercédès . . . I cannot live without you. I love you."

Before she could reply, the door of the library opened.

"Ah, Mercédès," said her husband as he came in. His sharp dark eyes showed no surprise at finding her in here, away from the festivities and with another—younger—man, who had somehow grabbed her hand yet again. "And Comte de Salieux."

Georges released her and blanched with guilt. He had no idea that Fernand cared little for his wife's extramarital activities—a fact that Mercédès had used to her benefit in more than one instance.

No, it wasn't Fernand's discovery of them that concerned her. Rather, it was the speculative expression in his eyes that made her lungs feel as though they'd frozen.

"Monsieur le Comte," she greeted him formally. Despite the fact that her heart was now ramming in her chest and her palms had become damp under the fine cotton of her gloves, she remained cool and poised. "I was just about to return to the party. If you'll excuse me . . ."

"Of course. I merely came to inform you that Baron Danglars is here with his daughter, Eugénie, and that, as it's my intent—" At this he paused and looked pointedly at Georges, who'd begun to edge toward the door, the bewildered look still on his face.

Whether that shocked look was due to Mercédès' dissolution of their *affaire* or the appearance of her husband, she wasn't sure.

"Perhaps you wish to find something to drink, Salieux," Fernand said pointedly. Georges left the room with a flap of his coattails, and the de Morcerfs were alone as their son's farewell party raged beyond the closed door.

Mercédès looked at the man she'd married eighteen months after Dantès had been taken off to prison. She hadn't wanted to marry him, but she'd had no choice. Even on her wedding day, she'd been sure her broken heart would cause her death, just as a damaged one had surely brought *Père* Dantès to his grave. After eighteen months of being badgered and cajoled by her distant cousin, she had agreed to marry him—not because she'd wanted to, but because she'd had no one and no resources, and had found herself in an impossible situation. Dantès was never coming back, his father was dead, and it had become clear that Villefort would do nothing to help her.

Fernand had been an attractive man, with the same Catalan looks as her own: golden skin, dark hair, and dark eyes. Part of the reason she'd turned to him was because it was expected that Catalans would marry among themselves. It was their culture.

But he had been pleading with her to marry him even while Edmond was alive; while Edmond was at sea on his last voyage, Fernand had come to her every day, trying to convince her to accept his suit. But she had loved only Edmond.

I will love him until the day I die.

She'd told Fernand that every day, yet still he asked. And then when the most horrible thing had happened—when Edmond had been arrested during their betrothal dinner—Fernand had remained quiet.

But then, months later, he asked again, and she refused him. And then he went off into the army, and when he came back, Edmond had been gone for a year, and *Père* Dantès had died only a month earlier, himself certain that Edmond was dead. Over the past eighteen months, she'd gone to Villefort so many times, begging for information, for any news, desperate for anything he could tell her.

When Fernand returned from the army, a hero for his work in Janina, he asked her again to marry him. And that time, she'd had no choice but to agree. Even when she told him the truth, and the reason for her acquiescence, his determination to marry her had not faltered. As she was to realize later, after some months of marriage, it suited his purposes to be married to a beautiful woman, thus proclaiming his virility for all to see.

So, despite the hollowness of her heart, the grief, and the knowledge that she would never love Fernand, she married him, determined to be a good wife to her cousin even if she could not love him. She owed it to him.

If only she'd known his true intentions then, and the real reason he wanted to marry her.

She and Fernand had been husband and wife for more than twenty-two years. Longer than Edmond had been alive.

Mercédès realized with a start that Fernand was looking at her, and that he'd blocked the door with his arm. "What is it?" she asked, keeping her voice steady.

"Am I to assume that Salieux is your current paramour?" he asked. His lips were tight under the dark mustache he'd taken to growing once he acquired his title. It was kept clipped short so that the hairs were sharp and bristly, and scraped sharply across one's skin. A great number of white hairs were beginning to thrust up from beneath the black ones. "I can fully appreciate your attraction. He is quite a robust, well-turned-out young man."

She refused to reply to his taunt. "Now, if you'll excuse me, I have been detained long enough."

"Mercédès," he said. He didn't move, and she could not pass by with his arm blocking the way. "You will be your charming, lovely self to Baron Danglars this evening. In whatever capacity is necessary." His dark eyes, which had long ago seemed so soft and gentle, shone hard and inflexible. "I desire a match between Albert and Eugénie, and I require that you do your part to ensure it."

Lips tight, stomach swirling, Mercédès gave him a short, sharp nod. "You can be assured that I will be hospitable and pleasant to Monsieur Danglars, but I will not suffer his clumsy hands on me."

She'd known of Danglars since he had sailed on the *Pharaon* with Edmond. He'd been the ship's purser, and Edmond the first mate, during a voyage in which the captain had taken ill and died. It had been Edmond's skill and diplomacy in sailing the ship back to Marseille that had earned him Monsieur Morrel's admiration—and had caused him to be named the new captain of the vessel.

Since Edmond had told her about Danglars' anger and jealousy over his promotion, Mercédès had been wary of the man before she even met him. Later, after she married Fernand, she realized that the two men had become known to each other in their business dealings. Still, the man's greasy demeanor, and his hands—which had grown pudgy, along with the rest of him—with their short-clipped nails and soft white skin, made her queasy when she thought of them touching her.

He'd tried. Oh, he'd tried. And Fernand—

"You'll do as I say, Mercédès," her husband said. "Or you will regret it." With one last meaningful look at her, he moved away so that she could exit the room.

She hurried past him, noticing that he was still close enough that her full, dome-shaped skirt and heavy crinolines brushed against his trousers.

"Mercédès," Fernand said just as she entered the hall, "now that Albert is leaving, I will be returning to your bed. Tomorrow. Be prepared to welcome me."

She froze, her hand on the doorjamb. Her heart gave a nasty dip and she turned back, wondering if her face looked as pale as it felt. "If that is your wish, then of course, husband. As long as you come alone."

His lips narrowed, along with his eyes. "You're no longer in a position to be making demands, Mercédès. Albert is leaving, and you have no more leverage. Now go be nice to Danglars and ensure that this marriage is to take place, and perhaps I'll consider your request."

"It isn't a request," she said, her heart pounding. "It's a requirement."

She would have darted away then, but he grabbed her arm and yanked her back into the library. The door slammed behind them, and Mercédès found herself being shoved against it. One of Fernand's hands cupped her throat, holding her there, and the other one circled one of her wrists.

"What ever happened to the quiet, unassuming, *desperate* orphan girl I married?" he asked, his voice deceptively sweet. His hand wasn't close enough around her throat to cut off her breathing, or to leave marks—he wasn't that stupid—but just enough to remind her of his strength . . . and the power he had over her.

"You were so biddable those first years of our marriage. You understood our agreement, and held up your end of the bargain so well. And then you got it in your head to run away from me. As if I wouldn't have been able to find you—Marseille was the first and only place I looked."

"I'll run farther the next time," she said, refusing to let her lips tremble.

"You dare not, Mercédès. Just as you learned before, you know now: You cannot get away from me, and you cannot have a life without your son. Just because Albert is leaving doesn't mean I can't prevent you from seeing him. I've left you alone—nearly alone—for these last ten years—relegated to merely showing you off on my arm as my beautiful, accomplished, distinguished wife. But now that Albert is leaving, I will return to your bed. And you will welcome me . . . in whatever fashion I require." He shifted the weight of his hand so that the palm pressed into the top of her chest, heavy and threatening. She coughed softly under the pressure. "Perhaps, since you are so attached to the comte, I will ask Salieux to join us."

Then, with a great heave, he shoved her to the side. She stumbled into a chair, losing one of her beaded mule slippers in the process. By the time she righted herself, Fernand was gone.

He'd left the library door open.

Mercédès smoothed shaking gloved hands down the front of her spun-gold taffeta skirt, then gingerly felt at the back of her head to see if her hair was still intact. A bit looser than when Charlotte had finished with it, the twisted mass was still pinned in place. The two locks that came from the front of her center-parted style had been drawn back in gentle swoops over each ear, and they too remained tucked into the complicated chignon.

She took a deep breath, refusing to let the tremors continue to shake her fingers, and tears to gather in her eyes. She couldn't let Albert see her like this.

One more night, and he would be gone.

And she would be alone with his father.

Fernand followed through on his threat to come to her chamber the next night.

Mercédès was exhausted from the party of the night before, and the emotion of saying farewell to her son earlier that day.

She had just been divested of her gown, crinolines, corset, and chemise, and had been dressed in a warm flannel night rail. Her maid was brushing her long dark hair.

"Charlotte, you are dismissed," said her husband as he came in the door.

The maid took one look at the set expression on the comte's face and, glancing at Mercédès, gave a quick curtsy and left the room.

Her mistress couldn't blame her: the comte hadn't darkened her door for nearly a decade—since Albert had become old enough to realize what was going on in the house—and Charlotte had only been with her for five years.

"Fernand," she said by way of greeting. It was neither welcoming nor frigid. It was a statement. After all, he was her husband. He had every right to come to her bed whenever he wished.

Mercédès was not foolish enough to attempt to deny him. During the early part of their marriage, she'd tried to love him—or, at least, to pretend that she didn't wish he was Edmond, to hide the tears that came after they copulated, to allow her body to try to respond to his. But she couldn't fully let herself go, and that was, ultimately, what caused his anger . . . and then the humiliations and torments that followed.

Fernand was jealous of Edmond. He always had been, and always would be—despite the fact that Edmond had been dead for more than twenty years.

"You can take that off," he said now, walking over to the bed, pulling off his own nightshirt as he did so.

This, she could do. This was simple. Hundreds, thousands of other wives had done so, did so, every night.

Mercédès unfastened the six cloth-covered buttons that marched down the front of her pleated nightgown, and pulled it over her head. She glanced at herself in the mirror as she made her way to the bed, where Fernand lay, naked and waiting.

Her skin was still golden, and mostly firm, except for the angry red lines from the bones of the corset that still marked her skin ten minutes after it had been removed. Her breasts had lowered a bit over the years, but they had become fuller after her pregnancies—four of which had ended in early miscarriage—and even more generous in these last five years, when her curves everywhere had become more pronounced. Her waist was much slimmer when tamed by the corset, of course, yet there was still a definite hourglass shape to her figure, and her belly made a gentle curve. But Mercédès knew that she was still a beautiful, desirable woman.

Standing in front of the bed, she divided her waist-length hair into two parts and tied it together at her nape, then again, and again, before pinning it into a makeshift knot at the back of her head, aware of how her breasts lifted tantalizingly when she raised her arms.

Fernand's eyes were flat as he watched her, and his cock lay like a large white worm, curled into the dark hair that spread between his legs. It didn't look as though it was ready to rise to the occasion.

Mercédès lowered herself onto the blanket next to him, and closed her eyes as he reached for her. Any vestige of affection she might have had for him had evaporated long ago, when he'd turned ugly and humiliating in their chamber. Now she merely lay there and let him do as he wished.

Or tried to do.

Her nipples reacted partly to his ministrations, and partly to the chill in the room—tightening, pointing—but when his mouth closed over one of them, and he began to suck loudly and avidly, she felt hardly any response twinge down in her belly. She made a soft moan, however, knowing that men appreciated that, and drew herself up to touch his cock. It had made a bit of an effort to come to life, but there was still much further to go. Perhaps if she took it into her mouth, it would hurry things on a bit.

But even after she closed her lips around it, and worked up and down over its head, letting her saliva lubricate the flimsy length, it was still loose and soft. His fingers dug into the tender skin of her back, as though to encourage her, but even her soft moans and teasing tongue made little difference.

It was the same story as before.

During the first months of their marriage, Fernand had been only a bit more easily aroused. It wasn't until a few months after Albert was born, and Fernand returned to her chamber, that she realized why mating with him was so difficult.

He preferred men.

Though he'd wooed and married a beautiful, desirable woman in order to display her as a symbol of his masculinity, and in an attempt to banish his homosexual tendencies, it hadn't worked as well as he'd obviously hoped it would.

Mercédès wouldn't have cared so much about his preferences—after all, she'd agreed to marry him although she loved another—if it hadn't been for the humiliations that ensued: when he could not find satisfaction with her, he brought others to their bed, most usually men—but sometimes a second woman would help provide enough stimulation for him.

The memories of those nights of twining bodies, limbs everywhere and grasping hands, too many mouths and the sight of Fernand bowing over the back of some other man, while Mercédès remained within his easy reach, had been burned into her brain. The shame of having to disrobe in front of another man—or woman—to be fondled and kissed and touched by her husband, or whomever else he invited. The gasps and deep groans, the slip and slide, the questing fingers and the demanding mouths . . . she preferred not to think about those dark nights, the way they'd made her feel, the humiliation of being beneath or next to two grunting men, or being entwined with another woman while her husband labored above her, in her. The way her body often responded to unsolicited stimulation, becoming aroused and titillated.

Even now she gave a shudder and tasted grease in the back of her throat.

And on those nights when Fernand didn't have a willing addition to their bed, and he was unable to find his release . . . his hand or fist would fly, his roughness would send her sprawling onto the bed or, worse, the floor.

A night like that had sent her running the next morning to Marseille those ten long years ago. But fear that he'd keep Albert from her had brought her back home.

After another night like that, a year after she'd returned to Paris, Albert had begun to ask questions his father didn't want to answer. Questions that had given Mercédès nearly nine years of peace from her husband's whims.

And tonight, the night after Albert had left, when Fernand found himself in the same frustrating position, he could not contain his anger and humiliation.

He raised his hand to strike Mercédès once—only once. But this time she was ready for him. She had a gun in her hand, procured from under the mattress. "I will be leaving in the morning for Marseille, for Julie is ready for her confinement. I shan't return until Albert is home. Now leave my chamber."

He did, dangling white worm and all.

And the next morning, once again, she left the house on rue du Helder. But this time, it was not a frightened flight. It was a calculated plan.

She'd decided long ago that she would never beg or plead again.

Mercédès visited with Julie Morrel and her husband, Emmanuel, when she arrived in Marseille.

"Will you stay away from him this time?" Julie asked her. Her belly was so round that it protruded higher than the walnut table next to her.

"Until Albert returns," Mercédès told her truthfully. "There is no telling what Fernand will say to Albert if I'm not there when he comes back. And while our son is home, he won't bother me." She didn't know why her husband had been motivated to come back to her bed, but whatever the reason, it appeared that his tastes had not changed over the years he'd stayed away.

How foolish of him to put himself in such a humiliating position again.

"And when Albert marries Mademoiselle Danglars? What will you do then?"

Mercédès shuddered. "I don't want him to marry Eugénie Danglars. There is something about the girl that puts me off, let alone that her father himself makes me ill. I don't believe Albert wants to marry her either."

"My brother, Maximilien, has returned from the army, just in time for the birth of his fifth niece or nephew," Julie told her, obviously attempting to change the subject to something more pleasant. "He is a captain now, and quite a hero, having saved the life of a nobleman while he was in Constantinople."

"Just like his father," replied Mercédès with a smile. "Doing good for others."

"And Lord Wilmore and Sinbad the Sailor," Julie added, glancing at the red velvet purse that sat in a small glass case on the fireplace mantel of her home. "I only wish I knew how to reach them, to thank them yet again for saving my father. We have never had any correspondence from either of them these last ten years."

Mercédès felt a little shiver. She had visited Marseille several times during the last decade and had spent an inordinate amount of time near the wharf. But she'd never seen the tall, bearded, exotic sailor again.

She'd been so foolish—she could have gotten with child; she

could have been carried off and raped or beaten and left to die, or even killed outright. Yet Sinbad had given her a gift by bringing back long-submerged emotions and sensations.

He'd helped her realize that she was still alive, and could still feel.

Which was why, although she would never admit it even to herself, when she ran from Paris, she came to Marseille and walked along the wharf, hoping.

And so, later that afternoon, on her fourth day in Marseille, Mercédès once again made her excuses to Julie and left for her walk. Her friend could have accompanied her, but at her late stage of pregnancy, a nap was more prudent.

Dressed in a simple day gown of pale pink wool, and a cloak of heavier wool to protect her against the bite of the November sea wind, Mercédès made her way along the streets, following the path she took every day. Past Morrel and Company, toward the tang of the salty air and the busyness of the docks.

She watched for a time, looking for the tall, bearded Sinbad and remembering the tall, lithe figure of Edmond striding toward her, lately from a ship's deck. The cold bit the tip of her nose, and her fingers had become stiff. The pungent smell of fish filled the breeze, bothering Mercédès, and at last she turned to go back.

But just beyond the bustle of the wharves, she felt someone behind her. Her heart began to thump in her throat, and the back of her neck prickled. She turned.

It wasn't Sinbad. It was no one she recognized. A man, perhaps in his middle forties, of average height and with the swarthy skin of a Greek, approached her. She realized he was holding a gun when he came close enough to prod her with it.

"Now you shall not be hurt, madam," he said calmly. "But you must come with me."

"Who are you? What do you want?" she asked, looking around. But no one passing by seemed to notice what was happening. There were four sailors, carrying a heavy crate hoisted on their shoulders. A cluster of women, giggling and pointing and watching the display of muscles from the aforementioned sailors, paid no mind to the single woman being edged back toward the docks.

"I am Jacopo," said the man. "Come with me." He poked her a bit harder with the weapon, and Mercédès had no choice but to follow. "You will not be injured if you do as I say."

"But what do you want from me?" she asked.

"I am taking you to my master." He directed her around a corner, and suddenly she realized they were at the far end of the docks, near one that was fairly deserted but for a single, well-appointed yacht that sat all by itself. Honey-colored wood gleamed in the sun, and startling white sails snapped under the sea wind. As she neared, Mercédès recognized that the small figurehead, carved of ebony, was that of the Greek goddess Nemesis.

Mercédès was prodded up the gangplank and found herself on the smooth deck of the small vessel. By now she was becoming truly frightened. At first, she had thought, perhaps crazily, that this was a trick of Sinbad's . . . that somehow he had found her again and wanted to see her. But there was no sign of the tall, bearded man, and before she had any chance to think, she was urged with the prod of the gun down a short flight of stairs. The passage was so narrow she had to turn sideways in order to fit her heavy skirts through, and she tripped on the bottom step, barely catching herself from falling.

She heard the shouts and calls, and the sudden shifting of the vessel, and realized that they were setting off.

"No! What are you doing?" she cried, pounding on the door that had closed behind her after she was shoved down the four steps. "Where are you taking me?"

No one answered for a long while, but she could tell by the rocking of the yacht that they had left the dock and were setting out to sea. She peered out the small porthole, watching in apprehension and disbelief as the dark patch that was Marseille disappeared over the horizon. At last she sank onto the narrow bed, staring into the falling darkness, wondering if she'd ever see Albert again.

At last, hours later, the door opened, and she was treated to the dark face of the man called Jacopo. She realized how much he looked like a pirate, with his unshaven face and red scarf tied over his head. "Now you may come up if you like, madam. We have food if you are hungry."

"What do you want from me?" she demanded much more bravely than she felt. She remembered now that ten years ago, Sinbad had saved her from being kidnapped by several men who'd threatened to do this very thing. Her mouth was dry, and her stomach churned so much she was certain she would never consider food. Yet fresh air was a must.

She came out onto the deck and realized that the sun had lowered quite a bit in the sky. The wind chilled her almost immediately, but she drew in deep breaths of the cool air. Besides Jacopo, there were only two other men on the small vessel.

They'd been sailing for several hours now, and behind them, she could see the outline of the rocky Château d'If, the island prison etched against the horizon. And behind that great craggy island, far beyond her sight, would be the shoreline of Marseille, and the village where she'd been raised along with Fernand.

Perhaps she would never see him again either. Her fingers shook and her stomach pitched, and it had nothing to do with the rhythm of the yacht.

"You are the Comtesse de Morcerf, are you not?" asked Jacopo.

"I am the comtesse, *oui*," she told him, her hands clasped. Yet she would not plead. "I wish to be taken back. My husband will pay handsomely for my return." She had no doubt of that. He did not wish to lose his wife—of that she was certain, for it was of great importance to him that he was wed to a beautiful woman he could show off in the ballrooms and theater, as well as in the privacy of his bedchamber.

Jacopo nodded in agreement, the tails of his headwrap flapping. "Indeed he will, madam. And that is exactly our wish. Or, I should say, the wish of Luigi Vampa."

"Luigi Vampa? Who is he?" Yet the name sounded familiar to her. A moment later she recalled the brief reprimand Sinbad had given her would-be kidnappers ten years earlier. *It would be best for you to release the woman, else I shall have to tell Luigi Vampa that you have tread beyond your boundaries.* Only the briefest of mentions, but since she had committed every detail of the event to memory, one that came to her immediately.

"A fearsome bandit." Jacopo's smile revealed a gold tooth. "But not a murderer, unless he is crossed. Nor does he involve himself in the slave trade, so you may consider yourself safe, madam. Now, if you do not wish to eat, you must go back below. We shall arrive at our destination in two days."

Two days!

It was indeed late in the second day that the yacht edged around the shoreline of Corsica and steadied itself straight on toward a small island. As they drew nearer, Mercédès, who had been allowed on deck, saw that it was little more than a massive rock. Straggling trees and a few tufts of grass were evident as they drew nearer, but other than that, the island looked completely uninhabitable.

"Monte Cristo," announced Jacopo with a flourish.

Mercédès looked with dismay at the rugged land. There was no sign of any buildings or even tents, nor anything remotely civilized. As the yacht came near the shore, she saw two goats stumbling along the ridge of ragged rocks, and then down below, in the beach, the black ashes of a fire's remains.

Surely they didn't mean to stay there?

"Where is this Luigi Vampa?" she asked boldly. "Surely a man who is as great a bandit as you claim doesn't live in such primitive conditions."

Jacopo laughed as if in delight at her pointed question. "No, no, Signor Vampa does not live here . . . but you are wrong if you believe these are primitive conditions."

Mercédès looked at him, brushing messy, tangled hair away from her forehead. Two days since she'd seen a brush or comb, or even a cloth to wipe her face! The marks from her stays must be permanent by now, and her dirt-hemmed, sea-crusted gown would never be the same. She'd given up wearing her gloves since getting on the yacht, and they were crumpled on the floor in a small puddle of seawater. "I see nothing but rock that's difficult even for the goats to maneuver. And do you mean to say that Signor Vampa, who is certain to demand a ransom from my husband, will not even be here to greet me?"

"No, not Signor Vampa. You will be kept here in comfort in the quarters of his friend while all arrangements are made for your husband to retrieve his wife. And now," he said, making an odd sort of *tsk*ing sound, "that is all I will say. You may ask the remainder of your questions to my master. Go below until we have dropped anchor, madam."

Another two hours passed before the vessel was secured enough for Mercédès and Jacopo to disembark. By then, the sun was resting on the edge of the sea, ready to dip beneath it, and she was hungry.

And nervous.

The yacht couldn't be beached, of course, so there was knee-deep water through which she had to slog—or would have had to, if Jacopo hadn't lifted her and handed her down to his companion. Mercédès closed her eyes against the mortification of being carried by the burly, sweaty sailor who looked—and smelled—as if he hadn't bathed for weeks.

Nevertheless, when she was let down on the beach, she felt more bereft than ever. How long was she going to be kept on this empty, rough place? Did she really have nothing to fear, as Jacopo claimed?

"My master desires that you join him," Jacopo said as he sloshed onto the sand next to her. "But you will have to be blindfolded, for he allows no one to know where his residence is."

Mercédès looked around yet again, and even though the light was growing dim, she could tell that there was nothing resembling a building or a house. The only possibility was some sort of cave, which certainly could be shelter from the elements, but didn't sound the least bit inviting.

"Excuse me, madam," Jacopo said, moving behind her. A

hood was placed over her head, not so stifling that she couldn't breathe, but enough to block out every bit of light. She couldn't even see through gaps in the bottom of the dark cloth.

Jacopo guided her over the soft sand, around choppy rocks, and up and down easy inclines. At last, after walking down, down, down and feeling the air grow cooler, Mercédès was halted. The hood was drawn away from her face and she found herself in . . . a miracle.

Aladdin's cave.

The cavern room wasn't large, but it was furnished just as comfortably as her parlor on rue de Helner. Thick rugs covered the floor; tapestries hung on the walls. Candles and sconces lit the room. There were two cushioned chairs and a long table, which presented gold dishes filled with grapes and oranges and other fruits she couldn't identify. Goblets encrusted with jewels lined the mahogany table, along with several bottles of wine, brandy, and other libations.

"The master thought perhaps you would like to bathe before joining him for dinner," said an oddly accented female voice.

Mercédès noticed a young woman with the darkest skin she'd ever seen emerge from the shadows. Her hair was completely covered with a brightly patterned scarf similar to the one Jacopo wore, and large golden earrings dangled from her ears. Her clothing was something that surely was out of *Arabian Nights*—loose fitting, silky, and gathered at wrists and ankles. "Come with me."

Mercédès felt as if she were in a dream—surely, this world of luxury wasn't really hidden beneath the rock of the small island! But the warm, bubbling water spilling into a marble pool wasn't a dream. It was heaven.

A pleasing scent rose into the air as the Nubian woman gracefully tipped a bronze urn to spill its liquid contents over the bubbling water.

"What is it?" asked Mercédès, sniffing delicately, as the young woman moved to her side to help her disrobe. The smell was orangey, yet floral, and very delicate.

"It is called neroli. Now let us hurry, for His Excellency awaits."

If it was a dream, it was one of the most heavenly Mercédès had ever experienced. Her hair, which had been pinned up for two days, was sorely in need of brushing and washing, and her scalp ached when all of the pins were finally removed. The maidservant's fingers massaged her scalp as Mercédès rested in the deep, bubbling pool, and tried not to worry about what was to come.

Thus far, she had no reason to disbelieve Jacopo.

Another ebony-skinned woman joined them, and soon Mercédès was being soaped and scrubbed and massaged by two pairs of hands. The slip and slide of fingers and suds, the lapping of the warm, incessantly bubbling water, and the easy, sensual scents all served to awaken her senses . . . yet to relax her at the same time.

At last, she was brought out of the bath and toweled and lotioned. Her hair was brushed, but not dressed; instead, it was left long and unbound in a fashion she hadn't worn since she was very young. A single tie, a leather thong, was wrapped around her thick, wavy tresses more than halfway down their length, creating a loose tail.

Instead of dressing her in the confining stays and heavy skirts, the two maidservants pulled a scandalously simple tunic over her head. It was rose-colored silk, with long, loose sleeves and a neckline that traced her throat, but opened in a deep, narrow slit. The edges were embroidered with black and gold, and tassels hung from the ties at the top of the slender vee. To Mercédès' relief, when she stood, the hem of the tunic reached the floor, for she was given nothing else to wear beneath it.

Now, suddenly very nervous, and exceedingly aware of the way the silk slid against her nipples, Mercédès was led from the bath room into yet another chamber by way of a tapestry-covered door.

She found herself back in the same chamber with the long table and golden fruit bowls, the thick rug beneath her bare feet, and the glorious hangings on the walls. But she wasn't to remain here, for the first maidservant—by now she'd learned her name was Omania—gestured for her to follow. Omania lifted another tapestry, and beckoned for Mercédès to go through the doorway thus revealed.

Heart pounding, palms suddenly slick, and her breathing much too shallow and quick, Mercédès walked silently across the rug and through the doorway. The tapestry fell into place behind her with a gust of air, and she found herself in a room even more splendid than the one before.

The rugs were even softer beneath her feet, and she realized with a start that they weren't rugs, but animal furs, piled thickly over the entire floor. The tapestries on the walls were decorated with Oriental swords, their hilts heavy with jewels and pearls, the curving blades etched with ornate designs. Lamps shaded by venetian stained glass hung from the ceiling, casting a soft, warm glow over a room that still held edges of shadow. She saw low, fat cushions of ruby, amethyst, sapphire, and emerald, decorated with fringe and tassels, embroidery and lace. A long, wide divan along one wall of the rectangular chamber was covered with more animal furs and smaller pillows.

Placed in front of the divan was a low, narrow table covered with golden platters, Japanese porcelain plates, glass bowls, jewel-encrusted goblets and pitchers, and food. The array of food was such as Mercédès had never seen before, and couldn't identify some of it. Fruits and vegetables of all colors, fowl of all sizes dressed and roasted, breads, cheeses, wine, tea . . .

Mercédès' examination of the room was halted when the tapestry across from her entrance shifted, and a tall figure came in.

She recognized him immediately; perhaps she'd expected it all along. He was dressed in wide dark red trousers and a simple white shirt. Over the shirt, his short black jacket had no sleeves, but by the glint at its hem, appeared to be decorated with golden threads and small jewels. He wore a black skullcap with a dangling blue tassel, and as before, his long dark hair was pulled into a straight queue that fell along his spine, well past his shoulder blades. The same heavy beard and mustache hid the sensual mouth she remembered, and the low light in the room obscured the details of his expression—but she recognized him just the same.

"Ah, Countess, so we meet again." The man who had called himself Sinbad the Sailor gestured to the chamber with an elegant hand, still cuffed with a gold armband. "Please make yourself comfortable."

Three

In Aladdin's Cave

Off the Coast of Italy
Monte Cristo Isle

When Sinbad settled on the divan and gestured for her to join him, Mercédès felt foolish continuing to stand in her flowing silk tunic while he appeared so comfortable. So she joined him, leaving a generous distance between them.

The particular fur pelt on which she settled was fine ermine, soft as the silk she wore, and thick and lush under her fingertips. At first, Mercédès had a difficult time finding a comfortable position on the divan—she simply wasn't used to the freedom of movement allowed without stays—much less perching on a piece of furniture that was so low to the ground, with no arms or back. At last she settled in a seated position, with her legs curled up to the side, covered by the skirt of her tunic, her long, damp hair gathered to one side. It fell in a heavy swath, pooling over the ermine pelt next to her hip. Even her toes were hidden.

"Please eat," Sinbad told her in that odd accent she couldn't place.

The meal tasted just as decadent as the chamber felt. At first, Mercédès wasn't terribly hungry; nervousness dried her mouth and tossed her stomach. But when Sinbad gestured to a plate of a brilliant golden-fleshed cut fruit that looked and felt like a rich peach, she realized how little she'd eaten in the last few days.

"What is it?" she asked him, after swallowing the delicious, peppery-sweet fruit.

"Mango," he replied, as if surprised that she didn't know. "Try this—papaya. And that." He looked at her with such a steady gaze that she was rattled. "Coconut."

He seemed relaxed, seated with his legs folded in front of him, knees bent and toes tucked inside. Yet it was dark enough in the room that she couldn't fully read his face—even what wasn't hidden by the beard and mustache—and she thought that perhaps his hand trembled a bit when he pointed to the various fruits. But his voice was steady and easy and exotic. She realized her nipples had hardened and poked through the thin silk that had seemed loose and flowing but, now that she'd been seated, seemed to cling everywhere. The slightest movement caused it to rub against her skin like a lover's caress.

Omania and her companion served them in silence, and Mercédès ate the roasted quail stuffed with rice, and a tiny, sweet grain mixed with raisins and dates. Bloodred wine splashed into her goblet and she drank it, and then water, before she had cheese and bread, pears, and figs.

"You were not injured or frightened during your voyage?" Sinbad asked. He ate, but sparingly.

"Annoyed, perhaps," she replied, keeping her voice as steady as his. "What is Signor Vampa's plan? And why are you here?"

"So inquisitive for a . . . guest." He flashed a smile, then drank from his own goblet. When he replaced it on the low table, he spoke to Omania in a foreign tongue, and she nodded. With a bow, she and her companion left the room. "I am here to ensure that your stay is comfortable . . . and pleasurable." He looked at her again, his eyes steady and piercing.

Mercédès felt a stab of lust in the pit of her belly, and her breasts tightened. She looked away. Her mouth suddenly went dry, and she realized her heart was pounding so hard that if she lifted her hand it would show the jolts.

"Has Signor Vampa sent word to my husband?" The sooner Fernand received word of the ransom request, the sooner he could pay it, and the sooner she would be released and back to her normal life, back to Albert.

"Ah, yes. We wouldn't want the comte to suffer in your absence, would we?" Steel laced his words, and he looked toward the table as if to conceal the expression in his eyes. "How terrible it would be for him to endure a moment of pain or worry. Are you so certain he will pay the amount of ransom demanded?"

"There is no question. And . . . is it possible . . . could you ask for a message to be sent to Julie Morrel? She is now married to Emmanuel Herbault, and near the end of her fifth confinement. I don't wish for her to worry that . . . that the worst has befallen me."

His demeanor softened a bit, and he gave a brief nod. "I have already seen to that, for I don't wish any harm to come to her or her family. And word has been sent to the comte." Then he looked sideways at her, a contemplative look in his eyes. "So you do not think that the worst has befallen you?"

"I'm not dead."

Sinbad nodded, but his eyebrows raised. "So you believe that death is the worst fate that can befall someone." He lifted an elegant hand, bringing a choice piece of pheasant to his mouth. The gold band at his wrist glinted in the low light.

"No, I suppose it isn't. One could be injured or ill and live the life of . . . of a rock, experiencing or enjoying little. At least with death, one is no longer conscious of the ills in one's life. . . . But with death there is no chance of improvement in one's condition or situation."

He'd been chewing thoughtfully, and now he swallowed. "Some consider death a welcome reprieve. For example, the man locked away in a dark prison cell likely wishes for death, rather than day after day of an empty existence. He might consider death an easier way than the madness that awaits him. The eternity of darkness and nothing."

Mercédès thought of Edmond, of course, and wondered if he too had wished for death before his demise . . . or if he'd believed that someday he would be free. Her eyes stung, and she looked away.

Sinbad continued to speak. "But perhaps there are worse things than death or imprisonment, Countess. If someone wronged you—for example, if something happened to your son—"

"What do you know of my son?" she asked, suddenly frightened.

"Nothing but what you told me, Countess. Ten years ago, when we last met, you told me you had a son of twelve. So he must be past his majority now." His voice was still relaxed, still exotic and lilting; yet she heard a trace of harshness beneath the superficial gentleness. "As I was saying, if something happened to your son—if he was set upon by bandits, for example, and mercilessly killed, what of revenge? Would you want the brigands who harmed him to die, or would you foist some other form of vengeance upon them?"

"I would want them to know the same suffering as I," she replied fiercely.

"Exactly so, my dear countess. And would not an execution—a rope around the neck, the kiss of the guillotine, a bullet to the head—be too simple, too easy? Would it not allow the evildoers to be released into whatever afterlife they might expect?"

"I said I *wanted* them to suffer . . . but they will be judged by God," Mercédès replied firmly. "It's not my place to judge here on this earth."

Sinbad smiled, his dark mustache stretching to show a glimpse of suddenly feral teeth. "But I know that God selects avenging angels—avenging ones and rewarding ones—and places them here on this earth to assist Him. And for great sins, very often the best justice is a long-lasting punishment. One in which the sinner lives with the results of his or her perfidy, rather than being released from his earthly responsibilities by swift death."

He met her eyes again. "Would you not want those who murdered your son to live with a pain and loss as great as your own? Wouldn't death be too simple, too quick for them?"

"I would want that—yes, I would . . . ," Mercédès replied, honesty compelling her to speak plainly. "But . . ."

Her voice trailed off. Sinbad was looking at her so steadily, so darkly, that the words simply disintegrated. "What an honest woman you are, Countess," he said sardonically. "Honest and loyal and true. You would wait for your love forever, wouldn't you?"

She had waited for Edmond.

She *had* . . . until she'd had no choice.

She knew Fernand had lived in fear for that first year or two after they married that Edmond would return, that he would be furious that Fernand had badgered her into wedding him when she'd promised to wait for him . . . but Edmond had never returned.

The sharp clap of Sinbad's hands startled her, drawing her from the deep, dark reverie of guilt and loss. "I can see that our debate is upsetting you, Countess," he said. "Let us move on to more enjoyable pastimes. Please," he said with a gesture of those elegant, gold-cuffed hands. "Enjoy Omania and Neru."

Mercédès realized that Omania and another servant, a male—presumably Neru—had returned, and cleared the table of much of the food whilst she and Sinbad conversed. They moved the table across the room, putting it against the wall opposite them. Neru moved another, smaller table next to Sinbad, and on it the servants placed some wine and several small bowls filled with grapes, mango, and a tiny jewellike red fruit Sinbad had called "pomegranate."

Now the two servants moved to the empty space recently vacated by the table of food, and stood in front of the divan. Omania had changed clothing, and was wearing a skirt made of nothing but countless strips of silk hanging from a golden girdle that settled below her navel. A large sapphire had been set in that small hollow. Her smooth coffee-colored skin was bare from hip to just below her breasts, which were bound with more strips of silk that wrapped around her neck, leaving her arms bare but for numerous golden bangles and bands. Her black hair hung in thick, springy coils from the crown of her head, where they were captured by a wide gold band studded with emeralds. Her feet were bare, but she wore gold rings on her ankles and toes.

Neru, a young man of approximately the same age as Omania—perhaps twenty—was garbed similarly to Sinbad. However, he wore no shirt under his short jacket, which hung open to display part of a well-muscled, hairless chest, and all of a flat belly, ridged with muscle. His arms were well defined and gleamed sleekly, as if they and the rest of his espresso skin had been oiled. His strong, broad feet planted themselves on the rug of leopard fur.

A drum began to beat low, drawing Mercédès' attention to an as yet unnoticed corner, where the other female maidservant who'd helped her bathe was sitting. The drummer's attention was trained on Omania and Neru as her sure hands beat an exotic rhythm.

"Countess." She heard the voice and turned to look at Sinbad. His shadowed eyes held hers.

Suddenly, the room felt soft and warm. And small. It shrank as he moved toward her, uncurling his legs and easing himself closer with the smooth stepping of his palms on the fur pelts. She watched his hands, tanned fingers spread wide and solid, sinking into the furs, and found herself unable to look away as they moved nearer. The drumbeat pounded low and steady in the background, deep enough that she felt it in the depths of her body.

Her heart rammed in her chest, and her own fingers trembled in her lap, crushing and dampening the silk. When his hand brushed against her silk-covered leg, she closed her eyes. Her breathing was unsteady, and she thought she heard raspiness in his breath.

When he kissed her, at last, the bristles of his mustache were the same soft ones she remembered. They brushed against the dry plumpness of her lips, a gentle tickling as if to invite them to open. And they did.

He was still on his hands and knees, their faces even and his head tipping to the side to better fit his mouth to hers. His arms bumped against her legs, and his weight on the divan cushions caused her to lean gently toward him, so she reached out to steady herself. Her fingers clashed with his among the fur.

The slick tangle of tongues, the sucking and nibbling and sliding of lips, the heat of his proximity, a spicy smell in his hair, the sweetness of mango and wine threaded through the kiss . . . a ferocious kiss, saved up for ten years. It was as if a door had opened and sensation burst through her body, awakening it.

Sinbad pulled back. "Enjoy," he told her, gesturing at the younger man and woman standing before them.

He moved back to his place, and Mercédès stared at him in the dim light, her lips parted, her eyes fastened on him, her breath still coming in little surprised pants. *Dios mio*, what he'd done with a mere kiss!

Turning away, Sinbad clapped his hands again, and Neru and Omania began to dance.

Mercédès watched as the couple's bodies began to undulate sinuously, gliding, shifting, rolling. At first, they stood next to each other, facing the divan, toes pointed toward their audience. Neru was in front of Mercédès, close enough that she could smell his musky scent and see the fine hairs of his brows, and Omania moved opposite Sinbad. Neru's eyes were closed, and his body moved as though drawn by the drumbeat, easily, sensuously . . . moving to the low throbbing that began to match the drumming of Mercédès' heart. His arms rose, his hips shifted sensually, and his belly rolled like the waves of the sea.

The mirror movements of the two dancers were beautiful and arousing, even before they turned to each other. But when Neru and Omania faced each other, the dance changed. They moved closer, eyes now open and trained upon the other. Palms flattened against each other, hips fitting together in a smooth slide, knees bent, torsos arched backward.

Omania turned away from Neru, and as she did, the scarf around her breasts unfurled, clasped somehow in his large dark hand. The colorful silk, patterned in red and gold and violet, wrapped around his fist and dangled to the floor. The woman turned back and Mercédès saw that her tight, high breasts were bare, thrusting dark, hard nipples and shifting in a sensuous, rolling movement as she kept time to the beat of the music.

Mercédès' mouth went dry when Neru's hands covered those two mahogany breasts with his large dark hands, the scarf still dangling from one of them. Omania tipped her head away, exposing the long line of her neck. The springy coils of her hair brushed her bare spine, and then down to dangle over the fur rug as she arched her back at an impossible angle, her hands finally reaching the ground behind her. Her knees bent, thrusting bare through the strips of silk that acted as a flimsy skirt. Neru drew his hands down her flat belly, over the navel that held the sparkling sapphire and around her hips, kneeling in front of her sex, between her knees.

With a few simple movements, Neru whisked away the golden belt that held the silk skirt. It was all Mercédès could do not to gasp at the sight of the other woman's hairless sex, rising smooth and beautiful, framed between Neru's thumbs, directly in front of her. So close, if she leaned to the edge of the divan, she could stretch out her hand and smooth it along his tight torso. His fingers were wrapped around Omania's slender thighs as her hips undulated in that same, easy rhythm.

As Neru bent his face to the exposed quim in front of him, Mercédès felt her own sex beating dully between her legs. When Omania gave a soft gasp as Neru tasted her, Mercédès suppressed her own little moan. Her nipples were hard points, her quim wet and slick, *waiting, needing*. . . . Her eyes fastened on the couple as though she could never turn away.

She could see plainly as Neru swiped his thick red tongue over the deep slit of Omania's quim, up and then down, feeling the strokes at the seam of her own sex . . . and then, as if choreographed, he slid his mouth up along her belly as Omania shifted her weight toward him, balancing into his face as she pulled herself back upright. When she was tall and straight again, he stood and the two entwined their arms, raising them toward the low, curving ceiling, and kissed. Her breasts were flat against the black of his jacket, and Neru pulled away to cup them again, to slide his thumbs over the jutting nipples there.

Through this all, the drum continued to beat incessantly, like the dull throb of sex. Mercédès' breath was coming faster; she felt as if she herself was in the midst of the sensual play in front of her. She could be, if she moved closer. Those hands, that tongue—that thick, strong, red tongue—could be pleasuring her.

This display of sexuality, of gentle, arousing dance and touch, was nothing like those nights with Fernand and his playmates. That had been . . . flat, rushed, desperate. . . . This was . . . this was . . .

Then Mercédès became aware of movement behind her, the warmth and weight of a man on the furs. She was still sitting on the side of her left hip, her legs curled up next to her, propped on her left hand, her hair making a damp patch on the ermine next to her—afraid to move, for fear if she did, she would be caught up in the whole dance. Behind her, engulfing her, his smell, that spicy scent that reminded her of one of the dishes she'd tried tonight, hovered . . . yet Sinbad didn't touch her.

Neru's short jacket was gone now, and Omania's delicate hands moved over his gleaming chest, over the flat nipples that sported fascinating gold rings. Mercédès stared at them, watching as Omania took one ring into her mouth, sucking and pulling on it so that the flesh of his nipple and areola tugged away from his body. It looked painful, yet . . . yet titillating. And if the flare of Neru's nostrils, and the soft little sigh, was any indication, he found it so as well. Her nipples surged and ached as she watched the rhythm of Omania's mouth on that golden ring.

The woman's hands were as busy as her mouth, pulling at the loose trousers Neru wore, and suddenly they slipped down, into a pool at his feet. Omania released the golden ring and bent to pull the last bit of clothing away, and when she moved back, Mercédès saw the long, proud thrust of his dark cock.

She must have made some noise, shuddered or moaned, for

Neru turned and looked directly at her. He smiled, his teeth perfect and white, and he held out his hand, brushing the air in front of her, beckoning for her to join them. Mercédès gasped and drew back, fascination and lust pounding through her as she tried to catch her breath. No, she shook her head, no.

But . . . yes. The lust rampaging through her made her feel as though her body was ready to burst—her nipples, her pip, even the lips of her quim were swollen and ripe and ready.

Neru continued to look at her with sultry eyes as Omania knelt in front of him, shifting slightly to the side so that Mercédès had an unencumbered view of the way she slid the length of his member into her mouth. The girl's jaws gaped, her cheeks looked hollow, and her eyes closed as she gripped Neru's hips, using him to balance her as she moved back and forth. Her small breasts moved and swayed, lifting and falling, as she moved, and her sleek brown haunches rose and fell in the same rhythm.

Mercédès closed her eyes, trying to steady her breathing, to pull herself out of the maze of sensations. But then there was the warmth of breath on the bare side of her neck, the whisper in her ear: "Open your eyes, Countess."

She shuddered and felt how close he was behind her now. And as she watched Omania suck and lick the cock before her, moving the foreskin up to reveal the burgeoning head, Mercédès felt two hands closing over her own aching breasts. At last. A burst of pleasure swelled, burning through her, ripening her pearl between her tight thighs.

His palms pressed into the stone-hard tips that jutted painfully, making the silk hot and damp over her skin. And then he released her, just as he released a long hiss of breath into her ear, moist over the side of her neck. She exhaled in deep disappointment, opening her eyes again in time to see the arch of Neru's neck and the pop of veins there as he gasped, shuddering his release into Omania's willing mouth.

Mercédès became aware of Sinbad's touch again. It was light as he grasped the material of her tunic, at the sides of her breasts, and began to shift it around and over them. The featherlight touch circled around her nipples, over the sensitive skin there, around and over, back and up and down . . . unrelenting in its gentle torture. She shifted, arching her back, trying to thrust her breasts closer to the material, trying to find some relief.

"Are you greedy, Countess?" he asked at her ear. His words were not so steady as before, and she let her head fall back onto his shoulder and felt the rampant pounding of his own heart beneath the back of her skull. "Are you watching them? They prefer to be watched."

With effort, she lifted her head and saw that Omania was on the floor in front of the table now, on a thick cushion. Her springy hair fell from its topknot, brushing her gleaming brown shoulders and reaching onto the floor behind her. She reached her hands up and beyond her head, lifting her breasts. Neru knelt on his haunches in front of her, his darker hands holding her thighs open as he bent his face to her sex. Mercédès watched, her mouth open, feeling herself panting softly, as he licked, slowly and thoroughly, arranging himself so that she could see every swipe of his tongue.

The rhythm over her nipples had stopped, and now Sinbad's heavy, warm hands moved down the sides of her torso, making the silk cling to her damp skin. One hand slipped around between her legs to feel there, through the silk. Mercédès shifted, lifting her hips to meet his questing fingers. He used his strong forefinger to brush over the top of her mound, pressing down over her labia, then gently stroking, up and down, up and down, through the quickly dampening fabric. Her breathing rose, her eyes closed, and she let herself rest back against him and felt his own short, hurried breathing.

Now his other hand had found its way back to her breast, and he slipped it through the deep vee of her tunic, closing his rough palm over real flesh. "Open your eyes, Countess," he said, his accent nearly gone in the low timbre of his words. They were little more than a breath, rough and hot now against her neck. His mouth closed over her skin there, fiercely, suddenly, scraping with his whiskers, and she gave a little gasp, a little jerk, and then everything exploded into a mass of shudders and jolts and long, sweet, undulating pleasure.

When Mercédès came back to herself, she realized she was still wrapped in Sinbad's arms from behind. Her eyes remained closed, and she felt damp and hot, yet alive and taut.

Yes, taut . . . for when he shifted against her, his hands moving over that horrible, sticky silk, her body tingled once more. Her breasts lifted, her pip swelled, ready, and her mouth watered.

"Countess," he murmured in her ear, "you're missing the show."

She opened her eyes reluctantly as he moved behind her, and saw Omania writhing on the cushions in front of her. As Sinbad shifted closer, Mercédès felt at last the ridge of his cock pressing into her buttock. Without another thought, she reached behind, closed her fingers over it, watching as the two performers in front of her at last collapsed into a sweaty, sated heap. Heat pulsed through the fabric of Sinbad's trousers, and the material was so thin she could feel the shape of his head, the ridges of veins, and deep below, the hard stones of his ballocks. Sinbad groaned when she touched him, his hands tightening where they'd settled on her hips.

"Ahh," he sighed, burying his face into her shoulder, his words smothered by her skin. She probed and stroked through the silk behind her, and would have taken the moment to pull the waistband away to slip her fingers down to touch his turgid flesh, but he kept her facing away, kept her hand there on his cock until she felt him stiffen, and then shudder behind her as the silk beneath her hands became wet.

His hands, tight on her shoulders, fell away, and she felt him sag back, propped up on his palms. When she turned toward him, his eyes were closed, and for a moment, with the bottom half of his bearded face shadowed, he looked so much like Edmond that she froze. Her heart actually stopped.

She was reaching to touch his forehead, with the thick brows and the strong curve that led into his nose, when he opened his eyes, startling her.

He held her gaze for an instant, just long enough that even in the unreliable light she saw a flash of what could only be agony. And then it was gone, and his expression turned back to that of the cordial, relaxed host.

"Shall I pour you a drink?" he asked, moving away on the furs. "Or perhaps you might like to try this." He lifted a small bowl.

A spoon protruded from the porcelain vessel, its handle ornate and heavy compared to the bowl of the utensil.

"What is it?" she asked, shifting, nearly groaning as her

legs ached from being in such a position for so long. The tunic bunched under her knees as she crawled closer to where Sinbad had retreated, nearly sending her off-balance. It was hot and clingy. . . . She wanted to remove it, but . . .

"It is the ambrosia of the gods," he told her, lifting the spoon to his mouth and eating from it. "It will take you wherever you wish to go."

Mercédès leaned toward him, and he fed her a bite of the chewy paste. She swallowed the odd-tasting mixture and then sipped her wine as Neru and Omania also ate from the spoon.

"What is it called?" she asked.

"It has many names, but the one you might be familiar with is hashish," Sinbad told her. "Now shall we relax? Here, there is more to drink. And if you like," he said, gesturing to yet another maidservant, who had appeared with a tray laden with a steaming bowl, "you may try a smoke." Mercédès saw the thin reed of various pipes curling from the bowl.

Some form of incense began to waft through the air, making the room again smaller, and warmer. The smell was unfamiliar to Mercédès, but it wasn't unpleasant; it had a sort of musky scent laced with a bit of spice. Neru and Omania, heedless of their nudity, knelt in front of the divan and faced Sinbad, as if waiting for his next command.

He gave a short nod, and the two rose and went to the small table next to their master. When they returned, each carried a small pot and a corked bottle.

Mercédès watched as Omania removed Sinbad's shirt with deft brown fingers, and then knelt to slide his trousers down, leaving him bare except for the gold cuffs at his wrists, and, to her surprise, a single ring on his right areola. A shock of lust spiked through her again—had he worn that ten years ago?—but then Sinbad reclined on the divan, settling in the shadowy corner on his belly, leaving the lovely muscular curve of his ass bare to the chamber.

Omania knelt next to him, and after dipping her fingers into the small pot, she poured oil from the corked bottle onto his broad back and began to rub. In the low light, his flesh glistened and moved under her hands, the ripple and shine of muscle and the dip and curve of his shoulders glowing. Mercédès wanted to shove the servant girl out of the way and touch him herself, but before she could make such a move, Neru knelt on the divan next to her.

She looked at him, suddenly feeling light of head, yet incredibly free and loose. Before she knew it, he bent his face to hers. His kiss, with those full, sensual lips and strong tongue, left her breathless and shaky; but then he sat back on his haunches and began to tug at the hated tunic.

It was her only covering, and she knew it would be so daring to remove it, her last shield. But she was the only one clothed, and her skin yearned to breathe, to rid itself of the heavy, damp cloth. She didn't protest as he lifted it up over her legs and hips, and before she quite knew it, she raised her arms so that it came up and over her head.

Relief . . . Her skin breathed once uncovered, yet felt warm and supple in the cooler air. Her heart beating strongly, Mercédès looked at Neru, wondering what was to happen next. But instead of kissing her again, he gestured for her to recline on the divan. Her skin tingling with apprehension and anticipation, she stretched out on her belly.

His hands were large and strong, and they moved over her

skin with long, sure strokes from shoulder to buttock and back up again. The oil he used created a heated friction, and sent off that same orangey-floral scent she recalled from her bath. Mercédès closed her eyes, giving herself up to the feel of this man's hands as they closed around her waist, sliding up to her shoulders and down along her arms to the tips of her fingers, and back. She felt glorious, alive, and aroused.

When Neru brought his hands back up from a long stroke to her hips, they slipped around between skin and fur, to cover her breasts. Mercédès caught her breath when his deft fingers veed around her tight nipples and wove them back and forth and side to side. His hot skin brushed up against her hips, his breath and the proximity of his torso warmed her bare back. Neru's fingers were rhythmic and relentless, tweaking and twitching her nipples against the ermine as her sex lifted and stretched again. Warm wet pooled in her quim; Mercédès shifted her legs so that they fell apart and buried her face into the soft furs near her restless fingers.

Before she knew it, Neru had rolled her onto her back and reared over her, his mouth descending to one breast as the other pulled the heavy, clinging strands of her damp hair away from her torso. When he closed over her nipple and sucked hard, she could no longer contain a gasp of pleasure. It came out like the long, low moan of wind before a summer storm.

The world moved and shifted, like pieces of colorful glass in a kaleidoscope: hot, dark skin touching her golden flesh; full, red lips opening over her nipple and sucking it into a long point; strong fingers sliding through the slick seam of her quim, flicking at her pip like a gentle tease. She closed her eyes, arching her hips and letting the pleasure overtake her.

Dimly, she heard a voice, a deep, sharp command from a great distance. Then the roaring sensations changed. . . . The heat shifted away, then returned. . . . The slickness of mouth and tongue disappeared, leaving one nipple hard and wet and cold, thrusting so tight it must be burning red. She opened her eyes as someone separated her knees, gently but firmly—but she had no desire to keep them closed. Her feet came off the divan, resting on the floor in front of it as large, warm hands stroked the insides of her thighs . . . lightly, so delicately, like a nasty tease, that she jerked and trembled in her sprawled position, trying to shift her hips, her thighs, her feet around . . . to find some kind of deeper touch that might lead her to what she needed.

Someone moved behind her—everything was a luscious haze of warmth and wetness, pressure and tug, rhythm and stroke—and strong, masculine hands came around, covering her tight, ripe nipples from behind. He pulled her back against him, supporting her spine with his torso, his taut arms bracketed around her, holding her breasts as he nuzzled sleek whiskers against her neck and shoulder. His long fingers slipped in and around her nipples, plucking at them, tweaking, caressing the very tips of them as his thumbs made light, sensual circles on the sides of her breasts. The hot length of his cock pressed between her spine and his leg.

Somehow, Sinbad's long, dark hair, smelling like cardamom and other spices, had come loose, and it mingled with hers, falling over her shoulder as he kissed and nibbled along her neck. She arched and shivered when he found that sensitive spot, just below and behind her ear, letting her eyes close once more as she fell into the rhythm of his fingers and the pulse of arousal.

The hands between her legs stopped their languorous strokes, settling firmly, fingers gently pressing into the tender flesh there. Then Neru's lips—it must have been Neru kneeling before her as Sinbad caressed her from behind—slid over one side of her labia, and his tongue snaked out in a surprise swipe over the seam of her quim. Mercédès startled, jerking under his hands, lifting her hips to press her sex to those full lips.

Did she hear a gentle chuckle in her ear? Her world became a maze of sounds—of deep sighs, and gentle moans, the soft suction, the faint lapping and rasping breathing; and Mercédès knew her own sounds of pleasure filled her ears most loudly.

Sinbad gently caressed her breasts, relentless with the teasing of her nipples to a point of near pain, but ultimate pleasure . . . and then easing a bit, just a bit, so her breathing could catch up. . . . Neru bent between her legs, his lips and tongue sliding in the deep, wet crevices of her quim, lapping through the pool of her juices slowly, so slowly she thought she would scream with the frustration.

She moved her hips desperately, feeling the orgasm come so close only to ebb away as Neru and Sinbad seemed to know just when to slow or ease back. Her body was tight and stretched, ripe as if to bursting—her nipples, her lips swollen from biting back the sighs and pleads, her quim lips, her pip . . . full, glossy and plump, ready . . . so ready . . .

And then Sinbad's fingers shifted away, and Neru's mouth stopped its lovely taunting, and Mercédès jerked restlessly, her hips lifting and rocking to the side, trying to find it again . . . but firm hands held her thighs steady. Sinbad's dark breath in her ear teased and infuriated her.

"Not yet, Countess," he said. But his words were harsh and forced, hot against her earlobe. She felt the rampant throbbing of his cock against her, the little swipe of moisture that had slipped from its head and stroked along her hip. He was ripe and ready too.

Before she could respond, grasp that cock and show him a little torture of his own, he moved like an eel, sleek and fast, and his mouth was on her breast, and his hand between her thighs. Mercédès gasped when his skillful mouth feathered over the sensitive, pebbling skin of her breast, arching up into the warm, wet cavern. She felt the movement, the gust of warm air over her damp skin when he breathed his own lust over it, and she reached, trying to find his sex.

He captured her hands, pulling them above her head, straight over and down into the furs, settling himself directly over her, hip to hip, breast to chest, mouth . . . oh, God, mouth to mouth with that strong tongue swiping deep and sure around hers. Limbs entwined, mouths smashing together, his cock throbbing against her quim, they kissed and touched and ground their bodies together.

She pulled her hands free, pushed away the mess of heavy, clinging hair plastered to their faces and bodies, and closed her fingers around his shoulders. Dragging her nails down, deeply into his skin, she lifted her hips, capturing his turgid penis between her thighs. He grunted and moved away, dragging the length of his dripping cock over her thigh, scooting to settle between her legs.

His tongue was flat and slow . . . oh, so slow . . . up and gently over her pulsing labia, up and down, slowly, excruciatingly slowly. Mercédès tried to sit up, to pull herself toward him and touch, but strong black hands closed around her wrists, holding them above her head again.

And again the tongue, and again, slowly up and over her quim . . . and then, with his thumbs, Sinbad pulled her lips apart, opening her swollen pip to the gentle lashing of his tongue. Mercédès was thrashing now, her hair over her face and shoulders, her lips parted and breath coming in desperate gasps as he played and teased and brought her to the edge again, and again . . . always stopping just before she went over until she was ready to scream.

But even through it all, she didn't ask. She didn't beg. She closed her lips on the words, biting them, knowing that it would come. . . . She was close, so close . . . ripe and ready, and at last, with one last teasing swipe, he steadied, settled, and used his tongue to lap and lift and jiggle her sex into madness.

She burst at last, her whole body arching, then convulsing against the hands that held and caressed her, against the mouth that ate at her and the furs that embraced her, pleasure hot and hard and strong trammeling through her body in a haze of flashing lights and satisfied groans.

Mercédès fell into a langorous darkness for a moment. Then she felt movements, shifting around her and short, sharp words . . . then the long, slow slide of a moist, hard body next to hers. Sinbad kissed her again, pulled her over as he rolled so that she sprawled, a sack of sated bone and muscle, over him. His cock rose strong and ready between her splayed thighs, and he said, "Ride me, Countess."

She pulled herself up, focusing at last, and saw no one else on the divan. They were alone, and her body hummed and prickled, and her mind had lost some of the dullness of desire. She looked down at him, but his face was in shadow; someone had extinguished more of the candles, leaving only a few across the room.

He moved his demanding hands to her hips and lifted her over him, easily. She spread her legs, settling his cock's head into the entrance of her quim, looking down as she placed her hands on his smooth, hairless chest, covering the gold ring jutting there.

She felt the slam of his heart beneath her fingers, the deep, desperate need of his breathing, and teased his cock with her slippery quim. He would have none of it; he grasped her hips and slammed up into her with the groan of a dying man. Mercédès matched the sound, her own gasp of pleasure riding into a long moan as he held her hips to thrust in again.

That was it. . . . He surged up a third time and let it go, and she felt the undulant pulsing inside her quim as he froze in the throes of release.

She collapsed on his chest, her mouth near that fascinating gold ring, and his hands fell away onto the fur. Their hair was plastered and tangled, and her legs ached from being spread wide, straddling him and holding herself up.

It wasn't long—not long at all, for her breathing had barely eased—when she felt him move against her, inside her. A little jolt of his hips, the change in breathing, the return of his wide hands to her torso, raising her.

He was growing hard again, inside her, and Mercédès felt her own response as her sex throbbed gently between them.

"Ride me, Countess," he said again. His voice was strained and flat, and she couldn't see his eyes—they were too shadowed. His fingers bit into the sides of her hips as he shifted her over him.

She moved, feeling the sweet swell of desire building again, rising and lowering on her thighs, her hands flat on his chest as he helped her shift back and forth, up and down.

"Reach up," he commanded. "High."

She did, settling back on her haunches, taking his thick length inside her, releasing it, lifting and falling, jolting back and forth in an increasing rhythm. Her breasts tightened, her nipples puckered and thrust, and his palms closed over them, warm and solid. She lifted her hands in the air, reaching toward the olive branches above from that day in the sun.

She reached and tipped and tilted, faster and faster, Edmond beneath her, the sun beating down on her, his hands on her breasts, the olive leaves just out of reach.

His hips thrashed below, his hands tight on her flesh, his breathing harsh and the shadowed planes of his face stark and hard. He was saying something, muttering it as if delirious, but she couldn't hear him, it was lost in the whirl of sensation and memory. Tears spilled from her eyes as she worked, and he worked, and they slammed into each other, hard and angry, grief-stricken and regretful and desperate. So desperate.

When she finally reached that last pinnacle, the hardest, most draining one yet, Mercédès slipped over, crashing into brightness, and she felt the tears pouring down her face.

She fell to the side, sobbing silently, and slipped into oblivion.

FOUR
The Return

Four months later
Paris

"*Maman!* I am so glad to be home," Albert said as Mercédès pulled him into her embrace. Instead of waiting in the parlor for him to be brought to her, she'd rushed to meet him in the foyer of their home on rue du Helder.

"At last," she said, burying her face into his neck, smelling the scent that had been her comfort since he was but an infant. She barely managed to keep the tears of joy from turning into ones of fear. Fear that she had almost lost the one that she loved above all else in the world. "Those bandits, they didn't hurt you?"

She stepped back to look at him, just to make certain. He certainly appeared unchanged, except for a more worldly, experienced air. His dark hair was combed neatly, his clothing was fashionable and pressed, and if his face looked a bit more mature . . . well, that wouldn't be particularly unusual after his experience.

"No, *maman*. They were unfailingly polite and even apologetic once it was made known to them that they had made a mistake."

It was March, four months after Albert had left to tour Switzerland and Italy. While in Rome for the Carnivale in February, he had been lured away from the festivities by an attractive woman, and then captured and held for ransom by her associates, a gang of brigands.

But by the time Mercédès and Fernand had received word of the demand, Albert had been set free, unharmed, and without his parents having paid the ransom. And then, to Mercédès' distress, an unconcerned Albert had continued his tour of Italy for another three weeks before returning to Paris.

"A mistake?" Mercédès asked. She knew her son would prefer to protect her from the sordid details, but she would not be stopped from knowing all of them. Could it be a coincidence that Sinbad had imagined the possibility of her son being attacked by brigands, and then for it to actually happen?

Albert seemed to realize how disconcerted she was, and holding her hands, he drew her to one of the pink-and-gold brocade sofas in the small parlor, settling himself next to her on a plump cushion. He even helped her to arrange her wide skirts so that they wouldn't be crushed, and he continued to clasp her fingers. "Mama, it was a mistake. Once the bandit realized I was a friend of the Count of Monte Cristo—"

"Monte Cristo?" Mercédès breathed, feeling the color drain

from her face, and then return with such a force that her cheeks felt very warm.

The name of the very island on which she'd been taken and kept in such a decadent, lush state by Sinbad the Sailor . . . and then abruptly and unceremoniously banished the day after her arrival. Indeed, Mercédès remembered only vague details from her time on Monte Cristo, deep beneath the rough, rocky surface—but what she did remember was enough to make her face flush even now. And to filter into her dreams in the night, waking her and leaving her hot and restless and confused.

"Yes, Mama. Franz and I had the pleasure of meeting the great Count of Monte Cristo while we were staying in Rome during Carnivale. In fact, if it weren't for him, we would never have had such a fine time, for he allowed us to use his carriage while we were there. He was staying in the same hotel, and learned that we had not—well, Mama, you know that Franz and I do not always make our plans in advance," he said sheepishly.

"When he learned that we had not found a carriage to rent, he offered us the use of his. What a grand gentleman he is, Mama! So learned and intelligent and very well-dressed and very, very rich. I have never seen such grandeur."

"And how did it come about that the Count of Monte Cristo saved you from the bandits?" she asked, her face having cooled to its normal temperature. "Surely we must pay him back for your ransom."

"But no, mama. You see, this bandit leader is indebted to His Excellency the count. When Franz learned that I had been taken, he was trying to find the money for my ransom, for we didn't have enough between the two of us, and there was no time to send to Father for it. He had to do it quickly, for the bandits insisted that if the ransom was not produced by the second day, I would be—well, Mama, it is of no consequence now."

"What? He would have killed you, wouldn't he?" Mercédès' fingers convulsed over Albert's, and her stomach squeezed anew.

Thank God. Thank God, her son had been spared.

"Well, that is what he threatened—but it did not happen, so there is nothing to be worried about now, Mama. When the count learned of my situation, for he was staying at the same hotel, and the news reached him easily, and he learned that the bandit's name was Luigi Vampa"—here Mercédès was forced to smother another gasp—"he immediately intervened. Not only did the count intervene," Albert said, his young eyes shining with admiration, "but he actually rode to the hideout of Signor Vampa and insisted that he release me at once."

"And you were released? And there was no ransom paid? And they didn't hurt you?" Mercédès couldn't stop herself from reaching to touch his handsome, beloved face. Albert was all she had left in the world that she cared for.

"No, Mama, as you can see, they didn't hurt me."

"And this Signor Vampa, he knows the man you speak of, this Count of Monte Cristo? What else do you know about this count?"

Albert's eyes were still shining. "As I said, Mama, I have never seen such power and wealth. He is a fine fellow, very accommodating and agreeable, and quite magnificent when he came bursting into the hideaway where the bandits had kept me. This Signor Vampa is an infamous brigand who strikes fear into the hearts of many in Rome and along the coast, for when he calls for a ransom, it must be produced or he will execute his victim," he said, seemingly unaware that he had just negated his earlier assurances. "But Monte Cristo had no fear of him at all, and there was no hesitation on Vampa's part when the count told him that I was a friend of his. In fact, as I have said, he was most apologetic for offending the count."

"What a debt we owe to this grand man," she said, real gratitude swelling in her chest, "for if not for him, you would not have returned to me."

"Indeed, Mama, I knew you would feel this way. And Papa too. And so I have invited him to come to Paris, and agreed to show him around the city, for he has never been here."

"Then Morcerf and I will be able to thank him ourselves. How splendid!" Mercédès spoke with heartfelt enthusiasm. The man who had saved her son's life would be more than welcome into her home, into her society, and she would show her gratitude in any way possible.

But she was still disconcerted about the connection with her own experience, of which Albert and Fernand knew nothing.

Could this Count of Monte Cristo have known that she was Albert's mother, and somehow interfered in Signor Vampa's plans for her as well?

For when he first abducted her, Jacopo had warned her it would take several days before the ransom request would reach Fernand, and then more days before the money could be delivered . . . and yet, she had been returned to Marseille a total of only five days after she had been kidnapped. She had spent a single night on the island of Monte Cristo, and when she awoke the next morning, she was already on the *Nemesis* being returned to Marseille. She hadn't seen Sinbad again.

There were days when Mercédès truly wondered if it had all been a dream.

Julie Morrel hadn't even known she'd been gone, for a message had been sent to her that Mercédès had decided to travel back to Paris for a short time, and so her friend hadn't worried about her absence.

But, no, this Count of Monte Cristo couldn't have known of the connection between Mercédès and Albert, for he had not even met her son until February . . . and her abduction had occurred in November.

And she had never met a count called Monte Cristo; she had only been incarcerated on an island with the same name. Neither Sinbad nor Jacopo had spoken such a name either. Perhaps it was simply a wild coincidence. After all, how could anyone be lord over such a piece of rock?

Mercédès realized that Albert had continued to describe his plans for meeting the count here in Paris, and she said, "When he arrives, you must tell me so that your papa and I might invite him to dinner."

"But, Mama, I already know when he is to arrive. On May the twentieth, exactly three months after we left each other in Rome. He will take breakfast with me here at ten o'clock in the morning."

Mercédès looked at him. "And you believe that he will be here for this appointment?"

"Mama, if you had met this amazing gentleman, you would have no question in your mind. He will be here. And you will meet him then."

She nodded, keeping her skepticism hidden. "An event I greatly anticipate."

On the twentieth of May, just past dawn, a magnificent carriage rolled along the most famous street of Paris, and stopped in front of the grand residence at number 30 Champs-Élysées.

The Count of Monte Cristo waited until the door of the well-sprung black velvet interior barouche was opened before taking his first steps onto a street of the famed city. He sniffed the air, noted that it smelled far cleaner than that of Singapore, but not nearly as crisp and pleasant as he'd expected for springtime, and nodded to the man who'd opened the door for him.

"Be prepared to leave again at precisely nine forty-five," he told him, and then strode up the walkway of his new residence.

Before he even considered raising his hand to knock, the door opened. With a flourish, a rather stout man with thinning brown hair and small, sharp eyes, very correctly attired and standing quite erectly, bowed. "Welcome, Your Excellency. I hope that you will find everything as you desire."

Monte Cristo nodded to his majordomo. "I am quite sure I shall, Bertuccio. You have never disappointed me."

"Your chamber has been prepared if you wish to freshen your toilette."

Although anyone who might have seen the count would have considered him more fashionably appointed than even the most fastidious of courtiers, Monte Cristo fully intended to attend to his appearance and preparation in the four hours before he renewed his acquaintance with young Albert de Morcerf.

"Haydée and Ali and the others shall be arriving shortly," Monte Cristo informed Bertuccio.

The other man bowed. "I shall see that the lady is made comfortable, Your Excellency. If you wish, I'll have a hot bath drawn for you. And perhaps a shave, if you require it." Even though Monte Cristo would have shaved already this morning, Bertuccio was aware of his master's meticulousness when it came to his appearance and grooming.

"I will bathe in one hour. Now I require some time alone."

By now the two had reached the massive chamber that would serve as the master's private apartments in the Paris mansion. Monte Cristo did not expect to be here above three or four months, at the very longest. And then he would leave Paris, leave all of this behind, and never return to France again.

Once Bertuccio closed the door and left him alone, Monte Cristo allowed himself to relax—something he did only in the presence of one other person on this earth, and even then, with some caution.

He examined the chamber, wandering through the spacious six-room suite appointed with a tasteful and luxurious combination of European and Oriental furnishings. Red-and-sapphire velvet brocade, edged with gold fringe, hung on the walls. Gold-and-silver brocade drapes were pulled away from tall floor-to-ceiling windows that overlooked the Champs-Élysées, as well as the colorful gardens that wrapped around the side and back of the mansion. The furnishings were similar to that which he'd become accustomed to during his decade traveling the Orient: low, flush with cushions, and sparing on wooden arms, legs, and headboards.

There was a spacious dressing room, an adjoining room

with one of the largest tubs Paris had ever seen, along with running water, and in a third chamber, the massive round bed piled high with tasseled pillows and silk cushions. A large mahogany table, complete with two lamps, ink pens, papers, blotter and ink, dominated one of the rooms. Potted plants and tall, formal flower arrangements brought the gardens into the apartments—a characteristic that, along with many windows and lots of light, Monte Cristo required of his living space. Bowls of fresh fruit, along with water, wine, and brandy, adorned at least one surface in each room as well.

Monte Cristo walked out onto the private balcony of his suite. Paris lay beyond, with its pale blond buildings like decorative cubes of Montrachet in the early-morning light, and the fountains and walkways of Marie de' Medici's famous avenue below. The Seine sparkled some few streets away, and the rising sun cast long dark brown shadows as it lifted over the city.

To his right, away from the river, rose the Arc de Triomphe, that massive archway celebrating the arrival of Napoleon in the city. Only four years since its completion, it blazed new and white in the bright sun as Monte Cristo's mouth firmed and his eyes narrowed. Any reminder of the emperor and politics—either that of the dead ruler or that of the Royals—lit a deep burn in his chest. Politics and greed and jealousy had destroyed the life of an innocent man. And now all of Paris was awash with talk about the possible return of the man's ashes to his city. Monte Cristo could care less, for he was concerned with another man's arrival: his own.

He was here, in Paris.

At last.

Monte Cristo grasped the wrought-iron balcony rail, marveling at the array of sins and miracles it had taken to get him here. Paris, the location in which he would wreak his holy vengeance on the four men who had betrayed Edmond Dantès and sent an innocent man to prison for fourteen years.

Twenty-four years ago, Dantès had everything to live for.

Now the young, uneducated man who'd once made love to his woman under an olive tree no longer existed.

He fingered the large onyx pin he always wore to remind himself of his duty—the duty he'd accepted in exchange for the miracles that brought him here. Inside was a list of names. Monte Cristo didn't need to open the pin's secret catch in order to review them, but he did, now, as he stood looking over the city. It seemed fitting, a necessary ritual.

The paper shuffled gently in the light morning breeze as he looked down at the small scrap and the names written on it. There were five.

Caderousse
Villefort
Danglars
Morcerf
Mercédès

The first four names were scribed neatly, with well-formed letters and without ink blotches. The last one was not. Though written with the same hand, the final name was scrawled so hard that the pen nib had scraped the paper.

His heart beating rapidly, his fingers trembling, Monte Cristo folded the paper along its well-worn creases and replaced it in the black brooch.

He would show no mercy, for none had been shown to him. A man's life had been destroyed by the jealousy, greed, and fear harbored by these four men. A simple letter, a blatant lie, that falsely accused Edmond Dantès of an involvement in a plot to return Napoleon to the throne had set the events in motion.

Danglars and Morcerf had written and posted the letter that claimed Dantès was involved in the plot because he was in possession of a missive describing the details of the emperor's intent to break free of Elba. Danglars did so because he wanted the captaincy of the *Pharaon*, and Fernand de Morcerf because he wanted Mercédès.

Caderousse had known of it, but had not come forward to expose them.

And Villefort, the crown prosecutor, had sent Dantès to prison because the missive that an unknowing Dantès had been asked to deliver incriminated his own father, and thus threatened Villefort's political position as a loyalist to the crown. The letter that Dantès had been duped into delivering had named Villefort's father, Monsieur Noirtier, as a participant in the emperor's plan to escape from Elba. If that knowledge had been revealed, Villefort's career would have been destroyed.

Greed, jealousy, and fear.

Monte Cristo had taken ten years to put his affairs in order, to plot and plan the revenge, to learn what he needed to know and to put enough time and distance between himself and the betrayers so that he could destroy them cleanly, and unemotionally, in the same way they had destroyed the innocent Edmond Dantès.

And Mercédès. She had waited for him—the man she swore to love until she died—for a mere eighteen months.

" 'Frailty, thy name is woman,' " Monte Cristo had whispered when he had learned this.

Frailty indeed. Eighteen months. She should have waited eighteen *years*, and more. But she had spread her glorious legs for Morcerf, and had spent the last twenty-two years moaning and sighing beneath the man, in his bed, while Dantès suffered through fourteen years of darkness and cold and despair, dreaming of her. Waiting for her. Wanting her.

All the while, she had been loving someone else. One of his betrayers.

Since she alone had loved Edmond Dantès, her betrayal was the greatest of them all.

His palms were slick, but he resisted wiping them on his trousers. No signs of weakness. The Count of Monte Cristo had *no weakness*. No mercy, no weakness, no second thoughts. No miscalculations.

A tremor ran through his body and he closed his eyes, leaning against the railing, again drawing in the fresh air of the early morning—something once he thought never to do again. Thank God for Abbé Faria's wrong turn in his tunnel of escape.

The old man had befriended the young, nearly mad Dantès and brought him back to sanity. He'd spent four years educating him, teaching him everything he knew as they secretly communed between their prison cells.

He shared with the younger man the secret of Cardinal Spada's family treasure buried on Monte Cristo island. For, as a younger man, the abbé had been the personal secretary of Count Spada, the last descendant of the old cardinal. He often spoke so wistfully of his family's lost treasure that, at first, Faria thought it was only a legend.

But after the count's death, Faria found a scrap of the cardinal's will inside the family breviary that Count Spada had bequeathed to him. That scrap of paper was enough for the abbé to puzzle out the location of the treasure, and to confirm its existence.

And when Abbé Faria died at last, he gave Dantès a final gift: freedom.

Dantès had replaced the abbé's body with his own, wrapped in the shroud for burial and left in his cell. When the would-be corpse had been tossed in the sea from the cliffs of Château d'If, he had managed a harrowing escape: one of the miracles that had brought him to this sunny day in May, on a balcony overlooking Paris.

Dantès had died, but the Count of Monte Cristo had been born.

Precisely one hour after Monte Cristo had closed the door of the private suite, Bertuccio knocked on it again.

Monte Cristo bade him enter, and the stout man did so, followed by a beautiful young woman dressed in Persian clothing.

"Your Excellency, I shall have the bath prepared now."

His master nodded in agreement, then transferred his attention to Haydée. "And so you have arrived in Paris," he said kindly. "Do you not think it a beautiful city?"

Haydée smiled, showing perfect white teeth and a tiny dimple at the corner of her mouth. "What little I have seen is beautiful, Excellency, but very different from Istanbul and Peking."

Monte Cristo smiled indulgently. "Now that we are in Paris, you must act as any young woman of Europe would. You will be my companion about the city. We will visit the opera and the theater, as well as attend some parties. You will, of course, require new clothing."

She was merely twenty years old, less than half his age, and a gloriously beautiful woman. The olive skin of her Greek ancestry was smooth and supple, and her hair black as ink and straight as the tail of an Arabian horse. Dark eyes slanted upward at the corners, giving her an exotic, mysterious look, and her mouth was slender and wide with a deep vee in the upper lip. Haydée was a princess—the daughter of the Ali Pasha, who had been the ruler of the westernmost part of the Ottoman Empire. He'd been assassinated in Janina in 1822, leaving Haydée and her mother to be sold into slavery.

The mother had died shortly after, but Monte Cristo had seen and purchased the young woman some years ago. He had had the pleasure of watching her grow into the loveliest of young women. He would soon be in a position to release her from servitude.

"Shall I assist with your bath today, Excellency?" the girl asked with a smile.

His attention swept over her, over the loose silken trousers and the tight beaded bodice that ended above her navel. "If you wish."

Perhaps her slender hands and cheerful disposition would distract him from the matters at hand.

Haydée smiled and bowed, leaving the room gracefully just as the door to the chamber opened again.

A massive man with skin of ebony and a bald head entered and approached Monte Cristo. He also wore the garb of the Orient: a loose, silken tunic belted over full trousers, a blinding white against his smooth coal flesh. His feet were bare. He wore gold armbands on his wrists and ankles, and two golden hoops in one ear.

He bowed in front of Monte Cristo.

"Ali," said the count, "I trust there were no problems with your arrival today."

The man shook his head, then spoke with his hands to give more details.

Ali had entered the service of the Count of Monte Cristo after the man had saved his life three years earlier. He had taken a vow of silence along with the mantle of his service until such a time in which he could return the favor; after which, he would return to his native Nubia.

"Very good," Monte Cristo said when the man finished. "I will return later this afternoon." With that, he rose from where he had been sitting and walked into the room where the bath had been prepared.

Haydée and two other servants were there. The pleasant scent of cardamom and lemon filtered through the air as Monte Cristo was divested of his fine garments. He gave instructions to one of the servants in regards to his new attire, and then climbed into the steaming tub.

The hot water streamed over his face and hair, and he closed his eyes, letting two pairs of hands minister to him. One set, impersonal and quick, soaped his feet and legs.

But the other pair of hands belonged to Haydée; he knew because she was scrubbing his thick hair, and he could smell the jasmine that she favored. She was so young and beautiful. He'd noticed her skin: smooth and supple, like a tanned deer hide, and the curve of her breasts and hips. Even her feet, which she kept bare whenever in the house, were elegant and brown and her toes encircled with silver rings.

He opened his eyes and realized that the other servant had gone, dismissed by Haydée perhaps. Turning to ask why she had done so, Monte Cristo found her face very close to his.

Surprise fluttered in his belly, followed by delight. Those lips were close enough. . . . Yes, she leaned forward and covered his mouth with her sweet one.

She'd never done such a thing before—and he'd never asked or even suggested it—but it was not unwelcome. He felt the rise of pleasure sweep over him as her lips opened against his and her slick tongue slipped through.

He realized he'd closed his eyes, and he didn't open them until she pulled away.

"What are you about?" he asked, a harsh note creeping into his voice as she sat back on her haunches.

She smiled as she unbuttoned her short, tight bodice. Her generous, high breasts spilled out, nipples pink and dusky against her olive skin. She wore a thin gold chain around her waist, and it settled over the curve of her bare hips, just above the low waistline of her trousers. Monte Cristo felt his mouth go dry and the sudden lift of his cock stir the water.

"You haven't been with a woman for months," she said, her hands moving to cover her breasts, lifting them to him.

He touched her with his left hand, moving his fingers over the warm skin, as his right hand lay against the other side of the tub, fingers curled easily. "How do you know this?" Her nipple puckered beneath his touch. If nothing else, she was willing.

"It is obvious, Excellency. Since you returned from Monte Cristo, you've not had a woman here, nor gone to one. I suspected, and Ali . . . well, he has confirmed it." She had the grace to look a bit ashamed at this revelation that his two servants had been in consultation about him, but Monte Cristo was too taken aback to react. And aside from that, her royal bearing held her in good stead even though she was bound in servitude. "Excellency, I wish to erase that crease between your brows," she said, tracing the offending line.

He closed his eyes in silent acquiescence and tried to settle his leaping pulse. The girl was a virgin, but she was his, and she offered herself to him. He'd never made any such overtures or hinted at any expectations in all of the time she'd served him.

And she was correct. He hadn't been with a woman since November.

The bathwater tinkled and surged, and he felt two narrow feet slide in on either side of his torso, then a warm weight on his belly, settled just north of his raging cock. Small hands moved over his chest, raising the hair he'd allowed to grow back, and then up and over his shoulders. She bent forward to kiss him again, and he didn't even have to raise his head to meet her lips.

As her hands and mouth were busy, he drifted on a sea of pleasure and memories. He opened his eyes once to see two ripe breasts in front of his face, offered to his mouth, dark and smooth. They were high and tight and young, but the ones he saw when he closed his eyes again were golden . . . the size of oranges, and no longer so high and tight.

His mouth tightened against hers, and she moved to kiss along his jaw, her hands smoothing up and down over his chest, but going no farther. Clearly, she was a virgin and wasn't quite certain how to go about the process at hand. . . . He took one of

Haydée's hands and closed it around his cock. Showed her how to move it.

Ah.

Desire surged again, and he almost spilled it right there.

With his eyes closed, he tried to focus on the young woman in front—on top—of him. But instead, he was pummeled with images and textures, sensations and sounds that didn't belong here . . . weren't part of this moment, this day, this woman.

Golden skin, not quite as firm as he remembered; hips flaring like that of a woman, not a young girl; long, wavy black hair unbound and damp mingling with his . . . her heavy, ratcheting breathing as Neru and Omania danced for them, which had been more arousing than their performance.

He'd brought her there to memorize her desires, fine-tune her body and needs, to *learn* her.

So that he could plan his revenge.

Ten years had passed since Mercédès first met Sinbad in Marseille. Ten years and countless women and experiences. And yet . . . when they were together on Monte Cristo, he'd forgotten his purpose, become caught up in the memories, the desires, the need.

So he sent her back, aborting his experiment.

Monte Cristo dragged himself back from those hazy, hashish-filled memories . . . of Neru kneeling between those slender golden thighs . . . of the way her breasts shivered and puckered while he touched them, caressed and teased her . . . of the long, undulating tremors that shook her beneath his own hands, the soft sighs and little trickles of tears. Of the way she'd mounted him, and reached high above her head, lifting her breasts as she rode him with skill and driving rhythm.

That had been his limit.

"Yes," he gasped now, shifting his hips as the slender hand moved over his cock, jerkily and haltingly so that he groaned with frustration and lust.

"Oh . . . ," she breathed, starting to move, to shift atop him.

"No," he commanded, closing his hand firmly over hers. He was still the count, even as the reminder of his own weakness caught him up in a typhoon of memory and sensation, as it built and fired and swelled until he reached the top. With a long, keening groan, he jerked one last time in her hand, spilling into the water and shuddering into stillness.

"Go," he said before he even opened his eyes. "Send Ali."

Mercédès was fully aware when the celebrated Count of Monte Cristo arrived at the de Morcerf home. However, she was still in her bedchamber, still dressed in her night rail, eating a small breakfast, and she was in no great hurry.

Albert had planned to have breakfast with the count along with two of his other friends—Franz d'Epinay, who had been in Rome with him, and Julie Morrel's brother, Captain Maximilien Morrel. They would eat and chat for some time before the gentlemen would move into the family parlor, where Mercédès and Fernand would meet the man who saved their son's life.

Dios mio, how could a woman thank such a man?

Did he have a son, a daughter, a wife . . . someone that he loved as much as she loved Albert?

Mercédès' thoughts were interrupted by a knock at her chamber door, and she gave permission to enter.

"Madam, this has arrived for you," Charlotte told her, offering a small parcel wrapped in gold foil and tied with a red ribbon.

With a quiet sigh, Mercédès took the package and nodded for her maid to leave. She was certain the gift was from Georges. He was quite persistent.

But it was her own fault. Last November, she'd returned from Marseille and her brief abduction and interlude with Sinbad, confused, exhausted, and feeling the emptiness of her life even more harshly than before. Most nights, her dreams were threaded with images—lush, sensual, arousing ones—from her experience in Aladdin's cave. In the morning, or even sometimes deep in the night, she woke alone in her bed, often in tears. Lonely. Frustrated. Empty.

And so, months sooner than she had planned when she left Fernand in anger, Mercédès returned to Paris and threw herself into a whirl of societal pleasures: soirees, dinners, balls, theater, and even, when no one would see her, slipping into the garden to indulge her guilty pleasure, digging in the soil, removing spent blossoms, and pruning rosemary and thyme.

And Georges had been here, waiting for her, intending to woo her back.

The sorrow she saw in his hazel eyes had been sincere, and Mercédès, herself feeling a similar bereft emotion, had foolishly allowed herself to be comforted by him.

Not that she'd taken him back to her bed . . . no, nothing that imprudent. But a stolen kiss here, an embrace there, just to feel the warmth and strength of a man's touch . . . yet even that didn't banish the emptiness that had pervaded her life. She was consumed by a feeling of unfinished business.

But he was clearly desirous of more, as evidenced by the gifts he'd been sending. And the long scrawled notes that accompanied them detailing his love for her.

She slipped the red ribbon from its mooring and lifted the note from the box. Inside she found a thick parchment paper, with his boyish scrawl covering the entire sheet. She put it aside for the moment, in favor of the parcel.

Inside was a rectangular brooch of garnet, set in filigree gold . . . rather simple, as compared to many of her other jewels, but Mercédès preferred a less ostentatious design than her husband did. It was beautiful, and, she realized with moist eyes, Georges did know her. He did care for her. He was devoted to her.

Why couldn't she care for him?

Because he wasn't Edmond.

He wasn't . . . Sinbad.

Mercédès gasped; she heard it like a little crack in the silent room. Sinbad? *Dios mio!* How could she even think such a thing?

It had to be the adventure. The seductiveness of being forbidden and dangerous.

She stood, suddenly resolute. That thought must be put immediately out of her mind. She looked contemplatively at the brooch. If she wore it, Georges would be in high spirits. He would take it as a sign that she was acquiescing to his renewed suit.

And perhaps that would be for the best. He would never hurt her. He cared for her. And she needed someone.

It was only a matter of time before Albert married—please, God, not to Eugénie Danglars!—and left their home for good.

Since her return from Marseille, she'd spent few nights at home, thus leaving Fernand no opportunity to claim his marital rights. He didn't dare complain that she attended house parties or slept at the home of her friend Amelie, the Comtesse Roleaux, for fear that Mercédès would leave again. But there was no certainty about what would happen once Albert left, and Mercédès couldn't continue to take advantage of Amelie's hospitality.

Having made up her mind, Mercédès rang for Charlotte. The door to her dressing room opened, and her maid came in. "I'll wear the dark red gown tonight. And the moiré day dress in gold to meet monsieur le comte."

Charlotte was quick and efficient, helping the comtesse dress, doing her hair in a properly intricate style appropriate for meeting a celebrated count. Thus it was past one o'clock when Mercédès stepped out of her chambers and found that her husband had already made his way downstairs to meet the Count of Monte Cristo.

A warm, grateful smile fixed on her face, and looking, she knew, particularly elegant, Mercédès walked sedately down the long, curving staircase that led to the main floor of their home. Undoubtedly, Albert had invited the count into the family parlor once they'd finished their breakfast—yes, she could hear the masculine voices from that room.

Unwilling to interrupt the conversation, Mercédès declined having the butler announce or introduce her, and as it turned out, it was just as well. She opened the door quietly and stepped in, at once hearing her husband as he spoke warmly about his soldierly experience in the Greek war of independence from the Turks, particularly the battle of Navarino—which was the occasion on which he'd garnered his aristocratic title.

She wasn't surprised that Fernand had chosen this topic of conversation. His inclination was obviously to set himself as the count's equal by describing his own ascension to the aristocracy with all its florid and dramatic details about his involvement in the overthrow of the ruler Ali Pasha.

Mercédès stepped into the little alcove—more of an antechamber to the room—closing the door quietly behind her. She saw her son, tall and handsome, standing at the fireplace mantel. He would be the first to see her, for he faced the door. And Fernand was standing with his hand on the back of an armchair, facing the count.

The Count of Monte Cristo himself was a tall man, and he stood near the ceiling-high windows in such a way that he was half thrown into shadow. From what she could see, he was wearing well-cut clothing, had dark hair, and stood proudly as he conversed with her husband and son. He had a smooth cultured voice with nary the trace of an accent as he responded to his host in flawless French.

Just as Mercédès was about to step fully into the room, to rush across to the count and thank him profusely for the gift he'd given her, the man moved. He shifted, and the shadows fell away, and she saw his face.

The world stopped: Everything froze. Her heart. Her breath. Her face. All feeling drained from her body, leaving her cold and clammy and dizzy. The room tilted, then converged into a pinpoint image . . . then shattered and fell away. Leaving only him.

Edmond.

Then her vision expanded sharply, and Mercédès felt her heart ramming so hard in her chest they must have heard it, pounding through her whole body. Her lungs were constricted; she couldn't breathe, couldn't swallow. . . . The world dimmed at the edges and then brightened again as if a great light was blaring in her face.

It was Edmond.

But . . . it couldn't be.

But . . .

She must have made some noise or movement that attracted the attention of her son, for Albert exclaimed, "*Maman*! At last you shall meet my dear friend the Count of Monte Cristo."

He was already striding across the room toward her, as if to take her arm and bring her in for an introduction. But Mercédès hardly noticed; she had begun to breathe again, her heart had settled into a more normal rhythm—albeit a harsh, jerky one. Her stomach felt as though it was tumbling down a hill. Her fingers trembled in front of her wide skirts.

She glanced at Fernand, who was looking at her oddly. There was no sign of recognition on his face. Perhaps she was wrong. Perhaps it was just the distance, the sudden shift of the man's face from darkness into light.

"*Maman*, are you feeling well?" Albert whispered, neatly turning his back to the other men so as to keep his question private.

"I . . . yes, I am fine. Merely a bit of a headache." Mercédès grasped Albert's arm a bit more firmly than usual, and allowed him to lead her toward the count as she gathered every bit of composure she could muster.

She must have been wrong.

"Your Excellency, I hope you will forgive me if I take the liberty of introducing you to my mother," Albert was saying.

"*Maman*, this is my friend and savior, His Excellency, the Count of Monte Cristo."

"Madame la Comtesse," said the count, already making a deep, correct bow as they moved to stand in front of him. "It is my great pleasure to meet you at last."

When he raised his face, Mercédès looked up into it fully for the first time. It was like being slammed in the stomach.

He was handsome . . . very handsome . . . yet forbidding, with high, sculpted cheekbones, wide, mobile lips, and a square jaw. His dark hair, the color of walnut hulls, was thick and brushed back high over his tall forehead. A bit of white tinged the hair at his temples and trimmed sideburns. Coffee-colored eyes fringed with dark lashes looked at her with impersonal congeniality and nothing else. Not a hint of recognition or even confusion.

His shoulders, in a rich brown morning coat, spanned wider and sturdier than those of the young man of nineteen she remembered, and the cuffs of his white shirtwaist showed slender tanned wrists and emerald cufflinks. He wore a large onyx pin in the center of his garnet neckcloth, holding the silk in place. A fine waistcoat of black, brown, and ivory completed his elegant ensemble, that of a man far removed from the simple sailor Edmond Dantès.

". . . have heard only the most complimentary things about you from your son," he was saying graciously.

Mercédès gathered up her composure, the tidy mask that she'd worn for years to hide the truth of her marriage and the intense hatred she felt for her husband, and smiled at him. There was nothing in his eyes to indicate that he recognized her. . . . Surely she hadn't changed that much.

Was he pretending? Or did he truly not recognize her?

Or was she wrong? Had she wanted and missed Edmond for so long that she was going mad, seeing things where they were not? After all, Fernand showed no sign of knowing him.

"You are too kind, Your Excellency," she replied. Was that really her gentle, gracious voice? How could it be when she was in such a turmoil? "But it is I who must throw myself at your feet in gratitude."

For the moment, her confusion and shock slid away, to be replaced by a most overwhelming gratitude. Whoever he might be, whatever he might know or not know of her, he had done something for which Mercédès could never repay him. "I cannot thank you enough," she said, tears warming the corners of her eyes, "for what you did for my son, Your Excellency. Surely, you saved his life. And if there is ever anything the Comte de Morcerf or I can do for you . . . you have but to ask." Her voice broke a bit at the end, becoming husky with emotion.

Again he gave an elegant bow, but not before she saw a flash of something shift in his eyes. "Indeed, madam, it was my pleasure to intervene for such a good and pleasant young man. I consider him a great friend of mine, and I would do anything for a friend. You have a fine son, you and the count." When he raised his face, his expression was bland . . . but she thought she heard a stony note in his voice.

Dear God, Edmond!

It had to be he. And here she was . . . here she was, married these last twenty-some years to Fernand, and with a son. A son that was not Edmond's, as she'd planned and dreamed and hoped . . . but a son that belonged to a man who was as cold and cruel as the sea. A man who'd successfully hidden his true self from her, with gentle wooing and false empathy as she mourned the very man who stood before her now.

The rich and powerful and esteemed Count of Monte Cristo. The room swayed again.

"Maman," Albert said, grasping her elbow, "would you care to sit down?" He was looking at her anxiously, and Mercédès again assembled control over herself.

"I do believe it might be the roses," she said, nodding to the large vases of tuberoses that spread their cloying scent in the parlor. It was as good an excuse as any, for there were six containers of them throughout the room. "Their aroma does make the air rather close."

"Well, I must be off," Fernand interrupted, giving a bow to the count. "I meant to be at the parliament session by two o'clock, and it is nearly half past by now. You must allow us to avail you of our hospitality quite soon, Monte Cristo."

The count bowed in return. "Indeed, I should be delighted. And also that of your son, for he has offered to acquaint me with the delights of your lovely city. And what better recompense could one ask for, than to be taken through such a metropolis than by a son of its own?"

"Of course. But we will also have a dinner party for you, and introduce you to our friends and society," Fernand continued magnanimously. "Then you will be received everywhere."

"That would be most kind. And I look forward to returning the favor at my own residence."

Here Albert interrupted. "The count has rented a home on the Champs-Élysées," he said. "And he has just purchased a house on the outskirts of Paris, in Auteuil, as well."

Mercédès hardly heard the conversation. She was feeling

numb again, as the reality settled over her. She must speak with him. Alone.

But how?

She couldn't very well send her son away; nor would he be so rude as to leave his guest alone for any moment.

Perhaps when his carriage was called, she might have the chance.

Decision made, Mercédès smiled at Albert. "My son, I must excuse myself now. . . . I do think the unseasonable warmth and too many sweet roses have made me feel weary." Hoping that her son would not remark on the fact that it was unlike her to be so sensitive, she turned to the count, steeling herself to remain cordial and impassive. "Your Excellency, I must thank you again for what you've done for us . . . and extend to you my welcome to our beautiful city. I hope you will enjoy your time here, and if you are in need of anything, please do not feel awkward about contacting us."

"It has been my pleasure to meet you, madam," he said, again with a bow.

Mercédès inclined her head, then turned to walk out of the room. She heard Albert offering to take the count about Paris immediately, and then Monte Cristo's reply that he must beg to decline, for he had to see to the settling of his new residence. "For I only arrived in Paris this morning," he said, his words clipped off as Mercédès shut the door of the parlor.

She ducked into another small room—the conservatory—and, closing the door behind her, alone at last, she collapsed against it. Violently shaking, her eyes welling with tears and a strange, twisting sensation pummeling her body, Mercédès leaned against the chilly wood of the door.

It was impossible.

Impossible on so many fronts, she could not begin to comprehend it.

Dimly, moments later, she heard masculine voices in the hall and the opening and closing of doors. Servants moved about, and she heard Albert explaining something in an obscured voice.

"Never you mind," said the count, his words clear through the door as if he were standing on the other side. Likely he was, for this room lay between the parlor and the front entrance. "You have already called for my coach. It will be here in a moment. Please attend to your message, and I will take my leave as soon as the vehicle is brought round."

"You are most gracious, Your Excellency," said Albert. "I shall call on you tomorrow."

"Indeed. And thank you for introducing me to your parents."

Mercédès waited for a moment, scarcely able to believe her luck. When she was certain Albert was gone, and that the only sound she heard beyond the door was that of the Count of Monte Cristo, she took a deep breath and opened the door.

He was standing with his back partially angled toward her, tall and straight, and, she noticed for the first time, with a steel-nobbed walking stick. He held a tall, dark hat in the same hand and with the other, he was checking the time on a circular watch that hung from a chain.

He looked up when she came out, attracted by her movement, and their eyes met.

"Edmond," Mercédès said in no more than a whisper. She took a step toward him, her hand outstretched. "Is it really you?"

He arched a brow and tilted his head with an arrogance that had not been present in the parlor. "Pardon me, madam?" There was a quizzical expression in his voice.

She balked for a moment, but reached to touch him, her fingers wanting to close around his wrist. "Edmond, don't you know me?"

There was a moment, a beat of pulse, that she felt the steady warmth of his skin, and the faint underlying tremors there. And then he pulled his arm away—not with a sharp movement, as if caught off-guard, but with a deliberate, demeaning extrication. As if it were hardly worth his energy to do so. "Madam, are you feeling quite well?" His voice was clipped and cold, and the look in his eyes flat and dark.

He was lying.

He had to be.

Mercédès would have tried again, but the front door opened there next to them, and the groom poked his head in, tugging his forelock. "Your coach, Your Excellency," he said, then stepped away to gesture down the walkway to the waiting barouche.

Monte Cristo placed the hat on his head and glanced down at Mercédès with another cool expression. It was as if his face was carved of stone. "By your leave, madam," he said and, swinging his cane, started out the front door.

She hurried after him, close enough to say, for his ears only, "I know it's you, Edmond. I know it."

But the door closed on her words, and she was left alone, staring at it as shock trembled through her again.

FIVE
The Bath

Later that day
Paris

Haydée remained tucked in her luxurious suite of rooms until after the Count of Monte Cristo left his residence that morning. The experiment in the bath hadn't turned out quite the way she'd intended, but at least something had happened. She'd finally touched a naked man, and it was just as lovely and arousing as she'd anticipated.

Of course, the little pip between her legs was still swollen and throbbing, teasing her now that she was alone in her rooms. Haydée knew what to do to relieve that discomfort, but she'd prefer to have someone else's quick finger do the work.

Ah, then. Perhaps she would call for a bath of her own.

Looking in the large mirror in front of her dressing table,

she smiled deviously. Her full lips curled up just a bit at the edges, her dark, exotic eyes sparkled, and her hair—long and dark and straight—hung in a perfect drape over her shoulders, curling just a bit at the ends. Her breasts . . . She let the soft robe slip away from her smooth olive shoulders so she could look at her bare torso. High and lovely, not too large and not too small . . . How could he resist her? She knew she was beautiful. She'd seen the way his eyes followed her when he thought she wasn't looking.

If only he weren't so damned honorable.

The bath.

She'd see how bloody honorable he was now!

Pulling the robe back up, she arranged it so that it draped just perfectly over her shoulders so that with the slightest shift of movement, it would slip down and gap open just enough . . . just enough for it to look accidental.

"Mahti," she called, rapping peremptorily on the door to her outer chamber. When her servant came, Haydée said, "I will bathe now. Tell Galya I require her assistance as well," she added with a smile. The other woman, knowing what that meant, flushed with pleasure and hurried off to do her bidding.

After Mahti opened the wide French doors to the next room, where the bath was, Haydée rang for another of the house servants. When he came, she gave him his instructions.

And then she settled back in her chair to wait.

She could hear the splash of water in the next room—how convenient indoor plumbing was! The scent of jasmine oil wafted in from the bath, and she heard Mahti and Galya gathering her clothing and other accoutrements. From her seat, she could see the vista of Paris spread out beyond the small balcony on which she'd hardly set foot, but the view didn't interest her as much as the accommodations in her chambers.

His Excellency was inconceivably generous to her, a slave who'd been saved by his money and his mercy from a horrid existence at the hands of her father's enemies. She often believed he had some secret reason for having her travel with and serve him, some motive as to why he treated her so like the princess she was.

Whatever the reason, it was not for her to warm his bed.

She'd been a mere twelve years of age when he purchased her in a private sale—the evening before she was to be auctioned off at a public market, saving her from untold humiliation. Haydée couldn't imagine how much money he'd paid for her, but it had to have been an exorbitant amount, considering that she was the daughter of Ali Pasha. Over the six years they'd been together, he treated her more like a treasure than a slave.

Now her lips curled down. She'd offered everything to him today, but he'd declined . . . some of it. Frustrating, yes, it had been. Confusing too. After all, she'd held his wickedly hot, thick cock in her hands . . . and it had been obvious he needed something.

And so did she.

A single sharp rap sounded on her door. Haydée sat up and called, "Enter."

The door opened and Ali walked in, tall and big and proud. Just looking at the broad shoulders in his blinding white tunic and the big black hands braceleted with gold bands made her mouth go dry.

He stayed near the door, but bowed regally to her. His bald

head was smooth and shone like an onyx marble, his full, soft lips fixed in a faint polite smile. His feet, always bare, were smooth, elegant ebony and decorated with a gold ring on one center toe, and thicker bands encircled his ankles.

Ali didn't speak, but Haydée had learned to read his sign language as easily as if he did. *You called for me?*

Ah. The insolence was there—in his eyes, in the very way those powerful hands signed to her. Haydée gave him a haughty look. "Yes, indeed, Ali. I find that the arrangement in these rooms are not to my liking. Perhaps you shall be so good as to move the furnishings about."

Of course. Those full lips firmed ever so slightly, sending a pang down to the very little pip that still throbbed between her legs, swirling harshly in her middle.

He said the words with his hands, but the subservient sentiment was not echoed in his eyes. They were carefully blank, and Haydée, who languidly lifted her arm to point to the bed, shifted so that her robe gapped, and watched his expression carefully.

Yes. Ah, yes, it was there.

She smiled deep inside, letting the knowledge tickle her belly. You've not seen anything yet, she thought. "There. The bed . . . it is too close to the window at that angle, and it catches the morning sun. I shan't be able to sleep as late as I desire if it remains there."

Where would you like it moved, mistress? His last gesture, the one for "mistress," he made with short, peremptory movements.

"Perhaps . . . there." She pointed to the wall opposite where the bed was now. Currently, her dressing table, covered with perfume bottles and jeweled hair combs and other feminine decorations, was in that position. He would be busy for quite some time. That wall also gave a perfect view into the room beyond, where her bath was nearly filled.

Perfect.

And just then, as if they'd been summoned, Mahti and Galya came to stand in the doorway between the two rooms.

"Excuse me, Ali. It appears my bath is ready." She felt his eyes on her as she swept past him into the inner chamber, letting her robe slip from her shoulders. She felt the heavy sear of his eyes on her bare skin as she walked away from him.

Slowly. Rolling her hips.

As she was climbing into the bath, which was positioned lengthwise in front of the doorway to the bedchamber, she saw Ali start to close the French doors between them.

"No, leave them open," she said, feeling her breasts jounce prettily as she turned toward him and propped herself up on the edges of the tub. "How else shall I give you directions?"

As he turned abruptly away, Haydée sank into the tub, closing her eyes, brimming with satisfaction. The steaming water enveloped her, and the sweet tinge of jasmine filled the air with every flutter of her hands. She closed her eyes and rested her head on the edge of the tub, her long hair flowing over the side and pooling onto the floor behind her.

Mahti gathered up the heavy tresses and twisted, then pinned them at the top of her head and left Haydée to relax for a moment. She heard the soft clink of bottles from the next room as Ali moved them off the dressing table, and she imagined those massive hands closing around such feminine and delicate knickknacks.

When His Excellency had sent her, dripping and unsatisfied, from his bath and ordered her to send Ali, Haydée had been annoyed and frustrated. But she'd managed to hide her feelings when, wrapped only in a soft towel, she approached the huge man, her face and body flushed and warm and humming.

So you've succeeded, he had signed when he saw her standing there, knowing whence she'd come. His handsome countenance, trimmed with a tiny square beard under that luscious lower lip, had been stony and calm . . . but Haydée was certain there was a pinpoint of emotion in those black eyes.

"His Excellency wishes you to attend him," she'd told him, wearing a haughty expression despite the fact that she was completely naked and vulnerable beneath the white towel.

Ali turned to go, but he stopped and looked at her again, slowly raking over her from head to toe. *Did you?*

Haydée summoned a slow, deep smile designed to hide her confusion regarding the fact that she still bore her maidenhead and to leave Ali just as discomfited. "Our master is no longer in need . . . although I cannot say the same for myself."

And then, her heart pounding and her mouth dry, she turned and flounced away.

And felt his gaze burning into the back of her, just as it had moments ago when she walked away from him into the bath.

Now, her eyes still closed as she enjoyed the heavenly feel of Galya's hands massaging her feet, Haydée smiled, but her grin was laced with frustration. If only Monte Cristo had taken her bloody virginity, then she would be free to do as she wished. But he owned her, and thus he owned her maidenhead, and it must be left intact until he chose to take it . . . or to sell her.

Or to free her.

He'd spoken of freeing her someday soon, and she both

yearned for and feared that day. So it was best not to think about it, and instead to concentrate on the matter at hand.

The clinking of bottles had stopped, and now Haydée heard the low, dull scrape of the dressing table being moved. She opened her eyes and, with a nod to her servants, knelt in the tub.

Water sluiced down her body, running between her breasts and around her thrusting nipples, and she wished for a moment that she'd told Ali to bring the dressing table mirror into this room. She wanted to see what he would see.

But she could imagine what vision would greet his eyes were he to look beyond the doorframe. And look he would, for she would ensure it.

As Mahti's fingers filtered around her mistress' nipples, rolling them gently and erotically between her knuckles, Haydée felt Galya smooth her small hands down along the sides of her torso, tracing the flare of her hips with the same slippery soap, then sliding between her mistress' parted legs. The water surged over her sensitive skin with every movement, in an ebb-and-flow rhythm that felt like the one her hips wanted to make, leaving her alternately warm and cold, wet and dry.

Haydée sighed as the long, sensual strokes on her inner thighs raised bumps on her flesh and the incessant tug and pinch at her nipples sent lust curling tighter in her belly. She thought of Ali, on the other side of the wall, just beyond the doorframe, and his massive black shoulders and strong black hands, imagining them here with her instead of the two little maids, and the coil burned tighter in her belly. She wanted to call his name . . . wanted him here, with her . . . his thick lips sucking on her, his tongue snaking in between the lips of her quim, his heavy cock raging in her hands.

Her pip surged at the thought, and Haydée suddenly tipped into orgasm—quick and sharp. Unexpected.

She couldn't contain the low, long moan as her body trembled beneath the capable hands of her maids, her wetness mingling with the water below. Then Galya's little fingers slipped around through the folds of her quim as Mahti came around to take one of her mistress' nipples into her mouth, prolonging the pleasurable shudders.

Haydée opened her eyes when lips closed over her nipple in a long, sleek tug, slow and deep, and the pull of pleasure there matched the slow pulsing between her legs. She looked down and saw the top of Mahti's dark head, hair piled high, cheeks sinking concavely with the strength of her suckle, and saw the hint of little breasts below bobbing enticingly. And then she saw the curve of Galya's neat little spine kneeling in front of her, sweeping into the flare of creamy hips and round, ripe buttocks stretching open in a tantalizing vee. She looked up at her mistress, question in her eyes, and Haydée nodded in permission . . . and need. That little victory had been only the beginning.

Galya slipped into the tub in front of her, facing her, sliding her strong legs beneath her mistress', her own thighs parted as Haydée settled on her crouching lap, her quim facing Galya's navel. Now Haydée's legs spread wide and folded over the sides of the tub, and her buttocks were hoisted up on Galya's lap so that her hips and the rise of her pubis were out of the water like a smooth, warm island. Haydée looked toward the doorway and saw only a fleeting movement of white along its edge, and the corner of what must be the bed as he moved it into place.

Trying to avoid her.

Haydée's lips curled. Any other man would be watching the three women.

When Galya bent to her mistress' quim, raising her hips with strong hands, Haydée groaned loudly, purposely. She kept her eyes focused on the doorway, half seeing and half lidded as Galya's tongue flew quickly and purposely over her little pearl, jiggling it, working it, teasing as the deep drive of lust built again.

She felt herself rise, the soft skin behind her knees pressing into the side of the tub as she raised her hips, shoving them closer to Galya's probing tongue, feeling the bite of the maid's fingers in the flesh of her buttocks. Haydée shifted back and forth in a restless, needy rhythm, her eyes fastened on the doorway, willing him to come back.

To see her.

To see what she wanted.

Mahti sucked, kneeling next to the tub, her free hand cradling the back of her mistress' neck, soft little sounds of pleasure grunting from the back of her throat as she fed. Haydée felt her body gather up again, her sex swollen and ripe, teased and tossed by a little wet tongue, the pain of the tub biting into her legs, the pull and release of her nipple matching the pull and release of her pip.

And then she saw him. Suddenly he was there, standing in the doorway. Watching.

So tall, so bald and black and sober. His face impassive, his eyes hot and focused, his hands hanging at his sides. He watched, his lips slightly parted, his nostrils wide, his chest rising and falling beneath the white tunic.

She looked at him. Matched his gaze with hers and held it. The pleasure built faster now, harder and deeper, and she let him see it. Let him see what she wanted, what she would give.

Her servants sensed the change, the urgency, and the tongues moved faster, harder, deeper, wetter. Haydée opened her mouth, drew herself up, thought of him, and then it came—the undulating swells, the hard ripple of release, the shaking, trembling of ecstasy.

When she opened her eyes, the bathwater was cold and Ali was gone.

Haydée was roused from what had been a restless nap on her newly arranged bed by a sharp knocking on her door. She sat up abruptly, pushing the hair from her face, and bid, "Enter."

It was Bertucci. "Mistress Haydée, His Excellency has returned. You . . . I think perhaps you should go to him." The little Italian man seemed to be wringing his hands.

Go to him? Haydée swung her feet off the bed. She was dressed in a loose, flowing caftan of pale aqua silk, her hair pulled back in a simple single braid. "Is he ill?"

"No . . . I do not think it is an illness. He seems . . . restless. Please. Jacopo is not here, and besides him and Ali, you seem to be the only one he—"

"Ali? Where is Ali?" Her heart seized.

"He's gone to attend to some matters in regard to the house in Auteuil. Mistress Haydée, I think His Excellency might welcome your tender presence."

Haydée felt the slightest warmth on her face. It had been

only this morning that she'd joined Monte Cristo in his bath; did the entire household now seem to think that her body was the answer to any malaise suffered by the count?

However, it would be another opportunity to rid herself of the nuisance of her virginity, so she acquiesced.

Bertuccio urged her not to take the time to change, so she went to the count's chambers dressed as she was. Of course, it wouldn't matter, for soon she would be wearing nothing more than the sapphire in her navel. She was determined.

"Enter," rumbled his voice when she rapped on the door.

Haydée opened it and came in to find Monte Cristo sitting in a chair, looking out over Paris from the interior of his room. He looked like a statue, not even turning his face to see who it was that begged entrance. His prominent nose was strong and straight, his lips set in a firm line, his eyes scanning the profusion of creamy architecture below, which blazed yellow from the afternoon sun. Thick dark hair curled around his ears and just brushed his high collar, which had been loosened, though he still wore his morning jacket. One long-fingered hand curled around the knob of his chair's armrest, and his feet were planted firmly on the floor, unmoving.

"Restless" was not a word she would use to describe the man before her.

What had Bertucci meant?

"Did you have a pleasant visit?" Haydée asked, taking a fat purple cushion from the divan. She placed it on the floor near his feet, just in his line of sight if he cared to look down and to the right. Arranging the pillow's tassels, she sank down on it and raised her face to look up at him.

For the first time, she saw the expression there, and now she understood why Bertuccio had called her. It was like granite, his face, but colder. Dark and harsh and set. Empty.

Frightening.

There was a long silence. Very long.

She was just about to draw up her breath to ask another question, or to say something gentle and amusing, when he spoke.

"Today I conversed with the man who killed your father. The one who murdered him in cold blood after gaining his trust."

Haydée froze. She'd been about to put her hand over his calf, to slip it up under the leg of his trousers and smooth it over the warm, hairy skin there. But she stopped.

"Who is he?" she managed to ask, her heart pounding madly.

"The Comte de Morcerf" was the reply. "You will meet him someday. Perhaps Albert, his son, as well. But you may not"—his voice became whiplash sharp, yet he still hadn't looked away from the vista outside—"say or divulge that you are the daughter of Ali Pasha in any manner. To them, or to anyone in Paris. Until such time as I permit."

Haydée's belly twisted deep inside her as she remembered that night in the caves where she and her mother thought they were safe . . . that her father had been set free from those who'd captured him during his exile. And then the shrieks, the shouts, the screams as he and his men were slaughtered.

After giving their word, and receiving one of safety and trust.

Morcerf. So that was his name. The man who'd assassinated and betrayed her father in the most dishonorable way.

She felt ill, and wondered how she would ever hide her disgust and fury if she met him. "I'll kill him myself," she murmured, her fingers closing as if to hold the knife that would do the job.

"Revenge must be slow and deliberate and fitting," Monte Cristo said quietly; and she was surprised that he'd heard her. "And it will be, Haydée. It will. If it is speedy, it is over too quickly, and the man will never know what—you have suffered. Will suffer."

She looked up at him, but his face was still marble.

"The sins of the fathers will be visited upon their sons," he said after another long moment. "For evil tendencies in the father will be passed on to the son, just as goodness and heroicism in the father is also given to the son."

Silence fell again. Haydée remained still, watching as her fingers curled into the thickness of the rich wool rug beneath her, crushing the pattern of rich red and subtle gold.

"All of them," he murmured, as if musing to himself. "Long and deep suffering." His voice became a bit louder and clearer. "And it shall be of their own making."

She wanted to ask *Who?* but something held her back, and she continued to watch the swirl in the rug's pattern next to the soft leather of his shoes.

"She as well," he whispered, his lips barely moving. "Most of all. By God."

The venom in his voice made a shiver zip from Haydée's scalp down along her spine, and unease pooled in her belly. She knew he needed comfort—she thought he did . . . but she didn't know how to go after it. He was so removed and harsh. Fearsome. She brushed against his leg and felt a faint trembling there in his muscles, as if he controlled some great fury.

"Haydée," he said suddenly, jerking her to attention.

Her heart pounding, she looked up at him, into flat, flinty eyes. Her fingers began to tremble and she was suddenly afraid of him in a way she'd never been. "Yes, Your Excellency," she managed in a steady voice.

"You are a treasure to me," he said.

She nodded, a huge lump growing in her throat.

"I do not want a repeat of the events during my bath today."

No! "But, Your Excellency, I wish to serve you . . . service you in every way," she cried, her hands clasping in front of her. For if her master didn't take her maidenhead, who would? Not Ali, damn him! He had made that quite clear.

"And you have done so. But I don't wish for that kind of service from you. You are my slave in name only, and someday that will be rectified."

"But . . . please."

"There are many young and handsome men here in Paris—doubtless you will meet them and perhaps find one to love"—this last word came out with a bitterness that made it different from the others—"if you choose. With my blessing. But I—" He stopped abruptly.

A flash of something akin to kindness softened his features, just barely. "There is a kind young man, a good one—he is the perfect example of evil begets evil and goodness begets same. His father was one of the three best men I've known, and he, Maximilien Morrel, is just as fine a person. A hero, they call him, for all of the lives he's saved."

Monte Cristo's thoughts were clear, but Haydée rebelled. She didn't want this faceless Maximilien Morrel. She wanted Ali.

And he wanted her too. He just wouldn't take her.

But neither would the count.

Not far from the Champs-Élysées, very near to the Jardins de Tuileries, was the very grand home of Monsieur Villefort. Such a residence was only fitting, for the crown prosecutor was an immensely powerful, well-respected man in the city, and had been since he had moved from a lower position in Marseille up through the ranks here to the capital.

Behind the stately house was a vast garden filled with oaks and maples, boxwood, sage and lavender, rosebushes, lilacs and lilies. Stone pathways and wrought-iron benches marked and divided the area. Its beauty and variety were always remarked upon during the spring, summer, and autumn months when the Villeforts entertained and their guests spilled out from the building into the thick green garden. What occurred among the bushes and behind the trellises and upon—or beneath—the benches perhaps was best left to the imagination; but suffice to say the garden was a popular place.

Perhaps a week after he had dined with the Count of Monte Cristo at the home of Albert de Morcerf, Maximilien Morrel approached a stone wall at the most distant part of this garden, where, among a cluster of apple trees and lilacs, there stood a little gate. It was barely wide enough for two men to walk through abreast, and its face was made of narrow iron bars, slats crisscrossed like regular little stitches, leaving small diamond-shaped openings perhaps the size of a child's fist.

The gate was locked, as it always was, with heavy chains; but

Morrel hadn't expected to find it open. He had expected to see the lovely figure of Valentine Villefort sitting on a small bench on the other side, however, and he was not disappointed.

She had not heard him approach, and so he just looked for a moment . . . just gazed upon the beauty before him. Her profile was to the gate so that she faced the house and the pebble path upon which she'd walked in order to be warned if anyone approached. No one could see her from the house, but it was not prudent to take a chance.

Looking upon her face took his breath away. Honey-colored hair fluttered in a soft spring breeze that brought the scent of lilacs, tickling her rosebud lips and dancing around eyelashes as dark as ink. Her heart-shaped face with its little pointed chin and deep widow's peak was turned away from Morrel, but he knew every detail, and contented himself with looking at her pert little nose and the long line of her neck.

He curled his fingers through the diamond-shaped holes of the gate, and it creaked ever so slightly. Valentine turned, her face immediately aglow with pleasure.

Morrel fell in love all over again, which was fairly difficult to do, as he'd adored her for months now.

"Maximilien," she said in her sweet voice, low and careful, "I was afraid you weren't coming today."

"I would never miss our meetings, Valentine," he told her. "You must know I live for them. You look beautiful today."

A faint pink tinged her cheeks as she ducked her head. "You always say that."

"You always are, but even more so today. Tell me, how are you? How is your grandfather?"

"I am fine, and so is *Grandpère*. I will tell you more about what he has done in a moment . . . but first, Maximilien, tell me about you. How have you been?"

"Missing you, of course. As always." His fingers curled through a lower hole of the gate, and to his delight, she shifted so that she might touch them. Warmth spread through his body—a pleasant shock—and he gently stroked the undersides of her fingers, enjoying the feel of her flesh. "As for what to tell . . . well, I have met the celebrated Count of Monte Cristo."

"You have? I have as well. He came to our house to call on Papa, after Papa called on him. There was an incident with a pair of wild horses—they belonged to the Danglarses—and they nearly ran away with Heloise, my stepmother. Somehow, the count's manservant was able to stop those wild horses and save Heloise and her son, right in front of the count's home. So, of course, Papa called on him to thank him. And the count returned the favor."

"He is a wonderful man, is he not?" asked Maximilien fervently. "I have had the pleasure of dining with him several times, and on other occasions we have ridden together about the city."

Valentine hesitated; he felt it in her fingers. "He intimidated me, Maximilien. He wasn't frightening or rude—no, he was the epitome of grace and all that is polite, but he had this cold expression on his face. An intensity that made me nervous."

Maximilien tightened his grip around her fingertips. "He is not like that to me. He is warm and friendly, and I like him very much. I would count him as one of my greatest friends, and if I were ever to be in trouble, I would go to him for help. He has indeed offered to help me." He shifted so that he could look through the gate holes and catch her eye. "I have considered asking him for his advice in regards to our situation."

Valentine's eyes widened, and her lips trembled in a soft smile. "You would trust him that much, then, that he might help us find a way to be together?"

"If anyone can help, it would be the count. I am sure of it. He is wickedly intelligent and immensely wealthy, and he does everything with such ease and skill. The man has power beyond belief, much of which I think comes from his own self-assurance. He does not care what others think of him, and so they cannot help but admire him. He could find a way to help us."

Now he saw Valentine's thick dark lashes drop, covering sky blue eyes. "Perhaps we might need his assistance."

Maximilien's chest felt tight, and he scrabbled at the gate with his other hand, wanting to touch her but unable to do so. His fingers thrust through as long and straight as they could, brushing the rough lace that trimmed the back of her gown. "What is it?"

"Papa wishes me to marry Franz d'Epinay, the friend of your acquaintance Albert de Morcerf. He is insistent."

The band around his chest tightened further. "No, Valentine!"

"But *Grandpère* Noirtier, whom you know loves me above all, knows that I don't wish the match. Though he is old and feeble, he has more power than my father. And he has called for the lawyers and has had me disowned from his will, which will leave me with a much smaller dowry. I believe he intends to make me undesirable to d'Epinay so that he will deny the betrothal."

"But . . . your *grandpère* cannot move or speak. How could he make his wishes known?"

Valentine, whom Maximilien knew loved her *grandpère*

nearly as much as she loved him, smiled at her would-be lover. "But *Grandpère* can speak with his eyes, my love. He blinks once for yes and twice for no, and as such, we have a whole manner of communicating." Her smile faded. "But my papa is still insistent that I marry Monsieur d'Epinay, and although my *grandpère*'s disowning me has struck a great blow to my dowry, it may not keep the monsieur from agreeing to a betrothal."

Maximilien felt a great wave of relief. "So there has been no contract, no formal agreement yet. That is good. Let us wait and see, and in the meantime, I will try to find a way for us to be together. You know I love you more than life, Valentine."

Heedless of the garden path stretching behind her, she'd turned to fully face him at the gate, and curled her own fingers through two different diamond holes. He brushed a gentle kiss over her delicate knuckles, and then followed it with little ones on each fingertip.

"How I wish I could touch you, my love," he said, resting his forehead against the gate, pressing his eyes to the openings there. A chill iron slat pressed into his nose, and he was close enough to see the fine hairs that grew along the edge of her temples, melding into thicker, darker honey-colored tresses.

She brought her head to the gate so that they were eye to eye, but she was also far enough away that he could focus on the parts of her face that he could see: pink lips, a smooth white forehead, two brilliant blue eyes, the point of her chin, the sweep of blond hair away from the tops of her temples.

"As do I," she murmured.

He ducked his head, breaking their gazes, but moving closer to her fingers, which still curled through the hole. Instead of merely kissing them this time, he gently took one of them into his mouth. Valentine's quiet gasp sent a shriek of desire shooting through him, and Maximilien closed his eyes as he slid her finger deeply into his mouth. She tasted sweet, of course, for it was Valentine.

He took each finger into his mouth in turn, sliding them in and out gently and slowly. Her fingers unbent, relaxed, sagged. He could hear, over the chattering of a nearby squirrel, the increase in her breathing. By angling carefully, he was able to keep her forefinger in his mouth, yet see through the small openings in the gate that her eyes had drifted closed, and her lips were gently parted. A rosy flush colored her cheeks, and with another adjustment, he was able to see the rise and fall of her chest. And he sucked and stroked, his lips full and his tongue sliding around her trembling fingers, over the sensitive fold of skin between them. His teeth nibbled faintly at their tips, clicking quietly against her nails, all the while his own need for her building into an incessant pounding as his hands clutched the gate.

At last, he pulled away, his cock pushing against the confines of his trousers, his own breathing faster than it should have been.

"Valentine," he sighed. His forehead slammed gently against the metal bars that bit into his palms.

"Maximilien," she sighed in return. The fingers from both of her hands—one set moist, the other dry—poked through the openings as if to grab at him. He couldn't help it. He brushed his face against them, and he felt the beauty of her fingertips smooth over a small area of his cheek. The only part she could touch.

"When will I be able to kiss you, Valentine?" he asked,

knowing that his voice was heavy with want and agony. "Touch you?"

"Oh, Maximilien," she said, and then he saw her mouth against one of the openings. "Kiss me now. Please."

She didn't need to make the suggestion twice. He moved flush against the gate so quickly it jolted on its hinges and the chains clinked. Maximilien pushed up against it and so did she . . . and they touched each other, piecemeal, where parts of their bodies pressed through. His fingers touched the upper part of her arms, then moved to another opening and brushed her waist and the impossibly wide skirts there. Her hands thrust into the openings—they were almost small enough to fit her fist completely through the holes. And below . . . her little shoes peeked under the edge of the gate brushing between his.

He fitted his lips to hers, framed by the diamond opening, pushing them as far through as he could. The sharp edge of the slats cut into the flesh around his mouth, but the discomfort was wiped away by Valentine.

Her lips were sweet and soft and just as delicious as he'd imagined. He did nothing more than press his mouth to hers at first, but that wasn't enough. It would never be enough. He pressed harder, and heard the clink of the chains around the gate again, and felt her mouth open slightly. Slipping his tongue through, Maximilien jammed his fingers through the openings on either side as far as he could, struggling to touch her cheeks, to pull her face closer.

Her lips parted wider, and their tongues slipped and slid around each other as an iron grid kept them from delving deeply and thoroughly. Her skin was soft as silk, and he even managed to capture a lock of hair for a moment, twisting it between his fingers.

At last, Maximilien pulled away, his cock raging between him and the welcome pressure of the gate. He was breathing heavily, and Valentine's gasps matched his.

"Soon, my love," she said. "Oh, soon, Maximilien . . ."

"I won't let anyone else have you," he promised. "Wait for me."

"Yes . . . yes. I love you."

"I love you, Valentine."

"In two days," she said. "Let us meet again in two days."

"Only death would keep me away," he vowed. He allowed himself one last thrust of fingers through the gate to brush her mouth and cheek, and then he took himself off.

Six

A Cluster of Grapes

Two weeks later
Paris

"The Count of Monte Cristo," announced Francois, the Morcerfs' butler.

Mercédès looked up at the tall, elegant man who had just crossed the threshold of her home, and now stood at the entrance to the parlor where all of the dinner guests had gathered.

The count was the last to arrive, and he cut a striking figure with his broad shoulders and erect posture. Although he wasn't the tallest man there, his presence seemed to make him that much more imposing.

"Good evening, Your Excellency," Mercédès said as he approached. She raised her gloved hand and looked him steadily in the eye—familiar eyes. Oh, God, they were so familiar to her . . . yet they were cool and empty. Polite.

"And to you, madam," he replied, raising her hand to his lips and pressing a deliberate kiss there. She felt it through her gloves. "You look incredibly well."

And then she saw the faintest flicker of . . . something . . . as he cast his gaze over her, then seemed to pull it away and onto Fernand, who stood next to her.

Mercédès had of course dressed in her finest and most flattering for the occasion, and she'd made certain Charlotte's handiwork was more impeccable than usual. It had been two weeks since Edmond—Monte Cristo—had visited their home, and this was the first time she'd seen him since. She'd heard about him and his activities through conversations with Albert, but there had been no occasion in which their paths had crossed again.

At first, after he'd left her house, Mercédès hadn't known what to do: how to act, what to think and feel, how to proceed. This was the man she loved—the one she'd never stopped loving and grieving for. And here he was, suddenly, after twenty-four years. With a different name, and cold, blank eyes.

He'd saved her son's life.

Had he known Albert was the son of his lover?

Why was he pretending not to know her—did he truly not know her? How could he not, when she'd recognized him instantly?

Perhaps it was amnesia, she realized. Perhaps he really didn't know it was she.

And perhaps that was just as well. For what could she do?

She was married—albeit unhappily. She had a son, a home, a life. She couldn't be with Edmond the way she'd want to. The way she'd promised and intended.

Would she want to?

Ah. But there was no doubt. Of course she would. She'd never stopped loving him.

She turned to look into the parlor, where Albert had just taken Monte Cristo and was offering him a drink. Yes, there was no doubt where her heart still lay. It pounded harshly in her chest, beneath the lemon-yellow gown. It broke when she looked at that strong profile, that handsome, familiar—yet unfamiliar—one. The pain in her chest was palpable, an actual squeezing and tightness of her heart and lungs.

Edmond.

Returned at last, yet still so far away.

"Mercédès."

The soft murmur, the gentle tug at her elbow, brought her back to the present. To the trap and the puzzle that was her life. It was Georges, of course, ever-present, and now at her elbow.

Mercédès pushed her anguish and confusion away and looked at him, leaning absently into his offered arm, relishing the support. God knew how badly she needed it. "Good evening, Georges," she said, forcing herself to look away from the figure that commanded her attention.

He smiled at her, his eyes soft like that of the pup Albert had raised when he was young. "You look ravishing tonight," he said, his voice low. "I don't believe I've ever seen you look so well, Mercédès. I thought my heart would fill to bursting when I saw you."

He was sincere, and what woman would not thrill to such

words—even if they were from an earnest, open man such as he. Mercédès smiled at him, turning resolutely from the tall, dark person in the parlor behind her. "Perhaps you will be my dinner partner this evening?" she asked. "I have already planned it so," she lied, knowing she would have to change the seating arrangements before they entered the dining room.

She wouldn't be able to eat a morsel if she were sitting next to Edmond.

Monte Cristo politely declined Albert's offer of a drink, and instead took the opportunity to mingle with the other guests at the Morcerf home. The Danglarses and the Villeforts were present, as well as a dozen others. He knew many of them, having been out and about at dinners and the theater and even one ball in the last two weeks.

He himself had just returned from hosting a dinner party at his new home in Auteuil, at which he'd entertained the Danglars family along with the Villeforts and several others. That had gone very well, and had left the Baroness Danglars and Monsieur Villefort—who had been secret lovers many years ago whilst he was married to his first wife—more than a little nervous.

Twenty years ago, the baroness and Villefort had not only been lovers, but they had also birthed a child. Villefort had taken the child from the baroness and buried it alive on the grounds in Auteuil, which was precisely the reason Monte Cristo had purchased the home, and invited them for dinner, under the guise of ignorance of the events that had taken place many years ago.

The house party had been only the first stage of his plan for revenge, and if Baroness Danglars' near faint and Monsieur

Villefort's pale, drawn face during the evening were any indication, all had gone well.

"Monte Cristo, would you not like to sample this fine brandy?" Morcerf asked, suddenly appearing at his elbow. Puffed up with his own importance as host, he offered a cut-crystal glass of the dark amber liquor.

Monte Cristo made a bow and replied, "No, thank you, indeed. I have no thirst at the moment. What a lovely home you have," he added affably. "And a lovely family." He purposely allowed his gaze to stray to Mercédès, who'd just entered the room on the elbow of an elegant young man.

She was magnificent tonight. A far cry from the simple peasant woman he'd been taken from—*taken from* because of this man next to him, trying to serve him and ingratiate himself to him, and two others in this very room!—so many years ago. She'd aged delicately, beautifully: Her skin was still smooth and unwrinkled, still the same rich tan of her Catalan heritage. He'd noticed none of the white or gray hairs that would show so brightly against such lush, dark hair, and it was pinned up in some intricate style that he imagined must have taken hours to arrange.

Her hair was adorned with the gold pearls from the South Seas and rare yellow diamonds he admired, for Monte Cristo was a connoisseur of gems and jewels, having so many of them in his possession. A fat, shiny curl rested over one smooth shoulder, falling onto the swell of her bosom. Her waist was pinched in, not so far as Haydée's would be in such a gown, but well enough, and then her gown spanned out in ridiculously wide skirts of soft summer yellow, decorated with a fall of spring green lace.

She was ripe and beautiful and elegant.

As Monte Cristo intended, Morcerf noticed that his gaze was trained on Mercédès. "Indeed. Mercédès has always been a lovely woman."

"You are a lucky man," Monte Cristo replied carefully, and realized that his fingers were closed too tightly. He loosened them deliberately, one by one. "And that young man with her?" he asked, knowing full well it was Georges, the Count of Salieux. He knew everything there was to know about the man who'd shared Mercédès' bed. He knew everything about everyone . . . except the details of the Morcerfs' intimate relationship.

He'd had no interest in that information.

"That is Salieux," Morcerf replied casually.

To Monte Cristo's eyes, the young man in question enjoyed an intimacy that he, were he the husband, would find unacceptable. Yet Morcerf didn't appear perturbed in the least.

Monte Cristo determined to press on. "A cousin, I presume?" he asked, making his own voice casual, dragging his attention away from Mercédès as she made her way through the room.

Yet he knew when she smiled, showing her one charming off-kilter tooth, as she paused to speak with each of the guests throughout the room. They laughed with her at something she said. She leaned in toward another cluster, and her face lit up anew. She brushed someone's arm as if to comfort. Her eyes gleamed and sparkled as she spoke, hands gesturing elegantly.

Monte Cristo forced his attention to Morcerf.

"No, not a cousin at all," the man said, baring faintly yellow teeth under a gray-speckled mustache. "An acquaintance of Mercédès."

Monte Cristo raised his eyebrows. "More than an acquaintance, I would venture to say."

Morcerf flashed a look at him. "Mercédès is my wife, Your Excellency. She does nothing without my permission."

Indeed. Monte Cristo wondered fleetingly if that included a visit to the Isle of Monte Cristo. But he continued the conversation, for there was something there that intrigued him. "How far does your permissiveness extend?" he murmured.

Morcerf looked at him with calculation, but not surprise. No, not surprise or offense. "You are Albert's friend. And savior."

Monte Cristo bowed his head in acknowledgment, but remained silent. His pulse was jumping, for this development was wholly unexpected.

And rather advantageous to a man in his position.

"And we are quite indebted to you," Morcerf added meaningfully.

But before the conversation could continue, a pleasant tinkling reached their ears. One of the servants was walking through the parlor, ringing a small gold bell that announced the imminence of dinner, and the guests began to file into the dining room.

With a precise bow, Monte Cristo left his host's presence, quite pleased with the direction their conversation had gone.

The meal ought to be quite interesting, for as was his custom, Monte Cristo refused to eat or drink at the home of his enemies.

Mercédès kept her attention well away from the dark-haired man who seemed to appear in her line of vision wherever she looked. She was relieved to be occupied, playing the perfect hostess at the table and throughout the evening. Her task was made quite simple tonight, thankfully, for the minister of the interior had made the announcement only this morning, at the National Assembly, that the ashes of Emperor Napoleon would at last be returned to his city in December.

Thus, she was able to carry on reasonable conversations—for the details were being repeated over and over again—while part of her attention was on the fat, sloppy Baron Danglars, who had known Edmond almost as well as Mercédès herself did. After all, they had sailed on the *Pharaon* together, long before Danglars had become obese from great wealth and rich food. She watched him for any sign of recognition, and saw none. In fact, Danglars appeared to be trying to ingratiate himself with Monte Cristo. He certainly seemed to be successful at it, if the wide smile and jovial responses he received from the count were any indication.

So neither Fernand nor Danglars recognized Edmond. Was Mercédès mad? Was she seeing something that didn't exist, forcing something that wasn't there?

She cast a sidewise glance down the table. No. She wasn't wrong.

Thankfully, Mercédès was distracted by a slightly off-color remark from Monsieur Farnaugh in regard to where he thought the ashes of the emperor should be placed, and she responded with a good-natured reprimand that drew chuckles from both Farnaugh and the others in the vicinity. Mercédès was known as a mild-mannered hostess who preferred to keep the dinner conversation appropriate for the ladies as well as for the men.

Then she reluctantly allowed her attention to drift to Monsieur Villefort, who sat near Fernand. He was a dapper man of a height that was, ironically, not much greater than that of his despised Napoleon Bonaparte. The very sight of him made her head light and her stomach hurt.

Villefort had been known as a loyal Royalist during the time Napoleon was incarcerated on Elba, although it was later learned that his father, Monsieur Noirtier, had been a Nationalist in support of the little emperor. Mercédès had only known Villefort by sight when they all lived in Marseille until she visited him after Edmond's imprisonment, begging for information about her fiancé. That was the last time she'd begged anyone for anything.

To this day, she'd wondered: had he even known who Edmond was? Had Villefort ever laid eyes upon the young man whom he so easily dismissed when Mercédès—and Monsieur Morrel too—had come to him for information?

If so, he certainly didn't recognize him now.

Despite her wandering train of thought, Mercédès was surprised at how quickly dinner was over. Conversation had turned from the emperor's ashes to the great floating pool on the Seine, Piscine Deligny, which would at last be open near Quai Voltaire for swimming. As they discussed the appropriate attire for such activities, the guests began to filter out of the dining room. Mercédès meant to follow as soon as she gave last-minute instructions to the servants.

She took longer than she'd intended, and when she finally was ready to rejoin the guests, Albert approached her.

"Mama, did you notice that His Excellency the count didn't eat one bite at dinner tonight?"

She had not; she had been too busy keeping her attention

away. "No, indeed," Mercédès replied. Horror and shame filled her that a guest in her house—particularly Monte Cristo—should be left wanting. "Was the food not to his liking? Are there items that do not agree with him or make him ill?"

"He claims that is not the case, that he was simply not hungry." Albert looked at her, his handsome face thoughtful. "It is true, the times that I have dined out with him, he eats very little, and even demurred when he came to breakfast with me, explaining that he'd eaten when the sun rose—but he does eat. And according to d'Epinay, who attended a dinner party at Monte Cristo's house in Auteuil, he ate quite well at that meal. But tonight he ate nothing. Nor drank any wine or water or anything."

"I will speak to him," Mercédès said, at the same time as a prickle ran over her shoulders. She would have to seek him out, to speak with him again. Beneath the gloves, her palms became damp as anticipation and apprehension washed over her. It was a perfectly reasonable excuse. "Do you know where he is?"

"When I took his leave, he was stepping out onto the terrace with Papa, expressing an interest in the gardens. I'll accompany you, *Maman.*"

The gardens. Yes, perhaps that would be best. "No, Albert, I think I shall approach him alone. In the event that there was a problem with the food or that he is ill, I'm certain he would wish fewer people to know."

Before he could respond, Mercédès swept past him and made her way through the small clusters of people until she reached the flat-stoned terrace, bordered by fragrant lavender plants that gave way to two different pathways. The sun had set some time ago, and the last vestiges of its warmth and light gave a purple-and-indigo cast to the gardens beyond. Soon, they would fade into black, except where occasional little lanterns hung at knee height.

As she walked across the terrace, she recognized handsome young Maximilien Morrel, who'd been invited at Albert's behest, looking up guiltily from an earnest conversation with the pretty Villefort girl, Valentine.

But Mercédès had no interest in whatever tryst might be happening between the two young people, for she was in search of a dark-haired figure that would tower above the hyacinth bushes.

She was just about to slip onto one of the darker paths when a strong hand came out of nowhere and grabbed her arm. Holding back a gasp of surprise, she turned to see her husband coming out of the shadows.

"Where are you going?" he asked. His fingers were tight on her skin.

"I must see to a guest," she replied, jerking free. Her arm ached where his fingers had clasped her. "According to Albert, the Count of Monte Cristo ate none of our dinner this evening."

Fernand seemed to relax. "Very good. See to the count, and stay away from Salieux tonight." He looked at her, his dark eyes narrowed. "And might I remind you that we are in great debt to His Excellency. You will make certain he is accommodated in any manner that he requires."

Mercédès drew herself up, her heart pounding. She did not think Fernand was speaking of the menu. "It is my intention to make certain that all of our guests are well-accommodated," she began coolly.

"The count. See to the count—I have just left him, and you'll find him near the gazebo where the grapevines grow."

Mercédès looked at him closely and saw the determination in his face, and since it suited her own purposes at this time, she started off in that direction without another word to her husband. Yet her stomach roiled deep inside, making her feel nauseated and uncertain. What sort of exchange had occurred between Fernand and the count that he should say such a thing?

Uneasiness prickled down her spine, but she continued. It was inevitable that they should speak again. And she'd thought of little else since his first visit.

Brushing past a lilac bush that needed to be trimmed, Mercédès found herself at the small white gazebo. It was draped with grapevines and nasturtiums that grew so heavily they obscured the openings of the little structure. At the base of the two steps that led into the building, one small lantern glowed from a low hanger. A flickering circle of yellow-white light colored the grass and pathway beneath it and washed up on the side of the gazebo and the ripe grapes that hung there.

"Does your husband know that you venture into the dark gardens alone?"

His voice, very close, almost made her jump. She was able to keep that reaction to herself, but the pounding of her heart made her jittery. Her mouth was dry, and her stomach swirled like wine being tested in a glass.

"Albert apprised me of the fact that you did not eat this evening," she said firmly to the darkness. "Was the meal not to your liking?"

He stepped out of the gazebo, halting on its top step. The broad, flat leaves of the vines brushed his dark hair but he stood there, arms folded over his middle. "I am afraid I was not at all hungry this evening, Comtesse Morcerf."

"But why attend a dinner party if you do not wish to eat?" she countered.

He was silent for a moment. "Why, indeed." The glow of the lantern splayed over his impossibly shiny boots and up along the dark trousers he wore, but the expression on his face was mostly in shadows. "So you sought me out merely in order to ascertain whether I was hungry, madam?"

"There was certainly no other reason, Your Excellency, despite whatever you might think." Mercédès was proud of her frosty voice.

"Ah. So devoted to your husband that you bristle at the very suggestion that you hurried into the darkness for some reason other than to ensure I was in no danger of fainting from lack of sustenance." There was an edge to his voice. "Or is it the young Count Salieux that you do not wish to disappoint, and not your husband?"

"Apparently, you are in no danger of fainting," Mercédès replied, resolutely ignoring his other comment. "But you did not even drink the wine at the table."

"No, indeed. I find that I have no thirst nor appetite tonight."

Mercédès stepped closer and reached up to pluck a bunch of the purple grapes that hung from the vine-draped gazebo. "Perhaps you would like to try one of our fresh grapes," she asked, looking up at him. "They're very refreshing and delicious. Certainly you could try just one."

"Please . . . don't hesitate. Eat them if you wish, madam. I prefer not to partake this evening."

Mercédès couldn't understand why he refused food and drink, and stubbornly, she decided that she wouldn't give up without a fight. Or at least until she learned the real reason for his reticence. "They are quite delicious," she said casually, slipping one into her mouth with gloved fingers. The juice burst over her tongue when she bit down, and it was fresh and sweet as she'd promised. "Are you certain you don't wish to try them?"

Monte Cristo was silent for a moment, and then he stepped down onto the second stair. "Perhaps . . . perhaps if you were to offer me one," he said, suggestion heavy in his voice.

She snapped a glance at him, but his face was inscrutable. His leg blocked half of the light from the lantern, so even though he was closer to her now, he was still in shadow. "Perhaps if you were a bit closer, I might be able to do so," she replied evenly. Her heart ramrodded in her chest at her boldness.

He stepped onto the ground, and they were facing each other. "Is this better?"

The tug, the rush of sensation from his proximity made the night air feel warm and cloying. Mercédès slowly raised her arm, a grape held firmly between her thumb and forefinger, and concentrated on keeping her hand from trembling. He was so close, so tall and forbidding, and he smelled of some exotic, spicy scent. And he was distant, yet . . . she felt a sense of deep, driving purpose simmering beneath his words and actions.

Suddenly, his hand reached out and captured her wrist in midair. The heaviness between them shattered into bright tension. "Take off your gloves, madam. I've no wish to taste cotton."

His grip was solid and firm, his fingers wrapping easily around her narrow wrist, and then deliberately flinging it from their grip as if disdainful of the modest covering. She looked up at him, annoyed, and hesitated.

"As your esteemed guest, I wish you to remove your gloves, Comtesse Morcerf," he said. "I dislike hand coverings immensely, particularly when they are touching food of which I am presumed to partake."

The request was a small thing, yet stubbornness lengthened her spine. Her lips firmed and she said, "Edm—"

"How long have you and that young whelp been lovers?" his biting voice cut into her words. "Salieux."

She was so startled by his question that she smashed the grape between her fingers. Its juice stained the gloves, seeping through to her skin. She ignored it then, trying to read the expression in his face, for the question—the timing, the tone, the topic—gave him away. Confirmed what she knew. It was Edmond who stood before her, her lost love. And he remembered her.

"So long that you cannot recall?" he pursued in a soft, coaxing voice. "Or one among many so that you cannot remember when one ended and another began?"

"You are mistaken," she replied, steady and controlled. He was trying to get a rise from her, and she would refuse it. "Salieux and I are not lovers."

"And now you lie to your guest. You cannot deny that you have welcomed him into your bed, Comtesse Morcerf. The evidence is there for all to see. The way he touches you, the expression on his face when he looks at you."

"Why," she countered, feeling stronger now, on a steadier path, "is it of such concern to you, Your Excellency?"

He seemed to withdraw slightly, yet he made no move to step back. "Because I do not share, Comtesse Morcerf. Although, apparently, your husband does."

Her mouth dried instantly and her gaze sharpened, caught by his harsh one. "My husband does not—"

"I have already requested that you remove your gloves, madam," he said, suddenly snatching at her wrist again. His fingers closed around it, pressing the little pearl buttons angrily into her tender skin. "Twice. Why do you continue to offend me?"

And with that, he adjusted his grip and stripped off the juice-stained glove, sending it whipping to the ground. "Where is the grape you wished to feed me?"

She realized she was still holding the bunch in her other still-gloved hand, and when he released her wrist, she plucked one of the small grapes from it with her bare fingers. It was smooth and cool, and she held it up in front of him. Looking up she found his dark eyes trained on her, and although it was too dark to read them, she sensed mockery in his entire demeanor.

"Here," she said, stepping closer and raising the grape to his mouth. "Crisp and sweet and clean."

Instead of opening his lips to take it, Monte Cristo curved them into a sardonic smile. He caught her wrist again, and brought her even closer. She stumbled slightly, her feet skittering against his heavier ones, and she felt the push of her skirts as they bumped against his legs. Her heart was racing again, and she brought the hand with the bunch of grapes up between them.

"I believe I'd rather watch you partake," he said. "I have no appetite. For food."

Mercédès allowed him to bring her fingers with the grape back to her mouth, and felt the warm brush of his hand against her chin as the fruit touched her lips. She opened them and the grape slipped in as Monte Cristo released her wrist. But he didn't move away; and she realized that her other hand had twisted and was now flush against the lapel of his coat, the cluster of fruit dangling between them.

She bit into the grape and the juice exploded over her tongue. He watched as she chewed, the expression on his face leaving no doubt as to what he was thinking. Mercédès swallowed and stepped back, suddenly unsure and discomfited.

He gave a short, sharp laugh and reached for her arm. "You needn't play coy with me," he said, his fingers closing firmly around her. He gave a little tug and she stumbled again, dropping the cluster of grapes and falling against him. His arms went around her, and his mouth crashed down on hers as he pulled her flush to his body.

She didn't push him away.

Her hands faltered for a moment, fluttering, then settled on the tops of his warm shoulders, moving up to touch the ends of his hair. His mouth wasn't gentle or tender, nor did he bother to coax her response. He took from her with a driving tongue, strong and deep and sweeping, and agile lips that fitted and moved around hers. His teeth scraped the edges of her mouth, the sensitive corners, as if he intended to swallow her whole, and Mercédès found herself hardly able to catch her breath.

And it was furious. There was an underlying anger and roughness in him, in the way his fingers curled into her arms and manner in which he pulled her up against his hips, shifting her so that she nearly straddled his thigh there, standing in the garden.

At last Monte Cristo released her mouth and raised his face. He was breathing heavily, his eyes dark and shadowed. His lips were parted, but firm and straight, as if flexed in annoyance. And he tilted his head, mocking her. "You must be gratified now, madam, for your intent has been accomplished."

Mercédès could only stare up at him, confused by his statement and still disconcerted and light-headed from the kiss. He released her and she took a reflexive step back.

"You wished for me to taste the grapes," he said. "And so I have."

She licked her lips, but every bit of sweetness from the fruit was gone. He stared at her, and she at last gathered back a semblance of control, even though her fingers were trembling. "What do you want?"

"I should think it is quite clear by now, Comtesse Morcerf."

If this was Edmond—and it had to be—he had become much more cruel and harsh than the man she'd known. Just in these last few moments here in the garden, gone too was the debonair, calm and controlled Count of Monte Cristo. The man who stood before her was a cold mercenary with anger in his face and arrogance in his voice.

He was dangerous, and yet Mercédès couldn't leave. She craved more of him, more of the man she loved—or had once loved. And that kiss had only been a taste. A sampling.

No more than a grape, when she wanted the whole cluster.

"My God," he said in quiet shock, his gaze intent. He reached for her more slowly this time, and she came easily into his embrace. The arms that banded around her were sturdy and strong, not bruising or confining.

She raised her face and met his lips, and they were softer this time. Not yet gentle, but firm and quick. Their mouths fitted together, tongues dancing and sliding hot and slick, her hands burrowing into the thick hair at the back of his head. He made a quiet, deep sound in his throat and smoothed his hands down her spine under her buttocks to pull her up against his erection. The pierce of lust in her belly had Mercédès pressing back against him, shifting her hips against the lovely hard cock many layers of clothing away.

Suddenly, he lifted her against him, her skirts bunching and spilling every which way, and she felt him moving, jouncing her against his body as he climbed the two steps into the gazebo, their mouths still fused together.

In the shadows, darker from the grapevines hanging over the openings of the small structure, Monte Cristo wasted no time. He let her slide down his body until her feet were on the floor, and then he spun her around, away from him, so quickly that she stumbled against his feet. He steadied her, his firm hands on her shoulders. Then he was sweeping them down the front of her throat and pulling roughly at the low, sweeping neckline of her gown. His fingers were cool and strong, sliding down beneath the lace that edged her bodice as he bent his face to nuzzle roughly at the tendon on her neck.

Mercédès sagged gratefully against his solid chest, tipping her head back and opening her shoulders so that he could find her nipples beneath the bones of her corset. She reached behind to finger through his hair, but he jerked, pulling his head away so that her hands brushed against his smooth cheek, and then fell back to her sides.

His lips were on her shoulder, his tongue warm and slick over the hollow of her collarbone, his hands rough and questing down the front of her bodice. He forced his hands between the boning and her flesh, tightening the corset around her torso as he slid his fingers to the undersides of her breasts. A thumb came up from beneath and stroked over her painfully hard nipple, sending more frissons of desire jetting to the center of her belly, and lower.

With another sharp movement, as though he had no patience, he yanked his hands free and gave her a little push. Mercédès lurched forward, putting a bit of space between them . . . and then she felt quick, impatient movements at the back of her gown, undoing the buttons there with sharp jerks.

"Edm—" She gasped, holding her bodice to her breasts.

"I am Monte Cristo," he snarled, with a particularly vicious tug at her stays. They loosened and Mercédès felt the breath of late-spring air over her skin, bared by a sagging gown and loosened corset.

Her heart was racing, her hands damp and her breathing rough as he yanked at her clothes, those large, warm hands moving over her skin and the fabric that covered it. She could do nothing but stand there like a doll being undressed, facing away from him and staring into the darkness. Feeling him strip away her clothing . . . and her discretion.

Suddenly, she felt the whole weight of her gown against her hands, and the shift of her corset and loosening of her chemise as they fell away from her breasts. She was naked from the waist up, except where she held the last bit of bodice to her breasts—all of her clothing settled around her hips. Monte Cristo moved his hands to her shoulders and twisted her around, then gently but firmly pulled her hands away and looked down at her. Her breasts, bare and proud in the darkness, could hardly be visible, but he found one easily, sliding his hand around to cup it, to tease her nipple again as he stepped closer to her.

Mercédès realized he was moving her backward, and she felt the hard edge of a bench behind her. Before she quite knew what was happening, he grasped her by the waist and lifted her onto the bench.

Her gown slid down farther, caught at her thighs and under his booted foot, and she gave a soft shriek. "No," she said, trying to hold up the last bit of her chemise.

"Ah, but yes, madam, I think so," he said, now looking up at her, where she perched on the bench, her face just above him. His face was barely visible in the darkness, but she could see a hint of his cheekbone and the unsmiling set of his lips, the thick curl of hair and the faint outline of broad shoulders.

Her hand rested on his shoulder and she closed her eyes as he tugged ruthlessly at the froth of lace and skirts and crinolines that billowed between them. She felt the warmth of him beneath his jacket, and the brush of hair against the back of her hand, the smooth stroke of his fingers as they moved up along her belly and the sides of her torso.

She was, suddenly, unbelievably, naked except for her stockings, standing on the bench of the gazebo in front of him. Somewhere next to her or below was the complicated froth of her gown and underthings, and . . . she didn't care at the moment, for he'd stepped closer to draw one of her nipples into his mouth.

Pleasure arched through her, forcing her eyes closed. On the bench above, Mercédès sagged against him, her hips against his chest, as he swirled his tongue around the taut tip of her nipple, playing sensuously over it, as if, suddenly, he had all night. Her body seemed to hum under his touch; she felt the gathering of desire tighten in her belly and twinge down to her core with every stroke of his tongue. Oh, yes.

His fingers dug into the bare skin of her back, beneath her ribs, holding her in front of him as he became more urgent, covering her areola with his warm, wet mouth. He sucked hard, rhythmically, drawing her nipple into his mouth deeply. From where her hands rested on his shoulders, she felt a rumble deep inside him, like a groan, and the barest tremors beneath her fingers. But all those details were lost in a sudden whirl of sensation.

He moved, kissing down around her breast and onto the smooth, jumpy skin of her belly and then back up to her other nipple, where instead of sucking, he merely teased it with his tongue. Around and up and down, the hot, slick strokes. The pointed sensual assault brought tremors to her body. He pulled away, and her nipples shone wet and hard in the night, cool from the moisture on them. When he slipped his hands down along her torso, she thrust her hips toward him even as her hands dug into his hair, smoothing along the wedge of his sharp cheeks to the slice of his jaw. She found his lips, sliding her finger along the parted seam of his mouth.

He opened, and she slipped it in, felt the deep rumble in the back of his throat as he sucked and licked and drove the spirals of pleasure even more deeply into her belly, down into her sex. It throbbed, pounding there between her splayed legs, damp and needy as he tongued the sensitive web of skin between her fingers.

Edmond. She said his name silently, above him, where he could not hear, could not see. *Ahh, Edmond . . . at last.*

A tear leaked from the corner of one of her eyes, still closed—closed against the reality that she was married to another man when the man she had always loved, had never forgotten, and could never have, was here before her.

Kissing her. Undressing her. In the gazebo of her gardens during a dinner party.

Mercédès thrust the thoughts away, focusing instead on the pleasure of the moment. His thick hair under her fingers, and then, as her hands moved lower, the crisp collar of his shirt, warm next to his hot skin. She was trembling in his arms when he pulled her off the bench—yanked, really, with that impatience that seemed to pervade his mood—into his arms. He covered her mouth, nearly smothering her, thrusting his tongue in and biting on her lips so that she knew they'd be red and soft and swollen like the skin of a wrinkled peach.

His hand slipped between her legs as he devoured her mouth, and found the shiny hard nub of her sex. Sliding in the wetness there, his fingers quested, slid up and around and between the folds of her labia, tickling the hair there and covering her entire quim with wide, slow strokes . . . oh, just nearly in the right place . . . close to the center of her existence at that moment . . . around and near and along the side of . . . but not . . . not where she needed it.

Not where she throbbed and bulged and begged.

Please, she thought, pushing herself against him, feeling through his trousers for the bulge that strained them.

"Ah," he sighed when she found it, both hands sliding down between them, surrounding the full, velvety cock that strained against the fabric. It was hot and heavy, and she stroked him there, cupping his ballocks and finding the smooth flesh of the tip.

He arched against her, and for a moment, she thought he'd come . . . but there was no wetness, no shiver of release, and she found herself tumbling back into the pleasure of his hands between her own legs. She whimpered quietly as he pulled away so that her hands came out of his trousers, and lifted her back onto the bench. She stood before him, and he grasped her thighs, pulling them apart so that her gleaming sex was bare in the darkness there in front of him. . . . She reached behind her, felt the beam from the wall of the gazebo, and caught at it with her hands as he bent to her.

Oh.

His mouth, there on the inner part of her thigh made her shiver and squeak softly in surprise . . . those soft lips, the hot moist tongue, firm fingers. . . . She arched toward him and shifted so that his mouth swiped over her quim. He paused to lick long and deeply through the crevice of her labia, nudging her pearl with a quick little tup that made her jump and arch and prepare herself for an onslaught.

And then he pulled back, his fingers still on her thighs, standing before her. She felt him draw in a deep breath, the quick clutch of his grip into her skin, and then it fell away.

She felt rather than saw him step back, away from where she stood on the bench like some sort of trophy on a shelf. Her arms trembled, and she let them fall, realizing her fingers were shaking, her body was still humming, and he wasn't pulling her back . . . he wasn't tearing off his own clothes. He wasn't touching her.

"Shall I . . . send for your husband . . . or your maid?" he asked. His voice was cool.

"Wh-what?" she asked, lost, groggy as if she'd just awakened. She could hear him moving—away, toward the steps beyond which glowed in the faint light of the lantern. Mercédès' knees felt weak, and she let them buckle as she half fell, half stepped off the bench.

"To help you."

Mercédès gathered her wits, shoved aside her pounding arousal, her unfulfilled need, and replied, "Why?"

"Surely," he said, a faint hitch in his breath, "you don't wish to return to the party . . . as is."

"What are you doing?" she breathed, suddenly realizing that, yes, he meant to leave. Leave her here, like this: throbbing, wet, breathless . . . naked.

"I've been gone from the party for long enough, I believe," he said, his words now calm. He was standing on the threshold of the gazebo steps, outlined from the waist down.

"But . . ." She struggled, caught herself, and allowed the anger to wash away the humiliation that threatened. "My maid. Or no . . . no, perhaps you should send Salieux to me. At least he will finish what he starts."

Monte Cristo gave a low, hard laugh. "Clever, Comtesse. I've already told him what will happen if I find him sniffing around you again. He nearly pissed his pants."

"What are you doing?" she asked, walking toward him, heedless of her nakedness. Somehow, she couldn't make herself call him Edmond, though part of her believed it would jar him. No, this was not her Edmond.

Whoever he might have been, he was now the Count of Monte Cristo.

"Nothing," he said. "I merely find that I have lost what little appetite I had."

And he disappeared into the darkness.

Seven
Haydée Stalks Her Prey

Later that evening
Paris

Mercédès returned to the dinner party with her head held high, her gown in place, and her hair as immaculate as it had been when she walked down the stairs earlier that evening. But there was fire in her eyes, and fury simmering in her veins. One of her gloves was lost in the dark bushes.

She hadn't been able to leave the gazebo until someone came to assist her to dress again, and thus she'd remained at the mercy of the man who called himself Monte Cristo, waiting to see if he would follow through on his offer to send Charlotte—or Fernand. It was at least fifteen minutes before her maid—thank God, not Fernand—appeared, peeking carefully around the doorway.

During those fifteen minutes, Mercédès traveled through a vortex of emotions. Her hands shook, her breasts ached, and her thighs moved wetly against each other as she stalked around the inside of the gazebo, at that point heedless of her state of undress. She cursed, she wept, and she vowed revenge on Monte Cristo—not only for leaving her here, naked and vulnerable, but also for the trick he'd played, the game, the tease.

The deliberate, ruthless taunting of her body.

That it had been deliberate, and not a sudden case of discretion and prudence, she had no doubt.

She was more certain than ever that Monte Cristo was none other than Edmond Dantès—for she'd kissed him, touched him, smelled him . . . tasted him. There'd been familiarity, and a sort of comfort, buried beneath the passion between them. Despite his harshness, she *knew* him. She remembered him.

But . . . why?

Why would he do such a thing?

Why would he come to Paris and play about society, and ingratiate himself with Fernand and Albert, and even Danglars and Villefort? And not admit his true identity? What did he have to hide?

As she turned the possibilities over in her mind, there in the dark and silent gazebo, Mercédès had the first niggling of worry in the back of her mind. Monte Cristo had been more than amiable to Albert, and had made himself a quick favorite among the other powerful members of society. He'd even made a friend of Villefort, who rarely deigned to interact with those whom he didn't know well.

The only person to whom he'd been less than cordial was she, Mercédès. Those dark eyes, that set face, the cool whiplash comments . . . all had been delivered to *her* with an edge—an underscored edge that had culminated in this moment of frustration and humiliation. She'd bared herself to him both literally and figuratively, and he'd left her vulnerable and aroused.

Perhaps he believed she'd done the same to him when she married Fernand.

Perhaps he was here because he was angry with her for doing so.

It was the only explanation that made sense of the way he'd acted, of the things he'd said—particularly about Salieux. There'd been an underlying jealousy when he spoke of Georges. Yet it was not the obsessive jealousy of a young man, but the disdainful annoyance of a more mature, confident one.

As if he'd allow no one to disrupt his intentions.

Mercédès hovered on the edge of great sadness for a moment. Tears burned at the corners of her eyes as she thought back to the beauty of their time together: two young, innocent lovers, ignorant of the separate futures that would be forced upon them. She thought she'd wept all she could for the interruption of their love, but the grief rose anew.

And then the sadness eased away to be replaced by anger. For whatever had happened to Edmond Dantès in these twenty-four years, she had been wronged too. Her future, her love, the life she'd desired had been torn away from her as well. In more than two decades, there'd been no news, no communication, no hint that he was still alive.

For the man to be as rich and powerful as he was, he had to have been accumulating the wealth and experience for years. Decades.

And not one word from him over that time.

That he'd been alive—how could she have known differently?

And then for him to come sweeping back into her life, with this cloud of vengeance resting on his shoulders, using her love and her body to humiliate her . . .

Mercédès swallowed another curse. She was damned if she would let him manipulate her like this. She'd not lived with Fernand de Morcerf for twenty-two miserable years—her own penance for making such a foolish choice—to be flummoxed by a plan of vengeance.

If he expected her to cower in the corner or to turn the other cheek, Monte Cristo was bound to be confounded. For Mercédès Herrera de Morcerf was no shy violet, no cowering mouse, no rug to be trod upon.

And so when she returned to the party more than an hour after she'd disappeared to find the Count of Monte Cristo, she held her chin high and walked with an elegant and easy swagger. She smiled, she chatted, she laughed, she flirted.

In other words, she was the gracious and elegant Comtesse de Morcerf.

And when she found Georges, despite the fact that he paled noticeably when she approached him and cast about frantically as if to find escape, she greeted him with a greater enthusiasm than she'd shown in months.

"There you are," she said, slipping her arm through his and giving him her warmest, most glorious smile. "I must apologize for disappearing for so long. There was a problem in the kitchen, and then in the wine cellar, and then—ah . . ." She laughed up at him and saw, with great satisfaction, that his reluctance was dissolving. "I shan't bother you with all of the tedious details of my hostess duties. Perhaps, now that I have put things well in hand, we might take a stroll through the gardens. I seem to have lost my glove."

Georges' eyes heated and a genuine smile, with the hint of deviltry that had first attracted her, quirked his lips. "Indeed, madam, I would be happy to assist you in your search." He flexed the arm beneath his coat so that the vee in which her hand rested tightened in a secret embrace.

As they strolled across the ballroom toward the wide-open doors, taking care not to exhibit any signs of hurry, Mercédès paused their progress so that she could speak to several of the guests. She would be discreet, as always, taking care not to make the exit with her companion hurried.

Monte Cristo was nowhere to be seen, and she entertained the thought that he might have been cowardly enough to make his escape before she returned to the party. But when she and Georges stepped out onto the terrace, she saw Monte Cristo's unmistakable figure, tall and broad-shouldered, and heard the rumble of his voice as he conversed in a small cluster of other guests. Impudently, Mercédès steered Georges toward the group, which included Maximilien Morrel and Franz d'Epinay but, fortunately, not Albert.

"Good evening, gentlemen," she said with a pleasant smile.

Monte Cristo's back had been partly angled toward her, but her voice drew his attention and he turned. As Georges' arm tensed beneath hers, Mercédès continued toward them, stopping at the edge of the group. "I trust that you have had a pleasant time this evening, and are lacking nothing with which to make it more comfortable . . . or satisfying." Her words were bland, oh so bland, and so was her smile . . . and she kept her eyes resolutely blank as she focused on Monte Cristo.

He was standing with his back to the house, so the light shone behind him and filtered through the wayward tips of the hair that curled around his ears, casting his face mostly into shadow. She couldn't read his expression, and his stance gave nothing away, but she had the satisfaction of knowing that he could not have expected her to approach him in such a manner, and with Salieux on her arm.

"Everything has been quite perfect, madam," Maximilien Morrel replied jovially. "Thank you for a delightful evening."

Mercédès gave a brief nod. "I'm gratified to know that. And so, if you'll excuse me, I must be off. I seem to have lost one of my gloves."

The gentlemen bowed, but Monte Cristo was the only one to speak. "In the gardens, madam? I fear you will find them a bit . . . chilly this time of night. Perhaps you might wish to wait until daylight." The warning in his voice was unmistakable, and she felt Georges hesitate.

Mercédès replied calmly, "In fact, I did find it quite drafty and unpleasant earlier this evening, but I've no fear that will happen in this instance. If you will excuse us . . ."

She turned and, with a subtle tug, directed Georges to walk with her, despite the fact that he appeared to be a bit disconcerted. Well, she would soon disabuse him of the notion that the Count of Monte Cristo had any control over her.

Once they were out of earshot of the others, Georges seemed to regain his confidence. In fact, they were close enough that the sounds from the party still filtered through the air so that Mercédès could identify the high-pitched laugh of Madam Villefort, and the answering guffaw of Baron Danglars. The remnants of light from the house reached this far, if only to give a faint illumination to the tops of the hyacinth bushes and boxwood, adding to the glow of the random lanterns hanging at knee height.

Georges led her into a small arbor that was covered by a wickedly thorny rosebush soon to be covered by a profusion of yellow flowers. Mercédès willingly went into his arms, her body already beginning to hum with anticipation and need, her aborted arousal quickly flowing back to life when his lips covered hers.

Arching her hips, skirts and all, into his, she closed her eyes and accepted the deep swipe of his tongue, feeling rather than hearing the soft grunt of his pleasured sigh. His arms tightened firmly around her, crushing her breasts against his solid chest as he delved more deeply, cradling her head with one hand. She matched his mouth with hers, smoothing her palms along the broad width of his shoulders—the other thing that had initially attracted her, those broad, strong shoulders—and closed her mind off to everything but the man holding her.

The gentle spiral began to unwind in her belly, slowly, and she kissed Georges with more passion, desperate for it to grow, so she could let it loose. In response, his hands moved, loosening their embrace and sliding around to find the swell of her breasts between them, cupping them through layers of clothing and boning. She arched toward him, wanting more, wanting the same pounding pleasure she'd had earlier that evening.

But the texture of his mouth, the taste, the way his hands moved over her breasts—too tentative, too worshipful, too slow and delicate—wasn't enough.

It wasn't enough.

The little rise of desire that had begun to rekindle in her belly faltered, even as she kissed Georges desperately. Even as his fingers gently moved down beneath her bodice, finding her half-mast nipples and stroking them, but the faint hum of pleasure merely turned into a buzz. Yes, her nipples hardened. Yes, the damp between her legs grew warmer, but it was not the same. Yes, her tongue slipped and slid around Georges' hot mouth, and she felt the insistent ridge of his cock pressing into the bone above her sex, but it was nothing more than reflex.

No whirlwind, no breathlessness, no spicy spiral that made her knees weak and her head light.

At last, she pulled away, and Georges' hand slipped out from her bodice. He reached for her again, the desperate avidity on his face evident even in the dim light, but Mercédès demurred, taking a small step backward.

"Mercédès," he groaned, grasping her hands, and falling onto his knees in front of her. "Please," he said, "let me taste you." His hands were moving beneath her skirts; she felt them over her slippers, then up along her stockinged legs.

"Georges," she said, feeling the welcome prickle of awareness along her thighs as his fingers came closer, "I . . . no, we cannot." A faint shudder of want tingled between her legs as he continued moving up along them. Her skin trembled beneath his touch, smooth and tantalizing on the sensitive flesh, and her mouth dried as she realized her arousal was growing.

"Please, Mercédès, my love. I want only to pleasure you," he said earnestly, the weight of her skirt and crinoline billowing up in an awkward pile of fabric over his arms. Only his face showed above the froth of lace and silk, shadowed by a nearby lantern. The sight of his full lips, moist from her kisses, and the pleading in his eyes caused her to waver. One of his fingers moved gently over the front of her sex, teasing the moist hair there, and sending more prickles of need scattering over her skin.

"Georges," she began, but he'd read the acquiescence in her face, and gave her a little push. She sank onto the bench built into the inside of the arbor, leaning back against the wall. A little prick of thorns teased the back of her head and the tops of her shoulders, but it wasn't sharp enough to bother her, for they grew on the other side of the trellis, and Mercédès had suddenly become much more invested in what was happening below.

He was between her legs now, his face hidden. A sudden eruption of fabric tossed up and onto her torso left her legs uncovered once again in the pleasant night air, and her view of the top of his head was obstructed.

But . . . her eyes sank closed as she felt the warmth of his fingers, the short, hot puffs of breath there on thighs bare above her stockings. Her pip swelled, suddenly pounding in anticipation, as full as it had been earlier at the hands of the Count of Monte Cristo. And when Georges pulled her thighs wider and put his face to her sex, she nearly came off the bench. She seized up and closed her eyes and thought about the hands and tongue of a tall, dark man . . . not a broad-shouldered, ginger-haired one.

One gentle stroke of a tongue over her engorged and sensitive tickler, and she was shuddering and undulating there, the orgasm short and sharp . . . and empty.

A reflex. A simple release.

And one she already regretted.

In the early hours of the morning, Haydée slipped from her chamber and padded along the carpeted hall.

At last, the household was asleep, and, she hoped, so was her prey. It had been a difficult night after their master returned from his dinner engagement, with Haydée and his manservant, Bertucci, bearing the brunt of it.

Haydée counted three doors from His Excellency's apartments, and at the fourth one, she paused, took a deep breath, and silently turned the knob.

Inside the small room, there was little but a set of drawers and a narrow bed placed along the darkest wall, far from the two windows. The rug beneath her feet, however, was just as lush as that in her own apartments. As she closed the door behind her, she realized that the bed was flat. Even though there was no light in the chamber, a starry sky that was beginning to pale in the East revealed that there was, indeed, no sign of a slumbering giant.

Confounded, she stopped and was just about to turn back when she saw him.

The pale light streamed through the window, coloring everything near it pale blue-gray, and shone on Ali. He was on the floor, surrounded and supported by numerous pillows and cushions piled in the corner.

She walked toward him, silent as air, and knelt. His breathing was deep and even, and she felt a wave of prickling anticipation sweep over her. A smile curled her lips, and she felt her eyes crinkle at the corners and her mouth go dry.

She had him now.

But first . . . she bent near and inhaled, her hands pressing into the cashmere blanket that draped over him. Her eyes closed and she breathed in his smell: unidentifiable, but strong and bold, spiced liked mint and tinged with the musk of patchouli.

Moving back onto her haunches, she pulled off her silk caftan—the only article of clothing she was wearing—careful not to disturb the air or brush it against his skin. She suspected

Ali, trusted servant and bodyguard of His Excellency, slept with one ear and one eye always alert.

She also suspected that he slept in the nude, and it was with delight that she determined this was indeed the case when she carefully lifted the single blanket on the side closest to the window. The cool blue light clearly showed smooth, gleaming ebony skin that made her mouth water and her stomach flip in anticipation.

Haydée expected him to awaken at any time now, but since he was mute, she had no fear he would shout and raise an alarm. Again, she smiled, a devilish curl to her lips as she slid her naked body onto the plump cushion next to him.

He was warm and solid, and she felt the moment he awakened and became aware of her presence. Ali went rigid—everywhere, she noted with satisfaction—and, with a low, guttural grunt, immediately tried to push her away. But by then, she was already sliding her slender body over his, straddling him with wide legs as he rolled from a side position onto his back in an effort to move away.

Slim and delicate she might be, and no match for his incredible strength, but Haydée was determined. She cupped his big shoulders with her hands and sinuously moved her body up and down along the length of his torso as she kissed in the folds of his musky, moist neck. Ali trembled beneath her, his chest rising and falling beneath her breasts, his cock—as gloriously huge as she'd anticipated—prodding in the gap between her thighs.

His hands came down onto her back, gripping her hips as though to remove Haydée from her position . . . but when he tried to lift her away, she clung tighter and rolled her hips. She felt his grip change, then, from pulling her up, to a brief caress, as though he couldn't stop himself. No sooner did he touch her than his hands jerked away as though burned.

She smiled against his throat, tasting salt and dark, hot skin . . . feeling the rampant surge of blood coursing through the veins there, the tension in the long tendon at his neck, and the low rumbling deep in his chest. He didn't touch her again; she could tell that his hands sort of hung helplessly above her body, as if afraid to reach for her for fear of what they would do.

"I want to be with you, Ali," she murmured, lifting her face above his. The light was filtering in more strongly from the window, and she could better see his expression: set and still as marble, lips pursed tightly and chin raised as he half turned away. "And it's obvious that you want me."

He angled his face as far as he could, his eyes closing, his mouth tighter, and shook his head slightly. *No.*

Though he didn't speak, she could feel the negation—the false, desperate negation—in his body language.

"Yes, Ali," she murmured, and she began to slide down his body, lifting her hips in the air and inching her breasts, shoulders, and face along his sternum to the rippled belly below. He was hot and sharp-planed and hard—a quivering mass of rock-firm muscle, salty and faintly moist, tense and dark.

He bunched up beneath her as she drew closer to the massive cock she crushed into his belly with the weight of her torso, and she smiled again and paused to look at him, enjoying the feel of his erection hot and firm beneath her.

Seeming to gather himself up, he made quick, jerky motions with his hands. *No. You belong to him.*

Haydée sat back on his hips, settling onto the tops of his thighs. The head of his cock poked out from where it was trapped beneath her bare sex, and she gave a smooth little move, sliding gently over it in the smallest of motions. The soft sound of wet suction, of bodies shifting against each other, sent a stronger thrill of desire zinging to her swollen pip. Ali's throat convulsed and he closed his eyes again.

Haydée, you belong to my master.

"He doesn't want me that way, Ali," she said in a low voice, serene in her control.

Yes, you've been with him. Tonight.

She shook her head and said, "Look at me, Ali."

He reluctantly opened his eyes, but she couldn't read what was there. Her only clues were the way he held his body so rigid it must be ready to shatter, and the irregular hitch of his chest every few breaths.

I will not take what is not mine. His signing was sharp and angry, his large hands whipping through the air, smacking and snapping together with vehemence. *I may be a slave, but I have honor.*

"Yes, I was with him tonight."

He demanded you when he returned. I saw the look on his face. He needed a woman.

"Yes, he did. And I went to him willingly, just as I have in the past. He asked me to run a bath for him, and he ordered me to remove my clothing."

Ali stared at her, his eyes unblinking, his smooth, hairless head shining in the slowly growing light. He licked his thick lips, and another wave of lust coursed down from her belly to her sex. She shifted, and he caught his breath.

She lifted her hands and cupped her breasts, and his lips parted. He breathed heavily.

Perhaps this was a better approach. "I stripped in front of him and waited for his next instruction," she said, keeping her voice low and hypnotic. "Then, as I watched, he seemed to dissolve from the cool, correct man we all know to . . . someone else. It was as if he'd released his control, and allowed his real emotions to come through. His hands began to tremble and the expression on his face became stark and cold. Furious." In contrast to her serious words, she plucked at one of her nipples, then began to toy with it. It grew harder, the skin around it wrinkling tightly.

"He was murmuring things I couldn't understand, as I stood there, naked, and the bath streamed into the tub behind us."

What did he say?

Ali was staring at her breasts, watching her play with them. She licked a thumb and forefinger, and then brought them to her nipple, sliding them around. His cock gave a little surge beneath her, and she shifted in response. Ali groaned and closed his eyes again. His huge hands had fallen to the pile of cushions above his head, palms up, fingers curled helplessly. The golden bands at his wrists gleamed in the dark.

"I could understand very little. He stared into the darkness, out over the city, his hands opening and closing at his sides. When he finally turned back to me, after I had said his name many times, he called me to come to him. 'Unclothe me,' he ordered."

Now she licked her fingers again—the tips of four of them—and slid them down to cup her quim, slipping them through the juices that coated the top of his cock. Ali swallowed hard.

You are his slave. You belong to him. His signing was weaker now; it was more difficult to read.

"I unclothed him," she continued, aware that her own

breathing was unsteady. It was no hardship for her to stroke herself with flat fingers trapped between her sex and his. Back and forth, slippery and slick, around that hard little pip ready to be released.

"I unclothed him," she said again, "and I knelt before him. His cock was hard, Ali . . . but not so beautiful as this one here. Not so long and thick and *ready*," she said, shifting so that she slid off his hips and onto the makeshift bed beside him. Freed, the erection lifted from his belly and Haydée closed her fingers around it, slipping in her own generous wetness. Ali gasped and shuddered, and she moved her hand up and down, up and down, quickly and firmly, watching his mouth open in shock. One of his hands flailed in the air toward her, but it was too late—three strokes, and the zip of juices traveled wildly up along his cock, under her tight fingers, then spurted onto his dark belly as he jerked and cried out.

Ali lay there, shuddering. Delighted with her success, and curious, Haydee bent forward and lapped up the sticky white puddle, tasting salt and something altogether masculine . . . an experience that gave her great pleasure.

Go away. He'd caught his breath and his head sagged to the side, but his hands spoke. *You've gotten what you came for. Now leave.*

"I touched his cock, and he flinched," she said, ignoring Ali's pleading. "Not like you . . . no, he turned away the moment I touched it. He snapped at me, told me to get up from my knees." Haydée spread her fingers wide and smoothed them from his belly up to the planes of his pectoral muscles and over his shoulders. "He doesn't want me that way, Ali."

Perhaps that is true now. But he will change his mind.

"If he does not take what I have so blatantly offered now, why would he change his mind?" she murmured, her face hovering above his. Her breasts hung over his chest, high above the tiny whorls of black hair sparsely scattered over it.

He can think of nothing but vengeance now. Later . . .

"Vengeance?" She bent forward and kissed him on the chin, letting her nipples brush his chest. They were tight and hard, and the demand between her legs had not ceased, but she was no longer in a rush.

On four men and a woman. That is why he looks at no other woman until he has flushed her from his mind.

"He needed release, but he wouldn't allow me to give it to him. I think . . . he took the matter into his own hands, for he bathed alone and I was ordered to sit and wait." Haydée cupped Ali's head between her hands, suddenly and fiercely, and turned it toward her. Then she lowered her mouth to his.

He was tense at first, but suddenly it was as if desire—or curiosity—won out. Ali softened his thick lips, covering hers with them and molding his mouth to hers. His tongue was strong and demanding, scoring the inside of her mouth as though he couldn't get enough of her taste. She closed her eyes, releasing his face and planting her hands on his chest, where she could feel the rampant beat of his heart and the heat from his flesh.

He kept his hands away, though, as if afraid to touch her. She mauled his mouth, tightening her thighs around his torso, biting and licking and sucking at those thick, fleshy lips, imagining what it would be like to have them eating at her quim, soft and full and wet. She groaned into his mouth, pressing the moisture of her throbbing sex down into his belly, grinding there as she smashed her mouth against his.

At last, he pulled violently away, pushing at her, breathing heavily, and she felt the prod of his cock at the base of her back. Panting, Haydée smiled down at him, and he looked away. She knew he could toss her off, push her aside with the mere flick of his hands . . . but he didn't. Instead, the massive man beneath her looked weary and beaten and vulnerable. His hands fell back onto the floor above his head again.

She reached a hand down to her quim and swiped three fingers through the drippings there. "When he climbed out of the bath, he called me over to him again," she said, bringing her glistening fingers near his face. Ali's eyes were closed, but they opened and his nostrils widened as he drew in her smell. "He lay on the bed and ordered me to use an oil to massage his skin."

Her fingers were close to Ali's mouth, and she gently drew them across the half parting of his soft lips. He opened them, and she slipped a finger into the warm wet, and when he gave a long, hard suck, she gasped in surprise. His tongue swirled around as though to lick off every bit of her dusky juices, making Haydée's head feel light and her belly tighter than ever. Her pip bulged, saturated in her wetness, and she pressed down into his taut belly with a little grunt. Not much longer, she knew.

She was breathy as she spoke again. "I smoothed my hands over his shoulders and back . . . but they weren't as broad as these." She'd pulled her finger from his mouth with a little pop of suction and trailed her hands over the expanse of his pectorals and collarbone, over the width of his upper arms. "Not dark and rich like these," she murmured. "When I touched his body, I thought only of yours, Ali. The warmth of your gleaming skin, the bulge of your muscles, the ripples in your skin. Your cock buried in me—"

Suddenly, she was on her back, slammed to the cushions. His fingers were like bands over her wrists, clamping them to the ground on either side of her hips.

With a rough knee, he shoved her thighs apart, spreading them and showing her dripping, glistening sex. It throbbed even harder, now that it was open and free, and he knelt between her legs. Using his hands, he gripped her wrists and closed his long fingers over her thighs, pinning her there unnecessarily—for she had no desire to move.

With a smooth motion, he buried his face in her quim, those thick lips eating at her swollen labia just as she'd imagined. Haydée gave a little scream and arched her back, trying to shove herself closer to his mouth, wanting him to jiggle her little pip, aching and pounding.

His tongue snaked inside her, then flipped up on the underside of her sex and teased it, working it quickly and expertly until she reached the peak and tumbled over in a mass of shivers and throbs.

Ali pulled his wet face away from her body, slowly releasing her hands and sitting back on his haunches. His cock was proud and long, straight out from his thighs. He looked at her a long moment, and then signed, *I'll not take what belongs to my master. It is his right as long as he owns you. Now go, or I will throw you out myself.*

Haydée struggled to her feet, still quivering and warm and sated. She walked by Ali and then stopped, standing next to his hunched body. Her hands rested on his broad shoulders from behind, and she bent to quickly give him a kiss on his smooth head. "I'll change your mind, Ali. Never fear."

Eight
At the Theater

The next morning
Paris

Mercédès stood in a cascade of water, and it poured down on her, hot and pounding over her shoulders and on the sensitive tips of her nipples. She raised her face and let the waterfall prickle against her cheeks and lips, and she smoothed her wet hair over the top of her head, feeling it slap against her back.

Suddenly, large tanned hands slipped around her waist, pulling her back up against a solid chest . . . and a thrusting cock, prodding below the crack of her ass. With a sigh, she rested back against his solid chest and felt wet, hot kisses on her bare shoulder as his hands moved up to cover her breasts.

She turned her head under the spray of water to see Edmond behind her, his handsome face taut with desire, young and lean, his lips full and moist from the cascade. As she looked at him, he merged into the older, harsher Monte Cristo, his hands pinging her nipples, making the sensation sing down into her belly.

Her desire rising, mingling with the steam, she tried to turn to face him, but a second pair of hands appeared, sliding over her shoulders to tangle in her sopping hair, and another tall, dark-haired figure was suddenly before her. Sinbad bent forward to kiss her mouth before she could protest, and she felt the bristle of his short beard and mustache as he fit his lips to hers, hands gripping her shoulders, molding his long body to hers.

Trapped, crushed, between them, Mercédès felt every inch of her body pressing into hard muscle and warm flesh. Between the beat of water, and the rise of steam, she could see little. Everything was a maelstrom of sensation: teeth nibbling gently beneath her ear, strong hands over the front of her nipples, fingertips tracing tiny little circles on them that made her squirm . . . sensual lips molding to her mouth, fitting, pulling, tasting . . . long legs behind hers, a cock raging against her from behind . . . and another one teasing at the front of her sex.

Mercédès tried to pull away, to escape from the delicious torture, but Sinbad held her shoulders while Monte Cristo cupped her breasts, their strong arms embracing her so tightly she could barely catch her breath. Wet flesh slipped and slid against hot, wet flesh, smooth curves crushed against firm, ropy muscle, limbs tangled and bent, her long black hair plastered everywhere.

Then Sinbad, with his dark-lined eyes and smooth, queued hair, pulled out of the kiss, and she drew in a deep sigh, struggling to push him away, hands splayed on his bare, smooth chest . . . but Monte Cristo caught at her wrists, and pulled them behind her back, holding them there with one strong hand as Sinbad knelt before her.

The water rained down, choking her as she opened her mouth to protest—or perhaps to sigh her pleasure—as firm fingers drew her thighs apart. Sinbad bent to her swollen pearl, his hands cupping the underside of her thighs as her knees buckled. She thrust herself toward his face, arching back into Monte Cristo's chest.

Sinbad licked all around, teasing her sex with his flat, warm tongue as Monte Cristo released her hands to return his own to fondling her breasts. He lifted them, pointing the nipples straight up into the cascade of water, holding them there, squeezing them, and she twitched, her hips moving as she felt Sinbad's tongue suddenly drive deeply into her quim. The incessant vibration of water over her nipples, the wringing of tongue in and out and around her sex rolled through her body, coiling and building and swelling unbearably.

Her hands fluttered around until they rested on the smooth hair of the sailor, who sucked at her pearl as the water pounded down on her . . . hard and strong and firm, he sucked, and drew that little pip into his mouth as if he would swallow it. She moaned and writhed and thrashed there, held firmly in place by four strong hands as the steam clogged her nose and the water filled her mouth, and at last, with one long, rhythmic draw, Sinbad tipped her over the edge into a burst of release . . . and she shuddered and sighed and sagged between them. . . .

Mercédès woke from the dream to find her sex throbbing gently, and her quim wet and slippery. She was breathing heavily, her heart pounding as though the two men had really been there. Her nipples thrust up into the blankets, sensitive to her slightest movement, as if they had actually been showered upon.

She swallowed and closed her eyes, reveling in the remnants of one of the most realistic, passionate dreams she'd ever experienced. The easy satisfaction stayed with her for a moment longer, and then it was gone when she remembered the events of last night's dinner party. And when she opened her eyes again, a dull gray light filtered through her bedroom window, matching her thoughts—thoughts that had plagued her until she fell into a restless sleep as the sun had begun to light the horizon.

An ugly feeling gnawed deep in her belly as she lay there, contemplating the pale green silk hanging on the ceiling above. She'd had no right to allow Georges to pleasure her in that way, not when she was enraptured with another man—deplorable as that other man had been.

Her throat was dry, and it crackled when she swallowed. She'd been wrong to take Georges into the garden—although, in her defense, she hadn't intended for things to go as far as they had. She'd truly only meant for Monte Cristo to see that she would defy him, that he would have no control over her.

After all, he'd left her body primed and ready for sensual touch . . . although it wasn't Georges' doing, and she should never have let him kneel in front of her and burrow under her gown. Their relationship could go no further, now that Monte Cristo had come to town.

For, much as she'd like to ignore him and his presence, Mercédès realized that until whatever needed to be resolved between them was put to bed—whatever burned in him so that he felt the need to torture and humiliate her as he had—she had no right to engage with any other man. No right to allow someone else to cloud what she was trying to understand.

And, in truth, there was no other man who'd made her quiver and come alive the way Monte Cristo had done last night—and not in her dreams and fantasies, but for real. In the gazebo.

She'd responded to him readily, immediately, as if her passion had never sunk far beneath the surface and was released as easily as a pin popped a bubble. No one else had ever made her feel that intense pleasure, that rightness . . . .

Except . . .

Mercédès stopped, a chill washing over her body.

Except Sinbad.

Something prickled in her fingertips; her head felt light, and her vision was confused. A band encircled her lungs.

Sinbad. Who'd taken her to the Isle of Monte Cristo.

She didn't breathe for a full minute as she considered the possibility.

Sinbad was tall, with long, straight hair and a beard and mustache—but that was simple to change. There'd been liner around his eyes, subtle, yet it could be used to give them a different shape and weight, and they'd only been together when the light was low and dim. Shadows could hide so much!

His chest was bare, but hair could be easily shaved. An earring in an ear could be removed, and the hole would hardly be noticeable unless one looked . . . and Monte Cristo wore his hair long, over his ears.

But the most damning thing of all . . . the clincher . . . was the way she felt when she had been with Sinbad those two times . . . the exquisite, full, deep-seated pleasure. A reawakening of her senses and emotions. A sort of familiarity and release that she'd attributed to . . . well, to the fact that he'd reminded her of Edmond when she first saw him from behind, fleetingly, but he had.

He'd reminded her of Edmond, even then.

Mercédès clapped a hand to her chest, making a sharp, hollow sound. Foolish! She'd been so utterly foolish.

How could she have not known it was he?

And then it dawned on her. *He'd* known it was she.

The realization took her breath away again, and it was as if scales fell from her eyes.

By God, he'd done it all. On purpose.

Her faced heated, then cooled as anger barreled through her. Her fingers were shaking. All of this—for revenge? On her? For marrying Fernand after Edmond had disappeared?

What had happened to turn him into such a man?

She breathed there for a moment, trying to control her anger, to understand how and why the loving, tender Edmond she'd known and loved could have turned into such a harsh and unfeeling man. One who'd lied to her, humiliated her—who knew who she was but would not acknowledge their past.

She remembered how Sinbad had trembled gently against her, how he'd been tender yet demanding, how he'd been in Aladdin's cave, the way he'd touched her and pleasured her . . . and how she'd pleasured him. How he'd called her "Countess" with that odd, sardonic note that made so much more sense to her now.

Her fingers were still shaking, but her mind had become clearer. If this were to be a game of vengeance, Mercédès had just as much a chance of winning as Monte Cristo did.

* * *

As he led Haydée to their theater box, Monte Cristo nodded to the many acquaintances he'd made since arriving in Paris. Both men and women stopped to greet him, and some to converse, but he never paused long. He preferred to wait for those who wished to speak with him to come to him of their own accord.

And they would.

"There are so many fine people here," Haydée said, sounding more ingenuous than he'd ever heard her. Her large, dark eyes were wide as they cast about the passageway, no doubt taking in every detail of the women's gowns, gloves, and other fripperies—rather than the paintings and architecture of the theater.

"You look just as lovely as any of them," he hastened to tell her. Monte Cristo was fully aware of the curious looks he and the lovely, exotic Haydée garnered as they promenaded to their box. He had no doubt that word would soon spread throughout Parisian drawing rooms of the Count of Monte Cristo and the stunning, mysterious woman he had escorted. "Do you see that man over there, the one with the violet waistcoat?"

"Yes. He looks as if he is someone very important."

"Indeed, he is. That is the author Victor Hugo, who has written a famous book called *The Hunchback of Notre Dame*. And perhaps you noticed the scaffolding around the Notre Dame Cathedral, that tall building with the two towers?"

Haydée nodded, her eyes luminous and interested. She had fairly inhaled the city's sights every time Monte Cristo took her out in the carriage; they were so different from Singapore and Peking, where she had lived for most of the last decade while he was on his travels. "Yes, I know the church you speak of."

"It's one of the most famous landmarks in Paris, but until Hugo's novel was published, the church had fallen into disrepair. It was only the notoriety of the book that shamed the city into restoring the building," he explained as they reached the door of their box.

In the week since the dinner party at the Morcerf residence, Monte Cristo had applied himself to several other aspects related to his purpose for being in Paris. He had waited to give himself some distance from the events of that evening.

Through some well-placed rumors and one very large bribe he'd ensured that the Baroness Danglars (who was a compulsive investor)—and through her, Danglars himself—had a huge loss in the stock exchange this week worth more than five hundred thousand francs. It was only a first step in his plan, and Madam Danglars had brought the loss upon herself through her own greed.

He'd also learned that the father of Villefort's first wife had died suddenly, which was not a surprise to Monte Cristo. Not more than two weeks ago, Monte Cristo had had quite an interesting conversation with Madam Heloise Villefort, the crown prosecutor's second wife, about poisons and their uses.

That was not all he'd accomplished in the last week, through his other silent manipulations, but the other lines that had been cast had yet to draw in their prey. All in all, events were unfolding just as he'd planned, and the nets would soon catch the four men who'd betrayed Edmond Dantès. The most delicious part of it all was that there would be no nets to catch those men if they had been good, honest, trustworthy men—thus, they would be caught in disasters of their own making.

And that was what confirmed for Monte Cristo that he was, indeed, acting as God's Avenging Angel.

Monte Cristo had ensured that his theater box was the most expensive, most visible one, located at the left side of the stage at nearly the same level as the actors. Ali had gone directly from the carriage to the box and awaited them, standing like a huge black sentinel at the entrance. No sooner had Monte Cristo and Haydée taken their seats on the plush green velvet chairs than there was a knock at the door.

He nodded at Ali to open it, and was gratified to see his first visitor was none other than Baron Danglars.

"Good evening, monsieur," Monte Cristo said, declining to rise from his seat.

Danglars came in and took an offered chair next to his host, glancing curiously at Haydée. "Good evening, Your Excellency."

Monte Cristo smiled pleasantly at him and said, "Ah, what a busy week you bankers have had on the exchange. I understand there was quite a disruption there this week. A telegram was misread, and some misinformation disseminated. Fortunately, it was corrected almost immediately, and likely caused no great harm."

He was aware that this was indeed what had happened, but he also knew that because of the baroness' proclivity for unscrupulous investing, she had asked her lover to make a huge investment based on the bad information. This information, which she'd dishonestly learned about the night before it was made public, had, in fact, caused her great loss. If she had learned the news at the same time as the rest of the city, she would also have heard its correction only moments later—as did everyone else—and would therefore have saved herself the great loss. Thus her greed had caused the Danglars household to choke down a massive monetary loss, one over which her husband must be furious.

Danglars nodded. "Indeed, it could have been much worse than it was. Still, for me, to be honest, Your Excellency, it was bad enough. In fact, I have suffered quite a few large ones in the last weeks myself."

Monte Cristo raised his eyebrows. He, of course, already knew this quite well, for he made it his practice to know everything . . . and to help such imminent events along rather more quickly.

"Oh, please don't think I mean to ask you for a loan—no, indeed," said Danglars. "But I do wish to ask your advice on one account. Since my finances are—shall we say, a bit out of sorts?—I have been concerned with finalizing the betrothal of my daughter to Albert de Morcerf. And I wondered if you had any advice—or opinion—on the matter, for I have recently begun to question the count's background. It seems so vague and secretive, and there have been rumors coming from the city of Janina, in Greece, where he fought in the army."

Pleased that his work was already coming to fruition, Monte Cristo steepled his fingers and allowed his gaze to travel out over the theater stalls as if he were deep in thought. As he did so, his attention was captured by a slender, dark-haired woman just taking her seat in the box directly across from him. Her head was turned away as she conversed with a companion and sank down into a chair, but he recognized her honey gold skin, the curve of her cheek and, most absurdly, the particular swell of her delicate collarbone exposed by a low—very low—lush red décolletage.

His fingers flexed against the wooden arm of his chair, and he calmly turned his attention back to Danglars. "And thus you speak of the devil himself," he commented, with a bored gesture toward the Morcerfs, and their three male guests, in the box. Mercédès was still in intense conversation with the man sitting next to her. He appeared to be quite interested in the large ruby that sat in the deep cleavage plunging into a bodice that surely only barely covered her nipples.

"Albert Morcerf is a fine young man, and I am certain he would be a worthy son-in-law. But if I were you," Monte Cristo said, focusing back on Danglars and the next nail in Fernand Morcerf's coffin, "I would send to Janina to learn as much as you can about the Ali Pasha affair before making any final decisions."

The count ignored the sudden jerk of tension in Haydée, whose arm rested against his, and simply nodded at Danglars, adding, "That would be my recommendation."

The fat baron stood, wiping his forehead with a handkerchief and looking immensely grateful. "*Merci*, Your Excellency. I shall take your suggestion to heart."

Monte Cristo inclined his head and didn't bother to watch Danglars as he pushed his way out of the box. Instead, he leaned over to speak to Haydée, turning toward her and placing a hand on the box's rail in front of them. "You must remember to give no indication of your relationship to Ali Pasha. . . . the right time will come, and I will tell you when. Now smile brightly and laugh as though you have never been happier."

Haydée complied, and Monte Cristo smiled warmly back at her, fully aware of the picture they made there in the most visible seats in the theater: an elegant, handsome, dark-haired couple seeming to be unaware of anything around them as they laughed intimately. Precisely the impression he wished to give.

The second knock on the door of their box brought a most welcome visitor.

"Come, come, sit with us, Maximilien," Monte Cristo said, standing to greet his young friend as he glanced quickly across the way. Now her head was bent toward another of the three men who weren't family members, and he could see the curve of her cheek as she smiled.

He was not surprised to see that Salieux was not one of the Morcerf party. Monte Cristo had paid a call on the young man the day following the dinner party. He clarified for the young man the consequences if he continued to be seen in the Comtesse Morcerf's company. Saliuex had babbled about visiting some family in Italy for an extended holiday, and the count had wished him a polite adieu.

Monte Cristo now shook Morrel's hand warmly and kissed both cheeks in a genuine display of affection. Since his arrival in Paris, other than those in his household whom he trusted, Monte Cristo had found no other soul whom he'd come to care for. "But what is it that bothers you?" he asked, immediately recognizing a subdued expression on the handsome young man's face.

Maximilien looked at him, his dark eyes earnest, yet carrying a profound wisdom from his years in the military. "I have just learned some terrible news."

"Please," Monte Cristo said, "unburden yourself to me, and I will help you in any way that I might be able to. Or, if I cannot help, I shall at least be a sympathetic ear."

The young man seemed to consider for a moment, and he was silent at first. During this time, Monte Cristo was reminded of his own intention of introducing Haydée to young Captain

Morrel, and he briefly contemplated doing so. But in the end, he resisted. It was to his advantage at this time for Parisian society—and one member in particular—to believe that he and the young woman were a couple. An intimate couple.

At last Maximilien spoke. "Please do not ask why or how I came to be in such a position—for that, I cannot divulge—but it happened that I was near the back garden gate of Monsieur Villefort's residence."

Monte Cristo was surprised, but not displeased, at the topic introduced. "I understand that there was a death in the family earlier this week."

Maximilien nodded. "In fact, what I learned today was that there have been two deaths in the last week—that of Monsieur Villefort's father-in-law and then, only two days later, his mother-in-law died at Villefort's home."

"Not Madam Heloise's parents?" Monte Cristo feigned surprise. Madam Heloise was the very young, second wife of Villefort, with whom he'd had that enlightening conversation regarding poison only two weeks earlier.

"No, these were the grandparents of Monsieur Villefort's daughter, Valentine. Her maternal grandparents. Her mother died many years ago."

"Indeed. And they were quite wealthy individuals, were they not?" Monte Cristo said. "I do recall hearing that. So this means that Mademoiselle Valentine will now inherit their fortune."

Maximilien seemed miserable. "But there is more to tell, for while I was at the back garden gate"—he stole a look at Monte Cristo, who took care to keep his expression bland, for he didn't care what reason the young man might have had for being in the vicinity of said gate—"I overheard a discussion between the monsieur and the physician, in which the doctor told him that the cause of the deaths was most definitely that of poison."

"So Monsieur Villefort harbors a poisoner, does he?" mused Monte Cristo, successfully keeping his satisfaction to himself.

"It appears so. But there is even more." Now Maximilien looked wholly dejected. "Not long after the physician was there to examine the woman's body, Mademoiselle Valentine was with her grandfather—Monsieur Noirtier, who is Monsieur Villefort's father and an old Bonapartist, who cannot speak or move—and she delivered a glass of lemonade to him. Before he could partake of it, the old man's devoted servant, who was feeling weary and thirsty, took it himself to drink. He became ill, and went into frightful convulsions and expired on the spot."

Monte Cristo looked grave. "So there have been three murders—poisonings—in Monsieur Villefort's home in less than a week. Based on what you have told me, it appears that Mademoiselle Valentine must be the culprit—for she has the most to gain from the deaths of her maternal grandparents, who were very wealthy, and her grandfather, Monsieur Noirtier, who also, I understand, has made her his heir."

"But no, it could not be V—Mademoiselle Valentine!" exclaimed Maximilien. "I-I do not believe she would do such a thing, for I-I met her at the Morcerfs' dinner party, which you also attended."

Monte Cristo raised one eyebrow. "Maximilien, my dearest friend, one can never be certain of a woman, the depths of her loyalty—or how far she will go in betrayal. That is one thing I have learned overwell. And it is said, and I believe it to be true, that the sins of the father will be visited upon his children. I am not altogether certain that Monsieur Villefort, for all of his power and social standing, is the fine and honest man he makes himself out to be. Perhaps his inclinations have merely manifested themselves in his daughter."

"I do not believe that is so. Mademoiselle Valentine loves her *grandpère* more than anyone in the world," Maximilien said. "She would not poison him."

Monte Cristo chose not to comment on Maximilien's supposed knowledge of Mademoiselle Valentine's affections; instead, he looked kindly at his friend. "I hope that you will keep me apprised of anything that might trouble you, my friend . . . but at this time, I sense only your kindness and misery toward three innocent people and their deaths."

Maximilien nodded, his face still grim. "Indeed, that is so. But"—he looked Monte Cristo straight in the eye, steadily and intensely—"there may be a time in which I find I may need more than a sympathetic ear, Your Excellency."

Monte Cristo leaned toward him, closing his fingers firmly around the young man's muscular arm. "And you can be certain, Maximilien, that if you ever come to me for assistance for any reason, for anything, I will move heaven and earth to help you. I give you my word, on my life. You have only to ask."

Perhaps there might have been a tear that glistened in his friend's eyes. Perhaps not. Regardless, Morrel's next words served to startle Monte Cristo so much that he almost jerked in his seat. "There has only been one other person I've known—besides my father, of course—who has been so kind and so generous to me and my family. I do not even know who he is, only his name: Lord Wilmore. My sister, Julie, and I have long thought that this man, who saved my father from certain ruin and suicide by forgiving a huge debt just at the moment of disaster, is none other than an old friend of ours: Edmond Dantès, who disappeared more than twenty years ago. I hope you will take this in the manner in which it is intended—that is, as a compliment, sir—but you remind me very much of him."

For a moment, Monte Cristo couldn't speak. He felt his face drain of warmth, and knew that it must have gone pale. But he quickly recovered, and replied in an uneven voice, "I will indeed take it as the greatest of compliments."

So it was true.

Mercédès couldn't keep her gaze from returning to the box across the stage from her, where Monte Cristo sat with an incredibly beautiful, young, exotic woman. Even when the play began, and her attention should have transferred to the actors only a short distance away, she kept looking over at them. They were easy to see, for although the stage lights had been illuminated with the commencement of the show, the other lamps throughout the theater remained lit as well.

So that was why he'd left Mercédès in such a state. This was what he had waiting for him. A woman half his age, half *her* age. Taut and firm and gloriously beautiful.

Mercédès had attended the theater tonight dressed in her boldest, most daring gown of bloodred, in the company of Albert, Fernand, and three of her husband's business associates—all men, none of whom were married. She'd heard that Monte Cristo meant to attend, and she wanted to give him something to look at.

Apparently, he didn't even notice her, for he spent the entire time chatting and laughing with the woman, leaning toward her as they shared some intimate conversation or amusement.

Her thoughts, which could not be focused on the play, turned to Georges, Count Salieux. What could have been quite a conundrum—for how was she to cut things off with him permanently after what had occurred in her own garden?—had turned out to be no problem at all. She'd heard through Albert that Georges had left on a sudden, long holiday to visit relatives in Italy.

She hadn't known he *had* relatives in Italy, which suggested that perhaps he'd left for some other reason—and she thought perhaps she might know what it was.

Regardless, his absence solved her problem, and allowed her to focus on the one at hand. She glanced across the stage toward Monte Cristo's box and found that he was looking at her. A thrill ran through her body, warming her face and spiraling in her stomach. Their eyes met and clashed for a long moment as Mercédès refused to look away . . . and at the same time, thought to herself: *What next?*

What was his plan?

From across the way, he gave her a bare nod, with no emotion attached to it—neither insolence, nor respect, nor cordiality; just a bare movement of the chin—and then turned his attention back to the play.

Had he simply planned to seduce her into a quivering puddle of arousal and then leave her unclothed and stranded during the dinner party? Why? To assert his control over her? To attempt to humiliate her? In either case, he hadn't completely succeeded.

Was that the extent of his plans for revenge? Were his goals now met?

Mercédès wanted to confront him, she wanted to grab his solid shoulders and shake the man to find out why . . . how . . . where he'd been all these years. Why he hadn't come back to her . . . and when he had, why he did so now, in this way.

This cold, unfeeling way.

A little shiver caught her by surprise, and Monsieur Hardegree, a Londoner visiting Paris, must have felt her shudder. He was immediately solicitous, and reached to drape her cashmere shawl more closely around her. His gloved hands brushed her bare shoulders, and she smiled her thanks at him, taking care to keep any hint of seduction from her eyes.

She settled back in her seat and felt someone's attention on her, but when she looked over, Monte Cristo wasn't even facing her. His back was to the theater, and he seemed to be speaking to someone behind him. But at that angle, his profile . . . it made her heart squeeze with pain. Edmond . . . it was so clearly Edmond, she wanted to cry.

But then he turned back, and it was Monte Cristo again, his demeanor harsh, rigid, elegant.

Mercédès thought for a moment. What did *she* want?

She wanted Edmond Dantès back. She always had.

She'd leave Fernand and his fine house and pots of money and salacious ways in an instant if she could have Edmond again. She'd live in a hovel, or on his ship, or wherever he wanted to live.

But Edmond, whatever had happened to him, was gone . . . and the man called the Count of Monte Cristo no longer resembled—except in a most superficial manner, in the barest of hints and the faintest of impressions—the man she loved.

And thus, as she thought about it, Mercédès felt less and less kindly toward him. Less and less regretful for the love they might have shared, for the years lost, the plans destroyed, the empty life she'd lived.

For if this was how he came back into her life—in mystery and coldness, and with vengeance—she wasn't certain she could love the man he'd become.

Her thoughts were interrupted by the play's intermission, and Mercédès accepted Monsieur Hardegree as her escort to the ladies' retiring room. Perhaps she thought she might have the occasion to see Monte Cristo as they walked along the promenade crowded with other members of society, all of them equally hoping to see and be seen. But, alas, she had not caught even a glimpse of the elegant figure of Monte Cristo, in his crisp white shirt, black frog coat, and gold-patterned cravat and shirtwaist, by the time she and Monsieur Hardegree reached their destination.

"I shall await your pleasure, my lady," he said in his delightfully British French, giving her an exact little bow.

Mercédès walked toward the room reserved for the ladies, and passed the largest, darkest man she'd ever seen, standing by the door. His bald head gleamed in the lamplight, and he wore a gold hoop in one ear, reminding her suddenly of Sinbad.

Inside the little room, women sat about and chattered, adjusted their gowns, and fussed with hair, and a few even dabbed rouge on their cheeks and lips. The antechamber was long and narrow, with gold-and-green brocade curtains pulled back to reveal a long mirror above an equally long and narrow table. Six plump chairs were arranged around two low square tables, and every surface was covered with vases of peonies and roses, filling the air with their sweet perfume as if to battle with those other smells of dusting powder, eau de toilette, feminine perspiration, and the results of the small, enclosed stalls beyond this gathering room. There was barely room for more than one woman, with her wide skirts, to walk along the gallery-like chamber

There was Mademoiselle Goutage, applying white powder to cover the spots on her bosom, and Mademoiselle LeFritier using kohl to line her eyes and color her lashes. Since her skin was pale and her lashes blond, it made quite a difference in her appearance—especially when it rubbed off under her eyes, giving her an exhausted look. Madam Foufant greeted Mercédès warmly, and they chatted for a moment before the other woman patted one last curl into its spot and replaced her gloves. As madam took her leave, Mercédès turned and noticed one of the doors of the private stalls in the next room opening.

A young woman came out, and Mercédès recognized her instantly as Monte Cristo's companion. Up close, the woman was even more breathtaking, and for a moment, Mercédès felt herself flush with despair and jealousy. She turned away from the woman—who was really no more than a girl—and turned her attention to her own reflection in the long, gilt-edged mirror. With trembling hands, Mercédès poked at her thick, dark hair and tried not to look at the other woman, who had come forward to also stand before the looking glass.

But then their eyes met in the reflection, and the young woman paused, holding Mercédès' gaze, and said, "Good evening." Her voice was husky and pleasantly accented. She gave a little nod, and Mercédès was struck again, horribly, with how exquisite she was: olive skin, tip-tilted eyes, thick, dark lashes that would never need kohl, blue-black hair just as heavy and shiny as her own locks, smooth skin and a long neck.

Mercédès was not one for rudeness, regardless of what position the young woman might have in her former lover's life or bed, however gorgeous she might be. Whoever she was, she was likely innocent of anything Monte Cristo had planned or had done. And besides . . . Mercédès thought she recognized a bit of nervousness in the young woman's eyes. "Good evening, mademoiselle," she replied with a regal nod, but returned to her own ministrations.

The young woman continued to glance at her under the guise of fixing her own hair. Mercédès noticed that the chatter had quieted in the room, and a few of the other women were staring at the girl—she looked as if she might be Greek—while whispering behind cupped hands. Ignoring them, and the girl, Mercédès adjusted her bodice to make sure it cut just across the tops of her areolas and no lower, and that the bows on her short sleeves were still lined up straight.

Meanwhile, the ebb of conversation seemed to be over, and whispers and low comments began to filter through the room more loudly. And then one comment rose above the others, settling over the room like a crack of sudden summer thunder.

"The retiring room for servants *and slaves* is down below. In the cellar."

Mercédès happened to catch the expression on the girl's face as she blanched. Confusion and hurt splashed across it, but she pretended to continue her primping as if she hadn't heard.

"If I had a slave, I would have her press my gown. Perhaps there is one nearby who might be able to assist," came another catty voice.

The young girl's hand trembled slightly as she reached to adjust the long strand of sapphires that hung from her ear, and her mouth twitched with quickly subdued misery.

Mercédès turned from her stance at the mirror. "I hardly think," she said, her flinty gaze skipping over the young mademoiselles who'd been gossiping, "that the Count of Monte Cristo would squire a slave to the theater. And if he did," she added when one of the little snips dared to open her mouth, "I do not expect that he would dress and bejewel her in a manner more elegantly than any other young woman here."

The other girls—for they were young, just as young as this Greek one—all closed their mouths. Red spots appeared on some of their cheeks, and Mademoiselle LeFritier had the grace to look away and flee from the room without any further comments. It was just as well, for Mercédès was well-acquainted with her mother, and Madam LeFritier was a lovely, polite woman who would be horrified at her daughter's behavior.

In front of the other girls, Mercédès turned to the Greek girl and said, "I am Comtesse de Morcerf, and I have had the pleasure of hosting the Count of Monte Cristo at my home."

The girl gave her a fleeting smile of gratitude, but kept her own regal poise as she gave a little bow in return. "I am fully aware of who you are, madam la comtesse," she said with a meaningful look. "And I am delighted—no, *privileged*—to make your acquaintance. My name is Haydée, and I am the ward of the Count of Monte Cristo." Her voice was dulcet and lightly accented.

Ward, indeed, Mercédès thought; but she held her emotions at bay. She had no right to judge or to make assumptions, despite the fact that Monte Cristo had treated the girl like anything but a ward. Nevertheless, her fingers curled into her gloved palms as she recalled how *he* had reacted when faced with *her* lover.

By now the other mademoiselles had fled the room, and the two women were left alone.

"You are very kind," said Haydée, glancing at the door as it closed behind the last billowing skirt.

"It was nothing," Mercédès told her, keeping her voice cool and steady. How she wanted to ask Haydée . . . so many things!

How she wanted to scratch at her almond-shaped eyes and tell her to stay away from Monte Cristo.

"They are young and cruel, as girls often are, and I do not believe that such incidents should go unnoticed," Mercédès said instead.

Haydée was still looking at her. "So you are the one," she murmured, her attention sharp and interested as it swept over her.

Mercédès raised her brows in surprise. "I am?"

The girl's look was calculating—but not in a cattish way. More of a contemplative one, as if some light were dawning over her. She gave a little nod and then a small smile, as if making a pleasurable decision. "His Excellency and I are not lovers, madam la comtesse."

If she would have claimed her nose were blue, Mercédès couldn't have been more surprised. But she retained her composure and allowed a little tilt to her own lips. "Is that so? He takes great pains to promote that misconception."

"That is true, but in private he calls me his daughter and treats me thus."

Suddenly realizing she'd found an ally in whatever competition there was between herself and Monte Cristo, Mercédès grasped the young girl's arm and gave it a little squeeze. "Thank you for telling me that, for whatever reason you chose to do so."

"My reason is pure selfishness, madam, if I may be so bold." Her smile was charming and Mercédès marveled that Monte Cristo had not fallen under its spell. But she had no reason to disbelieve Haydée, and so she smiled back.

"Whatever the reason, you have provided me with information that I may find very useful."

"I've no doubt you will, madam. And the sooner you do, the more appreciative I will be. Now perhaps it is best if I go, for Ali will be pulling his hair out. Or," she said with a dimple, looking more like a child than ever, "he would be if he had any hair to pull."

With a curtsy, Haydée swept out of the room with the air of a princess, leaving Mercédès to her thoughts.

They weren't lovers.

She smiled at herself in the mirror, noticing as she always did that little crooked tooth on top that marred an otherwise perfect spread of teeth and full red lips. She hated the way it dipped into her lower lip, almost like a little fang, when she grinned. But Edmond had thought it charming; he said it made her beauty real and accessible. Perfection, he claimed, would have been much too daunting.

Was that why he hadn't bedded Haydée? Or was she lying?

But there was no reason for her to lie. Mercédès quickly dismissed that thought.

She mused over their conversation for a few moments longer, then, with a start, realized she'd left Monsieur Hardegree waiting for her.

However, when she came out of the retiring room, it wasn't Hardegree who waited. It was Monte Cristo himself, leaning indolently against one of the gallery's half pillars, all of which lined the long room and were painted to depict the Greek gods and goddesses.

She lifted her chin when their eyes met, even as her heart gave a little leap and her palms dampened beneath her gloves. Had he been there long enough to suspect that she and Haydée had met? Even if he had . . . he wouldn't expect them to have the conversation they did.

Wondering why it mattered, why she shouldn't confront him right now, Mercédès nevertheless kept her gaze steady as he stepped toward her.

"Your husband asked me to escort you," Monte Cristo said, offering her his arm.

She briefly considered not accepting it, but realized there would be no purpose in doing so, and besides . . . she wanted to touch him. And for him to touch her. Because she knew that, whatever he'd done in the gazebo, however he'd left her, he still wanted her.

God knew, she still wanted him—though she would die before admitting it.

"Did he?" she asked, sliding her fingers around the solid warmth of his arm. He immediately shifted, pulling his elbow tight to his body so that her gown was crushed against his side and his trouser leg brushed her skirts. His close presence was overpowering: dark and strong, nearly vibrating with command. "How amusing, for it was Monsieur Hardegree who was my escort."

"Perhaps your toilette took too long, madam," replied Monte Cristo, "and he became weary of waiting for you."

"Ah, yes," she mused, stealing a glance at him, now quite certain that it was Monte Cristo who had suggested Hardegree's defection. "After waiting for a very long time, and without any word, one might begin to suspect that the one for whom one waits has found more exciting delights, and is never to return. And then whatever should one do? Spend the entire . . . evening . . . waiting in the gallery, only to find that the other wasn't about to return after all—and learn that one has missed the production?"

His beautiful lips tightened but he kept his gaze cool when he flicked it sharply at her, then away. "If one vows to wait, one should stay true to his—or her—word . . . and trust that the other will return as promised. After all, what is mere *entertainment* in contrast to one's *oath*?"

Mercédès felt a sudden wave of sadness and grief, but she didn't show it. Until she learned what he was after, why he was really here—and what had kept him from her for years—she would give no explanation for her choices—choices for which he obviously blamed and despised her.

But he clearly had known who she was when he approached her a decade ago as Sinbad. That, she could not excuse.

"And so you believe, monsieur le comte, that one should never give up hope that the other might reappear? Regardless of all evidence to the contrary, and any other occurrences that might arise to upset the situation?" She bumped against his side purposely as she looked up at him, making her eyes wide and guileless, and her lips part slightly.

"Above all, fidelity to one's word," Monte Cristo replied.

Mercédès was silent for a moment, contemplating her next response. The play had started again and the fashion watchers and gossipmongers had returned to their seats. Only an occasional couple or gentleman passed the two of them as they strolled along . . . and she realized, after looking around, that Monte Cristo had guided them beyond the gallery and the theater entrance to the side of the building.

"Fidelity to one's word," she replied thoughtfully. "Thus, above all, honesty and honor. I must concur with you in that. *Honesty* and *honor*, monsieur le comte."

He looked at her, his dark eyes delving into hers as if to read a deeper meaning. She saw that they had reached the dark alcove where the side staircase, used by ladies' maids and footmen, made a landing between the second and third floors.

They paused, and he swept her into his arms—just as she'd suspected he would, for there was little pretense in regard to their passion for each other.

Monte Cristo's embrace was strong and bold, and he crushed her between his body and the plastered wall. She slid her arms eagerly around his neck, feeling the warmth of his skin beneath the thick locks brushing his collar. His mouth swooped down on hers, no longer drawn hard and firm, but supple and demanding, pulling an immediate response from her even as it snuffed out her breath. She pressed up against him, her gown crushed and wrinkled between their hips as he drove his tongue into her mouth, his fingers curling into the jut of her shoulder blades.

Her eyes closed as she gave herself up to the familiar sensations shooting through her, curling in her middle, and twinging between her legs. The warm, slick stroke of his tongue and the urgent scrape of his teeth; soft, molding lips by turns sensual and coaxing to tight and harsh. The heat from his body and the scrape of wool sleeve over her delicate skin, the smell of Edmond mixed with that of Monte Cristo: slightly smoky and musky and citrusy, tinged with the aroma of wool and starch.

His leg pressed between hers, parting her thighs beneath the scads of fabric from her gown and crinolines, pushing boldly into the softness of her quim. Mercédès moaned softly against his mouth as she increased the pressure against his thigh, shifting her hips slightly in a little rhythm. Her head tipped back, the top of her coiffure catching in the rough plaster of the wall as he moved to kiss the generous expanse of skin exposed by her low bodice.

Warm, soft lips nuzzled into the hollows of her throat as he gathered her up closer, his knee sliding deeper between her legs, burrowing into the froth of skirts, her feet now on tiptoes as she kept her balance.

Edmond.

This was Edmond; this was how he had made her feel, how he had made her body hot and tight and needy.

When he tugged at the line of her bodice with impatient fingers, Mercédès battled herself back to reality, pulling from the deep place filled with strokes and licks and nibbles, and forced her eyes open. There was no one about. The area was dimly lit and quiet but for the gentle rasp of their breathing and the rustle of clothing.

Though her brain was fuzzy, and her body cried to be released—undressed, skin to skin with the man before her, filled and stroked and wooed until it peaked—she remembered what had happened last time. And the thought of being left half clothed in a theater was a chilling effect that helped to clear her mind.

Opening her eyes, she saw the top of his dark head as his

tongue slipped down into the warm cleft between her breasts, followed by the gentle bite of his lips on the inside of her cleavage. Her nipples were hard, surging under the confines of her corset, and Mercédès gave a little shrug so that they would brush up, over it.

Then she reached boldly for the placket on his trousers, smoothing her hands under his coat and over the stiff brocade waistcoat beneath. Monte Cristo startled at her movement, but when she found her way beneath the long tails of his shirt to the hot skin and rough hair, he pulled back, straightening in front of her. His knee edged out from under her throbbing sex, relieving some of the pressure there and sending a little chill over her body from the loss of his warmth.

But Mercédès' hands were busy down in the heat inside his trousers, and as her fingers came together over his flat belly and the indent of his navel, she reached up to kiss the side of his neck. Musky warm and salty, rough from the beginnings of stubble, and starchy-smelling from the crisp folds of his neckcloth, it was that frightening combination of Edmond Dantès, Sinbad, and Monte Cristo. She shoved her hands farther in, bringing him closer to her so that their bodies were nearly flush again. Combing her nails through the wiry hair that grew thick, and then down and around to cup the heavy, burning cock straining there.

He gave a quiet sigh, nearly a moan, and she swore she felt him surge in her hands. Blindly, she pulled apart his trousers so that her movements weren't restricted, and as her fingers slid along that glorious length of cock, over the bold veins and velvet skin, she found the softness of its head. With a little squeeze there in the warmth of his trousers, she pulled back the skin and traced the edge of that head, over the most delicate veins there beneath, and felt him gathering up beneath her touch . . . felt the little sticky drip from his cock's tip, and the tensing of muscles in his powerful thighs as she pressed against them, and the little sizzle as his seed moved up along the pounding erection.

If she had doubted his response to her before, she no longer did. Mercédès wanted nothing more than to drop to her knees in front of him, and take that long red-and-purple cock into her mouth and suck until he begged for mercy . . . shouted her name and admitted who he was . . . .

Her own sex was wet and ready, and her breasts tight beneath his hands, which had at some point begun to crush them behind her corset and gown. Their mouths met and she kept her fingers close around him, stroking arhythmically, unwilling to let him go, to release him, loving the feel of that solid cock in her hands . . . and knowing she held it, and him, in her control.

She cleared her mind again, remembered who she was, where she was . . . who she was with. She tightened her fingers around him and paused. Pulled away from his mouth enough to whisper, "By all that is right and fair, I should end this now."

He stilled beneath her, then captured her mouth again, holding her head with both hands. Grinding his lips against hers, he forced hers open in a rough, angry kiss—at once acknowledging her statement, and forcing her to respond with her own passion.

Mercédès kissed him back—she could never refuse it—and kept her hands tightly over his cock as it swelled and throbbed in the heat. She pulled her face away, looking up into his countenance, dark with shadows and fury, and said, "But I won't."

And she gave two sharp tugs on his ripe cock, felt him gasp and then shudder in an unexpected release. He surged in her grip and the hot, sticky seed splurged over her hands and into his drawers. She swiped her fingers over his shirttails and stepped away, breathing heavy, her body still humming, but satisfied, knowing she'd one-upped him here.

"Good evening, Your Excellency," she said in a cool voice. "I do hope you got what you came for."

And she turned, sedately and regally, and walked away . . . every hair in place, every inch the lady.

NINE

In the Bedchamber

Later that evening
Paris

After her little tête-à-tête with Monte Cristo, Mercédès returned to her theater box without an escort. Ignoring Fernand's annoyed glare when she entered the box, she sat through the rest of the play. Though her eyes were fixed on the stage before her, what was going on inside her mind had little to do with the lines delivered below.

The smell of him—it was still on her: on her hands, when she brought them up to her mouth . . . on her neck, when she turned her head a certain way . . . . Her lips were still full and plump, still throbbing from that last, rough kiss.

She considered leaving early, but decided it might give Monte Cristo the wrong impression, so she stayed until the very end. Mercédès declined an offer to walk through the gallery again during the second intermission, remaining in the box alone with the very attentive Monsieur Hardegree, who appeared to bear no hard feelings toward her for taking so long in the ladies' retiring room. She suspected yet again that Monte Cristo had engineered his replacement as her escort, likely with Fernand's approval.

Although she was well aware when Monte Cristo left his own box and when he returned, Mercédès barely glanced in that direction. She got the impression of annoyance wafting across the space between their respective seats, and smiled secretly to herself, wondering whether he was castigated or merely chagrined that she'd walked away from him, clearly the victor in that battle.

Either way, she was content.

Now, much later that night, she was back in her bedchamber, dressed for bed. Charlotte had removed all of the painful pins from her hair, and long, wavy locks fell past the seat on which she sat. The maid was just about to plait it in one arm-thick braid when there was a peremptory knock at the door.

When Charlotte opened the door, Fernand strode in. He was still fully clothed, and there was that unholy gleam in his eyes that Mercédès had come to recognize as one she preferred to avoid.

"You are dismissed for the evening," he told Charlotte.

Charlotte fairly streaked from the room, leaving her mistress with her hair loose and her evening's gown still hanging over a dressing screen.

"What do you want, Fernand?" Mercédès asked wearily, turning on her stool.

"You were with Monte Cristo tonight," her husband replied.

She inclined her head. "Was that not your doing, dear husband?"

"Of course it was." He eyed her narrowly. "What is your intention with regard to Hardegree? If you plan to entertain him tonight, I forbid it."

Mercédès stood angrily. "I am going to bed. Alone. Even if I chose to—entertain—Hardegree, it definitely wouldn't be here."

"You certainly appear as if you expect visitors." He gestured to her gown, which was little more than white lace from shoulder to hips, falling into a full silk skirt from there to the floor. "Quite a slut you've become," he added.

"Get out," she said.

Fernand grabbed at her arm and yanked her off the stool, sending it toppling to the floor. "You cannot order me from your chamber, Comtesse de Morcerf," he said, his face very close to hers. "I'm your husband, and you belong to me. I can do with you what I will, when I choose."

His mustache scraped her face when he mauled her lips with his, his fingers biting deeply into her bare arms. The kiss, if one could call it that, was brief, and when he pulled back, his eyes were bright and his breathing heavy. "You would take care to remember that."

He shoved her away, and she caught herself before she lost her balance, though she knocked her ankle painfully against the heavy post of her bed. By the time she looked up, Fernand had left the room, the door closing sharply after him.

Mercédès stared after, rubbing her throbbing ankle, wondering what that had been about. He came so rarely to her chamber anyway, and although it had appeared tonight he'd come to exercise his husbandly rights, his sudden departure was welcome yet confusing.

But a moment later, when there was another knock at her door, she felt a strange prickle over her back. Had he gone to get the whip? Her mouth dried, and she licked her lips, remembering the one time before he'd used the slender leather whip to increase his reluctant arousal at the expense of her buttocks and back. Because Albert had seen one of the marks on Mercédès' arm and asked about it, his father had not dared to use it again.

The sound of the knock had barely faded when the knob turned and the door opened and Fernand came back in. He carried only a long, dark bottle and two small glasses. But behind him . . .

Mercédès felt her face go white. Her knees gave out and she sagged against the massive wooden bedpost for a moment before pulling herself upright. Her fingers gripped the thick mahogany.

"We meet again, madam la comtesse," said the Count of Monte Cristo. He gave an insolent bow as he strode in. As if he owned the room.

Despite the fact that the chamber had shrunk and darkened alarmingly, Mercédès did not miss the glint in his eyes. Cold. Furious. It made her heart ram in her chest, and her mouth feel as though she'd stuffed huge wads of cotton into it.

Fernand, who still stood at the door, closed it behind him. Mercédès heard the ominous sound of the key grating in its lock. Then he turned, still carrying the bottle and glasses. "Please," he said to Monte Cristo with a gesture that encompassed the two chairs angled next to a small table.

Mercédès forced herself to gather her wits and her composure as Monte Cristo selected a chair while her husband removed his coat. The air thickened with tension, the mood starkly silent, waiting, as if for an execution.

Her uninvited guest stripped off his neckcloth with deliberate motions, his dark eyes flat and focused on her. The expression on his face remained unreadable as he shrugged out of his own coat and folded it over the arm of his chair. Then he sat down, stretching his legs indolently into the center of the room.

Standing straight and proud, her torso outlined by the fitted ivory lace of her night rail and its plunging neckline, Mercédès noticed the count's eyes watching her. Her hair, thick and full and dark, fell down over one shoulder, and when she took its weight in hand to push it back, her breast lifting, he watched. His jaw shifted ever so slightly.

Her heart pounded as she stood there, the silk skirt hot and cloying against her legs and over her hips, a trickle of dampness suddenly rolling down her spine. A soft clink of glass broke the charged silence, followed by the quiet shush of pouring liquid.

She felt as if she'd been thrust into a contest of nerves, and Mercédès realized with a rush that that was indeed what had happened. They were both waiting, measuring the other, as if Fernand wasn't even there. An intimacy stretched between them, sizzling in the space from chair to bed, man to woman, desire to pride.

But Fernand was there, and that was what made her palms damp and her stomach spin unpleasantly.

"Take off your gown," said her husband suddenly, standing next to his chair.

She saw the subtle movement of shadow over the count's

face, and it told her what she needed to know. If this were to be a battle of wills, she knew Monte Cristo's weakness . . . and she also knew Fernand's.

As for her own . . . she firmed her lips. She would not beg or plead. Never again.

Tipping her head to the side, she fastened her gaze on Fernand and allowed a seductive look to creep into her eyes—something she'd never done to him before. Ever. "Perhaps you should assist me, husband," she said.

The shock and delight that came into Fernand's face surprised her, almost distracting her. He slammed back his drink, emptying the small glass, and leaving it on the table, stepped toward her.

Mercédès lifted her hair, pulling it over one of her shoulders as she turned away from Monte Cristo . . . presenting her back to the count, and to her husband, so that he could unbutton her nightgown. Her heart still pounded; she could barely stomach Fernand's touch—sweaty, heavy, hot. Whatever his plan, surely Monte Cristo would not be able to watch them together for very long. She hoped.

The night rail began to loosen, its lace bodice shifting slightly.

"Stop" came Monte Cristo's smooth voice. "Let her do the rest."

The weight of Fernand's hands moved away, and Mercédès drew in a long, slow breath. Rough lace scratched the sensitive tips of her taut nipples. She felt two pairs of eyes boring into her spine, bared by the split halves of her gown.

She turned around slowly, feeling the sensual swish of silk against her legs and brushing over the tops of her feet.

"Drop it, madam," said Monte Cristo sharply. "I wish to see what I've purchased."

As an offensive strike, his comment was effective enough to freeze Mercédès for a moment. *Purchased?* She felt ill, but kept her face impassive. True or not, he'd said it to startle and wound her in this battle of wills—it was his parry to her thrust.

"I fear," she said smoothly, "that whatever the cost, you have grossly underpaid, my dear count." She let her nightgown fall in a sudden swish of lace and silk, pooling over her feet.

The quick intake of breath came from Fernand, but Monte Cristo wasn't immune—she could see that tiny shift in his jaw, and the subtle movement in his throat. After all, even Sinbad hadn't seen her fully nude, in full light.

And though her forty-year-old body was no match for that of Haydée and her taut, firm flesh, if Mercédès knew one thing, it was that a woman who was comfortable in her own skin, who knew its perfections and imperfections, its pleasures and capabilities, and who knew how to use it . . . who knew passion . . . could make a man cry with desire. Especially one who already desired her.

She put trembling hands behind her, artfully lifting her hair away, aware that the movement raised her breasts with their tight, chill-taut nipples. Keeping her attention from Monte Cristo, she focused on Fernand as she bent slowly, her breasts swaying, and picked up the pile of silk and lace.

She flung it casually toward Monte Cristo without even the flicker of a glance, and walked toward Fernand. Though every muscle, every sense in her body rebelled, she knew it was the only way. She had to make Monte Cristo angry—angry enough to intervene.

From the corner of her eye, she saw that he'd caught the gown, and held it in his lap. A brief, full glance told her that he watched her, even as his strong, dark fingers filtered the silk through them in a thoughtful rubbing motion.

Mercédès looked back at Fernand, and saw desire in his face. That was fortunate, and probably had something to do with the fact that she was more accommodating than she would normally be. Flashes of memories—of her arguing, fighting, crying, struggling—sideswiped her for a moment, threatening to paralyze her, but she pushed it away.

Not tonight.

Not tonight, for she was counting on the fact that Monte Cristo—who'd been so determined to rid her of Salieux, so openly annoyed when she was with Hardegree, so unwilling to share her with Neru when he was Sinbad—would never watch her copulate with Edmond Dantès' rival.

Never.

It was just a matter of who would break first.

The silk in his hands was still warm from her body, and when it had wafted toward him, he sensed her spicy, floral scent. Nothing as sweet and feminine as the jasmine Haydée favored, but muskier, spicier, mixed with what had to be lily-of-the-valley overtones.

Monte Cristo sipped his brandy and watched her smooth golden body, curvier than he remembered, in the hips and slightly rounded belly, and the full sway of her breasts. Despite the heat of the liquor, his mouth was dry and his throat tight. He relaxed his fingers, loosening the silk and forcing them to open slightly in his lap.

Beneath which raged his hungry cock.

He glanced over at Morcerf, and his skin prickled with abhorrence, but he kept his face blank. He would watch, perhaps even participate, in tonight's events from an impassive perspective. It was a means to an end, and he could stay removed enough as he watched—and enjoyed—her humiliation.

She surprised him for a moment, when she paused in stalking the prey of her husband, and suddenly turned to him. One moment, she was watching Morcerf, pinning him with those deep, dark eyes, and the next, she was there, in front of him.

Slender arms angled on either side of him as she closed her fingers over the arms of his chair and leaned forward, over him. Her long hair fell in a dark pile onto the white silk and lace in his lap, brushing over his hand. She surged forward, catching him by surprise when she covered his mouth with those sensuous red lips, slipping her warm, slick tongue over the front of his teeth until he opened and let her in.

The kiss was hot and brief, and she pulled away, her eyes half lidded so he couldn't read what was there—but he saw her pulse pounding in her throat.

"Enjoy the show," she murmured near his ear, her voice low and warm, filtering over his skin as she retreated.

Quick as a whip, he lashed out and grabbed her arm, yanking her back. He kept a cool lift to the side of his mouth, an unconcerned one, as he placed her hand over the bulge in his trousers. "I paid enough. . . . I expect a more satisfying performance than the one you gave earlier this evening." Then he shoved her away before his hands touched her anywhere else.

She barely stumbled, but her breasts jounced pleasantly, and there was a flash of something—annoyance, surprise . . .

something—there in her eyes. But then Mercédès was standing with a knowing, coy smile back on those lips, and she turned her attention to her husband.

Monte Cristo watched as she sashayed toward Morcerf . . . toward her husband . . . the man who looked as if he were half in shock and half drowning in lust. The man's throat moved as he swallowed, his Adam's apple convulsing as Mercédès lowered her fine, round ass onto his lap, her own legs turned primly to the side as if she were sitting sidesaddle on her mare, her knees facing Monte Cristo.

She bent forward to kiss her husband in the same deep, sensual way she'd kissed him only moments before. He saw the dark red slide of tongue, the quirk at the corner of her lips, the little laugh she gave into her husband's mouth, as though sharing a private joke.

She wouldn't be laughing if she were kissing him.

Monte Cristo reached easily, deliberately, for his glass and realized it was empty. He closed his fingers over the diamond-cut crystal and continued to watch. The only thing he hadn't investigated during the last decade was the state of Mercédès and Fernand's intimate relationship. Those details were something he didn't want—need—to know.

Now, it appeared, he would see them firsthand.

He lifted the bottle to pour a few fingers into his glass, as well as into Morcerf's, as he watched the other man's hands move up the smooth golden skin of her back, under that heavy, dark hair that smelled like lily of the valley. Mercédès had untied her husband's neckcloth and pulled it away, and was now unfastening his shirtwaist as he played with her breasts.

Monte Cristo watched placidly, sipping his brandy, as she

tipped her head back so that her hair spilled straight down behind her, over Morcerf's legs as he bent to suck on one of those dusky rose nipples. More lips and tongue, more sucking sounds, and a soft, little pleasure sigh from Mercédès.

He shifted slightly in his chair, and she looked at him, boldly catching his gaze for a moment before her lids sank closed and she arched her breasts closer to her husband. Her hands were on his bare chest now, his shirt open to show pale skin and a heavy dark patch of hair striping the top of his torso.

"Perhaps you could . . . hurry it along," Monte Cristo said, finishing his drink and setting the glass on the table with a dull little clunk. He looked at Mercédès, whose eyes had opened again. "It *is* getting late. And I had expected something a bit more . . . interesting."

She arched one eyebrow at him, then turned back to her husband. "Perhaps we should invite the count to join us," she said in a throaty voice. "Or do you think he wants merely to watch?"

Morcerf, whose mouth had been full of nipple and areola, pulled back with one long draw, elongating her breast, and then released it with a small pop. Monte Cristo looked at the swollen, red, glistening flesh and tightened his fingers over the silk in his lap, damp and hot in his grip.

"If there was something worth seeing, I would prefer to watch," he replied, reaching for the bottle again.

At that, Mercédès gestured toward the bed. "Come now, my dear count . . . surely you didn't pay merely to watch. Then you could do this. . . ." She took Morcerf's hands and closed them over her breasts, giving a faint little moan, a little arch, as his thumbs twitched over her nipples. "Or this . . ." Looking again at Monte Cristo, she removed one of her husband's hands from her breast and directed it down between her legs. He saw the shift of movement of the other man's arm as she slipped his fingers back and forth in that dark shadow between their bodies, then pulled them back up and brought them, glistening, back to her breast.

"We could all be moving together, dearest count . . . your skin to mine, your hands meshing with Fernand's, our legs tangled . . . two hard cocks . . . hair and muscle and heat and wet." Her low, mesmerizing voice curled in the air like smoke.

Morcerf's eyes were fastened on Mercédès as though he'd never seen her before. His breath was rasping loudly in the room, and Monte Cristo thought it likely that the man was going to blow his seed any moment.

"I prefer to watch," he said again, "if there is something worthwhile to see." He made certain that his voice sounded dubious and that his fingers did not shake when he reached for his glass. This sip of brandy he held in his mouth, feeling it burn and settle, before he swallowed it, reveling in the warmth that followed. His head was feeling lighter, and he watched as Mercédès slid her lush body off her husband's lap.

And come toward him.

As before, she bent down in a fluid motion, catching him a bit by surprise as her hands closed over the arms of his chair, covering one of his wrists with her small fingers. If he'd expected a coaxing, seductive kiss, he was disappointed, for it was just as savage and deep and bold as the first one. Her lips were soft and puffy and slick, and she used them to tease his, drawing them into her mouth, her tongue to slide over and around his, her teeth to nibble at his lower one as she pulled away. What was she trying to do?

"Feel free to join us if you begin to feel left out," she murmured near his ear. Then, giving him a burning cat smile, she moved away, removing her small hand from his wrist. "Fernand would be quite delighted."

Monte Cristo's chest tightened, and blood rushed through his veins. He wasn't wholly certain if it was from fury or that bloody kiss, and her taunting words and lithe, lush body. His fingers closed into the chair arm and he managed a cool smile. "I'll take it under advisement . . . but for now, I see nothing worth . . . joining."

Mercédès' smile did not slip. She turned away from him, giving him a proper view of her long, straight spine and the thick hair that brushed over skin that looked like a dusty peach, just above the sweet dimples of her ass and the flare of her hips.

Things happened quickly after that, it seemed. One moment, she was standing there, teasing and flaunting herself at him, and the next, she and Morcerf had made their way to the bed. His clothing lay in a heap on the floor, and Monte Cristo noticed the man's soft body, paler than Mercédès' more golden skin yet not so pasty as the English. Dark hair grew in that patch on his chest, and in two smaller patches on the backs of his shoulders and over his legs. His cock was full and hard, though it didn't look as if it were ready to burst at any moment.

Monte Cristo couldn't see well enough from where he sat; when the other two were on the bed, he saw only obliquely what was occurring. But, more important, he couldn't *be* seen.

He rose from his chair and ambled toward the bed in trousers tight in the crotch. As he approached, Mercédès slid next to her husband, sitting near his torso, planting her quim's dark thatch on the pale blue coverlet as she rested against his bent, hairy leg. Her eyes were closed, and she had her hands braced on the blanket as Morcerf shifted to suck again on one of her breasts, moving a curtain of hair back over her shoulder.

The other breast swayed beautifully, near Monte Cristo, near enough for him to touch. He gripped his glass and brought it to his lips for a sip, swallowed . . . and before he realized it, he was moving closer to the bed. Closing his free hand around the back of her head, shocking her into opening her eyes, he turned her toward him. Holding the back of her scalp, he ground a kiss against her lips, standing there with his legs pressed up against the bed and the brandy in his hand. As he kissed her, Monte Cristo felt the rhythm of Morcerf's lips as he suckled on Mercédès like a newborn.

"It's getting more interesting," he said, releasing her mouth suddenly enough that she jerked a little. "Good."

And he stepped back, holding her gaze, wanting her to remember that he was there. Watching.

Watching.

Then, suddenly, her hand snaked out and grabbed his shirt. She pulled, and Monte Cristo let her tug him forward so that his legs were against the bed again. "Leaving so soon?" she murmured, edging toward him on her knees, her fingers still curled in his shirt, hair tangling around her breasts.

This time when she kissed him, she pressed her whole naked torso against his and covered his shoulders with her hands. Her breasts pressed through the fine lawn of his shirt, and Monte Cristo felt the sudden sharp rise of lust as he slipped his arms around her warm body and crushed her against him, closing his eyes and breathing her in.

Mercédès.

He pulled away, dragging her with him to the bed, collapsing next to Morcerf, his arms still locked around her waist. Her breasts shifted between them as they fell, and her long legs slipped between his thighs, brushing against the swollen head of his cock beneath the tent of his trousers. He rolled her beneath him, trapping her head with his mouth on hers, smoothing over the silk of her cheek to the thrust of her chin, using teeth and tongue to taste and taunt, feeling the shift and slide of her curves, the warmth of her skin through his clothing.

He touched the smooth swell of her hip, the tender part of her shoulders. He tasted the hot, musky salt in the folds of her neck, the brandy on her tongue, and smelled the spice and flowery scent near the curl of her ear.

Her hair tangled around his fingers, under her body, between them, and he lifted himself away, off her and onto the bed again. No sooner had he moved to the side, slipping his hand down between her legs to feel the slick, full lips of her quim when the mattress dipped and another hand appeared, closing over one of her breasts.

Monte Cristo felt a cold wave over him as he looked up and found Morcerf's face close to his. The man's eyes were glazed with lust, and his lips were full and wet.

It reminded him why he was here.

Monte Cristo pulled away, distaste spinning through him as he read the interest in the other man's eyes, and saw that it wasn't just for the woman between them, below them. "Perhaps you would like to watch," he said.

Morcerf looked as though he might argue, and Mercédès shifted beneath them, but Monte Cristo's fingers were still at the heat of her sex. He smoothed them over the front of her, slipping in the wet there as he looked at her husband and said, "My turn. Watch."

The other man must have read his expression properly, for he shifted back on the bed, sitting up on his haunches, his cock straining straight between his thighs, his ballocks lifted tight and close in the shadow beneath it.

Monte Cristo gave him a cool look and settled back away from Mercédès. "Now, my dear comtesse," he said, looking down at her as he kept one hand on her chest, planted between her breasts. "We shall see how interesting things can get."

He couldn't help but notice that one nipple was redder and longer than the other, and gleaming wet. It took all of his control to keep from bending forward and sucking the other one to match. Later.

He scooted toward the edge of the bed, digging into his pockets to pull out the thin strips of silk he'd brought . . . for just such a purpose. He captured her wrists and stretched them above her head as she sprawled diagonally across the bed.

Then he sat down and looked at her, surprised that she wasn't struggling.

But she was looking at Morcerf, as if he were the only one there, and Morcerf had his hand around the length of his cock.

Monte Cristo's mouth dry, his lips tight, he gave a tug on the silk around her wrists, and looped it around the heavy wooden bedpost, binding her there. The position lifted her breasts, sending her nipples pointing sharply into the air, the long, sleek curve of her arms nestled in the swath of dark hair.

Mercédès glanced at him, and her eyes were half closed. "And so . . . who is to be first?" she asked and shifted, half rolling to one side so that her thighs clapped primly together. "The husband or the customer?"

Bloody hell if there wasn't a light of challenge in her eyes.

Morcerf moved toward her, and Monte Cristo saw the glint of moisture at the head of his cock. He watched impassively as the man moved his wife so that she lay flat on her back again, his hands closing over her legs as he parted them. Sliding closer, hand on his erection as if steering it, he crouched over her and bent to suck on the other nipple, the neglected one. The dark red head of his cock brushed in the dark curls at her quim as her knees fell fully away.

This was what he'd come for. He willed Mercédès to look at him, to turn toward him, so he could see her face . . . so she could see him watching, see that he didn't care, that he enjoyed seeing this.

Monte Cristo watched, stilling himself, hearing, feeling nothing but the rough pound of his heart as he saw the sweep of tongue, the demand of hands, the ready length steadying between long golden thighs. The muscles of his flaccid ass flexed as Morcerf shifted, his hand on her shoulder—

"Wait." His hand closed over Morcerf, pulling him away firmly. "I have a better idea."

The other man looked as though he might argue, but Monte Cristo gave him a steady look, and Morcerf eased back reluctantly. "You can have this"—he made a dismissive gesture at Mercédès—"anytime. I'll take mine while you watch."

This, he decided, would be better. To make her moan and cry and scream in front of her husband.

To make her beg.

Ten
Battle of Wills

Later that same night
Paris

When Fernand moved away from where he'd been poised between her legs, Mercédès felt an overwhelming sense of relief. It wasn't as if she hadn't had him inside her before, of course . . . but she much preferred not to, if she could help it.

And the last thing she'd wanted was to have to pretend to enjoy it, for the benefit of their guest.

For a moment there, she thought she might have miscalculated the look in Monte Cristo's eyes, and the irregularity of his breathing, and that he would have actually let it happen. But he hadn't.

And now . . . Fernand had moved away, out of her vision, and Monte Cristo turned his attention back to her.

The expression on his face sent a cool shiver down her spine, and for a moment, she was afraid. He looked dark and . . . in her state of half arousal and determination to manipulate this activity, the only word she could think of was "tortured." He looked dark and tortured: his cheeks hollowed by shadow, his mouth tight and firm, his eyes hooded and intense . . . yet flat. Expressionless in their intensity.

Or perhaps . . . intent on torturing. Her.

Mercédès swallowed with difficulty. All moisture had evaporated from her throat, and her lungs felt tight, pressured. Her heart shook her body with the force of its pounding, and a twinge of apprehension mixed with anticipation twisted in her belly.

Her arms, bound above her head, weren't stretched uncomfortably, nor was the silk binding tight. Her legs were still free, and she thought for a moment, as Monte Cristo leaned toward her, that he'd done that purposely . . . to give her a false sense of freedom.

His hands—warm, large, sure—came down onto the sides of her torso as he bent over her, gently gripping her hips as though to hold her still, his dark head blocking out the lamplight behind him. He moved too slowly, deliberately, as though to prolong her waiting—as if he knew she wondered whether he'd suddenly ravish her, or if his intent was to coax and tease as he'd done before.

Unlike the other kisses between them tonight, this one was softer, gentler. His lips fairly worshipped hers—in a way they hadn't since . . . She lost her thoughts, let herself spill into the sensation of slow, sensual movements . . . their mouths molding together and apart, slipping to the side with a subtle swipe of tongue over hers. She felt herself beginning to breathe into his mouth, against him, felt his fingers tighten on her flesh and the rise of response flourish in her belly and roll to her ready quim below.

"Like that, do you?" he asked against her mouth, his lips a hot, soft breath away. "Good. I look forward to hearing you beg for more."

He pulled back suddenly, in contrast to the manner in which he'd approached, and his hands began to move over her body with deliberate purpose.

He thought to make her beg.

The first time she'd truly pleaded with a man, cried and debased herself, had also been the last time she'd done so.

She'd learned what hell begging could wrought. What power and control it gave.

No. Monte Cristo was bound to be disappointed if he thought he could take her to those depths again.

When his hands smoothed up to cover both of her breasts, his torso, still clad in its fine lawn shirt, brushed over her skin, and Mercédès merely closed her eyes. She parted her lips, letting the pleasure of his mouth on her nipple puff out in a soft exhalation that wasn't feigned.

She shifted her hips, brushing them against his leg, bent next to her on the bed as he gently sucked her nipple far into his mouth, deeply, drawing in her whole areola. It was hot and slick and sensual, sending low, undulating waves of pleasure with each rhythmic draw. Long and slow and steady . . . She felt her breath begin to rise, and her other nipple tighten beneath the pad of his finger.

That finger circled around in tiny motions, teasing the very topmost, sensitive tip as her areola shrank and tightened beneath. The dualing sensations of slick tongue and teasing finger made her belly flip and twist, and sharp pangs of desire spiral down to her sex, which was already sensitive and swollen, burgeoning with need. He pulled away, his white shirt pale against rich, tanned skin and dark hair, his lips full and parted, his eyes bold and driven.

Locked on her gaze, he moved his hand . . . gently skimming her flesh, sending shivers scattering over the low swell of her belly . . . and down to the rise of her mons, to the delicate thatch of hair curling there. He watched her, and she couldn't close her eyes, she couldn't look away. Deep in there, behind the flat wall of his gaze, beneath the darkness and the torment, Mercédès saw Edmond. A hint of him, the man she knew . . .

He slipped his fingers down over the front of her sex, just brushing against the tips of the wiry, sensitive hair, creating little shivers along the insides of her thighs. She let her eyes slide closed as he fingered through the tangles, lifting them and sliding through the wetness spilling from her quim.

"Open your eyes," he said softly, slipping a finger deep inside.

Pleasure rushed through her at the sudden movement, and Mercédès shifted her hips in response as she opened her eyes.

"There . . . now . . . there." Satisfaction gleamed in his face, and he pulled out and then slid his fingers back in again, deeper, fuller, brushing against her pip as he did so. She arched gently, pushing against him, letting the pleasure spread through her.

Then he pulled his hand away, and moved down between her legs, spreading them with one easy movement. She allowed her knees to fall to the sides and felt the firm grip on her thighs, just above her knees, as he positioned himself between them.

The first touch of his tongue nearly sent her off the bed. It was so light and tentative on her swollen, ready pip, so quick and so *needed*, that she gave a little cry, jerking her hips there in front of him.

Dios mio.

That first stroke was fleeting, but then the tip of his tongue came back and teased her again with a soft flick, and another one, and another . . . and then as she began to gather up, to ready herself for the next, for the one that would send her ready body over . . . he moved away, kissing along the inside of her thigh with feathery kisses, light shifts of the tongue, gentle sucking.

Mercédès closed her eyes, her breathing faster, her nipples tighter, her pip pounding, exposed and ready. Of course. He wanted her to ask for it. To beg.

She felt Monte Cristo lift his face, and opened her eyes to look down at his dark ones just beyond the gentle swell of her belly. Their gazes met as he burrowed his nose back into the thrush of hair surrounding her sex, using his lips to gently nibble on her swollen labia, his chin and jaw brushing teasingly against her pip.

He seemed to be gauging her, and she let her eyes sink closed as the pleasure built again, slowly . . . inexorably . . . as he ate at her, sucked and licked, and snaked his tongue deep into her, dragging it out slowly, jaggedly, under her needy sex. An orgasm rose, then fell back, rose and nearly peaked . . . and each time, he seemed to sense the tightening of her body, the readiness and gathering of it, and just before she spilled over into the sweet release, he moved away, stopped the rhythm and the touch and let her slide back down on a ragged little moan.

Mercédès twitched and cried against him, beneath the easy touch of his hands against her knees as every aspect of her being centered there between her legs. Her breathing had become louder and more ragged, every exhale edged with soft little sighs . . . and she heard him too, heard and felt the change of his breath there against her sex.

She wanted to reach for him, to touch the man before her and to sense his own response, to know if he was near and wanted her too . . . but her arms were bound, and her fingers could only curl helplessly against the bedpost. She dared say nothing, for fear the words would turn to pleading . . . and so she battled with herself, and with him, determined that he would break first. That he would take what he wanted from her before she gave in to her desperate need.

Then he stopped, easing away and leaving her legs spread and cold, her quim open and wet and ready. She opened her eyes when the bed shifted and his weight moved, just in time to see Monte Cristo move around to the opposite side of the bed from where her hands were bound. She followed him, and her gaze brushed over Fernand, who stood at the side there, his hand furiously working his cock as he stared blankly into space. She focused her attention on her repulsive husband's slack jaw and glassy eyes for a moment as a way to pull herself out of the pleasure that blanketed her, ebbing now but waiting to be reawakened.

Which surely Monte Cristo meant to do in some other manner.

Then Mercédès' legs were being pulled; Monte Cristo

dragged them over the bed so that she lay sideways across it, her arms long and stretched, her hips settled on the edge of the mattress and her feet nearly flat on the floor. He stood between her knees, still fully clothed in contrast to her nakedness, and began to unfasten his trousers.

His face was just as unreadable as ever, and a shock of dark hair obstructed one eye, but she swore his sure fingers fumbled clumsily with the ties and buttons at his waist. . . . Surely, it didn't take that long to pull them away . . . and she felt rather than heard his relief when the purple erection surged free, raging there in the dark opening of his trousers. Mercédès felt a sudden rush of desire shoot down to her quim, and she gave a soft little moan.

"Ah," he said, the sound low and knowing. And a little raw. A little breathless.

He moved between her legs, grasping her hips to raise them as he poised there. She closed her eyes, ready, wanting, feeling her quim dripping and needy.

When he fitted himself to her, when he slid deeply inside, her breath caught and she was overwhelmed with need and pleasure and fulfillment, and she held her breath, ready for the onslaught . . . for the rise and spill of climax.

But he didn't move. He merely held her there, held her hips immobile with those strong fingers, breathing against her, throbbing and full—so damned long and full and familiar—inside her, close to her . . . but not close enough.

Not close enough.

Mercédès caught herself on a soft sob, tried to shift just so that he'd rub against her aching tickler and send her over . . . but he didn't move.

She opened her eyes to see that his were closed, his face like stone, the shadows of his cheeks deep and dark. He didn't breathe, and there, suddenly, in the amazing silence that gripped the chamber, came a deep, expressive grunt from the side.

Her gaze flew to Fernand just in time to see his head thrown back and the spurt of his release whip from the end of the cock he flogged mercilessly with his hand.

Mercédès felt her own body tighten in reaction to such a display of pleasure, and she shifted again, more urgently. More desperately. *Please.*

Monte Cristo opened his eyes, looked down at her, and smiled, hard and knowing. "Is there something you want, madam la comtesse?"

She looked away, her gaze flickering to Fernand, and she felt the cock inside her shift . . . just the slightest, easiest bit . . . and her whole body seized up, ready . . . and then fell back. She gathered up her resolve, her determination to snap his control. "Perhaps if you don't wish to . . . finish things, my husband should take over."

Monte Cristo's fingers convulsed against her, ever so slightly, but his expression remained dark and calm. "I think," he said, glancing over his shoulder at Fernand, who'd collapsed into a chair, "he has finished for the night. But . . . I am in no hurry."

Mercédès tightened herself around him and watched his face react. Subtle, but the surprise was there. "It's too bad you feel the need to have me restrained," she said, keeping her voice steady with effort. She felt as if she were to lose control, lose her focus, for one moment, one instant, she would also lose this battle. "Do you not trust yourself at my hands?"

In response, he pulled back and gave a sudden, savage thrust inside her, and she gasped at the beauty of it. *Dios. More, oh Dios mio, please . . .*

Mercédès bit back her cry and looked at him, and saw the same struggle on his face. *Good . . . oh, thank God.*

She shifted insistently, nearly throwing off his hold—she only needed one, maybe two strokes and she'd be there . . . *Please.*

"No, you don't," he breathed, pushing her hips into the mattress even more firmly, allowing her no room to move. "Ask for it . . . beg me."

"No," she gritted between her teeth, tightening her vagina around him again and giving a little flex of her buttocks to shift her hips. "Coward."

He laughed, harsh and short, and gave another sharp, hard thrust. Mercédès cried out and thrashed her head to one side, biting her lip at the surge inside. She wouldn't. He couldn't last much longer.

She arched her back, lifting her breasts slightly, focused on the throb between her legs. He was close. . . . she felt him filling inside her even more.

"Come with me, Comtesse," he said in a long, tense voice. "Beg."

"No," she said again.

He took a sudden, sharp breath and ground himself against her, pushing deeper. She sighed softly, erotically, and looked up at him. Desire blazed in his face now, as if he could no longer control it.

"I'll never beg you for anything," she said in a strong voice, using every bit of control to make it so. Forcing away the sensations that pounded through her, that twisted and dug and curled and promised.

"Never?" he said, and began to move in short, little strokes, barely shifting inside her, holding her in such a way that he came near, but didn't touch, her pip. Teasing. "Oh, you . . . will . . . ," he promised on a low breath.

"Oh . . . ," she cried. It rose again, her lust, burgeoning and billowing like a sail filling with wind, and Mercédès tossed her head to the side, biting her lip as he moved, holding her there, keeping her from matching him, from that pressure, that lovely pressure that would send her over. She focused, willed herself to live there, between her legs, where everything rose and rose and grew and surged and—

"Oh . . . no . . . you . . . don't . . . ," he gasped, pulling himself out in a sudden, desperate movement, leaving her swelled tight and shiny and needy. Oh, *Dios* . . . needy. She cried out, then bit her lip again to keep the pleas from erupting, tears leaking from her eyes as she rolled her face away.

Please.

He climbed on the bed next to her, his cock dark and rosy, slick and rampant with her juices, and she licked her lips, caught her breath, squeezed back the need, swallowed desperately . . . and drew in one long, steadying draft of air. Control.

"Come here, Count. Let me taste you and give you release." She licked her dry lips again, suggestively, dropping her gaze to that beautiful cock.

With a growl of rage, he moved quickly, his hand closing over his own thick, surging length and with two sharp movements, he finished, spilling thick white seed over her torso.

He gasped something as he came. She couldn't hear him, not really . . . but it sounded like her name.

Mercédès.

He left her there, tied to the bed, her sex glistening and plump between her splayed legs, his leavings sticky on her skin. He made Fernand go with him, and there she stayed, unsatisfied and needy, until Charlotte found her the next morning.

Yet, despite her thrumming, exhausted body, and the unseemly position in which she was found, Mercédès was complacent.

Monte Cristo had not succeeded in his desire for revenge. For in the end, it was he who'd given in.

ELEVEN

Behind the Iron Gate

One week later
Paris

Maximilien Morrel's fingers curled around the iron grate as he pressed his eye against it. "Valentine, my love," he murmured, wishing his fingers were long enough to touch her soft blond hair. "Are you well?"

She was, of course, sitting on her favorite bench, which had been angled more closely to the gate since the last time they'd met—but was still too far for him to reach. Her cheek curved with pleasure, and her thick lashes swept down, and as always, Maximilien was struck by her humble beauty. "I have missed you, my own love."

"And I you. But how are you? How is your grandfather?"

"He has given his blessing to our marriage," she said, suddenly turning her face directly to his so that he could see the full beauty of her smile. It took his breath away. "In eighteen months, we shall be wed, with his blessings."

Maximilien had never felt so full, so joyous, in all his life. "It is so? Oh, Valentine! I am the happiest man alive! And what of your father, Monsieur Villefort?"

Her expression checked, and her happiness faded a bit. "He is not so well. He isn't ill, but . . . of course with the three deaths in our house, and then the breaking off of my engagement to Franz d'Epinay . . . but surely you heard of that."

He nodded, feeling the cold, rough iron against his forehead and wishing with all of his might that it was her silky flesh that pressed against him, and not the bars between them. "The news has trickled out that your *grandpère* Monsieur Noirtier was the man who killed d'Epinay's father in a duel, many years ago during the Napoleonic uprising."

"Yes, it is true. And of course d'Epinay could not marry me after that—and as sorry as I am for him, truly, Maximilien, I must thank my grandfather for divulging this fact. But my father is devastated that such a profitable marriage has been canceled."

Maximilien couldn't help but feel a twinge of unease, for he knew Valentine's marriage to him would not be nearly as advantageous as her father would want. But Valentine was Monsieur Noirtier's heir, and if he gave permission, all would be well. *All would be well!* He would have her for his own.

"I have heard of another betrothal being broken in the last days," he said, hoping to ease the sadness in her face. "Come here, please, Valentine. . . . Let me touch you, and I will tell you that you are not the only one whose father's hopes have been dashed."

To his relief, she smiled again, those plump pink lips curving daintily, so delicious he was overwhelmed with the urge to taste them. But he had to settle for the tips of her fingers, tucked beneath his, through the small holes of the gate.

"Tell me, Maximilien. I love to hear your voice, and it has been so difficult this last week without hearing it. Things are so . . . strange . . . in my house, since those three deaths. I . . . the doctor . . . the last time he was here, he looked at me so strangely. As if he believed it could be I who did such a horrible thing as to kill my own grandparents!" Her last words caught on a sob, but she swallowed it back and looked through the grate at him.

"Oh, dear Valentine . . . no one who knows you could ever consider that you would harm anyone, let alone those you love. Please do not worry on it. All will be well, and we will be married in less than two years, and we will no longer have this terrible *gate* between us!"

"Thank you, Maximilien. . . . Now tell me the gossip so I have something else to think on."

He pressed a kiss to the tip of one of her sweet fingers, and as he nibbled on it, unable to let her pull it away, he spoke. "My dear friend Albert de Morcerf was intending to marry Eugénie Danglars, daughter of the bank baron. But earlier this week, Danglars told Count Morcerf that there would be no wedding between their children, and refused to tell him why. Albert, who didn't want to marry Eugénie in any case, told me that Danglars only said to his father, 'Be glad that I refuse to give you the reason.' "

He swiped his tongue gently into the webbing between her fingers, and she responded by giving a delicious little shiver.

"Maximilien," she sighed, leaning against the iron grate. Little parts of her body and gown seeped through the diamond-shaped holes, and Maximilien pushed himself up to the grate, likewise also pressing himself against it.

"Kiss me, darling . . . please . . . ," he said, finding a place where his mouth would fit at level with hers.

"Maximilien . . . ," she sighed, and as well as they were able, they kissed. Lips and tongue, cold iron bars between them, danced, receded, and thrashed together again.

He felt through the grate, his fingers brushing against and then curling around the silk of her gown where it fit to her waist, and he felt . . . he swore he did . . . the give of her gentle flesh beneath it. "Oh, Valentine," he sighed against her lips, against the cold iron, trying to bring her body even closer into the gate with the tips of his fingers. "So sweet . . . so sweet, you are. . . ."

She pulled away, and their noses bumped between the iron diamonds. They looked at each other, and he felt as though he might drown in her deep blue eyes. They shone with love and hope and, not for the first time, Maximilien wished he'd brought a saw to cut through the bloody bars between them.

"Tell me more," she whispered, her breath soft and sweet with mint.

He traced the silk hollows of her cheeks with fingers from both hands and said, "Danglars is said to have moved quickly and betrothed Eugénie to a young man named Andrea Cavalcanti, a poor young man who had been separated from his father since birth, only to find that he is a prince of Italy. The Count of Monte Cristo was the one who reunited him with his father."

"How kind of the count," said Valentine, but for the first time, Maximilien sensed a bit of hesitation in her voice.

"Monte Cristo is a good man," he told her. "He has already promised me that if we need any help, he will move heaven and earth to see that we are together."

To his surprise, she reached through the bars and touched his face. Maximilien sighed and let his forehead clunk against the gate, feeling the light, sensual touch as she brushed over his cheeks and jaw, then moved to another hole and, with one finger, traced over his lips, still plump from kissing her.

"It is just that . . . he seemed so friendly with my stepmother, Heloise," she said, then gave a lovely little gasp as he opened his mouth and her finger slipped in. "When he . . . visited . . . several weeks ago. And . . . well, I know she does not like me much, and would prefer that Father pay more attention to their son, and it seems . . ." She caught her breath as he flicked his tongue around and between her two fingers, just as he dreamed about doing to her quim.

The very thought made his cock strain harder against his breeches, and he nearly lost track of what she was saying. "It seems . . . ?" he prompted with a little laugh. "Come now. . . . Am I distracting you, my love?"

"Oh . . . indeed, you are . . . ," she sighed, "but you must take care, or I shall do the same to you."

Her voice carried a rare note of mischief in it, and Maximilien felt a fresh wave of desire and love course through him. Beautiful, bewitching, and lighthearted. What more could a man ask for in a wife?

"It just seems that if he is friends with her, and she does not care for me . . . then they're too much alike. I know that you're very fond of the count, but . . ."

"I respect him more than you can know," he replied.

She'd pulled her fingers away, leaving Maximilien straining for more . . . another taste, a deeper one, a longer, more erotic one. But then he noticed what she was doing and he felt faint. "Valentine!"

She'd begun to tug at her bodice, pulling it down low over one breast so that . . . *mon Dieu!* . . . so that more of that beautiful swell was revealed . . . and then the upper edge of her dusky pink areola. . . . Maximilien thought he might faint, but she stopped and looked at him. "Are you distracted, my love? Please . . . continue."

"I . . . he . . . the count is a good man, he is intelligent and kind, and he loves me—I'm sure of it." His words seemed to be forced between two very swollen lips and around a tongue that could not move properly. Suddenly her nipple popped out from the tight bodice, and there it was: her whole glorious, beautiful, plum-sized, pearlescent, blue-veined breast. There. *There.*

"Valentine . . . ," he groaned. His hand went to the iron bars, trying to reach through, but she stood just far enough away that he could only just brush over the tip of her nipple. His brief, bare touch caused her to snatch in her breath and straighten up.

"Go on," she said. But her voice was breathy and seductive, and when he glanced up, he saw that her eyes were focused down where her breast shone virginally white in the shadow of the wall and surrounding foliage.

"And . . . I cannot remember what I was saying, Valentine. Please! Have pity on me. . . ." He sagged to his knees before her, fairly hanging from his fingers on the grate, so that his face was even with her breast . . . and when she pressed herself against that very gate, her soft pink nipple and most of her areola poked through one of the holes . . . . Maximilien thought he would spend his seed right there in his trousers.

He didn't wait for an invitation. . . . He moved, putting his mouth on that luscious pink tip. At first, tentatively, like a first kiss, he pressed his lips to it, then swiped his tongue around. She caught her breath, then gasped, and she pulled away and he nearly cried out . . . but then, as if realizing that she'd aborted her own pleasure too, she came back, pressing herself even harder against the iron grate.

"Valentine," he sighed, drawing that delicate pink nubbin into his mouth as if he were a babe . . . all the way in, gently but firmly, delighting in her little gasp of delight, her little surprised sob . . . and he felt it grow hard in his mouth as he sucked and licked and mouthed against her. His own passion throbbed in the form of a cock raging against his trousers, pressing into the iron bars for relief.

"Oh, Maximilien . . . ," she sighed, shuddering against the grid so that it rumbled quietly in its hinges and against its chains. "Please . . ."

She could have no idea what she was asking for, but Maximilien did. "Come closer, love," he whispered. "Your hips . . . closer . . ."

He reached through the diamond shape where her quim would be, trying to push through the layers and layers of fabric there to find the place where her legs separated, and she helped by spreading them in a most unladylike manner, moving her feet apart. Maximilien looked up and saw that she was clutching the grate with her little fingers, sagging against it as he sucked at her breast and tried to find the way to her sex. The weight of skirt on top of crinoline on top of shift was too heavy for his fingers to move, levered as they were through the damned small hole.

"Please . . . ," she whispered again, and the grid clinked again as she pressed harder against it.

"Lift up your skirts," he whispered, his mouth dry, his voice raspy. Dear God, it was broad daylight, in the back of Villefort's garden. . . . The roof of the house could be seen in the distance, over the trees. . . . They could be discovered at any moment . . . but . . . oh Lord, he didn't care.

When that heavy mass of fabric—of lace and sky blue silk and the stiff crinoline and the finely woven chemise—when all were bunched up in her hands, pushed off to the side and held at bay as she sagged against the gate, her breast no longer poking through, he was able to slip his fingers through and find her.

Mon Dieu.

Oh! So warm and soft and wet . . . dear Lord, she was dripping and swollen and hot. He closed his eyes, pushed away the pain of his tight, shiny, purple cock and slipped his fingers around and through, into those secret, sweet folds and into her deepest part. . . . She caught her breath when his two fingers shot inside her, then eased out again, and then in again. . . . He used his thumb to find her tiny, hard pip; he couldn't see it, but as he rubbed it between his thumb and finger, he imagined it peeping shyly out from beneath its little hood and nearly ruined his trousers right then.

"Valentine . . . sweet . . . Valentine," he said, gently jiggling the little nub with the pad of his thumb, slipping around and pressing on it, and he felt her tensing, and her breath stopped and she seemed to wait. . . . He flipped his fingers out from inside her, around the hard, shiny pip, and suddenly she gasped and was shuddering against the iron bars, crying and shaking and laughing. . . .

His breath was heavy and fast, and when he drew his hand away from her warmth, he brought it immediately to his nose. . . . He had to smell her, to taste her . . . musky and sweet and feminine . . . Valentine . . . oh, Valentine!

"Oh God," he said, and fell against the gate. He kept his moist fingers by his nose, breathing in her smell and struggling to subdue the insistent, angry erection that he smashed up against the iron bars.

"Maximilien," she said at last. Her voice was a rough, surprised whisper, barely audible over the rustling breeze through the bushes around them. "I . . . that was . . . I love you."

"I love you too, Valentine," he said, bravely keeping his voice strong and steady. There would be time someday . . . someday for him to experience the release . . . but today was hers. "I will never survive eighteen months until we can wed," he added in a sudden burst of desperation. "I pray God something will happen to change that."

She looked through the grate, her eyes soft and glazed and hollyhock blue. "So do I, my love. So do I."

The evening she'd met the Comtesse de Morcerf at the theater, Haydée rode home in His Excellency's carriage alone. It had been no surprise to her when, after disappearing for a time during the first intermission, and then again during the second (after sending glowering stares across the stage at the comtesse), he elected to accept an invitation from the Comte de Morcerf instead of leaving for home at that time. And His Excellency hadn't returned to his house on the Champs-Élysées until after dawn, at which time he was, from what Bertuccio said, in very foul spirits.

Thus Haydée had ridden home alone in the carriage—alone, except for Ali, who declined to ride *in* the vehicle with her and instead chose to sit outside, up next to the driver.

All because he was too damned afraid to be alone with Haydée.

Over the next ten days, he continued to avoid her at all costs. Haydée actually found it rather amusing when, if she entered a room where he might be, he would immediately find an excuse to leave.

Or, if she would summon him to her presence for some manufactured reason, he would take care to bring another of the servants with him.

But after a time, she'd had enough of his blasted honorable excuses for not letting her touch him, and she set about hatching a plan to end this standoff once and for all.

If seducing him by making him a voyeur and watching her in the tub with her servants, or sneaking into his bed at night hadn't worked, then Haydée knew she'd have to resort to the last of the feminine wiles: tears.

And as it happened, an unexpected event occurred that gave her the perfect excuse to do so: a man broke into the home on the Champs-Élysées one night when the Count of Monte Cristo had taken his household to his other residence in Auteuil. The intruder was killed during his escape, and no one had been in the house but the count himself, who apparently had chased the man away . . . but Haydée decided to use the incident to her advantage.

The night following the incident, which she'd only heard about from Bertuccio and the other servants, Haydée selected her trap's settings very carefully. She was aware that Ali often prowled about the gardens late in the afternoon when the other servants were busy preparing for His Excellency's evening plans, and she arranged herself in a small gazebo in the very farthest corner of the grounds.

It was perfect for her use, for heavy vines and thick bushes grew around the small building, and it was tucked away just off the pebbled paths. But to ensure that her plot wouldn't be interrupted, she'd given strict orders to Bertuccio and Marie, the housekeeper, that no one but Ali was to come into the gardens for any reason.

Thus, when the sun was halfway back to its resting place, warm and yellow but not bearing down with its strongest blaze, Haydée settled herself on one of the large, plump chaises that occupied the gazebo. An odd thing to have in a garden house, really . . . but perhaps she was not the first one to choose to use the little structure as a trysting place. It really was perfect.

She checked to be certain everything was in readiness, including the special ring she wore, and then she began to cry. Loudly. Heartbreakingly, wrenchingly, forlornly.

Instead of burying her face in the cushions, she pitched her cries away, into the open, concentrating on making real tears and even turning her face blotchy and red. Ali was not easy to fool.

That was only one of the things she loved about him.

Another thing was the thick, dark length that he refused—unlike other men—to allow to lead him around and to influence his decisions. Damn him for being so insufferably honorable.

It wasn't long before, between gasping sobs, Haydée heard

the soft skitter of pebbles in the distance, and she let a particularly heartrending wail sally forth. And then she buried her face in her hands, ensuring that her shoulders were heaving convincingly.

Since he couldn't speak, Ali always made certain to create some quiet noise to announce his presence, and this time was no exception. A scuffle of feet on the dusty wooden floor of the building—along with the anticipatory prickling at the back of her neck—told her that he'd fallen for the bait.

Now it was only a matter of clinching the deal.

She felt him behind her, and imagined that he stood there, helpless and uncertain, confronted with a sobbing woman, opening and closing his fingers, beginning to step toward her, then hesitating and stepping back. So, after a moment, she lifted her head and gave a realistic start when she saw him standing before her, just as she'd imagined.

Haydée's mouth went dry as she looked over at him, big and bald and black, wrists cuffed in gleaming gold, looming there next to her chaise. Gorgeous. Inhumanly beautiful and powerful—yet looking as uncomfortable and out of place as if he were being fitted for a corset—and he was going to be hers. All hers.

What is it? he signed.

Haydée bravely held back another sob and used the hem of her tunic sleeve—a loose-fitting one-piece garment she'd chosen for just those reasons as her garb for this seduction—to dab at her eyes. Her hair she'd collected loosely in a long, low tail that fell down her spine, and she wore only a simple cord around the crown of her head, wrapping across her forehead where a single pearl dangled above the place between her brows.

"I . . . didn't know anyone was here," she said, ducking her face as though embarrassed. She waited until he touched her, featherlight, at the top of her head. Featherlight and fleeting, and she looked up again.

What is wrong?

She gave a few shaky sobs and then appeared to pull her wits about her, and sat up on the chaise. With a gesture to the other one—the one she'd prepared specially for Ali—she said, "Please sit down. You . . . it's hard to talk when you're looming over me."

Looking abashed, but with concern in his dark eyes, he sank down on the chaise, feet planted on the floor and arms akimbo over his knees.

Has someone hurt you? His hand motions showed subtle fury, as if waiting for some ugly confirmation before bursting free.

"No," she replied, sniffling a bit for good measure. "It's just that . . . last night, that man who broke into the house . . . Caderousse was his name, wasn't it?"

Ali gave a sharp nod, and she noticed that his large hand relaxed a bit.

"If he had come into the house while we were here, he could have . . . he could have murdered us all," she said fearfully.

No. I—Here Ali stopped, his hands slapping nonsense for a moment before they picked up again. *His Excellency, and all of us, would not let that happen. You're safe.*

"But he could have killed the count! And that"—she dabbed at her eyes again—"is what I fear the most! That he would be taken from me."

She saw the way Ali drew back, ever so slightly, stiffening. *His Excellency is no fool. He is not easily killed, nor bested. He has survived far more than you can imagine.*

"But it is possible . . . and then what would happen to me? Where would I go? What would I do? I am afraid to be alone." Haydée began to sob heavily again, sagging in her chaise so that she was about to fall off . . . unless he caught her.

Which he did. Gently, as though afraid to touch her, he caught her shoulders in his large, powerful hands. Haydée gave him no chance to think, to retreat; she fairly surged off her seat into his lap, snuggling her face into the musky corner between his neck and shoulder. Ahh. She closed her eyes and drew in a long, deep, lovely breath of the man she wanted above all others.

She gave a few more gentle sobs to camouflage her deep breaths, her growing sense of comfort and joy. Of course, with her face buried into his skin, she couldn't see any hand motions he might make, so after a moment, she raised herself from that most pleasant of positions.

Now she was sitting on his lap, her legs primly to one side of his thighs, his hands gingerly at her waist, barely touching her. The bulge in his trousers was a source of satisfaction to her rather than a surprise, but she took care to hide any evidence of that.

"He is like my father, Ali. . . . I cannot bear the thought of losing another father."

If anything happens to His Excellency, I will take care of you.

A wave of happiness swept over her when she saw the truth, the naked emotion in his eyes. No matter how hard he tried to hide it, to deny it, he cared for her . . . as more than a body, as what he perceived as a forbidden body.

"Ali . . . ," she began, but he stopped her with vigorous hand motions.

But nothing will happen to him, Haydée. I have seen him shoot a gun at an ace of diamonds, and put a bullet through the center diamond. His Excellency is well able to take care of himself.

Ali's eyes had gone flat, as though to obscure his feelings, and Haydée was momentarily quieted by his long speech. She'd never seen him "speak" so much. . . . He must have felt it was imperative that she understand.

But she didn't care.

She leaned forward without warning and covered his lovely, thick lips with hers, drawing in the dark taste of him gently but firmly. Her hand slipped around his neck, pulling herself up off his lap to delve deeply into the kiss . . . but then she settled back into place before he could end it.

He was breathing heavily, and those eyes weren't so shuttered and flat any longer. Haydée herself felt out of breath . . . and unsatisfied. But it was too soon to dive back into a kiss.

"I don't want His Excellency to take care of me," she said, leaning into him. As she'd expected, he tilted away as if to keep some distance between them, and with a little lunge, she caught him off-balance and tipped him back onto the chaise. Then, with a quick twist, she turned her ring and released its little needle, then reached up to wrap her arms around his neck again, and shoved the tiny needle into one of the veins in his neck as she did so.

He started in surprise, but a little nick like that would hardly be noticeable to a man like him, and she pretended nothing had happened, for it would take a few moments for the sleeping drug to work.

She smiled at him, running her hands back down over his chest as he half lay back, and she saw the flare of surprise and desire in his eyes. Quickly taking advantage of it by running her fingers gingerly along his massive arms, she moved up his body. "You are so strong, Ali," she said, close to his face. "I want you to take care of me. I would never worry if I was with you."

When he raised his hands, she covered the underside of his biceps with her wide fingers and smoothed up along those mighty arms—from shoulder to elbow to wrist, guiding his hands back above his head. She leaned forward to kiss him again, and in that moment felt him begin to relax under her body.

Ali shook his head as if to keep himself awake, but he was fighting a losing battle. The drug she'd used was quick and effective, even for a man his size, and Haydée had to wait only another few breaths before he was sagging sleepily in the chaise, his eyes closed, his breathing easy.

She then found it simple to raise his heavy arms and tie both wrists together at the top of the chaise, and then lash his ankles, one at each corner of the end of the divan. She would never have succeeded if he'd been awake and aware, she thought, as she fitted a belt over his hips to keep him from arching and bucking too violently.

Once Haydée was finished with that, she had to wait a bit longer for the effects of the drug to wear off. She helped the process by holding a little vial of eucalyptus and mint under his nose. It was perhaps ten minutes, or a quarter of an hour, later that he began to stir.

She sat and watched with a mixture of trepidation and anticipation as consciousness and awareness returned to his face. When he realized he was restrained, she actually held her breath for a moment as he struggled against his bonds.

His muscles bulged as he pulled at the leather cords, and Haydée swallowed hard . . . partly because of the fury in his face, and partly because . . . dear heaven, but he was beautiful and frighteningly powerful.

"I'm sorry, Ali, but I had to do this," she said, leaning forward to kiss him. "I don't want His Excellency. I want you. Only you. Forever. You."

He moved so angrily, with low, guttural grunts from his voiceless mouth that she thought for a moment he might pull the chaise into splinters. It jolted and shifted and lurched on the floor, and she watched in trepidation.

If he got free, would he kill her?

She should have tied him to a wrought-iron chaise instead of this one. It was made of bamboo, which she knew was used for houses and roofs in the Orient . . . but it was creaking a bit under his movements. . . .

Haydée's heart pounded in her chest and she swallowed hard, looking at his bulging eyes, dark and furious, his firm-lined mouth, no longer so thick and sensual, the incredible swells of his biceps and pectoral muscles—even in his neck, where the tendons were taut and throbbing and there was a tiny red dot from where she'd punctured him. Regret stung her for a bare moment, but she pushed it away. It had to be done if she was going to have this man for her own, forever.

For that was what she wanted.

"Please," she said, smoothing her small, olive-skinned hands over his gleaming ebony chest, "let me pleasure you, Ali. I want to touch you. I want to feel your skin against mine. And I knew this . . . this was the only way."

And with that, she pulled off her loose tunic with one

smooth motion and flung it. That left her completely nude, her breasts tight and lifted from anticipation, her nipples jutting up, her quim swollen and tingling.

No.

His mouth formed the word; she could almost hear it in the exhale of breath, low and deep and heartfelt. His head thrashed against the cushion beneath it, and he ended by turning away from her as his powerful legs jerked in futility.

Haydée's mouth was still dry, and her heart thumped madly. She wanted him. She knew he wanted her—he was just afraid to take her if she belonged to Monte Cristo.

But she didn't belong to Monte Cristo; he didn't want her. He wanted the Comtesse de Morcerf.

No matter what he said or how he acted toward the beautiful golden-skinned woman, Haydée knew the comtesse was the only one on his mind. The only one who could take that tension from his face, the emptiness that lurked in his eyes . . . the brittleness from his body. If he would let her.

And that night at the theater, His Excellency had told Haydée that she was free to choose her own lover. True, he had intimated that his choice for her would be Maximilien Morrel, but he had made it clear that she could seek her lover from any of the men in Paris.

Thus, Haydée pushed away any guilt she might have, any fear of consequences, and she slipped her hand beneath the loose waist of Ali's trousers, easing his immense cock from its dark, warm confines. Once free, it stood proud and hugely thick and ready, fairly vibrating with need.

Haydée cast a glance at Ali. His face was still turned away, but she could see that his eyes were closed. His breathing was rough, but steady, and she could see a shift of movement in his proud cheeks, as if he was gritting his teeth.

She placed her hands on that warm, pounding chest sprinkled with those unusual dark curlicues, like a scattering of small black circles over the upper part of his torso, beautiful, wiry, crinkly, and warm. She tumbled her nails through it, lifting the hair experimentally. Then she hoisted herself gently onto his body, which had begun to tremble faintly beneath her fingers, and settled herself just behind his massive purple-red-black cock.

"Ali," she said, stroking her drenched quim with her fingers until they too were dripping, "I am a virgin, and I want you to be the first."

He turned his face toward her and opened his eyes. She'd arranged the chaise and its pillows perfectly so that his head was in a raised position and he could see her without lifting his head. *No,* he shook his head. *No.*

She closed her soaking fingers around his cock and felt him lurch beneath her, then shudder violently, easing into soft trembling.

"His Excellency has no interest in my maidenhead, and neither do I. I wish to rid myself of it. Now." She gave a quick stroke down, then up, the wrist-thick column of his cock, causing him to jolt into little shudders again. Her mouth watered, as she thought about how it would feel when she fitted him inside her, and slid down deep and full. . . .

His eyes moved furiously, his face and head and soundless mouth, as he desperately tried to communicate with her. He didn't need to speak—she knew what he meant to say.

" 'He's my master. My virginity belongs to him. . . . You

are but a slave. . . .' Yes, Ali, I know your arguments," she said, keeping her voice smooth and seductive. She lifted her breasts, cupping both of her hands beneath them, offering them to him. "What if he changes his mind?" she added, then looked down at her left nipple as she used her thumb to tease over the front of it, drawing it even tighter into a pucker.

"But he has already given me leave to find a man to love," she said, leaning forward to kiss the sticky, moisture-tipped top of his penis. "And you are the man I choose, Ali."

He drew in a long, deep, hitching breath, and closed his eyes.

"You want me, don't you?" she asked, leaning forward again, his cock pressing into the side of her belly as her hands pushed into his chest. She felt the ramming of his heart beneath her fingers, and she edged forward more, lifting her bottom so that his penis scooted stickily along her body toward her smooth, wet quim. It jerked to a little halt right at the juncture of her thighs, right next to her swollen labia, then beyond as she lurched forward to cover his mouth with hers.

He twisted his face away, but she followed him, and suddenly those thick, lovely lips were open, devouring hers . . . taking her in, sucking and tasting and molding to her as she slipped her tongue into the wet warmth of his mouth.

Haydée groaned into him when he opened, when he fully took her in, and she ground her slippery, throbbing sex into his belly as her teeth scraped the sides of his mouth, as she swiped her tongue as long and deep into his mouth as she could.

Yes. Oh, yes.

Her hands moved up along the powerful lines of his shoulders, over the swell of muscle and into his taut neck, over the deep, warm hollows of his collarbone when she curved her fingers over wide shoulders. He was dark and spicy and ready. . . . She felt the gentle prod of his cock at the back of her ass as she moved back, lifting herself, and then, settling over him. She held there for a moment, feeling the width of his head as it pressed into the deep fold of her labia.

Ali's eyes were closed again, his neck tight, his lips parted, his chest rising and falling as if he'd just run leagues.

Haydée scooped her fingers deeply into her quim again, then rubbed her lubricant over the soft, velvety foreskin of his cock. Then she lifted herself, poised in a crouch, and fit him into her, just the tip . . . just the very tip of that massive erection.

He seized up, his chest stopped, his nostrils flared, his eyes open now, staring at the ceiling above. Her breasts were trembling, her heart was pounding so hard . . . her mouth watered, and her pip surged, tingling sharply.

And then she slammed herself down, as hard and fast as she could.

Pleasure . . . oh, wonderful pleasure such as she'd never known . . . a sharp cut of pain, and then . . . fulfillment. Fullness. Low, undulating, deep-within-her fullness.

Ali's mouth had opened in a low, guttural roar, and now she felt him beneath her, shuddering and vibrating. His eyes had sunk closed again, his teeth scoring into his lovely bottom lip, his nostrils wide, his skin glistening with moisture.

The pain was still pounding there, quietly, deep inside, but that fullness . . . that feeling of rightness and that tingle of need brought Haydée back to her knees again, and she lifted herself up over him again, and then slid back down to his thighs.

Oh, heavens, she thought she would cry at the pleasure of

it . . . again. . . . She raised and lowered, raised and lowered . . . slammed and lurched, slammed and lurched . . . and the pain eased, replaced by the whirling, mellow, rising lust.

Tears gathered in her eyes, her fingers clamped into his skin as she worked faster and faster over him, her pip round and hard, her insides tightening and slipping, until she heard him cry out, and felt the sudden jerk of his hips, and the uncontrollable shuddering and trembling inside her and beneath her . . . that low moan of reluctant ecstasy, the feel of him slamming himself up into her, even against the belt at his hips, drove her over the edge.

An orgasm such as she'd never known crashed over her, hot and wringing and long and deep. . . . She collapsed forward, her hands sliding on his slick chest, her heart stampeding in her chest, her mouth open and gasping and crying, her pip throbbing and undulating there against the side of his cock.

After a long moment, she pressed a kiss to his salty throat, lifted her head, and saw his face.

It was shadowed, sweaty, and blank. Devoid of emotion, shuttered, empty.

And she froze, the last vestiges of pleasure scattering like seeds on the wind.

What had she done?

Twelve
The Insult

The next day
Paris

Satisfaction and gut-level pleasure washed over Monte Cristo as he looked down at the list of four neatly printed names and the final off-kilter scrawled one.

~~*Caderousse*~~
Villefort
Danglars
Morcerf
Mercédès.

Only one was eliminated, by a single, neat line drawn through it, but his satisfaction came from the knowledge that the web was weaving tighter. It would be mere days before the worlds of Villefort, Danglars, and Morcerf disintegrated, collapsing upon them like the houses of cards they'd each built up to hide their greed and deceit.

Caderousse had been a fool to break into the home of the Count of Monte Cristo; of course, he could have had no idea that he was also Edmond Dantès, a man he'd helped betray twenty-four years ago by standing aside and letting his arrest happen. But the old thief had sown the seeds of his own fate: once he recognized Monte Cristo as Dantès, and he realized that the man had come back to haunt him, Caderousse fled the house . . . falling to his death from the second-story window.

There had been no need to worry the household about the attempted thievery, for Monte Cristo had been fully aware of Caderousse's plans to steal from him. In fact, he'd purposely planned and publicized the fact that his household would be in Auteuil in order to give Caderousse the opportunity to burgle his home, as a sort of subtle challenge to see if the man had given up his dishonest ways.

Clearly, Caderousse had not changed from the self-serving, thieving man he'd been since his betrayal of Edmond Dantès, and thus his demise was fitting.

And Monte Cristo had not needed to lift a hand in violence or anger against Caderousse; like Danglars and Morcerf and Villefort, his disaster was the result of his own choices, his own secrets, his own greed.

One of five. Eliminated from the list.

And soon, he would have a lasting vengeance on the rest of them—the ones who had actively plotted against him. A revenge longer and more lasting than a simple moment of execution, one more public than imprisonment.

Yet . . . Monte Cristo looked at the scribbled name at the bottom of the list and felt the satisfaction turn to a low beat of anger. Smoldering fury, deep within . . . a dryness in his throat . . . a maelstrom of remembered images, sounds, scents, textures.

Unlike the others, his plan for her had not materialized in the way he'd anticipated.

He'd had expectations, images of her crying and pleading for understanding, for sympathy, for mercy . . . begging for forgiveness . . . gasping for release.

His cock, the blasted traitor, lifted a bit, swelling in his trousers as he thought about those nights . . . the unexpected results and his own bloody weakness. His palms dampened, his mouth dried.

He knew it was a purely physical reaction, a bodily need, a simple function that made him respond to her the way he did . . . lose his head, forget his purpose, tumble into the moment.

But it didn't matter any longer. In a matter of days, his Campaign of Vengeance would be completed. He would leave Paris with Haydée, he would free her and release Ali from his vow, and he would never rest his eyes upon Mercédès Herrera de Morcerf again.

And despite the fact that his plans to dominate her physically, to break her, through humiliation and the betrayal of her own body—in the same way she'd betrayed Edmond Dantès, the man she had sworn to love forever—had not been fulfilled in the manner he'd expected . . . he *had* humiliated her. He *had* dominated her.

And he would yet be revenged.

For the sins of the father would also be visited upon the son.

And so would the sins of the mother.

Yes, indeed, Albert de Morcerf would feel the sting of vengeance for the wrongdoings of his parents. The disruption of his intended marriage to Eugénie Danglars was only part of the scheme to destroy Albert's father, pain that the young man would suffer as well.

Monte Cristo looked up at the knock on his door and bade Bertuccio to enter. He folded up his well-creased piece of paper and slipped it back into the large cabochon garnet pin he wore as his servant entered.

"Your Excellency, all has been prepared for our departure to Normandy. Monsieur Albert de Morcerf has arrived, below, and we await your pleasure in the carriage."

Monte Cristo nodded briefly, a renewed stab of satisfaction sending over him a feeling of well-being and purpose. He and Morcerf's son would be on holiday far from Paris when the world dropped away from Fernand's feet.

It had been more than two weeks since Mercédès had—for lack of a better term—entertained the Count of Monte Cristo in her bedchamber, and to her relief, she'd neither seen the man, nor heard from him. He wasn't even in Paris at this time; Mercédès knew this because he'd invited Albert to join him at yet another of his residences, this one in Normandy, and they had already been gone for two days.

She wasn't certain whether she should feel as if matters had been settled between them—for whatever his goal had been, certainly he must have felt some measure of satisfaction, even if she hadn't fully surrendered in the manner he'd demanded. After all, she'd been left there, humiliated and unsatisfied, for anyone to find.

Nor, miraculously, had Fernand made any reference to the events of that night. Mercédès, while perplexed about his silence, wasn't disappointed about his choice to ignore the events of that night. At first, he'd been furious about the humiliation of Baron Danglars' refusal to finalize the betrothal of Albert and Eugénie Danglars, which had already been announced publicly—but in retrospect, it was Danglars who'd ended up looking the fool, as the man he'd chosen to replace Albert as his future son-in-law had turned out to be nothing but a common thief masquerading as a prince. This discovery, to Danglars' embarrassment, had been made during the actual betrothal ceremony. Mercédès had heard that the prince had been sponsored by the Count of Monte Cristo, and considered how such a man as the count had made the error, mistaking a common criminal for a prince of Italy. Had it really been a mistake?

Mercédès had begun to wonder, in the last weeks, about these friendships—or, at least, acquaintances between Monte Cristo and the three men who had all been part of his life before Edmond Dantès' disappearance. Fernand had considered Edmond a rival for Mercédès' affections, although Mercédès had always loved only Edmond, and the men had had an uneasy friendship. Danglars had been purser on the *Pharaon* with him. And Villefort . . . Mercédès felt that familiar twisting in her stomach when she thought about Villefort and how she'd gone to him, asking for help and information about Edmond.

Begging.

She closed her eyes tightly, as if that would eliminate the memories, and turned her attention back to her original train of thought. Monte Cristo had ingratiated himself with those three men since his return to Paris, and now . . . odd things had begun to happen. Misfortunes.

Danglars' wife had lost a large sum of money on the exchange, and if rumors were true, the baron himself had lost even more money.

Mercédès had been greatly relieved when the betrothal between Eugénie Danglars and Albert had been canceled. But she couldn't help but wonder about it, especially since Danglars had gone ahead and betrothed his daughter to a man sponsored by the Count of Monte Cristo who turned out to be a common criminal. More embarrassment and humiliation for the baron.

And as for Monsieur Villefort . . . there was rumor that the three deaths in his household had not been accidental, but had, in fact, been murder. And his own daughter's betrothal to a wealthy young man had suddenly been canceled as well.

All of this in the last six weeks since Monte Cristo had arrived on the scene.

And now Fernand seemed to be very concerned with a newspaper story about Ali Pasha, whom he had helped protect when he was in the army in Janina. He was spending an inordinate amount of time in his private office, or at the upper house of parliament, and she'd seen very little of him.

But Mercédès cared little for Fernand's troubles or concerns and, as she'd been doing for more than two decades, stayed away from him as much as she could and occupied herself with her garden, and visiting with a few close friends. If Monte Cristo were involved in these misfortunes—and she couldn't quite fully believe that he had that extent of power and resources—it was no concern of hers.

For she had her own battle with him.

And as for that long night filled with memories that she preferred not to remember, but could not banish from her dreams—sounds, smells, sensations; skin to skin, lips on lips, heat and friction and dampness—Mercédès allowed herself little thought.

She refused to let herself dwell on the way she'd been left for Charlotte to find—arms bound, legs splayed, tight, cold breasts tipped to the ceiling. And Charlotte, who in that morning proved that she was without a doubt worthy of the high salary she was paid, merely untied her mistress' numb arms and immediately called for a warm bath.

So, for the two weeks since her bedchamber had been invaded by her husband and her former lover, Mercédès had resolutely pushed the thoughts away and concentrated her attention on the fully blooming gardens that needed to be cut and deadheaded. Certainly the gardeners did most of the work, but harvesting a few lavender branches and admiring the tiny yellow-star blooms on the few tomato bushes reminded her of simpler days back in Marseille, where she had worked in the gardens daily, and sat beneath olive trees with Edmond Dantès.

And thus it was that she was bent over a fragrant rosemary topiary, sticking several of its branches back into place so that the bird it depicted didn't look as though it was furred, when she heard the shouts from inside, the loud slamming of a door, and . . . Albert? Was that his voice raised in anger and shock? But he was supposed to be in Normandy with Monte Cristo. . . .

Mercédès stood, her heart pounding hard for no apparent reason.

"Father!" Now she heard Albert's bellow from the inside, the pounding of footsteps as he raced up the sweeping of stairs. He had returned early.

Unsure why she suddenly felt faint, why her mouth was desert dry, Mercédès gathered up the skirts of her oldest gown, crinolineless for comfort, and dirty now from where its hem had been trodden into the soil, and hurried toward the house. Disregarding the clumps of dirt that scattered from her slippers, she half ran through the French doors from the patio into the sitting room.

"Albert!" she called, and noticed that the house seemed particularly empty. And quiet. Except for the pounding of her son's feet.

"Slander!" she heard him cry from upstairs. "And libel! How dare he! Father!"

When he came bounding down the stairs, her son was alone. "Where's Father?" he said, and Mercédès saw that he was carrying the newspaper she recognized as *L'Impartial.* One that Fernand refused to read, for it was a product of the opposition government.

Albert's face was blotched red with fury, his hair mussed and hanging messily in his face. His eyes bulged with blue veins in their lids, and he looked as though he'd been traveling for days.

"I don't know, but, Albert, what is it?" Mercédès asked, uncertain whether he was accusing Fernand of libel and slander, or someone else of the crime.

"It's here, in the paper. I warned Beauchamp that if he ever printed anything like this again, I'd have satisfaction—and he did it a second time, this time with full-out accusation." Spit flew from his lips, he spoke so angrily. "The last article was bad enough, hinting that Father had something to hide, that he'd done something immoral when in Janina . . . but this! This horrible article, actually accusing Father of betraying the Ali Pasha outright! The man he was supposed to protect—Father would never have done that! Never!"

Mercédès didn't know what to think or to say. Something inside her was whirling and spiraling, and she felt absurdly faint. What had Fernand done? What had he *done*?

"Mama," Albert said, "you didn't know anything about these articles, did you? You haven't seen them—the first one was earlier this week, and I warned Beauchamp at the paper. . . . I told him. And then I got word in Normandy that this article had appeared. . . . The count of course allowed me the use of his best horses to get me back here immediately. Mama, you must sit down. And you must tell me where Father is."

"He is at work, at the upper house, of course," she told him. Her brain was functioning so slowly. She took the paper from Albert, and saw it, splashed over the front page: the story that Fernand de Morcerf had bought his count's title by betraying and foully murdering the man he'd been sworn to protect . . . that he'd sold the man's wife and daughter into slavery . . . that he'd been believed to be a hero when he received his title of comte . . . when, in reality, he was a murderer.

"It's not true, Mama," Albert was raging. "Don't look like that! It's not true, and this will be retracted! I'm going down to the paper now, and then I'll find Father. I cannot imagine how he's taking this, but he won't be alone. There's talk on the streets of a hearing to be held tomorrow, at the chambers. So quickly, but it's best to clear his name immediately."

Mercédès couldn't stop him. She watched the tails of his coat flap as he dashed from the room, and her heart shattered.

Not for Fernand, never for him. Never for that man.

Not for herself, for how her life would change if these accusations proved to be true. And she had no doubt they were, for she knew the kind of man Fernand was.

No, her heart broke for her son, who loved his father so, and would no longer be protected from the knowledge of what the man was really like.

Haydée sensed an air of anticipation about His Excellency as they settled in the coach, on their way to the opera again.

She had a strong feeling that, unlike the last time they attended the opera, the Morcerfs would not be in attendance this evening. Only yesterday she, Haydée, had appeared at a hearing at the chamber of the upper house in the Palais du Luxembourg to testify that the Comte de Morcerf had indeed murdered her father and sold his wife and daughter into slavery.

The Comte de Morcerf had been convicted and humiliated, and had left the palace in disgrace. For all she knew, he was locked away in some beautiful house somewhere here in Paris, with his kind wife, Mercédès.

But His Excellency, here in the carriage with her, had a certain aura about him, as if he were waiting for something. Something else. For it had been he who, returning early from Normandy, had ordered her to appear at the upper house, and to at last tell the story of what had happened to her family. And to point out the man who had betrayed them.

Monte Cristo looked particularly formidable tonight, handsome and dark and sleekly groomed, yet that harshness, that intensity that had been a part of him ever since she'd known him—but which had grown more noticeable since their arrival in Paris—seemed to simmer just below the surface more than ever.

Haydée felt as though something ugly was to occur, and that he was merely waiting for it.

"I hope that you shall be happy, at last," she said suddenly, there in the dimly lit carriage.

Monte Cristo turned his sharp-planed face toward her, and even in the low light, she could feel the spear of his eyes. "What do you mean, Haydée?"

She wasn't afraid of him, despite the frigidity in his voice. And since she'd unburdened herself in front of the upper house of Parliament, she felt freer. Her tragedy was now fully known.

If only Ali would stop averting his eyes whenever she came within his sight.

If only he would not have that flat, empty look in his face.

Her eyes suddenly filled with tears, and she pushed those worries away. She couldn't dwell on them now . . . though, dear heaven, her heart felt as though it was being shredded every time she saw him, she sensed there was something else at stake tonight in relation to her guardian . . . something bigger.

"I mean, Your Excellency," she began carefully, blinking rapidly to get rid of the tears, "you have been set upon this scheme of vengeance for so long . . . perhaps at last, now that it is done, you will find happiness."

For a long moment, as a taut silence stretched, Haydée feared she'd spoken out of turn. After all, she was a slave, even if he didn't really treat her like one.

"I do not think I know what happiness is," he said at last. Instead of being soft and contemplative, his words were cool and emotionless. "But I must believe that, having carried out God's will as His avenging angel that He'll look kindly on me when I'm no longer on this earth."

The carriage lurched to a stop, ending the conversation abruptly. When Haydée alighted from it, she tried to brush against Ali, to catch his eye, as she moved past him . . . but he set his dark gaze resolutely over her head. His face was sober and still, and she felt another stab in her heart.

Her moment of fulfillment, of deep, soul-crushing passion, had been so fleeting . . . and now meant absolutely nothing.

She had begun to understand that emptiness that seemed to pervade the Count of Monte Cristo.

Whatever it was that he expected to happen didn't occur as they strolled to their box—as always, the most prominent in the theater. Monte Cristo greeted everyone politely and even graciously, and of course it was Maximilien Morrel to whom he gave a kiss on each cheek and a heartfelt embrace.

Haydée saw some of the edge ease from the count's face now that he was in the presence of Monsieur Morrel. She was glad that the lonely count had at least one person about whom he truly seemed to care, and who showed the same affection for him.

It wasn't until the first intermission that the door of their box slammed open.

Haydée jumped and spun around in her chair, but the count

merely craned his head. "Ah, Albert," he said calmly, "I trust my horses brought you safely and speedily back from Normandy—what was it, two days ago?"

"I am not here to exchange false courtesies or to extend the pretense of friendship," replied the young Morcerf. "I have come to demand an explanation."

Haydée noticed, as the man stalked to the front of the box in what was clearly a confrontation, that he was pale and trembling. His voice carried easily beyond their box, and other operagoers were looking on in curiosity. Two other young men, both with set, serious faces, followed Albert Morcerf into the box, and she saw the way Ali shifted, making certain he was in their view.

"An explanation? At the opera?" Monte Cristo asked.

"Since you have hidden yourself away, it seems the only place that I can find you to demand an explanation for your perfidy is here," replied Albert Morcerf, still in a voice he took no care in subduing.

"I've been at my home all day," responded Monte Cristo mildly. "I would not consider bathing in one's own home 'hiding away.' Now, if you would kindly leave until you are in better control of your faculties, perhaps—"

"Do not play word games with me. I shall get you out of your home, and on my terms, for certain," Albert responded, and Haydée noticed that he was holding a white glove in his hands, twisting it about angrily, nervously. She thought that there must be some hidden meaning to this, for she saw the count's attention flicker to that white glove. "I demand an explanation for your actions, for disclosing these *lies* about my father—and you must understand that I—"

"And you should understand," interrupted the count silkily, "that if you wish an argument with me, *you will get it.* But I might also remind you that the truth is the truth, and accosting the bearer of such news will not change that. And, might I also suggest, Monsieur Morcerf, that it is also a bad habit to announce one's challenges from the rooftops so that all can hear."

Haydée heard the others outside the box, all of whom had been watching from their own seats, gasp. It was true: The name of Morcerf had been shouted from house to house during the last day, as the downfall of the Comte de Morcerf became public knowledge. And now the Count of Monte Cristo had all but announced to the city at large that there was an altercation between the two.

There was a sudden movement from Albert, as if he were about to step toward the count, the white glove brandished in his hand, but Maximilien Morrel caught his wrist in midair. The white glove fell to the floor, and as a silence more complete than during any performance descended over the theater, Monte Cristo reached over and picked up the mangled glove.

"Monsieur Morcerf," said the count in a horribly still voice, "I will consider your gauntlet thrown. Know that I will return it to you at dawn. Now leave or I will have you thrown out."

Thirteen
The Visitor

Later that night
Paris

Later that night, Haydée sat alone on the terrace in the back of the house at number 30 Champs-Élysées.

She and His Excellency had returned from the opera no more than an hour ago, having left during the second intermission amid the stares and whispers of the other theatergoers. There had been no sign of Albert Morcerf, but within the ripple of murmurs, she'd heard the sibilant syllables of his name following them out of the theater.

The chair she'd chosen here on the terrace was made of curling, curving wrought iron, and its handle was cool under her fingertips as she closed them around it. Other than that, she tried not to feel anything, for she feared if she thought about what had happened . . . and what was to occur at dawn this morning . . . she would suffocate.

In her lap lay the paper His Excellency had given her upon their return—and the very reason she'd fled the confines of the house, needing to breathe fresh night air. It was the only way she could keep from crying and screaming.

She could not bear to lose another father.

A quiet noise drew her attention, and she looked up as one of the doors opened onto the covered, flat-stoned patio on which she sat.

Ali.

Her stomach burned and she looked down at the paper in her hands; it was too dark to read the words there, but she knew what they said.

When he touched her shoulder, she shook her head, willing him to leave. When he did not, when those strong fingers curled a little more deeply into her shoulder, she said, "I want to be alone. Go away, Ali."

He removed his fingers and, before she quite knew what was happening, yanked her out of the chair and onto his massive lap as he sat on a stone bench. His arms were large and warm and so strong around her, and Haydée felt a bit of something stir within her . . . deep in her belly . . . but she pushed it away.

She couldn't let it bubble up, let the hope rise again.

Then she became aware that the light filtering from the house illuminated Ali's face, and her own, on the bench where they sat. Firmly, he turned her so that she faced him and could see his strong, solid face and the gleam of his ebony head and chin and cheeks. His hands moved sharply, briefly.

He won't die.

Haydée shook her head, the tears starting to well there again. "There's always a chance," she said.

He was challenged, so he will shoot first. He won't miss. He never misses.

"But . . . what if Albert Morcerf shoots out of turn? I couldn't bear it, and, Ali . . . it's not because I love him like—" She caught herself from finishing and snatched in a deep breath, then steadied her voice. "He's like another father to me, and I don't want to lose him."

He made you free. He's protected you by making you free.

She looked down at the paper, still clutched in her hand. Yes, he'd always said he would make her free, and now he'd done so—but free to do what? He'd never treated her like anything but a daughter, and there was no other place she wanted to be, no one she wanted to be *with*—

He told me what you said.

Haydée looked at Ali now, realizing his mouth was so close to hers . . . so close, and she could feel the warm, gentle brush of his breath, scented minty with caraway seed. She almost gave in to her need and moved into him for a taste, but she didn't. No, she couldn't do that to herself again.

You asked him to free me instead of you. His arms tightened around her, and she felt the soft touch of his hand over her hair, still coiled and braided, French-style, at the back of her head. *Thank you.*

"But he didn't listen," she replied, and shoved the paper at him. He pushed her hand back to her own lap.

There are things you don't understand. Things like honor between men.

"I don't care about honor," she raged, suddenly feeling the sorrow and fear ready to burst forth. "Honor caused my father to die. It caused him to believe in a man who had none and who killed him in cold blood. Honor is nothing."

Suddenly, she was bawling into Ali's tunic, her body shaking, his arms tight around her. He smelled so good, felt so strong and warm and close, and that little swirling sensation in her belly began to uncurl and simmer there. And she held her breath and forced it away.

The next thing she knew, he was kissing her, carefully, sensually . . . in a manner that had never been between them. As if he wanted to show her how gentle he could be, his full lips molding softly to hers, his hands open wide over her narrow back, pushing her close to him.

Haydée felt the stirring of his cock between them, shifting in his thin, silky trousers beneath her thigh, and a sudden spear of lust shot to her sex as she remembered the feel of him inside her. Oh, wonder.

She pulled away. She wanted to be with him. She wanted him so badly her fingers trembled and her breasts were tight, and her quim was awakening . . . but not this way.

Not because he thought he owed her. Not because of his foolish honor, believing that she should be thanked for asking for his freedom—for offering to exchange.

She wanted him to want her as an equal. As one he loved, and with no qualms, no regrets, no hidden agendas.

"No," she said, pulling herself away from him. The taste of him was still on her lips; they tingled and pounded now, and she wanted nothing more than to bury her mouth back against his. "No, Ali, not . . . this way," she said.

Then, before he could respond, a sudden altercation in the house drew their attention.

"I must see him!" a voice cried urgently. A woman's voice.

Haydée scrambled off Ali's lap, her heart pounding. Thank goodness. She was off toward the house, her gown, now crushed and wrinkled and off-kilter, tripping her on her first step before she caught up her skirts.

"I'm sorry, madam, but—"

Haydée interrupted Bertuccio's calm placation as she hurried into the foyer, which was just beyond the sitting room that opened to the patio. "His Excellency will see her," Haydée announced, slightly out of breath—due perhaps more to the kisses than her running. She felt Ali as he came up beside her.

"But, Mistress Haydée—"

She laid a hand on Bertuccio's arm, and with a quick, comforting glance at the Comtesse de Morcerf, she drew the majordomo aside. "If you recall, I assisted you in attending to His Excellency when you needed me to do so," she said quietly, and much more calmly than she felt. "You must trust me that he will see the Comtesse de Morcerf."

"He instructed that he was not to be disturbed. He will be furious if his orders are not obeyed."

"I will take it upon myself, Bertuccio. It was I who sent the message to the comtesse, notifying her about the count's challenge, and I who will bring her to him. If there is any ire to be dealt with, I shall do it." And with that, accompanied by a thudding heart and a calm certainty, she turned to Mercédès. "Come with me. I'll take you to him."

"Thank you, Haydée," Mercédès replied. For a woman who must be terrified about the prospect of her son meeting the

Count of Monte Cristo in a duel only hours away, she looked remarkably composed. Except for the strain around her mouth, and an unusual brightness in her dark eyes, she looked just as beautiful and gracious as she'd been at the theater.

Haydée could fully understand why His Excellency could not forget this woman.

With a quick glance at Ali, who'd moved to stand behind her, Haydée took Mercédès' arm and led her up the stairs, fully aware of Ali's solid footfalls on the steps behind her. If there was to be any problem with the count, Ali would be there to assist.

But Haydée did not think that His Excellency would turn the Comtesse Morcerf away.

No indeed, for this confrontation had been a long time coming.

The house at number 30 Champs-Élysées was even more opulent and exotic than Mercédès could have imagined. Despite her desperation, and the knowledge that her world was crumbling around her, she noticed the fine furnishings, the elegant decor, and the colors and textures that bespoke great wealth and impeccable taste, all with the flair of the Orient—for it seemed easier to let her mind soak up these details than to think about the future. She noticed black lacquer tables, painted with golden grass and shiny red birds. Low tables and many cushions, flat chairs and teapots. Rich, sleek mahogany and olive wood. Bamboo and silk hangings. And some more familiar French and Spanish pieces as well, to set off the Chinese and Indian styles.

Of course . . . for Sinbad had exuded that same aura of the Far East. He must have lived there for years.

Mercédès took a deep breath to ease her racing pulse as Haydée opened two wide, ceiling-high doors at the top of a flight of stairs and, with a little bow, gestured for her to enter.

The doors closed silently behind Mercédès, and she was alone in a vast chamber. Her first impression was the undercurrent of spice—a pleasant, warm scent hovering in the air. She stepped away from the door and looked around. The area was lit by moonlight outlining tall windows across the room, and a few lamps scattered about, giving a soft yellow glow, tingeing gold the upholstery on two low chairs next to a knee-high table. A desk stood nearby, its smooth surface broken by an ink bottle, pens, and a small lamp.

She saw a large bed at the opposite end of the room, its curtains pulled wide and its lake-colored silk coverings shining in the light, piled with tasseled pillows and lush cushions. Mercédès realized with a start that she must be in the count's bedchamber.

And it was then, as her gaze skittered fully around the room for the first time, that she noticed the chairs in front of the tall windows. And the strong profile of the man seated in one of them, looking out over what would be dawn in a matter of hours.

"How did you get in here?" he asked. His voice, calm and deep, nevertheless held a tightness that clipped the words as they broke the silence.

"Does it matter? I'm here now." Mercédès walked toward him, her heart racing, her palms dampening under her gloves. She *felt* him. . . . It was if a skein of threads stretched between them suddenly, taut and vibrating . . . but fine and as easily broken as a cobweb. "Why do you sit in the dark like this?"

He shifted slightly in his chair, not to turn to look at her, but, apparently, merely to move his arm to a more comfortable position, for he seemed to keep his attention focused on the window beyond. "Is it dark? I can see everything quite well. The fear in your eyes, the proud lift of your chin. Your gown is a pale green. It reminds me of the depths of shallow sea near Singapore. It's covered with much too much lace, and too many—what are they called? Those pieces, like little waves near the bottom."

"Flounces."

"Ah, flounces. I can even see the tiny pink flowers on the flounces, the dark green braid the color of olive leaves, and pale blue trim along the edge of the neckline and sleeves. It's all quite clear to me, down to the texture of the tiny plaits in your hair. But then . . . when one has spent fourteen years in darkness, day and night, night and day . . . one's eyesight in the dark becomes remarkably clear."

Mercédès had come to stand before him. "Fourteen years?"

"Fourteen years in Château d'If." The bitterness in his voice made her stomach quail. "Why are you here?"

"I'm fairly certain you know why I am here," she replied. She knew she should be on her knees, begging him, pleading with him . . . but she just couldn't. Not . . . yet. Not when this odd quivering sensation buzzed in the air between them, lifting the hair on her arms, making her insides lurch and her heart thump. Not when he was so cold and unfeeling. "If you were smart enough to uncover that which my husband took such care in hiding, and to unravel it just as you obviously have . . . publicly and dramatically . . . then you have no need to ask why I am here."

"You're here to ask me why I destroyed your husband. And

to ask me not to meet your son at dawn, with pistols and my seconds behind me."

She couldn't make out the nuances of his expression, but he sounded bored. Careless.

Mercédès walked over to the nearest lamp, and turned it up as brightly as it would go. Now, when she turned back, she could see his face, the closed expression, the firm lips, the intensity in his eyes. She felt the tension vibrating from him. "I care nothing for Fernand. And if it was because of you that his own perfidy has become public knowledge, then I hold no grudge against you. And in fact I can see that justice should—and must—be done." She saw surprise release briefly in his face, but she continued. "But I am here to b—ask that you spare my son. That you not meet him tomorrow."

"But it was your son who insulted me, madam."

"But you will kill him." With an effort, she kept the sob from her voice, kept it steady and strong.

"Of course I will." Now he turned and faced her, his face warm and golden in the lamplight, but etched sharply with shadows and anger. And pain. Pain, lurking there in the depths of his eyes. But no mercy.

Mercédès felt her heart lurch horribly. He truly meant to do it. "But . . . why? What has Albert ever done to you? He is young and innocent of his father's immorality."

"It is written in the Holy Bible that the sins of the fathers should be visited upon the sons—to three generations. And aside of that, the loss of his son will further injure your husband."

"And me," she whispered, suddenly empty. "And *me.*" She looked down at him, and their gazes locked solidly. Determination and faint mockery flared in his dark eyes; they were no longer as flat and emotionless as she'd been used to seeing. "You would take my son from me?"

His gaze did not waver. "I have waited many years to make this trip to Paris. I'll not be dissuaded from this."

Her lips would barely move, they were so cold. Her whole body suddenly felt as though she'd been thrust in an icy sea and her hands began to tremble against the sides of her gown. "Edmond, what has befallen you that you could do such a thing?" She knew her voice came out in a soft wail, a low, horror-stricken one, but she didn't care. It was incomprehensible to her. "What has happened to you, Edmond Dantès?"

His eyes closed for a moment, severing that unsettling connection between them. "Edmond Dantès . . . it has been so long since I've heard that name. Spoken it." He opened his eyes, and they blazed up at her from where he sat. "Edmond Dantès is dead. He died a decade ago."

"No," she said, sinking to her knees next to him. She reached up and grasped his wrist where it rested on the arm of his chair, closing her fingers tightly around it. "Don't lie to me, Edmond. I know it's you. I know you're still in there—behind that mask, that tight, fake, closed, dark mask of politeness, of inscrutable politeness. I know you're there. I knew it the moment I saw you . . . and you know it is I, Mercédès. The woman who has always loved you."

"Loved me?" He jerked his hand away, snapping it so hard that she lost her balance and lurched toward the chair. "How long did you wait before you spread your legs for Morcerf? How long?"

Anger sliced through her. Anger and horror and disgust. And deep grief. He could have no idea what she'd gone through.

She pulled awkwardly to her feet, tripping on her gown as she replied, "You know how long I waited until I married Fernand, Edmond. You know because I told you . . . Sinbad."

"Sinbad?" There was a faint note of admiration in his voice. "How long have you known?"

"Long enough to wonder why, if you had come back to Marseille in disguise ten years ago, you didn't tell me it was you. You didn't tell me, Edmond. . . . You didn't come back to me when you could have." Now, suddenly, she was sobbing, shaking, and she reached out blindly, her fingers closing over the heavy brocade curtains to steady herself as she looked down at him. "*You let me think you were dead.* For twenty-four years."

"You were married to Fernand," he replied harshly. "What was I to do? You waited a mere eighteen months for the man you said you'd love forever."

"I waited as long as I could . . . but then I had no choice," she said softly, still gripping the heavy velvet, leaning her cheek against it. She couldn't tell him why; it was better that he believed she'd grown tired of waiting than to know the truth about her, and the choices she'd made, the bargains she'd wrought. "I had no word from you, nothing. Villefort would tell your father, Monsieur Morrel, me, *nothing* of you. It was as if you'd disappeared, Edmond. Vanished. Your father died a year later of a broken heart, certain you were dead. I would have done anything to find you, Edmond. Anything. I believed . . ." Her breath hitched, catching her words. She gathered herself together and continued. "I believed if you were alive, you would contact me—"

"I was in Château d'If. There was no contact. There was nothing, Mercédès—nothing but dark and rats and worm-filled bread and brackish water. There was no light, no voices, nothing but stone walls and one threadbare blanket. No hope, no words, no life. Nothing. Nothing but the memory of the woman who swore she'd love me forever. That was the only thing that kept me sane for those first four years."

Her lips trembled so hard she could barely speak. Her stomach roiled and pitched, and she felt as though she would never be right again. Oh God. What horrors he must have lived through. "But why, Edmond? How did you get there? And how . . . how did you ever get out?"

"It was your husband, in part, who sent me there. He and Danglars and Villefort."

Villefort. Her stomach pitched anew. "What—how?"

"I didn't know for certain while I was there, but once I escaped, I was able to confirm the suspicions that I'd formed with the help of a fellow prisoner, Abbé Faria." A tinge of sorrow laced his voice; then he continued in the flat tone he'd been using.

"Fernand and Danglars conspired against me—Fernand because, of course, he wanted you, though I cannot understand why, now that I know he prefers men—and Danglars because he thought he should have the captaincy of the *Pharaon*. Greed and jealousy, Mercédès. Greed and jealousy sent an innocent man to the deepest, darkest of prisons for fourteen years.

"The captain of the *Pharaon*, who died while we were on that last voyage, gave me a letter to deliver to a man in Paris by the name of Monsieur Noirtier. You may know him as the grandfather of Valentine Villefort, and the father of Monsieur Villefort. As you know, I was not able to read, and I had no way of knowing that the letter was information for the Bonaparte sympathizers who were helping Napoleon in his escape from Elba. But somehow Danglars and Fernand discovered that this letter was in my possession, and they wrote an anonymous note reporting it to the crown prosecutor—who was, of course, Villefort.

"Villefort called for me—that was when the officers came to take me from our betrothal party—and questioned me about the letter, which I immediately gave him and told him I had no idea what it said. He would have released me. In fact, he had already done so, and I was walking out the door when he opened it and read his father's name. Because the letter incriminated his father as a Bonaparte sympathizer, Villefort knew that this knowledge could never come to light, for it would ruin his own position as a crown prosecutor and career as loyalist to the king—and since I was the only other person who could possibly know the information in the letter, he sent me away in secret to the prison.

"I never had a trial. I never saw anyone where I could plead my case . . . and for a long time, I thought it was a mistake that would be corrected. But it never was."

By now, Mercédès had released her grip on the curtains. She'd slid to the floor, and was in a pile of skirts and crinolines, staring up at him, at the man she'd loved, with horror and disbelief. Her cheeks and bodice were soaked wet from tears, and she felt them plop in a steady stream onto her hands, seeping through her gloves. "My God, my God, Edmond . . ."

He seemed not to hear her, for he continued steadily, as if nothing would stop him from telling the story. "The only reason I was able to escape was because of my fellow prisoner, Abbé Faria. I thank God for the day I met him, for it was he who kept me from descending into madness, and who stopped me from committing suicide when he accidentally tunneled into my cell. He thought it was the way out, and he was horribly, thankfully wrong." Here again was a different note in his voice, a bit of wry humor; and then it was gone.

"We visited each other in our cells secretly for ten years, during which he gave me a complete education and told me about a secret treasure buried on the Isle of Monte Cristo. When the abbé died, I was able to replace his body with my own in his burial shroud, so when the jailers came to take his corpse away, I went instead. I thought they meant to bury the shroud, but instead, they wrapped chains around my legs and threw me off of a cliff, never knowing they had done so to a living man. I managed to escape from the chains, somehow, miraculously, and that was when I knew God wanted me to live.

"And that my purpose was to avenge the wrongs done to me . . . and to repay those who had done right by me."

"That was why you gave the purse of money, and the diamond, to save the Morrels' shipping company," Mercédès said quietly. "As Sinbad, and as Lord Wilmore."

He gave a brief nod. "Yes. And so . . . now . . . here we are."

"You came to Paris to destroy the men who sent you to prison. And . . . and me."

Monte Cristo—for even now, she wasn't certain she could ever think of him as Edmond again—gave her a steady look. "Danglars' house of cards, which was built by the same money loaned, and reloaned, and reloaned, is about to fall down about him. In two more days, he'll be finished, completely destroyed. All because of his own greed and dishonesty.

"Villefort's daughter is a suspected poisoner, and in perhaps another day, a young man will step forward—you may have heard of him, for he was engaged to be married to Eugénie Danglars. He was thought to be a prince, but, alas, he is nothing but a common criminal. And he will step forward, likely tomorrow, to announce that he is the illegitimate son of Villefort and the Baroness Danglars, birthed in secret and buried alive, *left to die*, some twenty-two years ago. It is only a matter of days before Villefort is finished."

Mercédès could not control a gasp of horror. Left to die? Buried alive?

"And your husband . . . he has lost his job and his position, and his wealth will soon follow. And his hotheaded son will soon be taught a lesson—"

"Edmond!" She lurched toward him, grasping at his arm from her crumpled position on the floor. "You would truly do that? Send an innocent man to his death? My son? Please, Edmond, please. I beg you. . . . I'm . . . begging . . . you." The tears were falling fast and hard, and she heard the same desperation in her voice that she'd had when she'd begged Villefort all those years ago. Begged and pleaded for some news, something about Edmond. Anything.

She felt the flexing of the count's muscles beneath her fingers, the slight shift, the barest tremble. Then, suddenly, all of the tension drained out of him. He looked down at her, his face dark and tight. But contemplative and suddenly—suddenly—quite arch and smug. "I won't shoot at him. But you must give me something in return."

"Whatever you want. Name it, Edmond. Whatever your revenge against me needs to be, I willingly give it in exchange for the life of my son."

"Eighteen months you waited for me . . . and so I desire eighteen months of you. . . ." His voice was smooth and sleek, like a coiled snake. "As my slave—my willing, subservient, groveling slave. Eighteen months of doing my every command, following my every whim." He looked at her, his eyes burning into hers, and she felt a deep shiver inside. Damp sprang anew to her palms, and her mouth dried and her throat tightened.

So. He would have it at last. Have her the way he wanted her, have his revenge, have her under his control. But to save the life of her child, there was no question what she would do.

"I'll do it," she told him without hesitation, without fear.

For nothing could be worse than she'd experienced at the hands of Monsieur Villefort. Nothing.

He seemed to relax further, to release his last remaining bit of tension. He glanced out the window, and she saw the faint color of dawn over the squat cream-colored buildings. "You will return here tonight at eight o'clock. You'll need no clothing, only one dress and perhaps one night rail. You won't need a maid. Do give my regards to your husband."

She stood, pulling to her feet on stiff legs, awkward from the weight and volume of her skirts. He made no move to assist her.

Fourteen
Acceptance & Regret

Early the next morning
Paris

As dawn approached, he planned for death.

He wore a dark coat with a crisp white shirt under it. A simple, subdued neckcloth of bloodred, appropriately, and a dark brown waistcoat. Fine trousers of rich brown, and butter-soft leather boots the color of ink.

No one would say that the Count of Monte Cristo appeared less fashionable in death than in life.

He walked over to the chair in which he'd sat only hours ago—when Mercédès had begged for her son's life—looking out once again at the city spread before him. He couldn't help but recall the day he'd first arrived here in Paris and stood at this very same span of windows, watching the sun prepare to rise.

How much he'd accomplished in these last two months. Nearly everything he'd planned had been seen to its fruition . . . or soon would be. Caderousse was dead, though by no fault of Monte Cristo. Danglars, Villefort and Morcerf were only days—perhaps hours—from their final ruin.

And the beauty of it all was the knowledge that these men had created their own downfalls through years of deceit, dishonesty, greed, jealousy—even beyond what they'd done to poor Edmond Dantès.

All Monte Cristo had done was help expose the ugly underbelly of the lives they'd chosen to live.

His only regret was that he wouldn't live to see it happen, that they would never know who'd exposed their true beings. That Edmond Dantès had come back for his revenge.

Yet perhaps it was best this way, that his life should end at the hands of Albert Morcerf. Monte Cristo smoothed his fingers over the back of the chair, letting his hand drop to the sleek wood of its curved arm as he moved to sit down in it once more.

In retrospect, he couldn't believe that he'd given his word to Mercédès—after all this, all of his years of planning and plotting, burning with the heat of vengeance, he'd softened that little bit, edging back from his goals, changing the ultimate ending he'd planned. He'd die instead of Morcerf's son, and his empty life would end.

As the one challenged in the duel, Monte Cristo would have the honor of shooting first. He would aim in the air and fire harmlessly into the trees. Then Albert, who was better than a fair shot, would take aim and put a bullet into Monte Cristo's heart, finishing the destruction his mother had begun years ago.

And yet . . . for the first time that he could remember, he

felt . . . easier. Lighter. Just the slightest bit, but enough that he noticed the lessening of tension in his chest, the ease in his neck and jaw. Something like serenity.

He would have no blood on his hands.

Glancing down to where his wrist rested on the mahogany arm, his fingers slipping around under it, he remembered how Mercédès had gripped his hand there just a short time ago. Her pale green skirts were piled awkwardly on the ground around her, her oval face tear-streaked but determined, her rich, thick hair still twisted and braided and coiled into some impossible design . . . from which only a few wisps had dared come loose. Her eyes. Dark and sorrowful, boring into him . . . seeing him.

Seeing . . . what?

A little shiver skittered over the back of his shoulders, and he realized his hands were trembling. He saw those lush lips, red, always so red and wide and inviting, her pert chin, the slightly tilted tooth, that smooth golden skin . . . felt such warm curves beneath his palms. Remembered the delicate smell of some flower she preferred.

Monte Cristo swallowed, gathered his thoughts back together, reminding himself . . . and felt the slow burn of anger replace the tease of lust, of memory, that had tugged at him. Tried to soften him.

She was the one piece of his plan that would be left unfulfilled, the one bit of vengeance unserved . . . and perhaps the one that dug the deepest. Of all of them—Caderousse, Danglars, Morcerf, Villefort, Mercédès—it had been her face that had haunted and mocked him the most. The one that disturbed his sleep so deeply.

They'd all been heinous. But Mercédès . . .

Monte Cristo shuddered in his chair as dawn broke along the horizon.

He should have done what he wanted to do: what every tendon and muscle and urge, every bit of consciousness, drove him to. He should have dragged her into his arms and kissed those mocking lips, made her cry and sigh and beg for him, taken her to the bed and driven himself inside her until he could forget. Until he was sure she never would.

Then perhaps he could go to his death satisfied.

Resolute, he stood, walked to the desk, and picked up the box that held his dueling pistols.

If, by the grace of God, he made it back alive, then he would know his vengeance was not yet complete.

And God help her if he returned.

Fifteen
The Punishment

Later that afternoon
Paris

"His Excellency has returned."

Mercédès looked up, her heartbeat jolting into hard spikes. She'd returned to the count's house as requested—required—some hours ago, well past dawn, and had been shown to his chambers again, only this time they'd been empty. Still smelling of his essence, still vibrating with his presence . . . yet empty.

Left to her own devices, she'd paced and sat and paced more. . . . She'd opened the windows and the large door that led to the balcony, and walked out there for a time, breathing in the summer air, looking over at the sparkling Seine dotted with boats . . . then back into the lush chamber, wondering what would happen here tonight.

And every night for the next eighteen months.

When she had left the home of her husband earlier today to come to Monte Cristo, she'd told Fernand she would never return. She and Albert, after he had returned from meeting Monte Cristo, had both packed the few things they wished to keep from their lives as Morcerfs, leaving him and his false, superficial life. Albert would join the army, and she . . . she would live out this eighteen-month sentence with Monte Cristo. Then she would go back to Marseille and live the simple life she'd always intended. The one she'd been meant to live.

Now the door had opened without a knock—the first sign that Monte Cristo indeed meant to treat her as a servant, rather than a guest—and Bertuccio walked in as he delivered his announcement. He was followed by a young woman dressed as a servant carrying a pile of cherry red silk.

"He is uninjured," said the majordomo after a moment. Perhaps he'd expected her to ask . . . but Mercédès hadn't needed to. She already knew from Albert that he'd return alive, but no other details about what had occurred. "He is uninjured, and he will expect you to attend him momentarily. Galya will assist you."

Mercédès bowed her head in acknowledgment, keeping her face blank and her bearing regal until Bertuccio closed the door behind him, leaving her alone with the maid. He needed to give no further instructions, for it was obvious that the maid was to help her don what appeared to be a simple red gown, little more than a man's long shirt, shapeless but for a slender belt that tied at the waist. It covered her from neck to floor.

Perhaps ten minutes after the maid left, the door opened again. Mercédès heard it behind her; but she'd turned so that her back was to it, and the view of the city was spread in front of her. Monte Cristo might expect her to do his every bidding, but she would not dance attendance upon him. Not when he'd held her son's life as ransom for her servitude.

The door closed with a soft click of finality that seemed to hang in the air for a moment, then was banished by the soft swish of trouser legs brushing against each other.

"You told him everything."

Whatever she'd expected, it hadn't been that half-bewildered, half-angry statement. Unsure how to respond, she remained silent, continuing to stare out over the streets and houses below and beyond, at the shimmer of the river, the vendors and their carts of food . . . as her fingers slipped nervously over the front of the silk tunic. The back of her neck prickled, and she felt him moving into the room, toward her . . . but keeping a distance.

"When you left here last night, you went to Albert and told him what they did to—Dantès. What his father did. You knew he would call off the duel."

"Is that what happened?" she asked at last, still watching the sailboats beyond. There was one with a white sail and blue stripe that zigzagged from shore to shore with amazing speed. "He called off the duel?" Albert hadn't given her the details, only that Monte Cristo was unharmed.

"He refused to shoot. He apologized and asked my forgiveness."

"So you forgave *him* for the sins of his *parents*. How merciful of you."

"I forgave him for insulting me." His words were short and sharp.

Mercédès said nothing, and remained resolutely facing away, still waiting. Waiting for a command, waiting for a touch, waiting for something. He moved again, closer, and she heard the quiet whisk of clothing, then a soft flutter that sounded as if something had been tossed away, onto a chair, perhaps.

"Yet you aren't surprised. You knew I would come back, hale and hearty, and yet you returned here."

"To fulfill my part of the bargain. To serve my sentence, to fulfill your need for vengeance. To complete your plan." Now she turned toward him, knowing that anger sparkled in her eyes even as she kept her demeanor calm and undisturbed. She wouldn't let him know how the blood was racing through her veins, how her stomach curled and twisted in a combination of apprehension and anticipation, how even now, the sight of this man who was no longer Edmond Dantès—yet *was*—still managed to move her. To make her mouth dry and her heart slam harder, and her fingers itch to touch his warm skin.

He stood half a room away, yet it was as if he were pressing against her. His eyes bored into her, dark and sharp, as though trying to read her and understand why she didn't cower from him. He'd removed his coat and neckcloth and now wore only dark trousers and his white shirt, along with boots and a waistcoat. His hair fell in disarray, in long, straight spikes that brushed his cheeks and jaw, giving him a sort of animalistic look. His sensual lips, the top one straight and narrow, the bottom one full, as though he'd just bitten it—she looked away, down at the hands that were working on the buttons of his waistcoat, and she straightened her spine. She couldn't allow any wistfulness to surface . . . or he would destroy her.

"Where would you like me, Your Excellency? On my hands

and knees, or spread on the bed?" she said coolly, reaching to pull the pins from her hair.

His fingers paused, then continued their task as he gave a curt nod toward her. "Take that off."

"As you wish." Her eyes boldly meeting his, challenging, she untied the slender belt and let it fall to the floor. "It seems to me we could have eliminated this step by dismissing the maid after she removed my shift—instead of giving me this to wear." Her fingers shook, but she held the neckline of her tunic firmly and whisked it over her head. The flair of the silk sent a light breeze over her, tightening her nipples and provoking little shivers over her skin.

Monte Cristo's gaze moved over her naked body as he pulled off his waistcoat. "An excellent suggestion, that. I'll make certain to clarify it in the future." He sat on the bed and began to pull off one of his boots—a task with which he would normally have his valet assist. Stubbornly, Mercédès made no move to help.

He glanced up at her with those dark eyes as the first boot thumped to the floor. "As for the future, and my other expectations: You'll attend social engagements with me. On my arm, in the eyes of society—and make no mistake, the nature of our relationship will be clear to all."

"And how will I be dressed during these occasions? Thusly?" She gestured to her naked self. "That would cause quite a stir." Monte Cristo yanked off his other boot and dropped it to the floor a bit more loudly than the first one, but he did not respond.

Mercédès felt the need to goad him further; she wanted this tension, this waiting, to stop and for him to do something besides give her those flat, emotionless looks. She knew something else lurked beneath them, and by God, she wanted it out in the open—whether it be passion or anger or sorrow, she wanted something from him . . . something, so she knew how to let herself feel. "And will you also invite your friends to join us as well? The Comte de Pleiurs would be quite interested, I do believe. And Monsieur Hardegree, before he returns to London."

He stood suddenly, and she saw that his fingers had curled into his palms. Then they relaxed and he replied, "I'm sorry to disappoint you, but that will never happen. Come here."

"Shall I play the valet for you, master?" Mercédès asked, walking toward him, her heart thumping madly.

But when she reached to touch the placket of his trousers, his hand whipped out to close tightly around her wrist. He gave a sharp pull and she bumped flush into him. One strong hand came up behind her neck as he released her wrist to wrap his other arm around her waist, and then he bent his stark, angry face to hers.

His fingers bit into the soft sides of her nape, and his mouth was just as hard and firm. No contest, no mercy, just strong, deep plunder that left her breathless and pulsing. He pulled back just as abruptly, releasing her, and without another word, with no change of expression, he began to unfasten the placket of his trousers. His lips—full and dark red—were slightly parted, and she heard the soft whistle of breath between them as he stared down at her while his fingers fumbled with the buttons.

Mercédès licked her lips, suddenly dry, but puffy and warm from the kiss. She couldn't read him, but God help her, that kiss had left her wanting more.

With rough movements, he opened his trousers, sliding them and the drawers beneath down lean hips. His cock lifted from their depths and was suddenly before her, between them, raging purple and red.

She didn't need to be told what he wanted. . . . She sank to her knees on the thick rug and lifted her palms to slide them under his tight, dark-haired ballocks, curling her fingers around the demanding erection above them. He gave a quiet sigh, and she felt his body lurch softly against her, as if in surprise, or relief, that she was touching him.

He was heavy and warm in her hands, and Mercédès tightened her fingers around his length, moving the foreskin back and forth in a light, teasing motion . . . just enough to reveal the crown of his head. When she leaned forward to slip the soft, round tip into her mouth, she felt the sensation of him tensing everywhere, against her, as if waiting for . . . something. For her to stop, to pull away, to tease—as he'd done to her?

But then she forgot about the games, and tasted the salty drip of moisture on her tongue, felt the warmth of his flesh stretching her lips, and when he gave a low, desperate groan, she felt a matching wave of arousal slash through her. He was thick and firm, and he swelled more and sighed again as she sank and rose against him, tilted and tongued, pushing and pulling his hips in a long, slow, easy rhythm that had him trembling against her face. His musky male smell, sharply familiar and arousing, filled her nostrils, and the velvety heat of his cock tasted heavy and salty in her mouth.

With a sudden cry—a low exclamation—he shoved his cock into the back of her mouth, and as she gasped, she felt the shot of his seed spurt into her throat as he pulsed against tongue and lips and teeth.

When he finished, he released her shoulders roughly and

turned away before she could speak. The sticky, salty taste still in her mouth, Mercédès rose to her feet and stood on trembling knees, fully aware of the way her nipples had grown taut and her quim moist.

"On the bed," he said curtly, still not looking at her.

As she walked over, her stomach spinning and her heart slamming hard in her chest, she heard the quiet *whoosh* behind her and knew he'd taken off his shirt. A soft shucking sound followed, and the hair on the back of her neck prickled. He was as naked as she.

"What is this?" she asked, looking at the bed as she slid onto the haphazard pile of cushions and pillows. "I see no restraints? No ties? How surprising." She rolled onto her back and propped herself on one elbow, one knee bent in the air and the other leg extended straight in front of her, facing the side of the bed.

He walked closer and now she could see him, completely naked in full light for the first time in nearly a quarter century. She suddenly couldn't swallow; her throat constricted and her tongue felt like a piece of cloth: clumsy and dry. If Edmond Dantès, at nineteen, had been tall and wiry and lean, tanned on the arms and in the vee of the chest, sparse hair growing there and along the line of his belly . . . all with the promise of growing into a fully mature man . . . the Count of Monte Cristo had more than fulfilled that promise.

Still lean and slender in the torso and hips, he was now darker with hair, which fully covered his upper chest and grew to a long slim line to the curling bush that held his cock and ballocks. His shoulders were wide and square, his arms had grown thicker, curved with muscle, and his thighs . . . powerful and wide, jutting from the sharp edge of hips and a flat, hairy belly.

As if skin were a premium, there wasn't a bit of pudge or paunch anywhere on his body; it was lean and golden and tight, like that of a statue. Tighter than any man she'd seen naked.

"Turn over," he said. His voice sounded uneven, and his eyes did not meet hers.

Her heart gave a little jump of nervousness, but Mercédès did as he bid, rolling onto her belly so that she lay across the bed, head at one side, feet facing him at the other. The pile of cushions was to her left, near the head of the bed.

"Spread your legs. And your arms."

The pressure against her pounding sex was a relief, and she shifted so that she tilted her hips and pressed it more firmly into the bed beneath her. She spread her legs in a gentle vee, and reached beyond her head until her fingers curled over the edge of the mattress, pulling herself flat. Turning her face to the side, she rested on her cheek and tried to see him . . . but he was standing at her feet, out of sight.

There was silence for a long moment, and her apprehension and tension grew when he made no move to touch her. The skin over her back prickled, rising in little bumps, as she anticipated him. Would he suddenly shove his cock inside her quim, from behind? Would he take her in the ass? Would he slash at her with a whip?

Her heart was pounding faster now, and she felt the trembling begin deep inside, and fought to keep from showing it. None of it would be new to her. . . . It had all been done before.

She'd survived it. She could survive this—whatever it would be.

The silence stretched, and she wondered suddenly if he'd

gone silently from the room and left her there to wait and worry. Just as she thought to lift her head, he spoke. His voice was hard and brittle. "Don't move."

She sagged back against the bed, gripping it with her fingers, still fighting the tremors that threatened to burst forth . . . yet aware of her swollen pip, of her wet quim and pointed nipples . . . all of them seeming to throb harder as she waited.

Waited.

When he touched her finally, she started and gave a little cry. His hand closed over her nape, as if to hold her there—not harshly, not strong enough to make her feel stifled or want to fight for her life—but enough to make it clear that she wasn't to move. Then his other hand smoothed along her spine, in a wide, languid stroke, down over her buttocks, raising those little flesh bumps all the way. She trembled as his hand came back up, lighter, nearly tickling her but sending shocks to her little pip, where it swelled against the bed. She spread her legs wider, trying to increase the pressure there, to find some relief. . . . His hand moved again, slowly, teasing and tickling, around the other side. And this time, he slipped his fingers down between the vee of her buttocks, down into the slippery warmth there. She groaned and shifted, trying to fit those questing fingers deep inside.

His hand tightened a bit over her neck, and he removed his fingers from her quim. "Be still."

With a soft little moan, she bit her lip and closed her eyes.

He lifted his hand from the back of her neck, and she braced herself. . . . The bed dipped and she felt him climb over her, his legs between her spread ones. Suddenly his cock was pushing against the cleft of her ass, and his hips pressed into her buttocks as he slipped his hands down around her breasts.

Then his mouth was on her shoulder, and she nearly jerked again when she felt the soft, gentle tickling of lips and tongue on the sensitive skin there at the crook of her neck. Sensation erupted over her body, and his fingers tightened over her nipples, there between them and the bed. She shifted her hips and felt his penis slip against her more, closer to the place she wanted him to be.

His mouth moved up along the side of her neck, his hands held her breasts, lifting her shoulders, gently arching her back up into him, pressing her quim into the bed. The arousal was becoming unbearable; Mercédès bit her lip and squeezed her eyes closed as he kissed, and slowly sucked at that spot . . . that place below her ear . . . the one that made her insides quiver and curl and her body shudder and tremble in anticipation.

If she begged him now, would it end this game? Would it make the next eighteen months easier, would he take her without the teasing? Would he satisfy her?

Did she have any reason to wait? She'd already lost.

Just as she opened her mouth to say it, to plead with him, to cry for release, he moved quickly, rolling off her and flipping her onto her back. The next thing she knew, his lips were on hers, hard and rough, cutting off anything she might have said, pushing the back of her head into the pile of cushions.

It was as if he wanted to devour her, to take her whole into his mouth. His fingers closed over her wrists, pulling them wide beyond her shoulders, pushing them into the cushions, as he ate at her lips, and she lifted her head to kiss him back, to suck his tongue deep into her throat, to inhale his taste and smell and touch.

His torso arched over hers, his legs and hips on the bed next to her splayed legs, and at last he released her arms. Her wrists ached from where he'd gripped them, but she moved her hands to touch his hair—his soft, long hair, which fell in a shaggy brush against her face. He pulled away from her mouth with a long, loud smack, and she saw his face for a brief moment before he fell upon her breast, taking the nipple into his mouth with long, hard draws as though he wanted to devour it too.

But the fleeting expression she'd seen on his face sent a cold shiver beneath the pangs of lust curling in her belly. Sharp and hard, it hadn't been one of desire as much as determination and pain.

Then she was caught up again in the tug at her nipple, the fingers that slid over her quivering belly and down between her legs to slip and surge in the wetness there. She moved her hands from the back of his head over the broad warmth of his shoulders, tracing their angular curves over arms that bulged as he braced himself on the bed over her.

The next thing she knew, their bodies were smashed together, tangled and hot as he rolled on top of her, gathering her into his arms and raising his face to kiss her neck. His cock pushed against her, and she lifted her hips and felt it slip against her quim, sending a quick, hard shudder through her.

Please. Now.

As if he read her mind, he moved suddenly, shifting up and away from her torso, sitting back on his haunches, he grasped her hips, sliding them up onto his thighs. Looking down, his fingers biting into the tender flesh of her back, he shifted, his cock long and proud, raging between them, and slid himself inside.

Mercédès cried out with the pleasure of it, yet deep inside, she held back, bracing herself for his teasing withdrawal, for the game to begin again.

But he held her hips, and he thrust in and out, so deep and hard that her whole body jolted against the cushions, and they fell over her, muffling her soft cries, sopping the tears that had begun to leak from the sides of her eyes. The building desire rose, tightened, clutched inside her as he slammed and rocked. . . . She felt the grip of his fingers in her skin, knew there would be marks, but she shifted and bucked and moved with him, her own fingers digging into the brocade coverlet beneath her until at last . . . at last . . . with a soft scream, she found her peak—he brought her there, took her over—and she tumbled into a vortex of bone-deep pleasure and shudders undulating from within and without, her toes curling into the bed behind him, her fingers pulling up the coverlet, her face buried in fringe and cushions.

And then with a deep, angry grunt, he shot his hips forward in one last, hard slam, as if to shove himself up into her belly, and she felt the pulsation of his orgasm ripple through her insides. When his hands fell away, the cusions shifted, uncovering her eyes. He sagged back onto his haunches and gasped for breath as if he'd been running for leagues . . . for years. . . .

"Mer . . . cé . . . dès . . . ," he whispered in a hollow, desperate voice. "Why . . . ?" To her shock, to her great horror, she saw the streak of tears glistening on his face before he turned, pulling out of her and stumbling away from the bed.

SIXTEEN

The Dismissal

Later that day
Paris

"Edmond?" Mercédès sat up in the bed, saying his name tentatively.

"Go."

"But—"

"I no longer have the stomach . . . but first, you must tell me . . ." He seemed to gather himself together. His voice was still raw, but not as desperate, not as agonized as it had been moments before.

He'd moved to stand, still naked, at what appeared to be his favorite place—near the light, the windows. Something he must still crave after spending fourteen years in darkness. The sun had moved over the house and would be low in the afternoon sky, just beginning to touch the tops of the brown-roofed houses in the distance if they were to look west. "Morcerf is not Albert's father."

Mercédès caught her breath. "No." She had never revealed Albert's true parentage to him until last night, when she explained everything—or nearly everything—about Fernand and Villefort and Danglars—and what had happened to Edmond Dantès.

"You not only betrayed . . . Dantès . . ."—his voice dipped on the word, as if he could barely acknowledge his ownership of that name, that person—"with Morcerf, but with another as well? How many? How long did you wait before you spread your legs? *How long?*"

She looked over at him. Her vision was damp and blurry, but she spoke clearly. "I never betrayed Edmond Dantès. Everything I did was because I loved you . . . but you believe me tainted with the same brush as the men who would have seen you dead. So let us get on with this—this vengeance of yours, so that eighteen months from now, I will be able to walk away and wash my hands of anything and anyone associated with Edmond Dantès."

"Who was it?"

There was no sense in keeping it from him. "Villefort."

A low, agonized cry ripped from the back of his throat, and when he turned to look at her, his face was ravaged. So drawn, so tight, so black and angular. Frightening. "My God . . . of all . . ." He caught himself, steadied, pulled back that infamous control. Yet still his voice shook. "He had freed me . . . sent me on my way. . . . My bloody hand was on the damned doorknob . . . *on the doorknob* . . . when he opened the letter and read it. And then . . . he called his guards. . . . I thought they were taking me home . . . back to you . . . but they took me to a boat instead. I thought it was a mistake. . . . It would be rectified . . . an error. . . . The boat took me to d'If. . . ."

His shoulders were trembling, his hands clenching and relaxing, his damp eyes burned with loathing. "And you were fucking him? Those months and years I was in d'If, *you lay with the man who sent me there?* You gave him pleasure from the same body that I loved? That I could not forget?"

Mercédès had tears streaming from her face. She reached toward him. "No, Edmond . . . it wasn't like that. I . . . went to him. I begged him for information about you . . . for any news. He—"

"Leave me. You must leave now, Mercédès," he said in a terrifying voice. "Or I cannot guarantee your safety. I cannot—*Leave!* If I had known . . . if I had known he was that devil's son—*Go!*"

He fairly shouted that last word. Mercédès had never been frightened of him before—as Edmond Dantès, as Sinbad, even as the Count of Monte Cristo at his most forbidding. But now . . . he looked so murderous, his face so hard and black and furious.

But she had to try, to make him understand. "Edmond, please," she said, stepping toward him, her hand outstretched. "He forced me—in exchange for information, he made me—"

"Go!" he shouted, shoving her hand away. "Get from my sight!" He pushed past her so close she felt the swish of air, his entire body visibly shaking as he stalked out of the chamber. The sharp crack of the door slamming into place echoed in his departure, and all was silent.

Fingers trembling, she pulled on the tunic and stared at the splintered door. Should she wait? Perhaps . . . but the memory of his face, black and tortured and violent, haunted her. Edmond would never have lifted a hand against her. But . . . she was no longer sure she knew the man he'd become.

She had to tell him . . . whether he would understand or forgive her—or even believe her—she didn't know . . . but she had to make him understand. Somehow.

Mercedes opened the door and found herself in the corridor. As she stood there, footsteps approached from below and momentarily, Bertuccio's head appeared. His face was grave, and at first Mercédès thought it was because he'd heard the altercation, heard Monte Cristo order her to leave.

But the expression on his face told her he was surprised to see her standing in dishabille in the corridor, yet not so surprised that he could not deliver the message he'd come to impart.

"Pardon me, madam la comtesse, but I have just received some disturbing news. I . . . regret to inform you that the Comte de Morcerf has . . . expired . . . in his home, due to a self-inflicted gunshot."

"I am not certain His Excellency is available to see you," said Bertuccio to the young man at the door.

Haydée recognized the visitor as Monsieur Maximilien Morrel, that particular friend of the count's. The only one who seemed able to bring a relaxed light into His Excellency's eyes, and who seemed to provoke sincere affection from him.

"It's a rather urgent matter," Morrel replied, crumpling his fine buckskin gloves with worrying fingers. He wasn't wearing a hat, nor did he have a recently removed one in his hands, implying that he had arrived in great haste. "I would be most grateful if you would announce my presence, and that I desperately wish to see him. It's a matter of life and death."

Haydée stepped forward and said to Bertuccio, "I believe His Excellency would see Monsieur Morrel, of all people. Perhaps you will accompany me?" she added, looking with clear invitation at the young man.

The majordomo seemed ready to argue; but truly, what could he say? The count had been incommunicado from the entire household since the Comtesse de Morcerf had left the day before. Only Haydée had been admitted to his rooms a short time ago, to deliver the news regarding Morcerf's suicide. She'd found Monte Cristo sitting in his favorite chair, staring out over the city, deep in thought.

He'd looked up at her, turning from the morning sun, his face deeply lined with sorrow and regret. "I've been wrong, I think, Haydée," he'd said quietly. His voice was devoid of emotion. "All this time, I thought . . . I thought God had sent me to wreak vengeance on them all. Yet it was she—Mercédès—who reminded me of honor, of selflessness . . . and who reminded me that He too is merciful.

"She told me what she did . . . for me. What she gave up, how she must have suffered . . . but I didn't hear her. I didn't really *hear* her. Her words have been echoing in these chambers since yesterday, and only now have I truly heard them. And understood. About mercy. And honor and selflessness. How I was wrong to judge her for her choices, the difficult decisions she made.

"And that it is not my place to judge and condemn *anyone*—especially those who are innocent." He'd heaved a great sigh, then turned back to the city's view beyond. "Yet . . . I cannot imagine a life without the need for revenge burning inside me. What is there for me now?"

But when she'd tried to speak, to comfort him, he'd dismissed her, firmly but with cordiality. "I need a bit more time, Haydée . . . to figure out how to live. And what I can do."

And so now, with an excellent excuse in the form of Captain Maximilien Morrel, Haydée welcomed the opportunity to look in on His Excellency again. Perhaps the young man for whom the count seemed to have the most genuine affection could entice him back to life.

No one tried to stop her from interrupting the master. Now that she had been made a freewoman, the remaining servants seemed to accept her as the lady of the household.

All except for Ali, who had been stationed outside the count's private apartments since yesterday afternoon after the comtesse left. He seemed nearly as out of sorts as the count did, and he would make no eye contact with Haydée when she came into his presence. Not that she had tried to speak with him or interact with him . . . not since the night before the duel, when he'd found her crying—for real this time—on the terrace, and had tried to kiss her.

She was simply too confused about what to do regarding the man she loved, now that she was a freewoman and he was a slave. She'd learned that the last thing she wanted was an unwilling man, one she had to order or trick into loving her. She was no longer certain about the difference between what he desired, and what she thought he did—or wanted him to.

As she led Monsieur Morrel up the wide sweep of stairs from the ground floor to the first story, she couldn't help but wonder again why the count had sent Comtesse Morcerf away after less than a day. Haydée had been told that the woman would remain for an extended time, and she, at least, had expected His Excellency to be in much better spirits after being with her.

In fact she had been certain whatever it was between them would be resolved, if not after the bloodless duel, then after several hours of serious fucking. The last thing Haydée had expected was for him to cut short his liaison with the woman he obviously still had great feelings for . . . and send her on her way.

At the top of the stairs, Ali stood guard, his massive body settled on what looked to be an extremely uncomfortable chair posted just outside the door.

"I have brought Monsieur Morrel to His Excellency on a matter that he has described as regarding life and death," Haydée told Ali in a cool, businesslike tone. She swept past him and grasped the knob of one of the French doors without waiting for his response.

Ali moved gracefully to his feet, all dark and smooth and strong, his extensive shadow falling over her and onto the door. He closed his fingers around her arm, not tightly, but enough to gain her attention—for she had barely looked at him, and had not allowed their eyes to meet. She couldn't . . . not right now.

With a sharp jolt, she pulled from his grip and turned the knob as she raised her hand to give a warning knock. "Please, wait here, monsieur," she said to Morrel, holding up a slender hand.

Ali did not try to stop her; perhaps that hadn't even been his intent. Yet her arm felt warm and strange after his touch. She knocked again, a bit harder, trying not only to capture the count's attention, but also to dislodge the tingling on her skin.

At last, she heard the peremptory "Come" from within.

Opening the door, she peered in. The count was standing at the windows, at what appeared to be his favorite spot in the room. "Your Excellency, Monsieur Morrel has arrived. He desires to speak with you on a matter of great urgency."

Monte Cristo seemed to shake himself from some deep meditation and turned to look at her. The afternoon sunlight glowed behind him, streaming through the window and filtering through his thick mass of messy hair. He wore only a simple white shirt and trousers. The shirt cuffs were undone, hanging over his dark hands. Even his feet were bare, and the three buttons at the throat of his shirt were open.

"Maximilien?" Whatever burden he carried seemed to lighten a bit, and the lines of his face eased. "It will be good to see him. I will tell him all, unburden my heart. Yes, send him in. And . . . I think perhaps I will eat something, Haydée."

She bowed and, moving backward from the room, gestured for Morrel to enter. The young man did so with such speed and alacrity that she wondered how he had resisted earlier. "My God, Monte Cristo, are you ill?" she heard him say before closing the door behind her.

No sooner had the latch clicked than she turned and started toward the stairs—intent on personally asking Bertuccio to arrange for some food and drink for his master—when Ali's strong hand reached for her again.

This time, she did not shake off his touch, but stood there, next to the door, looking down at her slippered feet, waiting.

Two large black feet, banded with gold cuffs, moved into view beside her own narrow, blue silk ones. They sidled up, trapping her feet between his large toes and the elegant arches into which those digits swept.

"I'm sorry, Ali," she said in a low voice, still looking down. The cream of his loose trousers, the hems embroidered with gold designs that she'd never noticed before, was pale and simple next to his rich dark skin and the cerulean blue of her gown. "I should never have . . . I was wrong to act as I did."

His other hand had closed over her shoulder, and now he held her on both arms. But still, she didn't look up at him. She couldn't.

He gave her a little jerk, just enough to get her attention, and at last she lifted her gaze to see him. His eyes were wary, shuttered . . . yet she saw something else there. Hope, perhaps. Or a question.

He released her to sign. *I will be leaving soon.*

The bottom dropped out of her stomach. She tightened her fingers into the sides of her gown. "Where are you going?"

Home. Back to my home.

Her mouth was so dry, her stomach churning so hard, that she thought she might vomit right there. She'd thought to have more time . . . more time with him, to see him, to talk to him, to smell him . . . to give them another chance. Her another chance.

Haydée wanted to say something easy and light, to wish him well, but the words wouldn't come. Instead, she could do nothing but look up at those thick pink lips and think about never tasting them again.

Will you go with me?

"Go . . . with you?" She could hardly believe it; there were all sorts of things blazing through her mind.

But before she could respond, the doors to the bedchamber flew open and out strode the Count of Monte Cristo. Dressed, combed, booted, and determined. Maximilien Morrel followed him, his face much lighter than when he'd arrived.

"You're sure of it?" Monte Cristo was saying. "Someone is trying to poison Valentine Villefort?"

"There is no doubt, after three other deaths by poison in the household," the young man replied as they stopped on the landing. "Valentine and I have kept our love secret for so long because her father would never allow us to be together—but I knew I could trust you with the knowledge. I knew you would help us. And now that you have told me you're Edmond Dantès, as well as Lord Wilmore and Sinbad the Sailor—the men who saved my father from ruin and death—now I know for certain I was right to come to you."

"Indeed. I've been so . . . foolish," Monte Cristo said, that last word so quiet that Haydée was certain she was the only one to hear. "I could have been the cause of her death," he muttered to himself as his young companion walked back into the chambers to retrieve his gloves, neither of them appearing to notice her and Ali.

"The sins of the fathers visited upon their sons . . . How could I have believed in that—believed in the destruction of innocent lives? I would have been no better than Morcerf and Villefort themselves. Thank God, Mercédès helped me to see . . . how foolish I've been . . . . And now . . . yes, I will save Valentine." He said this last more loudly, speaking to his friend as he reappeared carrying his gloves. "This, then, is a reason to live. Love."

Morrel would have started down the stairs, but Monte Cristo stopped him. "I will save her. I vow it. But you must trust me. Will you?"

"As I would my father," Morrel told him, grasping the count's arm.

"Now I will go on to see Valentine myself, for you cannot go there, of course, if you are to keep your love secret. But never fear. All will be well in the end."

Monte Cristo was nodding now; it seemed as if he spoke to himself. "All will be well." Then he looked up directly at Haydée and Ali for the first time and said, "Ali, I have need of you for one more task. Will you, my friend?"

Ali gave a willing bow and stepped away from Haydée to follow his master. As she watched the count bound away, down the spread of stairs, she was relieved that he seemed to be purposeful again. Yet . . . her sharp gaze had not missed the lines of grief and weariness that seemed to have gone deeper in the last day, as well as the glint of anger that still limned his eyes.

His Excellency had found a new purpose, yet something disturbing still ate at him.

But even that unpleasant realization paled in comparison to the fact that Ali wanted her to go home with him. Wherever and however it could be possible, he wanted her to go with him.

For the first time in weeks, Haydée felt alive. She went through the rest of the day with a glorious smile on her face and warmth in her heart. She sank into bed that night, knowing that the next day Ali would return and she would be able to tell him how joyful she was to be going home with him. It didn't take much for her to drift off to sleep, for she was no longer worried about what the future might hold.

She awoke suddenly.

Moonlight glowed from beyond her windows, tingeing her

bedchamber with all shades of gray and blue and silver. Someone was there . . . large and sleek and silent. Spicy and rich.

Her heart leaped and her stomach twirled as the thick, low cushions that made her bed dipped slightly to the side as he climbed on next to her.

"Ali," she murmured as his head moved closer, shining in the moonlight. The gold hoop at his ear glinted as he reached for her, and she eagerly wrapped her arms around his thick muscular neck. "You've returned."

She'd had a bit of an awkward day after he left with Monte Cristo, having been unable to immediately accept Ali's invitation to go home with him. She didn't care where it was or what it was like, she wanted to be with him. But he'd been called away as she stood there with her mouth open, stupidly repeating his question . . . left to wonder if he thought she'd been shocked or repulsed, rather than delighted. Oh, most definitely delighted.

As she was now, with his thick, soft lips that had found the thrust of one hard, long-neglected nipple. He sucked firmly, magically, using his tongue to swirl around it and tease over the crinkles of its base before drawing nearly her whole breast into his wide, hot mouth. Haydée shuddered and trembled beneath him, as his fingers slipped down over the low rise of her belly and up again onto the lift of her smooth mound, and then down into the heat and wetness of her quim.

There was nothing . . . *nothing* . . . like the pleasure, the knowledge, of a man's touch, she thought dazedly, as he slipped those knowing fingers down and around and between the folds of her skin, spreading her thick juices over her swollen flesh slowly, tortuously. As if he had all the time in the world. Her pip was hard and ripe when he found it under its little hood, the perfect pressure of his fingertip jiggling and teasing her until she writhed beneath him, gasping against the musky skin of his jaw.

She felt the smile on his face as he bent to kiss her again, sucking her top lip deeply into his mouth as he continued to play and stroke and finger between her legs. The sweet, low rise toward her orgasm built, higher and higher, twining through her body as her legs fell open, her nails dug into his arm, her mouth opened in short little pants.

Oh, my . . . oh . . . Her hips moved against his hand, desperate and needy, and she heard his low masculine chuckle next to her face.

"Ali," she gasped, biting her lip to keep from screaming.

In response, he moved his finger from her and shifted quickly and smoothly to bury his face between her legs. He didn't wait, didn't ease into her: Instead, he devoured her, his full, mobile mouth closing over the wet, swollen folds of her quim, sucking and nibbling and licking. . . . Oh, wonderful, nudging and slipping and teasing without pause, as though he'd saved up his hunger forever. She gave a little scream as he found her pearl, ripe and full to bursting, and when he gave a long, undulating pull on it, vibrating it between his full lips and teasing it with his tongue, Haydée felt everything, every part of her, fill up, then explode and fall away into a long, sweet, shuddering tumble.

Her mouth was dry from breathing through open, gasping lips. She drew her tongue over them, wetting them, and suddenly he was on top of her again, his mouth, moist and musky and tasting of her, eating at her lips, thrusting his tongue between them, long and deep and sleek. He grasped her hips, and she lifted them, using her hand to slide between them and wrap around that incredible length and width of cock, hot and heavy.

She guided him to her, then removed her grip as, with a long, easy thrust, he filled her. Tears sprang to her eyes at the beauty of it, the sensation of being one with him, joined so deeply and so fully . . . and then he began to move, and she too, their breath hot and gasping as he held himself over her body, the muscles of his arms bulging like small boulders under her fingers as he thrust in and out, sliding easily into her and out, deep and long and sweet.

He moved faster, and she did, raking her nails over his arms as she tried to pull herself closer, wanting to crawl up and into him, into his hard, rich body, spicy and musky and smooth and powerful . . . in and out and up and down until their movements were frantic and crazy and the only sound was the slam of their bodies together, the soft sucking sounds of her juices holding on to him.

She felt him release, shooting hard and fast inside her, and she met him with her own peak, with one last thrust of her hips up toward him, one last gasp before she fell back onto the cushions, her body sifting lazily into the nothingness of pleasure.

He held himself up on his strong arms for a moment longer. Then he too sagged down, trembling under his skin, and rolled to the side, bringing her with him.

"I love you, Haydée."

For a moment, it didn't register through the haze, the satiation of her pleasure . . . but then . . . She would have bolted upright if he hadn't had those impossibly powerful arms holding her against the slabs of his chest. "You can speak?"

She felt him nod against her, his arms tightening when she

tried again to sit up and look at him. "Those are the first words I've spoken in more than three years."

Haydée lay there, her hand open on his warm chest, his skin damp with exertion, the deep *ka-thump* of his heartbeat beneath her ear. "Why . . . why did you not speak for three years? Does His Excellency know?"

"Indeed, he does." Haydée was distracted for a moment by the richness of his voice, with an exotic accent that made his syllables short and clipped on the end, yet deep and husky. It was heavy and dark, and it matched him perfectly. "I am from Nubia, as you know—but what you do not know is that I am what you would call a prince, or a duke, of that country. My family is very powerful and rich, and a little more than three years ago when we—my father and mother and siblings—were on a voyage to the Indian Ocean, our ship was destroyed during a large storm. I shouldn't use the word 'ship,' " he added in his formal, clipped voice accompanied by a soft laugh, "for His Excellency disabused me of the notion when he saw the remains of our vessel. It was little more than a yacht, in fact, and had been unable to survive a great hurricane in the sea. Monte Cristo saved us—all of us—and in return, I, as the eldest in my family, and as is the custom in my country, pledged myself to him in service for ten years.

"At first he wanted to relieve me of the obligation, but I insisted on repaying the debt as a matter of pride and honor. It is what would have been expected of anyone in my country—and such a long period of service was due to the fact that it was not only my life that he saved, at the jeopardy of his own, but also my entire family's. When he saw that I was intent on it, he at last agreed, but with some modification, and asked that I serve him as his personal guard until such time as he concluded this business in Paris. As is the custom with my people, I took a vow of silence for the duration of my time in service to him, and that is how I came to be here. It took me some time before I was able to communicate easily by signing, but since His Excellency wasn't fluent in my native language, nor me in his, we began our relationship with hand gestures."

Haydée could scarcely accommodate the details of the story. "And now?"

"Now," he said, those soft thick lips moving to slide over her delicate temple, "I have been released from his service, and I wanted the first words I spoke to be the ones that told you how I felt."

"And you did not . . . that whole time, you never spoke. Even when . . . even . . ." Her voice trailed off as she remembered him bound against the chaise in the gazebo, how he'd fought and struggled, and yet had never said a word. Though he could have.

A man who would keep his vow under such duress . . . She shivered, remembering how she'd wronged him and weakened him.

"I nearly did," he said, and his lips moved against her skin so she knew he was smiling again. "But I focused on the day when I'd be able to tell you all, and then I . . ." He stopped, pressed a kiss against her cheek. "You nearly destroyed me, Haydée. I couldn't make you understand that my honor rested on my service to Monte Cristo. . . . I couldn't take from him. I would not have been able to live with myself if I had."

"I'm sorry I forced you," she said. "I regretted it almost the moment it was over."

"I know. I could see it in your face, but I was angry, and I wanted you to know that you'd hurt me. But I never stopped loving you."

"And now . . . you are free to go?"

"Yes. His Excellency has released me. I may go back to my people, or I may stay and work with him. Not as a servant, but as an equal."

"He has finished his business here in Paris, then," Haydée said, smoothing her hand over the planes of his chest, gently tickling the tight whorls of black hair there.

"Yes. Tomorrow, he says, shall be the last of it, and then he will be free to go."

"Go where?"

Ali shrugged against her, his arms squeezing her tight. "I do not know, and I'm not certain he does either."

"I have known him for nearly a decade, and I've never known him to be uncertain or indecisive of anything," she said sadly. For now that she'd found her completion, she felt more aware of her master's deficits. "But I think you are right. He has lived with nothing but his drive for vengeance for so long. I don't think he knows how to live without it. He is a very unhappy man. And I think the one person who would make him happy . . ."

"The Comtesse Morcerf?" Ali said, smoothing his hand along her hip. "Yes, perhaps . . . yet I don't believe he is ready to be happy yet. At least, as happy as I am." His fingers slipped around to find the hot juncture between her legs. "No, indeed. It is my pleasure now to partake of all of those treasures you so boldly flaunted, and freely shared, nearly to my undoing. I love you, Haydée."

"I love you, Ali."

SEVENTEEN

Confrontation in the Garden

One week later
Marseille

Mercédès crouched in the small garden, pulling up the tenacious weeds that had taken over the plot during the last decade of neglect. June was too late to start many of the plants she liked, but there was still time to plant tarragon and sage seeds, both of which grew quickly, if she could clear out a sunny area in this small, fenced-in yard. Much of it was shaded by olive and oak trees, or by the house on one side, and the tall wood-plank fence that was meant to keep the deer and rabbits from feasting on tender seedlings.

A new shadow fell across the rich Marseille soil, sending Mercédès twisting around and back onto her heels. She had to shield her face against the sun to look up at him.

It wasn't Albert—he had left two days ago to enlist in the

army, refusing to use any of the fortune that had passed to him upon Fernand's death. Like Mercédès, he would rather create his own life than take something from such a man. He even disdained his father's name, opting to take Herrera, Mercédès' surname, for his own.

No, it wasn't Albert standing over her. Even though the bright stream of sun shadowed the details of his face, she knew those shoulders, that proud bearing. Her heart skipped a beat, and her stomach plunged. "Edmond."

His boots rested on the stone path behind her, scuffed and worn, spread apart as if he needed stability and power in his stance. "Mercédès." He said her name as if he'd saved it forever and then suddenly needed to feel it on his tongue. Softly, tentatively.

Surprise and apprehension had leached her mouth dry, and she swallowed hard. Certainly, she had expected some response from him in regard to the letter she'd sent after he ordered her from his residence in Paris—a summons, perhaps, which she would have ignored . . . but she hadn't thought the powerful, aloof Count of Monte Cristo would travel to her. To her poor, little cottage in Marseille—even if it had once belonged to his father and been left to her upon his death.

It was just as well that the sun blinded her when she looked up at him; it made it easier for her to remain cool and unaffected. She didn't want to see his face, to remember the angles of his cheeks, the fullness of his beautiful lips, the depth of his hot gaze. It would make her too weak, too susceptible.

"You received my letter," she said by way of response, closing her fingers around a stubborn chicory plant to tug it from the soil. The flowers were good for steeping into a coffee, and also for stomach ailments . . . but this was not the location she wanted it to grow, for it was greedy and would take over the garden.

"Yes." His voice was careful, as if afraid to reveal too much. "Mercédès." This time, it was a plea, a gentle one, beckoning. "I—" He broke off, shaking his head as if to clear it.

And then he moved toward her, reaching down to pull her to her feet, soil-dampened skirt, muddy fingers, chicory plant, and all. "Mercédès," he said as if he would never tire of doing so, drawing her into his arms . . . and, *oh, Dios,* she let him. She ignored her sense, her head, her logic, her grief and anger . . . and she allowed herself to be folded up into his arms, deep into his embrace.

Her legs were stiff and weak from crouching, but he held her against his strong body and she drew in the smell of him—the one of cardamom and cinnamon and musk and, faintly, of Edmond and lemon trees, and the salt of the sea.

Or perhaps that was only her memory of him.

She closed her eyes as his mouth found hers, knowing that her upper lip was salty and moist from the sun's heat, aware that her hands and the dirt clinging to the roots of the chicory would soil his tailored wool coat, but unwilling to give this up . . . this moment.

For after, she would have to face the truth, and her future.

But for now . . . now it was Edmond again, his mouth so firm and hungry over her own eager lips. She closed her eyes against the blazing sun, seeing its bright remnants in blue spots on the insides of her lids as strong hands crushed her against a tall, powerful body. One that had haunted her, one that had taken from her and challenged her and teased her.

Edmond.

She couldn't say his name aloud, couldn't allow that intimacy. But she kissed him back, accepting the strong swipe of his tongue as it thrust deeply into her mouth, and dancing her own around it until he groaned against her. She touched his hair, sliding her hands through it, her fingers warm from the sun, feeling the neatness of his skull beneath her touch.

Before she knew it, the blinding sun had given way to shade, and the rough bark of a tree was behind her, catching on her hair, which she'd braided and pinned into a coil at her nape. The world of seedlings, soil, and sun had slid away to one of slick heat and rising desire, the fumble of fingers at the back of her gown, smooth and strong over the bare skin above it, and the heavy pressure between her thighs.

She leaned to him again, her nose buried in the warmth of his neck, drawing him in once more, tasting his salty skin while the back of her gown fell open under his hands. Her breasts were tight and ready when he slid his hands around to touch them, shoving down beneath the confines of the corset she'd begun to wear more loosely now that she had no one to impress, lifting them out so he could feel them and rub his thumbs against rigid nipples. Her dress fell to her hips and she felt the ruthless tugs at the back of her stays, and they eased and sagged, and then she was there in her shift. . . . There in her little private garden at the cottage in Marseille, she was kissing Edmond . . . Monte Cristo . . . Sinbad . . . and tearing at his clothes.

They were on the ground then, beneath the tree and tumbling over its thrusting roots, mouths clashing and hands seeking, suddenly skin to skin from muscular, haired legs to soft, round shoulders. There was no holding back this time, no game, no teasing or taunting. . . . She moaned when he found her breast with his mouth, sucking gently, erotically on her nipple, slipping around it with his strong tongue as his other hand traced the curve of her bottom. He moved again and pushed her gently down onto the uneven ground, the shady grass cool beneath her skin, the top of her head brushing against the base of the tree.

His hands smoothed from her breasts to her hips, and his mouth followed, soft and worshipful over her belly, which shuddered delicately under his light touch. The heat of his breath warmed her, and as he drew nearer to her quim, she arched up, lifting to him, her breathing heavy and urgent as she looked up at the spread of leaves and small green apples.

She read the way he touched her, the apology, the tenderness in his fingers and the steady, firm sampling of his lips as they moved along the inner parts of her thighs, sucking gently, tasting her warm skin. She twisted and sighed against his hands, shivering and needing, wet and ready. So ready. Ripe and swollen . . . and when his tongue found her tight pip, flicking hard against it, Mercédès gripped his shoulders hard and surged up into his mouth.

He sucked on her little pearl, sliding his tongue under it, darting in and out and around, driving her mad with the swirling, building pleasure focused there in that tiny, needy place. She writhed and cried, the lovely soft spiral of lust sharpening and unfurling into full-blown pleasure, billowing and growing and rising until he gave one last deep, long, *strong* draw, holding her there at the precipice until at last she spilled over, crying and shaking and moaning beneath him.

"Mercédès," he gasped, surging back up to cover her body with his, his mouth musky and wet, sliding over her chin and to her lips, taking and tasting as he fitted his hips against hers, groaning desperately into her mouth as her hands reached down to close around his cock. She stroked him, slipping his head in and around her quim, feeling him tense and shudder against her, his body damp with holding back, strong and heavy and rough against her soft skin.

She would have lifted her hips to slip him in, but he pulled away suddenly, leaving her cool and spread wide, and for a moment, she was confused . . . but then he slung her up into his arms, and she fell against his solid chest as he began to walk toward the little cottage.

Inside, he strode smoothly to the room she slept in, placing her on the little bed so that her hips rested on its edge and her feet on the floor. Standing there in front of her, he drew her legs long and straight behind him, sliding his hands beneath her ass to raise her hips from the bed as he stood against it. He looked magnificent—long and lean, the planes of his chest dusted with dark hair, the smooth curves of shoulder to biceps to forearm shadowed by the late-afternoon light. His hips were narrow beneath the width of his shoulders, and his belly flat. His cock jutted straight from the shock of black hair as he looked down at her, his eyes gleaming hot and his lips full and moist.

Mercédès shifted her hips in his hands, feeling the gentle bite of fingers in her bottom, and suddenly he moved, slipping himself in, her eyes closing with the intensity of the pleasure. He gave a quiet, desperate groan as he eased fully into place and held there . . . just breathing, his hands beneath her, the soft twitch of his cock deep inside.

She opened her eyes then, and saw his face stressed and

tight, his mouth drawn flat and his eyes . . . *Dio,* his eyes so deep and dark and haunted. They frightened her.

And then he began to move, slowly at first, as though to take great care, to savor it, and Mercédès closed her own eyes, and felt pleasure release within her as her fingers splayed over the warm, tight skin of his back. Long and easy, he moved away—then hard and strong to fill her up again. She gave a soft cry when he thrust back in, felt his own responding moan rumble through the back of his lungs.

And so it was, easy and slow he rocked against her, and she lifted to meet him. Pleasure brought tears to her eyes, and she let them leak from there, trickling onto the quilt beneath. It was bittersweetly familiar and yet foreign to feel him against her, inside her, filling and releasing her in a smooth, slow rhythm. Their breathing rose, became more ragged . . . her skin flushed warm and his muscles tightened under her hands. . . . It wasn't enough. . . . She wanted more. . . .

Suddenly, it was as if a string broke and released them—he surged up onto the bed, bringing her with him, lifting her away from the edge and falling over her. Mercédès' feet slammed onto the soft mattress, and then they were thrashing together, wildly smashing body to body, hip to hip, gripping and scratching and urging and riding until he cried out, and she groaned, and they fell against each other, sated and sagging, sweaty and musky.

Mercédès came back to herself when she felt the gentle kiss on the side of her neck, the feathery stroke along the curve of her back. She realized what she'd done, and allowed . . . how everything had fallen away in favor of nostalgia and memory.

Monte Cristo raised his face, and she saw streaks of moisture running down his cheeks. She didn't know if they were rivulets of tears or of perspiration, but it didn't matter.

She wouldn't let it matter.

Before she could speak, he bent toward her, covering her mouth with a tender kiss that took her breath away, started the curl of pleasure again in her belly, and she closed her eyes against it. Passing a hand over her face, she smelled the remnants of chicory and sex. He withdrew and slid onto the bed next to her with a soft, heartfelt sigh.

Mercédès lay there, listening to him breathing, for a long while, staring at the plaster ceiling above, the light brown spots from the leaks, the cracks from the settling walls, and memorized the moment, taking herself back to twenty-four years ago when she lay next to Edmond Dantès.

Finally, he spoke, breaking what had grown into a charged silence. A waiting, for all of the things that yet needed to be said. "He raped you."

A shiver ran over the back of her neck at the sound of the blunt, real words, but Mercédès didn't allow them to sink further into her consciousness. This wasn't how—or when—she'd imagined this conversation would begin, but it was too late.

She steeled herself against the reality of the statement, for she couldn't relive those days, those months, at the hands of Villefort; she'd worked too hard to build a wall around the memories and keep them barricaded from her dreams. It had been the only way she could carry on, and, later, to exist in her life in Paris, interacting with the man everyone admired and sought after, when she knew the depths of his ugliness.

But he was not the only man whose ugliness had been revealed to her. Fernand. Villefort. Even Monte Cristo himself.

"He raped you, and yet you returned to him." There was no accusation in his voice, only disbelief, and pain, and sorrow as he pulled up onto his elbow to look down at her. "Your letter—I thought I understood, after you told me, but . . . your letter." He drew in a breath, closed his eyes for a moment. "You returned to him again and again . . . and he used you and raped you. You could have stayed away. You could have revealed it, told someone, Mercédès."

At last, she couldn't hold it back. She sat up abruptly, pulling away to sit on the edge of the bed, half facing him, half toward the shuttered window that allowed the summer light in. "And then I would have had no chance of word of you, Edmond. I bore it—the pain, the humiliation, the degradation—for more than a year because he made me believe he could help me. That he would have news, that he would find you and bring you back to me. I was nothing but a poor Catalan girl then—ignorant and naive, and he used that against me. But I let him because I still had hope. I thought that even if he didn't tell me, I might learn something by being in his office . . . by searching through his files and papers when he wasn't there. When he left me, bruised and aching—and sometimes bloody—there in the storage room behind his office, when he'd go to meet with his colleagues, I took the opportunity to search."

She realized her hands were shaking, the quilt mangled and crushed in her grip. She sucked in a ragged breath and swallowed, closing her eyes against the tears that threatened. It was a long time ago. The only good thing that had come of it was Albert. Yes, the son of a man she hated, but he was her son. Wholly, wonderfully, beautifully hers. And he'd proven his worth, his character, by rejecting everything Fernand had given him.

"Did Fernand know?"

"He knew that I was with child, that that was the only reason I agreed to marry him. He knew he would likely never father his own—I'm certain your investigations turned up the information that he preferred men. Or at least, very stimulating episodes. And I was afraid . . . afraid that if Villefort knew I'd gotten with his child that he would do something horrible."

"As he did with the child he fathered on Madam Danglars not so long afterward? He buried it alive in order to keep it a secret, and it was Bertuccio, the man who later became my majordomo, who found the babe and raised him. Later, after the boy grew up and ran away to seek his fortune, I located him and brought him back to Paris so that he would reveal himself."

Mercédès nodded, for she had heard the news from Maximilen Morrel and his sister, Julie. "And so Villefort's career was destroyed by the revelation of the son he thought he'd murdered come back to life. And now the death of his beloved daughter, Valentine, and the suicide of his second wife has driven him irrevocably mad. Danglars has become bankrupt and has run off to Italy. And Fernand is dead, by his own hand—yet the weight of your own hand is clear in all of this."

Now she pulled awkwardly to her feet, her knees weak and trembling as she stood over him where he sat upright on the bed. "And so you have come here now to finish your vengeance on me, then? The last of those who wronged you? Oh, of course . . . and our children too. For they must bear the burden of our sins as well."

"No, Mercédès, no." His voice was taut. "No. I'm done . . . done with that. I was wrong. I came to see you. To tell you I love you. Could you not see it? Feel it?"

"Ah, yes . . . you allowed both of us to receive pleasure at last." Her lips twisted as she reminded herself who he'd become.

"Mercédès, I came to beg your forgiveness."

"You have it, for what you did to me, for what you believed about me. Yes, I can forgive you that—for how could you have known I whored myself for you? You could not have known, and in light of all that had been done to you by Danglars and Fernand and Villefort, I can at least understand why you should think it.

"But you do *not* have my forgiveness for planning to kill my son. And for letting Valentine Villefort die. They were innocent people—innocent of all of the perfidy of their fathers—and yet you planned to destroy their lives without a second thought. And your friend Maximilien Morrel, who trusted you . . . who came to you for help, and whom you betrayed by letting him believe you would save Valentine. All in the manner of revenge." She stepped back, away from his devastated face, but she kept her eyes on him. "*I loved Edmond Dantès.* But I do not love the man he's become—burning with vengeance, ruthless, and destructive. Cold and calculating and unfeeling. You are no better than Fernand or Villefort."

He scrambled off the bed, tall and dark and hard, reaching for her. "Mercédès, no. I've come to the end of it all. It's done. You . . . and your letter . . . helped me to realize how wrong I was."

She pulled away before he touched her. "Yes. Yes, it is. It's done, Your Excellency. It's done, and now you feel the guilt, the compassion, the regret." She felt the burn of tears in her eyes, but she held back the emotion. "But it's too late. Nothing will change the fact that you would have killed my son, merely for being the flesh and blood of a man—and woman—who wronged you. And that you stood by and allowed Valentine Villefort to die in order to add to the destruction of her father's life.

"But the worst, Your Excellency, is that you betrayed Maximilien. You led him to believe that you could have saved his love, and you did not. He put his trust in you because you'd saved his family once before, and you betrayed him, just as you were betrayed by trusting in Villefort. So, yes, it is done. I am done."

His face was a mask of stone. "You don't understand. I had—"

She stood at the door of the room, aware that her last words to him would be said between two naked bodies. "No, Your Excellency, I don't understand. And I have no wish to. I have loved and lost Edmond Dantès . . . and loved and lost him *again.* I will have no more of it. Edmond Dantès is dead, and the Count of Monte Cristo is abhorrent to me. Now leave. Leave me to pick up the pieces of my life yet again, and to find a simple and worthwhile way to live."

She closed the door behind her.

Mercédès was sitting on the single chair in the small kitchen area when he came back out, fully dressed. When she heard him draw in his breath to speak, she held up a hand to stop him. "No."

"Mercédès," he said, his voice strong and harsh, "I ask you to do one more thing for me—no, not for me. For Edmond Dantès. For the man you once loved."

He waited, and she did not respond. She was so weary and heartsick!

When she didn't speak, he continued in that urgent, hard

voice. "I have made an agreement with Maximilien Morrel that he should come to me in three weeks, exactly one month after the death of Valentine Villefort. He meant to put a bullet in his head immediately upon hearing the news of her death, but I made him promise to wait until he comes to me for our meeting, after one month . . . and then if he still wished to end things, I would help him to make it painless.

"For there was a time . . . many times . . . when I desired the sleep of death myself. And I can understand the attraction of it."

"You need not fear that I wish to end my life," she replied coldly, wishing he would leave. Go, before she softened again and reached for him, curled her body around his strength and begged him never to leave her again . . . Edmond, Sinbad, Monte Cristo. "The Count of Monte Cristo has not that much influence on me."

"No," he said harshly, and she felt rather than saw him flinch as if to move toward her—but then he obviously thought better of it. "No, that is not what I meant. But my last request to you is that you accompany Morrel when he comes to meet me. And then . . . and then I vow that I will never darken your door again. Will you do that? Come with him?"

Mercédès lifted her shoulders in a deep sigh. "I will do it, but only for Maximilien. Not for you. Never for you."

Eighteen

The Revelation

Three weeks later
The Isle of Monte Cristo

The sight of the craggy rock of an island brought back a wave of memory for Mercédès. She stood on the deck of the yacht *Nemesis*, the same one that had brought her here nine months earlier. The same sailor, Jacopo, captained the small vessel.

Mercédès had made him promise to let her take Maximilien Morrel's remains back to Marseille with her after their meeting with Monte Cristo. She realized Jacopo was in service to the count, but she believed he would keep his word.

Next to her, on the small deck, his own fingers curled in a death grip around the rail, Maximilien stood. He'd stared out beyond the horizon since the moment they'd boarded the yacht, two days earlier in Marseille, going below only briefly to sleep when his knees could no longer keep him upright. His face, red and beaten by the sun, his hair a matted mass of windblown curls, and the gauntness in his cheeks bespoke his grief and longing.

While Mercédès dreaded the imminent meeting with Monte Cristo, she knew that Maximilien pined for it. It was only his vow to his friend that kept him alive. Despite the fact that Monte Cristo had failed to save Valentine, Maximilien continued to love and respect him because of what he'd done for his family in the past by saving Morrel and Company from disaster and his father from suicide. The young man had told Mercédès he would never forget that, and even now he truly cared for Monte Cristo.

When the boat scraped over the jutting rocks, Jacopo anchored it and, as he had before, helped Mercédès through the water onto the shore. Maximilien followed eagerly, his strides long, if not jerky from the sudden change from sea to land. "Where is he?" he asked, glaring up at the low rocky cliff above them. "Where is Monte Cristo?"

This time Jacopo did not obstruct the view of the visitors; instead, he led the way, smiling and silent, through a rough passage of boulders cut by wind and sea, and down around a corner. They found themselves facing a well-hidden door made of rocks, and when it opened, Jacopo gestured for them to enter.

Maximilien recalled his manners and bowed Mercédès into the opening, but she slowed and slid her hand around his arm for comfort—though she wasn't quite certain whose comfort she meant it to be.

Inside, down a slanting passageway, they walked, and finally found themselves in the same chamber, with heavy hangings on the wall and a long table of food, where she had seen Sinbad.

Monte Cristo was there, waiting.

Despite her best efforts to remain untouched, her stomach plummeted, and her eyes feasted on him—so tall and commanding, dressed as though he were about to be inducted into the *Académie Française*. His hair was a bit shorter, combed back elegantly from his high forehead and arching black brows. His face was clean-shaven and smooth. He swept her up in his gaze immediately, and she felt it score over her as if to ascertain that she was as he'd left her.

She was not. But she wouldn't let him know how she grieved. It had been hard enough to lose Edmond Dantès once . . . but to lose him again to his thirst for vengeance felt like more than she could bear.

"I trust you had a comfortable voyage," he said, breaking his attention from Mercédès and turning to Maximilien. "I am so gratified that you've come." He moved forward to pull the younger man into an embrace in a manner so unlike the Count of Monte Cristo that Mercédès gaped.

Maximilien returned the affection, it was clear, despite the fact that sorrow still pulled at his expression. "There is no other face—save one—that I would want to see before I expire," he said, looking at the count.

"Please sit," Monte Cristo invited, and Mercédès was certain she saw a glitter of tears in his eyes, but she hardened her heart to his emotion. It was too late. "May I provide you with refreshment?"

Mercédès looked at the table, heavy with exotic fruits and bread and cheeses, but she refrained from partaking.

"Monte Cristo, I am here. I've come, as you asked, and now I ask that you let me do that which I must . . . that I have wanted to do since I saw the marble face of my beloved Valentine. Please . . . let me join her."

"You shall do as you wish," the count replied, again his gaze sketching over to Mercédès. "But first, I must ask you. . . . How do you feel?"

"But, of course, you know how I feel!" burst forth Maximilien. "I feel the deepest, harshest, unrelenting grief and unhappiness that one can ever imagine. That I'll never find sunshine again. That my lungs will never take another breath. That my heart cannot stand to beat any longer. I wish only to end it all." Tears streamed down his cheeks, and Mercédès, having had enough of whatever it was Monte Cristo was playing, leaped to her feet.

"Edmond, stop it!" she cried, tears threatening her own eyes. "Whatever game you play, you need do it no longer. We're here, as you have asked—it is clear Maximilien is at his very end. . . . Why do you prolong it any further? You do him, and yourself, no service."

Monte Cristo's eyes had flashed to hers when she called him by name, and his lips moved in a humorless smile. "So I am Edmond again," he said. "Is it futile for me to hope this means your love for him might yet be resurrected?"

"It is more futile than to hope that Valentine Villefort might walk into this room," Mercédès raged.

And at that, the most astonishing thing happened. The count's face lost some of the granitelike hardness that never seemed to ease from his countenance, and his brief smile became more genuine. "As you wish, madam."

And at that moment, the heavy tapestry depicting the Blessed Mother holding her staff and a small globe moved aside to reveal the slender figure of a young woman.

It took a moment for Maximilien to comprehend what his eyes saw, a split second before he lunged toward her, crying her name and gathering her into his arms, laughing against her head and streaming tears over her face.

Mercédès turned to look at Monte Cristo, her own mouth open, her eyes bulging, and a hint of softness lightening her heart. He was watching the reunion of the young lovers, and there was indeed a gleam of tears in his eyes.

When he turned to look at her, one of the tears spilled over and made a single, tiny trickle down his cheek.

"Edmond," she said, hardly aware that she'd used his name again, "I don't understand."

"I knew who planned to poison Mademoiselle Valentine—it was her stepmother, Villefort's second wife—who had done so to all of the other unfortunates who died in their household. She wanted her own son, not Valentine, to inherit Villefort's wealth, and so she was to make certain of it—after ensuring that Valentine's grandparents expired and left their money to her first."

By now, Valentine and Maximilien, who, entwined on a cushioned chair, had not a breath of space between them, were listening as Monte Cristo told his tale. "I spoke to Valentine in secret that night you came to me, Maximilien, and I kept watch over her bed and the water in the glass next to it. When her step-mother came and replaced the liquid with poison, I retrieved it and gave Valentine a different medication—one that would put her into a deep sleep and slow her heart so much that it would appear she was dead."

"He told me to trust him, and not to be frightened, and so I did," said Valentine, beaming at the count in a way that made

Mercédès soften even more. "He promised that all would be well, and that Maximilien and I would be reunited forever—after he was certain my father wouldn't find me." She looked at her lover again. "And so the Count of Monte Cristo has saved two lives—two that would have ended in death if he had not intervened."

"But . . . ," Maximilien began, but whatever he was about to say was swallowed by such a joyous smile that Mercédès felt her own joy twinge deep inside.

"Why did you not tell him?" asked Mercédès, beginning to understand that things had changed. "Why did you allow him to live in agony for four weeks?"

Monte Cristo—Edmond—looked steadily at her. His eyes were sad and old. "I have learned that the only way to understand, to fully know, happiness—regardless of one's lot or place in life—is to experience fathomless sorrow. Complete loss of hope. Incomparable devastation and grief. Only then can one see what happiness is, and find it, no matter where or how one lives. For there is no real happiness or unhappiness—only comparison between the two."

Their eyes met and held, and she felt the last bit of bonds loosening inside her.

"Mercédès," he said, moving toward her, falling on his knees at her feet, "I have felt that incomparable sorrow and fathomless grief. I've spent the last ten years living and breathing the fury of revenge with anger and hatred to fuel me . . . but I've learned. . . . You taught me." His voice broke. He swallowed and took her hands, looking down at them. "It was you who made me realize that I was wrong to be so vengeful—though it took me some time to stop fighting it. Can you forgive me, Mercédès? For it all?"

Looking down at his sleek, dark head, she reached forward and pulled his face up to hers. Covering his lips in a kiss of forgiveness, she closed her eyes.

Edmond Dantès had returned.

About the Author

Colette Gale is the pseudonym of a historical novelist. She lives in the Midwest with her family.